THE
DESTINY
EQUATION

KENNETH TAM

PHEALAN CAINE
DEPUTY SUPREME CONSUL OF EARTH

THE
DESTINY
EQUATION
THE EIGHTH EQUATIONS NOVEL

KENNETH TAM

ICEBERG

Published in Canada by Iceberg Publishing, Waterloo

Library and Archives Canada Cataloguing in Publication
Tam, Kenneth, 1984-
    The destiny equation : the eighth equations novel / Kenneth Tam.
ISBN 978-0-9865017-8-4
    I. Title.
PS8589.A7676D47 2010   C813'.6   C2010-900090-0

Iceberg Publishing
55 Northfield Drive East, Suite 171
Waterloo ON N2K 3T6
contact@icebergpublishing.com
www.icebergpublishing.com

First pocket paperback printing: July 2009
Special international edition: January 2010

Cover Artwork: Wesley Prewer
Cover Design: Kenneth Tam

For Atlas.

FOREWORD

We come to the end.

The Kroggs, after all, came good, and rightly so. The Larosians have rallied and come forward with all the force they can muster, and what remains of humanity is determined to stand against the plague. But is that enough? Can anything be enough when something so vast sweeps down against you?

To the Earthers, that question hardly matters. This is the ultimate test of who they are, and what they stand for. When there is no hope, can they continue to hold a perspective that's rooted in innocence and idealism? I wager they can, but you'll have to read to see.

And what about Omega? Can the plague be stopped, or is this really the end of the Earthers, and the beginning of his new dominion? I remember wondering the very same as I tried to figure out how all this would conclude. I recall questioning how it would be possible for the Earthers to defeat an enemy with such incredible reach — who has armies of billions, the ability to control minions when they're galaxies apart, and foresight enough to predict Earther plans long before he goes into battle.

Omega is the ultimate opposite of the Earthers: too evil to be true, and yet still true. The first Earther, Setter's ancestor, was named Alpha Caine, and while I wish I could claim that I'd thought that through (the Earthers beginning with Alpha, and ending with Omega), I honestly didn't. In retrospect, the symmetry is rather striking.

What you're about to read, then, is a battle of opposites in just about every sense that matters. It's good and evil, to be sure, but beyond morality, this is the clash between different world views, different approaches to life, and different levels of maturity. And the ending, I personally think, is profoundly happy. That modifier — 'profoundly' — being an important one.

How many people will be left to see it, and where they'll see it from... I invite you to read and discover.

And then there's the Postscript, which is part of a plan that's been developing since those words — you'll probably recognize them when you read them — were first uttered back in *The Earther Equation*. Stay tuned in future years to find out what that's all about.

There's not much more for me to say, so I'll move on to the thanks that are so very well deserved as we come to this final installment of the series.

Now as before, we begin with Cody Herauf. After originating the Kroggs and Larosians, and building such a rich tapestry around their war, Cody was crucial in helping me understand how the former nemesis could become an ally. As we saw at the end of *The Nemesis Equation*, the Kroggs remain grateful to the Earthers, who not only proved their equals — often betters — at war, but who chose to keep them alive, when they could have easily destroyed them.

So the Earthers are rewarded for making a principled decision, and now, both of the magnificent races that Cody created stand shoulder-to-shoulder with Earth's protectors. Thanks to my old comrade for helping make this happen.

I've sung Wes Prewer's praises throughout this series, and I must do so again here. His work on cover art remains peerless for its relentless attention to detail, and for the patience and effort he puts into it. If you close this book and look at the Earthers ships standing above their homeworld, waiting for the final battle, you get a true taste of the scope of what's to come.

And though we lost some of Wes' characters in *The Nemesis Equation*, more of his heroes remain with Earth's defense forces, and will make their stand alongside veterans like Jax Furgus, Artie Tigar, and Dran Nightclaw.

Wes has made this series better by his very involvement in it. He is a true friend, and a hell of a comrade. I'm indebted to him, and I invite you to stay tuned to www.icebergpublishing.com to see what other artwork and writing he has in store. You won't be disappointed.

From the beginning, I've said that Peter Caron's contributions to this story have been fundamental. I hope I've done enough to point out just how that's been the case, because my friend Peter deserves as many thanks as I can manage to give — and more besides.

As a sounding board, an analyst, a strategist and a friend, he's pointed to things and asked questions, or offered suggestions, that made these books possible. So thanks to Peter for the Freetowners, for Omega's strategy, and for the countless thoughts and contributions that have enhanced different dimensions of this saga since the start. I'm glad a character based on him gets a cameo in this book — a fitting, if modest, tribute in recognition of all he's done to get us here.

They don't make friends any better.

Now's the time to thank my parents again. They are my business partners in Iceberg Publishing, they've been my friends as long as I've lived, and they've encouraged me, supported me, challenged me and taught me.

I'll never work with better people, and as far as I'm concerned, that's saying a lot, because I've been fortunate to work with some of the best folks around outside Iceberg's walls. Thank you guys.

Last, we come back to Atlas. I've explained before that he was just a dog — just a silly German Shepherd. By the time I came to draft this book, his era had ended. Lymphoma caught him, and he fought it — and fought hard. But he was big and strong... and that meant the only thing that could beat him was his own immune system. He died in 2006, having spent most of that year fighting it with chemicals, drugs, surgeries, and every other manner of treatment we could try. And through all that suffering, he never stopped enjoying life. Even when he could barely breathe, he'd find moments to be happy.

Atlas taught me you should chase your dreams with a smile, because you'll never regret the adventure. He taught me that on the last day of your life, you should find time to smile, because you'll never get another chance. And he reminded me of something I learned from my grandfather: that even in the last dark days of your life, you can still find ways to make a difference — to teach the people you're going to leave behind, so that they'll be better individuals after you're gone.

All that from a dog. All that, I daresay, from an Earther. Someone who saw life from a truly alien point of view, one we humans may never fully appreciate, but one with merits that we shouldn't ignore.

The day Atlas died was like the day I lost my grandfather: it was profoundly happy. It was agonizing, and yet with all the pain came a new sort of light. That light endures now.

And as the Earthers make their last stand against Omega, they'll need to find light of their own. This plague afflicts the universe like Lymphoma took root in Atlas; like Alzheimer's assailed my grandfather.

The Earthers will find their own profoundly happy victory, and in the end, we'll see how well that cynical, self-absorbed bastard Omega likes the beings he created, took for granted, and abused.

It all comes down to this.

And win or lose, the Earthers are ready to fight.

PROLOGUE

Earth space was full of purpose.

Much destruction had already taken place there, and much more seemed to be at hand. Omega was coming, and the Earthers and their allies were going to try to stop him, once and for all.

The preparations for that last battle were evident everywhere in the system. There was no panic, just a quiet and grave certainty that a movement of destiny was soon to take place. The Earthers knew that the last battle was nearly upon them… and they didn't know how it would end.

Sitting in his pinnace as it climbed out of Earth's atmosphere, Supreme Consul Setter Caine, leader of the Earther people, silently reflected on the possibilities. This wasn't the first time the wolf had sat in a pinnace, climbing to his ship waiting in orbit, and wondering about the fate that awaited him and his people.

The last time he'd thought this way had been over four decades before, on the eve of the arrival of the human Quest Fleet. It had been a much simpler time then. The Earthers had been a young and idealistic race, facing none of the issues that now plagued them…

Setter winced as the bad pun crossed his mind, and sitting across the aisle from him, a giant bear named Ursla chuckled.

You need to be more vigilant with your internal dialogue… puns like that undermine the serious thinking you're doing.

"Don't get carried away with the telepathy thing," Setter managed to smile despite the gravity of his thoughts. Of course there were new challenges before the Earthers — Omega had unraveled the Genesis and Freetown colonies, had shattered the Larosian Empire and was now armed with ships and weapons augmented by Krogg bio-technology — all challenges that Setter, as First Lord of the Admiralty forty years before, could hardly have envisioned, let alone overcome.

But Setter wasn't the same wolf who had fought the Quest Fleet forty years prior, and his Earthers certainly weren't the same people.

For one thing, thanks to the drugs created by Celia Lazarus — now the Earthers' leading expert on Omega — every Earther had access to the telepathic center of his or her brain. That was rather important.

Beyond that, though, was the great history of the last forty years. The

Earthers had learned much from their war against the Kroggs — they'd learned about sacrifice and confidence, about doing what they promised they'd do, and doing it in a way that reflected their beliefs. The lessons had been learned at the expense of the blood of many friends... but they'd been learned all the same.

And they had earned new allies along the way. The humans had stood with them the longest, but they were now falling victim to Omega far more easily than anyone else. That was perhaps to be expected — the plague had originally been designed to kill humans, after all.

There were the Larosians, the noble alien race that lived by honor and now stood by the Earthers in the same way the Earthers had stood by them during the Krogg War. And there were the Kroggs, reformed since their defeat, and determined to become close allies of the race that proved the undoing of their old, fanatical Queen.

The Alliance of these four races — Earthers, humans, Larosians and Kroggs — was a formidable one, and perhaps it would be a match for Omega.

Perhaps, when the plague came to Earth space and faced the Allies' best fighters, he'd be destroyed...

No. No that couldn't happen, really. Omega was too immense, too powerful. A sentient plague who, thanks to a botched attempt to destroy him, had been able to take control of uninnoculated bodies, Omega had billions of minions. To wipe him out would require eliminating not just each of them, but each cell infected with him across the cosmos.

No Alliance of races could hope to achieve that sort of end through a feat of conventional arms.

So when Omega came to Earth, all the Allies could hope to do would be to turn him back — to keep him from occupying the planet, from killing every last Earther he saw. Because that's certainly what he wanted to do.

Killing the plague, once and for all, would inevitably be Setter's job. Setter and Ursla, along with Sarah Manchester, Pat Conroy, Graham Manchester, and Christine Schaeffer had missions to accomplish. Theirs was a long-shot plan, but it had a chance of succeeding.

And if it did succeed, it would mean the end of Omega.

Setter's eyes flicked to the case sitting on the seat next to him — to the box containing Celia Lazarus' *cure*.

If that cure worked, it would be a miracle... if it didn't...

Come on now, no point thinking like that. We haven't even left yet.

Setter blinked himself out of his thoughts and looked across the aisle at Ursla again, "You going to give up on talking altogether?"

Laughing brightly, Ursla shook her head, "I'll start talking when you stop pondering morosely. This is either going to work or we're all going to die... which I admit isn't a particularly confidence-inspiring state of affairs, but we might as well laugh anyway."

With his eyebrow climbing, Setter slowly started to smile again. Andra Ursla had that right — he couldn't change his plan now. Everything depended on it. So perhaps it was best just to smile in recognition of the fact that they did indeed *have* a plan.

A couple of weeks earlier they wouldn't have even thought it possible to plan anything against Omega, but now they had a real chance.

That's better, see, Ursla offered her telepathic encouragement, and Setter nodded in agreement.

Looking out the view port next to his seat, Setter at last caught sight of his destination. Battered and still hewn open by Omega's ramming assaults at Freetown, *ENS Orion* stood nonetheless proudly at grav anchor, its scorched hull still glinting in the light of the sun.

Wounded but still ready to fight, just like us, Setter thought to himself.

The pinnace closed to land.

As Setter and Ursla descended the ramp from their craft, the cure case locked under the Supreme Consul's arm, a familiar figure approached them.

First Lord of the Admiralty Labrador Forepaw had been Setter's Flag Captain aboard *Orion* when the Quest Fleet had arrived, and now he greeted his two old friends with a smile and a nod.

"Battered but proud," Lab said as he waved to his former ship. "It doesn't get easier to see it in such bad shape... but knowing now that it'll get a chance to fight again... makes me feel better."

Replying with a smile, Setter nodded, "It really couldn't be another ship. It has to be *Orion*. Same way it has to be us."

Lab looked back at Setter and his smile ebbed away, "Yes... you're right about that."

A pause was in order, and the silence gave Setter just a second to listen to the emptiness of his old flagship. There was no one else aboard *Orion* — the ship's great hull was empty but for these three and their pinnaces.

"Zed has confirmed that the automation systems are all in place, including the final program. He says he can't promise it'll be fit for an intense gunfight, but it should get the job done for you," Lab continued after a moment.

Zed Dune, probably the best engineer in the fleet, had personally overseen the rigging of this ship for its mission. If the enterprising white wolf said *Orion* could do the job, then Setter believed it.

"Good," the Supreme Consul said at last. "We'll depart on schedule. Meantime, Andra and I better start getting things set up here."

Lab nodded, "I'll be back on *Venerable* if you need me."

With parting nods, Lab headed back to his pinnace. Ursla and Setter exchanged glances, and then went to work.

There was much to be done.

CHAPTER 1

Omega-Natosh smiled.

The chief avatar of Omega's corporeal forces, the infected Larosian remained the plague's favorite means of expressing himself physically, though Omega-Gillian — once Gillian Hodge, Graham Manchester's wife — had many charms.

But no, none were better than the first Larosian Omega had infected after he'd spliced himself with Krogg DNA.

Because of that preference, Omega had decided almost instantly that it would be his Larosian avatar who must cross swords with Setter Caine, when the stupid wolf came to Genesis and the most perfect setting the plague could have imagined.

Omega's minions worked to clear the memorial of bodies as Omega-Natosh watched on. In his confusing and omnipresent way, Omega was all of them at once — the minions and the avatars were all part of the same being, much as a human's fingers and eyes were all part of the same body. Some parts were just more complicated and important than others. Where the Natosh avatar was akin to a major organ, a minion was a fingernail, or something like that...

Though, Omega realized, he needed to stop thinking about himself in quite that way. It was making him hungry to eat human, but he had to ration his uninfected human supplies. So many of his would-be torture victims had been added to his army for Earth, he didn't have many left for play.

The bodies being cleared out of this Genesis War Memorial were testament to that. Liz Hastings had commissioned this vast cenotaph just after the Krogg War, with Harvey Bingham's help. Dug three meters down into a park in the planet's capital city, the huge circular area had walls faced in black rock, and on that rock was etched the name of every human killed in the war against the Kroggs, *and* every Crusader who'd died on the Quest.

That had been a ballsy move, adding the Crusaders to the list. Bingham had insisted on it, because he'd been trying to unite Genesis society. They had tried to sanitize their history, to make it seem like the millions of Crusaders who'd died in their vain attempt to take Earth at the beginning had actually been casualties of the Krogg War.

Obviously the people of Genesis hadn't adopted that rosy picture of the past... they'd had a coup, after all.

But whatever the memorial had or hadn't done for the people of Genesis, it would be a fitting arena for Omega-Natosh's duel with Setter Caine... once it was cleared of all the corpses that had been tossed into it.

My own little coliseum, how quaint...

Such poetically appropriate sites didn't exist on Freetown or Ecclesia, despite the duels that would be fought on both those planets... but that didn't matter. Omega would still get the satisfaction of bringing Setter Caine into the ring, and killing him... or better yet, beating him but making him wait and watch as Earth was picked clean of Earthers, and then that stupid colony at New Halifax was cut to ribbons.

Perhaps the descendant of the first Earther would end up being the last of his kind... that would be poetic.

Omega's taste for clichéd poetics was definitely growing. He was becoming increasingly fond of stupid Shakespearian theatrics ever since Setter's surprise offer, and was more than happy to indulge the Earthers.

To *cautiously* indulge.

When Setter had walked into the basement of Fengate Hospital on Earth, and had made the offer to Omega-King — the avatar Omega had created from the minion *Renown* had captured in the Larosian galaxy — the plague had been quite surprised.

"Let me fight your avatar... Natosh... let me fight him face to face," Setter had said. "Let Graham fight Gillian, let Sarah fight Paine. Let us come to them, wherever they are... let us fight them face to face."

Omega had accused the wolf of getting the stupid idea from old human movies, but on some level the notion of fighting big, overly-dramatic duels had appealed to him too. There was a reason the humans of the times that had birthed him — the twenty-first century — had so loved shows and movies where the bad guy and the good guy faced off in a bare-knuckles fistfight at the end. It made for awesome storytelling, and better yet, it gave them a chance to vent their anger at each other.

So Omega had taken Caine's suggestion under advisement. He'd thought about it for a while... and more importantly, he'd carefully probed the minds of every Earther he could reach to try to figure out what Setter's plan was.

The wolf was predictable and a fucking boy scout, but Omega knew better than to assume he was simply an idiot, or desperate enough to think that if he somehow beat Omega-Natosh in single's combat, the plague would spare his people.

No, there was obviously something Setter, Sarah and Graham thought they could accomplish by coming face to face with the avatars, so Omega wanted to figure out what that was.

It hadn't taken long.

The Earthers had lapped up the drug that restored their telepathy like thirsty dogs, but not all of them seemed to have Setter Caine's discipline. Their plan was all too evident, based on what Omega-King had gleaned from the hospital staff.

And it would be oh so very satisfying to see the look on Setter Caine's face — up close and personal — when the daft idea simply didn't work.

So Omega was going to let the three leaders come to his avatars, and he was going to get particular joy from killing them... but slowly, and only after he showed them how foolish their assumptions about him were.

And while he was doing that, he'd also be assaulting Earth. That was breaking the terms of the deal, but no one actually expected Omega *not* to attack Earth when Setter arrived on Genesis. The Earthers had made him promise, and he'd sworn with scout's honor just for them, but they knew he was lying. He could see it in their minds.

They were counting on their top secret super-duper plan to stop him from overrunning them when the attack came. They were counting on the mighty Setter Caine, and his human lackeys the Manchester siblings, to deliver an epic movie-worthy saving 'cure' at just the right moment, when Earth was about to be overrun.

Sad, stupid, over-idealistic fuckers.

They'd learn how foolish their hopes were, and then they'd die.

Omega was *so* looking forward to it.

He had 5,000 ships and an army of nine billion — just about every human from Genesis and Ecclesia who hadn't been eaten had been turned into a soldier minion, and many more cloned. He was going to carpet Earth and the Earthers with death, and he was going to love it...

This would be an ending worthy of story.

And once it was over, Omega would be sure to create a race to whom he could tell that story... or perhaps he would figure out the secret behind the Earthers' ancestors and explain it to them, before he ate them too.

Whatever happened, it would suit his twenty-first-century sense of over-dramatic and cliché endings. And it would crush the hopes of the goodest and cuddliest creatures to ever deface the universe.

Omega-Natosh grinned at that prospect, and his minions continued clearing the cenotaph of the dead.

Less than two weeks from now it would be finished.

CHAPTER 2

"It is well that he has given us these two weeks. Our strength here will be 1,200 ships by the time his attack comes."

Warlord Kragran was standing in a room that, decades before, he would never have expected to see: the cabin of Admiral-of-a-Fleet Narosh, on the battleship *Carnarvon*. Narosh was sitting as he received his guest, but none of the chairs in the room was of the right shape or size to accommodate Kragran, with all his protruding blades. That was fine; the Krogg was happy enough to stand.

The Warlord's words — spoken in English, instead of sent telepathically to the Larosian — drew a nod, "As long as he keeps to the schedule, we will have over 200 ships here as well. Not as many as your fleet, Kragran. But a help."

Narosh was still not completely comfortable with the Krogg, though he was becoming more accustomed to having the former hated enemy as an ally. The Larosian squadron that had gone to the defense of Krogg 'A' had been moved without incident to Sol in the Hyper Motherships of the new Krogg Navy. During that cruise, they'd worked together and probed each others' minds at length, and Narosh's Earther-augmented blood felt right around the Kroggs...

But old pain died hard. The Kroggs had killed Praaxus and the Son, and while those acts had been directed by their Queen, Warlords like Krag had done the legwork.

If not for the common desire to defend the Earthers here, it seemed quite unlikely that Narosh would have spent any time with Kragran... but the Earthers were bringing Kroggs and Larosians together.

For his part, Krag was more enthusiastic about joining forces with the Larosians. Redemption was foremost on the mind of every Krogg — becoming an ally and proving that the influence of the Queen had been broken was critical to his people. If the Larosians could welcome the Kroggs back, there would be no better proof of how completely things had changed.

But Krag knew better than to rush the building of such a partnership. He'd waited patiently for forty years as his people had changed and rearmed, and now they were ready for war... patience paid off, it seemed.

And indeed, Omega's patience in waiting two weeks was benefiting the Allies. But would the plague truly conform to the agreement?

"What do you think of this plan of Caine's, Narosh? It seems... unusual to me, and it assumes a lot from Omega," Krag chanced the question to his counterpart, fixing his single eye on the Larosian's pair.

Narosh sat back in his chair, his mind briefly churning on the question, and the Earther cells that had lived in his bloodstream for forty years seemed to tremble slightly.

What did he think?

The Son had once dueled with a sub-Queen of the Kroggs, and that had seemed right at that time. A great battle of telepaths, the fight had ended in the destruction of an entire solar system... such was the amount of telepathic energy that a strong mind could harness. The duel had broken the Kroggs' campaign, and sent them into a seemingly hasty flight.

Which had, in fact, led the Larosians to find the hyperspace corridor to Genesis, and to add the Earthers and humans to their war against the Kroggs.

That duel had felt right to Narosh. The Son of Praaxus had been his friend, and yet it had made sense to watch him go to his death in single combat.

This plan — the plan created by Setter Caine and his Earthers, along with the humans — felt quite different. It felt desperate — almost intentionally so. And if Narosh could detect that desperation, the plague must have been able to sense the same.

Reading those surface thoughts, Krag agreed without words, *I have to admit I feel the same way, Narosh.*

Unfazed by the telepathic contact, the Admiral-of-a-Fleet nodded, *But if anyone can make it succeed, it must be Setter Caine.*

"Absolutely," Krag voiced his opinion. "And we will help protect this place while he carries it out."

Nodding again, Narosh considered the situation in his mind. The Earthers were building up a defense fleet with blinding speed — 150 of their vaunted *Venerable*-class ships of the line would be ready by the deadline, along with more than 1,000 other ships, most of Krogg War vintage, and 50,000 of their gunboats. The Kroggs would add their 1,200 ships to that force, and the Larosians more than 200 of their battered but tough old vessels. The Genesis human ships would be sent to hold New Halifax, as they were clearly not equal to fighting Omega, and what remained of the Freetown Navy would stay at Earth.

It would be a remarkable effort, then — the sort that hadn't been seen since the death of the Queen.

But it would provide fewer than 3,000 Allied ships to face Omega's new fleet of 5,000. Setter had been able to pierce Omega-King's barriers sufficiently to know what the plague had coming, and those 5,000 ships were terrifying. But not as terrifying as the nine *billion* ground troops Omega had at his disposal — they were genuinely horrifying, even to the proud Larosians and fierce Kroggs. No one could figure out how the plague was planning to move that many minions through space, but all telepathic scans showed that he had great confidence in his ability to do so.

Mounting a defense against that many landing troops — almost five times the Earther population of the planet — was virtually impossible to comprehend, let alone carry out.

But the Larosians and the Kroggs were honor-bound to try. They would not surrender to Omega's forces, nor give up on the Earthers who had done so much for both their races.

Both Kragran and Narosh were committed to that, and so they were meeting regularly now, building a rapport they hoped would help them fight as friends when the battle was joined.

"Captain-Elite Tovarrin wants to start joint combat exercises, if you're agreeable," Narosh moved his mind on to practical matters, and Kragran nodded thoughtfully.

"I'll have Kragthar assemble a Legion Horde or two for combined training," the Warlord's words were thoughtful, and they impressed Narosh with how little hiss they contained. The Kroggs had certainly come far since Narosh had first fought them, but he shook away that distraction as Krag smiled hungrily. "Imagine the fearsome kills of a combined force, my friend. Stealth Guards fighting alongside Warriors... it would be a great and powerful sight to behold. Many minions would die."

The Warlord clearly did still enjoy the prospect of good killing — some things didn't change — but Narosh had to agree with the sentiment.

"It would be a formidable arrangement," the Admiral agreed. "And we'll have a couple of weeks to figure out how to make it work."

"Indeed," Krag said. Then the Krogg's smile stretched further and he seemed to shake his head in disbelief, "It really is wonderful, this union between our peoples, Narosh. If the Earthers can bring *us* together, imagine what other good they can do for the universe... once we stop Omega, of course. If they can bring us together, and if we can help them in future... imagine what good can be done."

The word 'good' coming from a Krogg struck Narosh as strange for a moment, but he shook away his old prejudice again and simply nodded.

"We'll build a new galaxy, once we beat Omega," the Larosian's words were lined with a confidence that he wasn't certain was genuine, but which the Krogg accepted as truth.

"A great future. We must win."

Yes, they certainly had to do that.

CHAPTER 3

Pat Conroy looked at the kit that sat on his bed, still packed and where he'd dropped it twenty minutes before. He'd just returned from New Halifax, where he'd seen his parents and a number of old friends. He'd thought so very little of those people over the past weeks and months... they'd long ago moved to New Halifax, away from the Church and the government, living in the enclave of humans on the Earther colony.

He'd made sure they'd stayed there, too — New Halifax had seemed to Pat to be the safest place for them when a war between Freetown and Ecclesia had appeared a likely problem.

Well, that had never come to pass. But safe those people remained — safe as anyone could be right now, anyway.

Pat had taken a week to go to New Halifax and spend time with them, because after abandoning Freetown, Sarah hadn't wanted to see him. She'd locked herself down cold, and so she remained, unfeeling and unwilling to let him in.

It was a state he'd seen her in so often, and given the circumstances... given all the friends he'd seen Omega kill at Freetown... he'd needed to see some familiar faces, and get a little reminder of what a family was supposed to be...

Returning to Earth, Pat had been determined to use that reminder to cut through to Sarah, but as he stepped into their cabin, she instantly chilled him away. She had been packing an overnight kit, and as she moved back and forth from her closet to the open duffle on her bed, Pat had dropped his own bag where it now lay, and had tried to find out what she was up to.

They were going down to Earth for an overnight visit. Setter had a plan and had put it into motion while Pat had been away. She'd explain it while they were on Earth. Graham would be there, with Christine. This would be the first time they all saw each other since Graham had stormed away from them to rescue his wife at Genesis. And this could be the last time Sarah saw Graham, because he was also part of the plan.

The more Sarah had recited the words 'the plan' to Pat, the more nervous he'd become. Sarah had never stopped being the one who charged the guns. As President she'd gotten better at moderating her habit of taking risks and trying to continually prove herself... but after all that had been lost, it seemed inevitable that she was going to take a high-risk mission, and get herself killed.

Pat's plans to sit down with her, to get through to her as a husband did with a wife, were gone. He'd go with her to Earth and see what this *plan* was… and if he had to, he'd put a stop to it.

Without saying much himself, he picked his kit up off the bed and joined Sarah as she left her cabin and headed for her pinnace.

He wasn't really sure if she even noticed he was with her.

Christine Schaeffer had never been to Earth, and yet somehow she felt at home there.

It must be all this Earther DNA swimming around in me, she thought to herself as she stepped carefully over some slippery-looking rocks, and ended up dropping a boot into something squishy that tried to suck it from her foot.

This place — *Newfoundland* — was remarkable. She was surrounded by trees, it was cool and damp with a wind blowing, and yet she felt more alive here than she could ever remember feeling anywhere else. It was a raw place, and part of her blood — a new, Earther part — sung as she felt the foreign and yet familiar caress of the wind, and breathed deep the air.

Despite the skin suit under her clothes — the suit with the strobing stasis field that kept her nerve endings from registering even a slight breeze as a hot fire — she could feel something wonderful about this place.

After weeks of sensory depravation aboard ships, and of visits to truly alien worlds, this was *living*.

Unfortunately, Graham Manchester didn't seem to be having quite the same reaction to it.

"Be careful, those holes will pull your boot off," he said dispassionately, passing Christine as they continued their hike up towards their destination.

"Why don't the Caines have…" Christine started to ask why there was no roadway going up to the Caine estate when she realized she knew the answer.

If she could feel this alive here, even while trapped in a skin suit that dulled every touch, then what if she'd been free of that — what if she'd been normal again? It would have been magical. And what if she'd had even more Earther DNA in her? It would have been magnificent.

Providing an opportunity for a walk through the woods was undoubtedly one of the reasons why the estate was situated where it was — in the middle of nowhere. It was located in the midst of all the things its builders most loved.

So no road.

Very eloquently said, and completely correct too.

Christine had been drawing her boot out of the hole that had attempted to rob her of it when the thought entered her mind. She froze instantly in place. She didn't know that voice, but it sounded friendly.

One of the Caines?

"Over here," a voice erupted in answer to the question she'd pushed to the surface of her mind, and as she looked right to see the speaker, she saw an Earther waving through the trees.

Graham stopped and turned to look at the arriving wolf, raising his own hand, "Phealan, good day."

Drawing her boot clear and finding solid ground on which to plant her feet, Christine watched the wolf make his easy approach.

That was another reason the Earthers didn't need roads, or even trails: they were born for this terrain, and their feet never missed the mark.

You're much too generous... believe me, I've had spills! Phealan favored Christine with a smile as he came to a stop alongside her and Graham. "Welcome both of you. You'll be the first to arrive — Sarah and Pat are still on their way down."

Graham shook the young Caine's hand, and then Christine extended hers as well, receiving Phealan's firm grasp with some comfort, "It's a pleasure to meet you."

Phealan's smile remained, "You too. I've come to know a bit about you... through your sister."

The warmth inside Christine died abruptly, and Phealan's instincts — not his new telepathy, but his trusty Earther instincts — instantly detected the chill that ran through her. He refused to say anything in front of Graham, so he let go her hand and waved back the way he came, "Come with me, I'll take you an easier way."

Graham said nothing, and simply started off in the direction Phealan had indicated. Christine's eyes had drifted sideways and she stared at nothing.

Claire. How often have I thought of Claire since I left her?

It wasn't that thinking of the younger Schaeffer sister would have done any good while Christine had been lost a galaxy away, or had been going to Krogg 'A' with Graham... it would have done no good to dwell on the fact that the sister she loved so much was alone in an alien place, with no parents and no friends...

But how did I shut her out so easily? How...

She stopped herself.

Then she realized how easily she was able to stop such troubling thoughts, and that reality nearly panicked her.

What about her parents? She'd lost them, they were gone... and she wasn't mourning them. She wasn't feeling the pain of their loss, she wasn't feeling a deep longing to see her sister... she was at peace with what she had done, what she must do...

How can I be at peace with that? Gods help me... I...

All this time away, she'd been fixated on Graham, and on herself. How had she forgotten that her sister was all alone? Why hadn't she come back sooner? Why... why couldn't she convince herself now that anything she'd done was wrong?

She didn't feel like a big sister anymore... she barely felt human...

I'd heard the crash treatment was causing some strange side-effects, Christine. This may be one of them, Phealan's thoughts interrupted her own. *I'm sorry it's startled you... but what you're describing is normal for Earthers.*

Christine's eyes jolted back to Phealan, and she pushed new thoughts to the top of her mind, *But I'm not... I mean I was a good sister... if you love someone you don't forget them...*

Phealan's smile became tenuous, and instantly Christine's Earther-like instincts sensed a shift in him. His mind sent her a picture, that of his mother, and then all the feeling he'd had for her — all the warmth and love and joy.

And then she felt how it had been to have that snatched painfully away... an awesome, staggering pain that she recognized as being one she'd felt too.

Then he forced the pain to be silent.

It didn't go away, she realized, but it didn't dominate him, or make him panic, or anger him. The pain became a *part* of him, part of his character... but he didn't let it consume him.

That was his Earther way... and that was her way now too. A way different than anything she'd known before.

Like I said, sorry it has come as a shock. Hopefully now that we're all telepathic, we can lend a hand in getting you more accustomed to whatever's happening to you.

Christine swallowed nervously, "I'd... like that. Sometimes I don't know who I am anymore."

Phealan nodded in the direction Graham had started, and the young wolf smiled again, "I know that feeling too. We'll figure it out in time, I suppose."

With a sigh, Christine managed to keep from shaking her head, "I sure hope so."

They headed towards the Caine house.

CHAPTER 4

Setter Caine's kit was packed for his trip to Genesis. All the things he'd need were in it, including a printed photo of Elandra and Phealan — a picture that, during the last war, Ursla had confiscated in order to force him to think clearly.

This time, as the war came to an end, he'd need that photo. He'd need to remember his wife, and to see his son.

Orion would be shipping out for Omega's homeworld in just over forty-eight hours... he was determined to enjoy the last couple of days he had at home. On this second-to-last night, he was hosting Sarah and Graham, the other leaders destined to play to Omega's ego and set the final trap.

This plan. Good grief, if it could be called a plan...

The cure from Celia Lazarus, the addition of telepathy to the Earther arsenal... It was all promising to a certain extent, but at the same time it felt as though this mission was too ridiculous to succeed.

Duels with avatars? It was like something out of Shakespeare... it wasn't the way a war was supposed to be won.

It had been how Andros Grieve — the great old bear — had defeated the Queen on Krogg 'A', but that was different. Thirteen days from now, Setter would be invited to land on Genesis, to fight a duel against Omega. Of course, Omega had promised to spare Earth if Omega-Natosh lost, but he and Setter both knew that the minute Setter arrived, if not before, Omega's fleet would attack Earth.

The gambit, though, was that Omega would fall into their trap... that letting Setter, Sarah and Graham close to his avatars might be his undoing. It was such a slim hope...

Stop thinking like that, dad... I'm bringing Graham and Christine in from the woods and when she sees Claire, we might have to help.

Setter's uncertainties were interrupted by the thought from his son, and checking his own instincts, the elder Caine realized he could sense the tension building around the house. Christine was coming, alright, and Claire Schaeffer — the houseguest of the Caines' since Pat had brought her in after the fall of Genesis — was in no great shape to receive her.

As much as Phealan had worked with Claire, helped her open up enough to talk and sometimes even feel, she was still consumed by a formidable mix of hopelessness and anger, much of it repressed. There was no telling what would spill forth from the young, damaged human upon the appearance of the sister she felt had abandoned her.

It was the sort of drama that Setter didn't need at the moment... and yet he had to be a part of it. What the Schaeffers had suffered was much worse than what he and Phealan had been through, and if the wolves could help, they would.

That was the way they did things.

Setter left his room and hurried down the stairs, finding Claire stretched out on the couch, staring at a holo channel with news about Omega.

"You going somewhere?" the girl asked sharply, not even casting her eyes in Setter's direction.

"Soon," he confirmed in a soft tone. "Right now I think you should get up."

"I'm watching something," she disagreed.

Get up.

"Fuck off, and get out of my head," she now turned on Setter with an angry stare.

Initially, when Claire had been so sharp, Setter and Phealan had only been able to assess her with their instincts. Those instincts were excellent, but being able to actually read some of the thoughts crossing her mind was much better.

She was trying to start a fight, because if the Earthers started an argument she could use the opportunity to vent about all she'd lost. But Setter and Phealan were never baited — Earthers rarely were. She didn't get a chance to vent her rage, and Setter wasn't sure if that was a good thing or not.

Maybe it would mean that everything had just been saved up for right now — for when Christine returned.

The sounds of boots coming up the deck stairs didn't draw Claire's eyes at first, as she was fixed on Setter's gaze. Then his eyes darted over her shoulder, so she looked back.

Confused, she got to her feet.

Graham had stepped aside to reveal Christine standing at the top of the stairs. Phealan came up behind the elder Schaeffer sibling, but quickly stood aside as well.

Christine simply stopped and stared, dropping the duffle she'd brought. Both sisters' eyes told an epic story of agony and loss.

Setter's instincts were instantly flooded by a sort of misery with which he'd become all too familiar, and he had to take a breath to focus and make certain the feeling didn't take root in him.

He watched Claire walk towards the deck door, then followed ponderously, not sure what to expect.

No idea how this is going to go, Phealan confirmed his own uncertainty. *Any thoughts?*

Setter offered a telepathic shake of the head, *No way to know...*

Claire stepped out onto the deck and shivered as a burst of cold wind hit her. She stared at Christine for a moment, then walked past her and descended the deck stairs, setting off at a run into the woods.

Surprised, Christine turned and watched her sister go... then, as if finally registering what she'd just seen, followed at a run.

Setter and Phealan stayed where they were, wondering what precisely they should do, but Graham made the decision simple for them, "Christine will sort it out."

The chill that came with those words had nothing to do with the wind, and Setter recognized the pain in the Manchester's tone. He'd heard it before, when Graham had come to him at Gibraltar, demanding that someone be sent out to save Sarah.

"How's the pain?" Setter turned to the junior Manchester, and Graham stared back before answering.

A rare smile graced the human's lips, and he let out a very long breath, "Completely unbearable. You understand."

Graham then stepped up in front of Setter, and took his old mentor's hand in one of his, placing the other on the wolf's shoulder, "There's nothing left of me, you see. Only you really understand what I mean."

Setter nodded slowly. He'd known Graham through truly the worst of times, and the best. Graham, whose own parents had been killed when he was so young, had always looked to Setter for father-like wisdom. Even other Earthers couldn't compare.

"Thank you," Graham said now, with meaningful emotion filling his voice. "Thank you for giving me this chance to see her. To kill her. To end this."

The tormented words were painful for Setter to hear, but he understood. Graham's life now was about revenge and nothing else. Under this plan, he'd be going to Freetown, and there he'd duel with his wife, the avatar, and he'd either kill her or die.

Or both.

It was all Graham could have wanted, and it was part of the plan, without him even having asked for it.

"We didn't plan it this way for you," Phealan said softly, stepping up next to his father. "But we knew you were the only one who could make Omega believe we meant what we were saying about having scores to settle."

Graham took a deep cleansing breath and nodded, "I know that. But thank you all the same. And dammit, Phealan, well done coming to the fore like this. You're a remarkable young wolf."

Feeling the weight of responsibility somehow released from him — at least for this moment — Graham extended his smile and released Setter's grip so that he could shake Phealan's hand again.

"The air is good here," Graham took a few more deep breaths, looking up at the gray sky. "I wish I could have been here more over the years."

"You might be back, yet," Setter said quietly.

Graham looked back down at Setter and his smile faded. He'd released the emotions he needed to, and his calm, cool façade was returning — even if the Caines could see through it, perhaps no one else would.

"Do you expect to be coming back, Setter?"

The Supreme Consul of the Earther people smiled a genuine smile and shook his head, "I know I won't be back."

Graham nodded, "So do I."

Claire had spent weeks on the Caine estate, and thus knew it reasonably well. Christine only managed to keep on her sister's trail because of her new Earther skills... the very skills that had kept her distant were now bringing her physically closer to Claire.

That's just too damned poetic. I feel like I'm in a novel... maybe Pat will write me into one of his histories, if we live through this...

There she was, sitting on a log with her back to Christine. The elder sister was upon the younger in an instant, moving so quickly and silently that Claire didn't realize she'd been caught until she felt the log shift from Christine's weight lowering onto it. She tried to bolt again, but her sibling's firm grip held her down, and then pulled her close.

Trying to remember how to be a human sister, Christine wrapped her arms tightly around Claire. The younger girl wasn't impressed, and her fists thumped Christine's chest and leg as she tried to yank herself free.

"You left... you're dead... you left me..."

The words were repeated over and over again, and every time they came out they were more anguished than the last time. The struggling eased, and Christine pulled her sister closer and whispered her apologies.

Claire finally gave up fighting, and her arms tried to crush the life from Christine. All the pain that had been bottled up between the two of them started to spill out, Christine's Earther aspects standing aside to let her feel human again, if only for this moment.

Everything that had happened since Pat had grabbed her from that Panatorium. The injury, the regen, the coup, her parents...

Christine at last lost her composure. Her parents. Mom and dad. Mom and dad. Mom and dad.

Mom and dad.

All at once Christine started sobbing, and she buried her face in Claire's shoulder while Claire did the same back.

It felt so good to be back together. Even in the midst of all Omega's threats, the universe didn't seem to matter. Christine didn't know how she'd stayed away for so long, or why. She had become less and less human but now, at last, she had some of her old self back. And she had her sister. Claire was all she had left of her humanity.

And to Claire, Christine was the same. Phealan and Setter had been impossibly warm to the younger girl, and she tried to keep them away because she hurt so bad. But now, with Christine back, hurt and pain could be shared, the way they had always been.

"Remember when all we cared about was clothes and boys and stupid stuff?" Claire recovered from a deep sob to ask that question, and Christine laughed through her tears.

"You're not coming on to Phealan, are you? He's like thirty years older than you and he's a wolf!"

They laughed. They laughed so hard they cried some more.

And they refused to let go of each other. Both of them got the feeling that this might be one of the last human moments they would ever share, and neither meant to waste it.

CHAPTER 5

"Weather's good today."

Pat's words barely registered with Sarah, but she nodded anyway, presuming that she didn't need to reply verbally. The last time she'd been here, Setter and Elandra had been able to help her find peace. Now Elandra was dead, and she knew there was no peace. She just wanted to get this over with and go back to *Joseph Barron*.

So help her, she had no idea how she'd deal with Graham. What was she going to say to her brother... the man who, driven by emotions, had abandoned his post, and been a petulant and petty recluse in another galaxy when she'd needed him here?

What if he'd stayed? Maybe a sure hand leading the fleet would have saved Freetown, or more importantly, the Genesis refugees that Omega had massacred or abducted just short of the Sol system. He could have made a difference here, but instead he shirked his responsibilities and went off on a personal quest for *revenge*.

That was unforgivable, in many ways. Sarah had learned long ago that she must do the opposite. Now she hid from her life and her emotions specifically so that she would not lose her path. She'd done that once when she'd abandoned her fleet at Gibraltar during the Krogg War, and had vowed never again. But Pat had almost shaken her of that resolve when he'd nearly died on Freetown. She had to stay distant from him now, in these last days of her life.

The mission ahead would be the biggest she'd ever been a part of, and one on which she'd mercifully die. That was almost certain. She couldn't let her feelings for Pat surface or they might make her hesitate in her duty. Keeping them down would make this so much easier.

"Would be nice if the wolves were around... always like to see the wolves," Pat was continuing to try to get her attention, but Sarah wasn't taking the bait. Her walls were up, her focus was set, and she walked right into Setter Caine.

"Just me," the gray wolf said with a kind smile as Sarah smacked into him. Pat couldn't help but laugh at the absurd sight of his wife bouncing off Setter's chest after he'd emerged quickly from behind a tree.

She cursed her distractedness in the same second that her foot slipped off the rock she'd been on. As she toppled backwards Setter's hands closed around her waist at the same moment that Pat's caught her back. She was suspended for a second in that awkward state before she was pushed upright, and Setter drew his hands away.

"Welcome back. We heard you coming... heard your thoughts, I mean. So I thought I'd come out to meet you."

"Earther telepaths indeed. Still getting used to that," Pat's tone was relatively light, and it was immediately clear to Setter that the Irishman was still trying to keep Sarah's spirits up. Sarah, though, seemed without spirits at all.

Hers was a coldness Setter recognized — similar to Graham's, but different at its core. Graham's dispassion came from fury... from the loss of someone close to him. During the last war, it had been the threat of losing Sarah. This time it was his wife and unborn child. But Sarah was different: hers was a cold born of isolation.

Setter could intellectually understand these reactions, but he could never take them to such extremes as the Manchester siblings had. And now these two would meet again, and somehow Setter doubted the reception would be as good as the one Christine and Claire had shared.

They were both so very wary now.

Perhaps peace could be made between the two of them — Setter would try to make it — but he wasn't certain it was possible. These two were both about to set off on the most dangerous of missions. If they'd been Earthers, they'd have made the most of the time they had left together.

But they weren't, and as Setter studied Sarah's expression, he saw that his young human friend was stony faced and trying desperately to remain so.

"Graham up at the house now?" Pat asked the question with no subtlety, knowing it would send a jolt through Sarah.

Setter nodded in reply, "He arrived a couple of hours ago, and Christine and Claire have had a fine reunion..." he paused and looked back at Sarah, "...a better reunion than Sarah and Graham will have, I think."

Sarah's face tightened, and she opened her mouth to protest the seemingly unkind words, but Setter invaded her mind with a private message, *Promise me, Sarah, that you will try to make peace with him. Don't freeze him out just to be stubborn... it would hurt me personally to see the two of you part as enemies.*

Those words were quite possibly the most brutal ones that Setter Caine had ever delivered to a human friend. Sarah's lips trembled as they filled her mind — he'd played the one, nasty trump card that Earthers never played: guilt. He was going to guilt her into being open to Graham.

"Why?" she protested, realizing her chances of countering Setter were slim, but trying anyway.

"Why what?" Pat frowned, so Setter sent him the same message and his eyes widened. "Gods, Setter, that's low."

"I don't care if it's low. You two aren't Earthers, but you should both be mature and sensible enough to realize that the end is near, and you need to make your peace with each other while you can. Any kind of peace."

Sarah fought hard to control her emotions, and she was successful. For many decades she'd trained herself to repress them — through youth, war and peace. And now it was paying off.

"We'll part as brother and sister," Sarah's words still had a chill, and Setter nodded.

"That's something. Come with me."

Graham didn't want to stare as Christine and Claire sat hugging each other close on the couch in the Caines' living room. He was outside on the deck, but he couldn't help but watch and be impressed by the closeness of the sisters. They deserved to be together, so Graham would ask Christine not to come on this mission with him, even though she'd already told him she would.

She'd told him that before she'd come back to Claire. The two needed to be together now.

"Let her make that decision," Phealan was beside Graham suddenly, and had clearly been reading his mind.

Graham's eyebrow climbed slightly, and he looked at the young wolf, "I cannot ask her to join a one-way mission when she's all Claire has in the world. It would be very difficult for both of them."

Phealan smiled sadly and took a deep breath, "The day after tomorrow, my father is going to ship out for Genesis, and he's never coming back. Ever. He's going to die out there with Andra, while I'll be here. And he's all I have left in the world. And I'm all he has in the world. But that's what he's doing."

"Yes, but you're Earthers," Graham's words were quiet. "You're different."

For a fleeting second, Graham remembered the words of his long-dead friend, Savanna Felix. What a great Earther that cat had been... willing, like all Earthers, to die. Able to mourn, able to move on, able to let go.

Earthers were superior to humans in every conceivable way. They could sacrifice themselves and their loved ones...

"So can humans," Phealan said softly, linking his hands behind his back in a way that reminded Graham of Setter. "And either way, she..." he nodded his head towards Christine, "...isn't human anymore. I can see it in her, the same as you can. Some of her humanity remains, but so much of what I feel from her is Earther. She's not going to let you go alone."

Graham sighed, "I'll recommend against it."

"And she'll go anyway. The same way she did when she followed you onto *Carnarvon*."

That drew a shallow frown from Graham, "Why does she do that?"

Phealan managed a sad chuckle, "If you'd clear your head, you might figure it out... but you have something else to worry about right now."

Graham turned his head to question the words, but he realized he could see Sarah and Pat emerging from the trees below the house.

Dad's trying to get her to open up, but she's even worse than you are right now. She has frozen out Pat and everyone else.

"So did I," Graham replied quietly.

"But you just told me you're worried about Christine. Sarah's worried about nothing aside from the mission. She hasn't even explained the plan to Pat."

"Isn't he going with her?" Graham's question deepened his frown, and Phealan's eyebrows rose as he shook his head.

"She hasn't asked anyone yet. But it has to be him."

Graham nodded. This plan was going to gut so many of the people he cared about — it was going to kill so many of his family, be they related by blood or spirit.

But the losses on their particular mission would be miniscule compared to those that would occur in the battle for Earth that would be its dramatic backdrop. Omega was going to take a mighty toll as he fell.

Sarah was coming up the stairs now, her eyes fixed on Graham, and he met her stare. Their chills competed for dominance, each sibling pouring all the ice they could muster into their gazes. Who was more damaged... who was in more pain... did it matter?

Really, I wish you'd stop wearing your pain like a badge of pride, Phealan offered the thought frankly, but neither sibling reacted.

"Sarah," Graham's greeting was not warm, but nor was it entirely cold.

"Graham," Sarah's reply was remarkably warm... compared to others she'd given of late.

Neither contained any genuine emotion, though, and as Setter climbed to the deck and came to a stop next to his son, he couldn't help but feel a pang of regret. He'd tried. They probably wouldn't realize what they'd missed until they were both locked in their respective duels. Then they might well regret this aloofness...

Sarah hugged Graham, and Graham hugged back. For a moment, Setter had hope that the ice walls would fall.

That hopeful second ended when the siblings parted, having gone through the motions but both still totally isolated from each other.

Pat stepped in and extended his hand to Graham, and as the junior Manchester took it Pat yanked him into a big hug.

"Sorry about the last time we saw each other, Graham. Good to see you, again."

More hope filled Setter, and then faded as the hug parted and Graham nodded, "You were right not to go with us to *Genesis One*. But it is good to see you again. Both of you."

Pat nodded, "There you go. Hope for the future"

"You haven't heard the plan yet," Graham observed, almost sounding regretful. "You're going to have to go with Sarah, for all our sakes."

The plan. The stupid, hated, damned plan.

"Come in and we'll explain it to you," Setter waved towards the door, and they all went inside.

CHAPTER 6

Pat hated the damned plan.

He knew it was their best shot at defeating Omega, but he hated it.

It required that they come face to face with the junior avatars — with Omega-Gillian and Omega-Paine, as well as with Omega-King down in Fengate Hospital, though that would be the easiest of the three. And, of course, Setter had to face Omega-Natosh.

And Omega was agreeing to let them come? The plague was no fool. He had to know that Setter had an ulterior motive when suggesting these duels. He had to know what they intended, or at least part of it.

But if he did know, and was ready for it, then all of the people on the Caine estate this night — Phealan and Claire excepted — would die staring at avatars who would mock them and torture them... knowing they'd failed.

It was a fate Pat would have wished on no one, and yet he knew he had no choice but to play his part. Because if the plan did work... if it *somehow*, miraculously worked... well then Omega would be gone.

Civilian or not, he was still a leader, and that was the sort of risk he had to take.

More importantly, Sarah was going, and he couldn't let her go alone. Ever.

Standing on the deck, wearing his jacket to ward off the night's chill, Pat breathed deeply and tried to remember the happy days with Sarah. Some of those great times between the wars... such good times.

It really did seem a lifetime away, as much as Pat hated that clichéd turn of phrase. And the odds were it was all about to end. But Pat wasn't going to let that happen without a fight. They weren't necessarily going to die, and if he could manage it, Pat would find a way to beat the odds...

But this *cure*? The whole thing was such a long shot.

To be relying on something as new and untested as this...

"We're not experienced telepaths, but we have to rely on that," Setter was suddenly leaning against the railing next to Pat.

"A telepathic fight is fine... but this cure? You think he's not going to see the whole scheme coming?"

Setter smiled against the night and sniffed the air the way a wolf would, "I can only hope my mind's strong enough."

Pat let his chin drop, but then he nodded, "Aye. This idea, though, that the cure injected into the avatars will filter down…"

His words trailed off, and Setter nodded, "I know, it's not the most likely thing we've ever come up with. But Celia's done a lot of work that shows there's a chance. Christine's cells being in flux… I don't understand the medicine of it, but she says it's plausible."

Plausible, sure.

"I… I don't say this or even allow myself to think it much anymore, but I wish Elandra was here to explain it to me," Setter said that softly, and Pat looked sideways at the wolf.

"Aye. Sorry again, my friend," the Irishman patted the wolf on the back, and Setter smiled sadly.

"Well just imagine," Pat tried to turn up the mood, "this cure might work. It's plausible, after all. Imagine that."

Setter chuckled and returned the pat on Pat's back, "Yes, my friend, it'd be a great day. I can't count on that, though."

"Aye," Pat agreed.

The pair fell silent for a few moments, and the clouds cleared out of the sky overhead long enough for the stars and the reflections of orbiting ships and stations to be obvious in the night sky.

"We've never been in a fight this massive, have we?" Pat asked, almost smiling. "Gods I hope I get to write this history. What a marvelous story it'd be."

Setter glanced at the Irishman, "You'll tell it well."

"Ha," Pat shook his head. "No, I'd be serviceable, maybe. The story itself is mad, though… the return of a plague that was never really gone, the God complex that bastard has. The rallying of the old allies and the enemies… all your good deeds of the last war coming back to your aid. Has all the right messages — the good ones I'll want my kids to learn. It's like watching destiny unfold right in front of you."

"Destiny," Setter smiled. "I don't know what I think about destiny. But Omega certainly thinks this is his. I'm sure that's one of the reasons he's letting us come to him. He's convinced he's meant to win while looking me in the eye, like it's an old movie with a spy and an arrogant supervillain."

"I was thinking that very thing earlier," Pat agreed, then paused. "Did you pluck that allusion out of my head?"

Setter chuckled, "Paranoid, Pat?"

"Damned right I am. I'll be wearing so much riot gear when we get to Ecclesia, to keep that bastard out of my mind…"

With a laugh, Setter nodded. Again they fell silent, and the wolf took a deep breath of the cold night air.

"Pat, you're probably the most Earther-like human I've ever had the privilege of knowing. I'm not sure if you think that's a compliment, but it's been a pleasure and an honor to call you friend for all these years."

"Oh shit, now don't start talking like that. We're both dead now."

The swearing was for effect, and Setter laughed. Pat joined him, and the two stared at the night sky.

Christine and Claire fell asleep cuddled up next to each other, and as Phealan tossed a blanket over them, he remembered what it had been like, years and years before, to sleep cuddled up like that with his mother.

Sarah had gone away to a guest room, but Graham remained, and as Phealan turned from the sisters he saw that the junior Manchester was staring at them.

I miss being able to be so comforted, the human put that thought on the surface of his mind, and Phealan read it telepathically.

Well, Sarah's here. You're the only one keeping yourself from her.

Graham shook his head. *I'd say she's doing her share too. It's undoubtedly ridiculous, but even under these circumstances we'll not have the warm reunion that I think we both wish we could have. I know you can't understand. It's senseless... but it's the way we are. We won't realize how much we truly regret this until we're both facing death on different planets.*

That does strike me as ridiculous, Phealan agreed. *It's pointless to separate yourselves now.*

It's pointless, but it's the way we must do it. I'm sorry my friend.

Phealan could see the coldness building in Graham again, and he could sense the same from Sarah. Claire had been damaged, but she'd been young and resilient... and she hadn't been dragged down by the subsequent horrors in quite the same way.

With time, Sarah and Graham could find each other again.

But they didn't have any more time... not now. Perhaps not ever.

Setter was taking *Orion* out the day after tomorrow. They would go a week after that — and it would be a week of solid preparations. This was their last night on the same planet without responsibilities...

And despite Setter's and Phealan's hopes, the barriers between the Manchesters wouldn't be cracked in that time.

"You'll find your peace," Phealan said those words reassuringly, and Graham nodded.

"Yes I will. In death, I should expect."

Under other circumstances, the young Caine would have disapproved of the negativity.

But tonight he knew that the sentiment reflected some realism.

CHAPTER 7

Several hours later, and circling high over Earth in the *Venerable*-class ship of the line *Victory* — fresh from the yards, and still being fitted out — First Space Lord Fox Magnus let out a deep sigh.

He really had no business being displeased — the remobilization was going incredibly well, and the yards had moved onto such an epic war-footing that they'd have 150 *Venerables* by the time Omega's deadline arrived.

Those ships had proved virtually invulnerable during Omega's assault on Krogg 'A', so having such a large force of them was fantastic.

But 150 against 5,000?

Of course, the numbers weren't quite that bad — they'd have around 3,000 ships by the time Omega was expected — but even so, there was much to do to get ready.

To get ready to *win*.

Despite the odds, Fox genuinely did expect to survive this fight, and to see Omega gone. He believed in the plan with the enthusiasm that ex-sloop skippers could often have for long shots. Which made his sigh all the more inappropriate... he was probably just tired. His head was also still sore from the knock it had taken weeks before, during the destruction of *Chimera*.

"Fox."

He blinked and looked to his right. Thena, his wife, was trying to draw him back to the meeting.

"Oops, sorry."

Today was Fox's day to host the major commanders' meeting — all the leading Admirals who would be commanding parts of the fleet in the coming battle with Omega were with him aboard *Victory*, including Varnia Lupus, Jax Furgus, Dran Nightclaw, Ami Dune, Zed Dune, Artie Tigar (with limbs restored... but tender!), Minnie Maximane, Ed Jeffries of Freetown, Kardrath of the Krogg Navy, Novash of the Larosian Fleet, and last but by no means least, his old friend Chronos Claw.

It was an impressive collection of warriors, and they'd all been working hard over the past weeks to assemble battle groups that suited their strengths.

When Omega came, it was expected his 5,000 ships would run straight at Earth, so they could drop their billions of minions. The 3,000 ships commanded by these officers would obviously try to interfere in that process... but they'd have to be very smart about it.

As First Lord of the Admiralty (not First Space Lord), Lab was going to command the entire operation from *Venerable*, but he was going to be charged not just with command of the 2,600 ships, but also with command of the orbital stations and the 50,000 gunboats Earth would launch.

Fleet command — command of the warships — would go to Fox. He'd be under Lab's orders, but it would be up to the dapper little fox to exercise operational command of the mobile squadrons.

Hence the meetings. They had to make the most of their available ships.

Chronos and Varnia would split the *Venerables* save for Fox's First Battle Squadron. Nightclaw, Jax, Ami, Zed and Artie would split the 1,000 recommissioned Krogg War ships, while Minnie Maximane would command what was left of the inter-war ships — the *Champions* and other first and second-generation post-Krogg War ships.

Kardrath would, obviously, command his Krogg Navy, and Novash would be in charge of the Larosian Fleet. Their superiors — Kragran and Narosh respectively — would be concerned with both the space battles and the land battle that was sure to come.

Omega's troops were going to get to ground, that was inevitable... but the Earthers would still win.

"Fox."

Chronos took his turn prodding the First Space Lord, and Fox Magnus blinked again and shook his head, "Sorry, was thinking."

"Yeah, we know, we're all telepathic now remember?" Jax sounded as crotchety as ever. The old cat liked this plan for one reason: if it worked, it'd gut the plague.

If it didn't, really, they'd be no worse off than if the plan hadn't existed in the first place.

Nothing to lose.

"Stop being so grim, would you?" Artie prodded the old lion. "We can hear what you're thinking just as well as we can hear him."

Yeah well I'm allowed my internal dialogue! Jax shot back.

"Don't make me have Kardrath and Novash separate you two," Ami Dune interceded, and the Larosian and the Krogg sitting down the table looked at each other almost sheepishly.

Fox slapped the table lightly with his open hand, "I actually want to see that. Could be entertaining!"

There were laughs all around — his joke wasn't terribly funny, but it was taken in the right spirit.

"Good that you admit to yourself that it wasn't funny," Thena murmured next to him.

"Hey!"

•••

In one of the briefing rooms in Antarctic Base, Beckett Lupus was sitting at a similar table with his Generals. They had their own daunting challenge... perhaps the most daunting of all.

The Earther Marine Corps, even with a rapid expansion drive over the past two weeks, still numbered only 454,000 troops.

That number was, to Beckett Lupus, quite remarkable: every Earther who'd ever served with the marines had seemed to come back, some of them over 220 years old. Even so, fewer than half a million troops was no sort of match for the *billions* Omega was bringing.

Sitting with his old friend Colonel Cadmus Howler, along with General Karyn Kudlee, General Cedric Lion, Lieutenant General Garnett Wiskar, Warlord Kragthar, and Captain-Elite Tovarrin, Beckett was acutely aware of the challenge before them.

The Earther people were mostly staying on their planet. Some were going to evacuate to New Halifax, but many would remain. Those Earthers who were staying expected to fight when the minions landed — fight with all the natural fearsomeness and ability that came with being Earthers. Beckett's job, and that of the marines, was to make certain they had as much help as possible.

But trying to defend an entire planet was not a simple matter.

"So you've sent the humans on?" Captain-Elite Tovarrin asked the question verbally, and it drew Beckett's attention.

"Yes... after what we saw on Freetown, I doubt there'd be much point keeping their troops around. Their marines represent at least one percent of the surviving human population... they need to survive," Beckett nodded as he explained his thinking.

"Ed Jeffries will be keeping some of the human fleet here, but the Genesis marines are going to New Halifax for ground security," Kudlee added. "And to be evacuated if necessary."

Nodding, Tovarrin sat back in his seat. The Larosian was enjoying his first real experience in dealing with Earthers — he'd met some when they'd come to his world aboard *Carnarvon*, but now he was seeing how they lived, and how they thought. It was remarkable, and he enjoyed the proximity.

"I cannot come up with any good deployment suggestions, I'm afraid," Kragthar leaned forward on his box-chair, managing to lay his bottom pair of arms on the tabletop without jamming his bone blades into it. "With the number of minions Omega has, I can only assume he'll try to land everywhere."

Beckett nodded at the Krogg's apt observation, and contained (yet again) some surprise at the quality of the alien's English. The Kroggs certainly had come a long way since last he'd seen them... back on the plateau of the Queen's spire, behind a battle line of the Guards Brigade of the Heavy Division...

A long way indeed.

And of course Kragthar was entirely correct. When Shappa Elias Bactule had conducted his invasion of Earth, he'd had but 100,000 troops, and had confined his landings to this very base.

The chances of Omega being so obliging were non-existent. Having billions of minions would allow him to put a massive number of troops in every population center on Earth — to attack everything in force.

Of course, every city had layers of shields, and huge numbers of energy cannon were being installed on the ground to cut through minions as they fell from the sky... but it really was like trying to stop the rain. Even the protective shield-and-gun arrangement would only change where Omega landed — the way that water ran off an umbrella and still fell to the ground, the minions would likely manage the very same.

So with 454,000 marines, eleven million Krogg Warriors — everything the new allies could muster by the deadline — and 121,000 Stealth Guards, Beckett and the officers assembled here had to protect an entire *planet*.

His planet.

Earth.

Beckett inadvertently let out a sigh, and sitting beside him, his old friend and comrade Cadmus Howler forced himself to smile, "Yeah, we have our work cut out for us."

Nods of agreement came from everyone around the table.

Lab Forepaw, Varnon Broadpaw, Narosh and Kragran sat in Lab's office in the Admiralty House building, looking at a glowing three-dimensional map of the planet.

"Every city's defensive shield will be tougher than Freetown's... but I can't expect they'll last very long," Lab was referring to the thousands of cities and towns that were marked by glowing white icons on the holo globe, and Varnon and the aliens nodded in turn.

"Beckett's still trying to figure out how to deploy us... I'll leave that to him, as he's much better at it than I am. But Varnon, your civil defense model is definitely the one we'll have to use."

First Consul Varnon Broadpaw nodded again as he studied the map. Every Earther would be armed — *every* Earther. Those who couldn't fight were going to New Halifax before this mess started... the couple of billion who remained would all be ready to defend their homes. Regular, ordinary, everyday Earthers were being issued swords and rifles, and even now, marines were moving around teaching and advising on tactics.

One marine would teach a dozen Earthers in a city, and each of them would teach a dozen, and each of them a dozen... eventually, all the latest techniques would trickle down to every remaining Earther.

Combined with the natural martial instinct that seemed inherent in all

Earthers thanks to their predatory ancestors, that would hopefully be enough...

To help.

"It's not so much a plan as just 'make everybody fight'," Varnon said quietly after a moment. "How's the installation of the gun batteries going?"

Lab nodded, "Pretty well. All our manufacturing capacity that isn't going into ships or boats is building them... there'll be almost a million guns pointing skyward by the time Omega gets here."

A million... not bad... yes, Varnon could accept a million...

Narosh couldn't help but laugh, and both Earthers and the Krogg glanced at him in slight surprise.

I'm sorry my friends, the Admiral-of-a-Fleet started telepathically, then switched to words, "It's just so remarkable, your industry. It took our Empire more than sixty fully industrial worlds to maintain our Navy. From one planet, one base of production, you are producing a mighty fleet, and an endless streams of weapons. It is truly impressive."

Varnon let out a breath and replied with a small smile, "It's always been one of our strengths. But. Well, we may have enough equipment, but we don't have enough people to use it."

Kragran leaned forward in his seat, "Yes, but you have enough to make a good fight."

Varnon's eyes darted to Lab's, and the First Lord of the Admiralty half-shrugged, "True... and if the plan works, that's all we'll need to do. Keep them busy for long enough..."

The mention of the plan brought silence to the table again, but Krag broke it, "When the time comes, my Warriors will defend your Earthers with all our fury. And I know Narosh's Stealth Guards will fight with their utmost."

Narosh agreed immediately, "We'll be here."

Lab and Varnon both took some comfort from those assurances, but of course, none of it might be enough.

When Omega came, few things really could be *enough*.

CHAPTER 8

"Do you *have* to go back?"

Phealan overheard part of Claire's conversation with Christine the next morning, and he winced at that question. Christine did have to go back to her preparations — she was necessary to the plan. It had to be her, or else the gambit would become even more transparent.

That meant leaving her sister behind... though because she and Graham didn't have to ship out for Freetown for another eight days, she would be able to come back and see Claire again...

Still, that didn't make it any easier to leave right now. After being reunited for less than twenty four hours, Claire was having to say goodbye to her sister yet again... and that could never be easy.

Despite that reality though, something about Christine remained cool and assured... Phealan could detect it as he silently observed her. She definitely had a lot of Earther character in her now. It was making such a difference in the way she handled things. Maybe it'd help her survive this mission, and come home after the plan was done.

"You're going to get evacuated to New Halifax, I'll see you just before you leave... and we'll meet there once the battle's over... just a couple of weeks," Christine was saying now, and Phealan's ear twitched.

All humans were being evacuated from Earth, their minds having proved far too vulnerable to Omega's landed minions to allow them to stay. He didn't savor the thought of sending Claire away — *again* — but it seemed best for her.

And it was only until the battle was over, as Christine had said. If all went well, then Claire would come back to Earth. If it went badly, she'd join the surviving Allies in a retreat to the Larosian galaxy through the New Halifax corridor, which would then be collapsed behind them.

Phealan didn't dare chance a guess at which would be the ultimate outcome. He had his part to play in the plan, and he'd continue to focus on that...

No, actually, he would focus on the outcome.

Everyone else in Earth space seemed wary to be confident, Fox Magnus excepted. Phealan was a firm believer that the first place a battle could be lost was in one's own mind... that tired old adage held so much truth it couldn't be ignored.

Phealan had to believe that they were going to win. If the Earthers had learned anything in the last war, it was that sticking to their beliefs and trusting their instincts was vitally important. Now he had to stick to his. They'd win. They had to win.

As that thought crossed the young Caine's mind, Sarah and Pat emerged into the living room behind him, followed by Graham. The siblings were still cool, but kind words had been exchanged.

They'd still regret all they'd not said, Phealan was certain of that, but at least they'd had a chance to spend time together. Over the next week, they'd see precious little of each other...

Phealan knew these feelings all too well.

Separation under grim circumstances had dominated his young life. He hadn't fought a war — not himself — and he'd certainly never faced the death of so many. But he'd learned much in his father's absence during the Krogg War... and added to that, somewhere within him, it felt as though there was a wealth of wisdom that wasn't his own. Perhaps he had an old soul, as it was sometimes called.

There was really no time to wonder about that, though. He was just glad he had it.

We're all glad. You've got the most even keel of all of us right now, Setter's thoughts appeared in his son's mind, and Phealan chuckled.

That's how desperate we are, I know.

They ceased their telepathic joking as Phealan turned back towards the living room and saw his father arrive there. The exchange of final farewells began.

Pat went to Setter first, and with a hug the Irishman said goodbye, "You die well out there, my friend. And thank you so much for doing it."

It was not the sort of goodbye Setter had ever received before, but now he nodded and drew away from Pat, "Come back here, Pat. Good luck."

The Irishman stepped back and looked directly at Setter for a moment. Then a smile crept onto his face, "We'll make the bastard feel it."

That was sure enough.

Phealan appeared next to Pat, and they hugged too, "See you again sometime, somewhere, kiddo. You'll do damned good."

With a smile, Pat left the Caine house. He didn't want to wait inside now that he'd said his goodbyes.

Sarah came next, following her husband. Her hug to Setter was much more reserved, but beneath her powerful façade of ice, Setter could feel a spark of the warmth that she really did feel for him. It was good to feel that tiny sliver.

She said nothing as she broke their hug, and then embraced Phealan. It was only as she headed for the door that she stopped, turned around and stared at the two wolves, "I wish..."

Swallowing hard, she managed to get the words out, "I wish you'd been at Genesis. I wish you'd been there so we could have stopped all this where it started. But I'm glad you're going back there, because I couldn't. Good luck."

Setter held up his hand, "And to you, my old friend. You'll do us all proud... you'll do *me* proud."

Sarah's face twitched almost unnoticeably at the last words, and she quickly turned away and headed out, putting the warm sentiments behind her before they cracked her resolve. She and Pat set off through the woods.

Turning away from the door, Setter realized Graham was standing next to him, and the cool look on the junior Manchester's face seemed a little less concrete.

"I'd say I'll miss you, but I wager we'll both be killed around the same moment," the human said softly.

"Not a bet I'd want to take," Setter smiled. "A little hope doesn't hurt."

"I suppose it doesn't," Graham agreed. Then he extended his hand to the wolf, "Do good out there, Setter."

Taking the hand, Setter nodded and looked into Graham's eyes. The junior Manchester was ready for this, more so even than his sister was.

"You do good too, Graham," he answered simply, and then the ArcGeneral stepped away.

Stopping next to Phealan, the human repeated the handshake, and then he put a hand on the younger wolf's shoulder, "You're going to be the most important Earther in the world pretty soon. And none better for it."

Phealan smiled, then patted Graham's shoulder in return, "We'll see. Good luck. Face her, Graham. You may yet come back stronger."

Graham stared at Phealan for a second, then he nodded, released the younger wolf's hand, and headed out the door.

Christine and Claire were still entangled on the couch, but Christine was slowly pulling away from her sister, whispering comforting things in her ear.

"I'll be back to see you again, I promise... but I have to go for now..."

Claire's grip on her was understandably iron — Phealan probably couldn't have physically shaken it off. Claire did *not* want to lose her only sister, her only family left in the whole world.

She held onto Christine for dear life, crying desperately, while Christine tried to keep a stern façade. That didn't work — Christine was riddled with Earther character, but over the past day she'd also become a sister again. She didn't want to go, and yet she did, and trying to make Claire understand that was difficult...

So Phealan abruptly decided to help.

Pardon this... I'm sorry to be rude, but I think it might be of some use.

Claire and Christine were shocked to suddenly find themselves standing in a white place — nothing but bright whiteness in all directions. Up, down, front, back... even underfoot, everything was bright white, without texture or shadow.

"This is the telepathic plane... I think that's what we're supposed to call it," Phealan appeared out of the light standing aside from the two, and he looked between them. "You can spend hours here... days theoretically... and only seconds will pass in the real world. Less than seconds, sometimes. Take some time, Christine, and explain it to her. Up here, I think you'll be able to convey emotions better than down there. Your minds are connected directly."

With that, Phealan vanished, at least from their corner of the boundless plane.

Setter frowned when silence fell over the sisters, and then he glanced at his son and noted the blue swirling that had filled Phealan's eyes. He'd taken them up to the telepathic plane... what a good idea. Of course now in the physical world, they were all essentially statues, so if he wanted to speak to his son, he'd have to go in too.

Stepping forward and turning, he looked into his son's blue-swirling eyes, then reached out and put a hand on his shoulder. That was the fastest way to connect...

Phealan was waiting patiently, far away from the sisters so that they could share their private thoughts and feelings without fear of observation. Setter appeared beside him as he waited, and the son smiled at the father.

"I love this telepathic thing. So many more options."

Setter smiled, "Certainly. I should have thought to bring Sarah and Graham up here. They could have used the time."

"If I get the chance, I'll do it after you leave. You could probably even be in on it."

With a nod, Setter agreed. Even as far away as Genesis, the Larosians had explained that there was no reason why strong minds couldn't reach each other on this plane. The elder Caine certainly hoped that was true... he needed it to be true.

He was going to leave his son behind on this mission. Being able to see him here on this plane, despite being ten days away, would be good.

Essential, even.

"How long has it been?" Phealan asked after a stretch of minutes, and Setter carefully checked his mental timekeeper.

"About twenty minutes in plane time... feels like much less out there."

Phealan nodded, reaching out with his mind towards Christine, "She's close to done. I think she's been able to explain to Claire what's happening to her."

Setter nodded, "Good. Well, she can have all the time she needs."

"Absolutely," Phealan agreed.

CHAPTER 9

"I can walk, I can fight."

Celia Lazarus felt slightly outgunned when her patient made that protest, but she held her ground, "You've only had that leg for two days."

"It'll be ten days by the time Omega gets here, I can fight."

Elizabeth Hastings had a new leg — again — and was determined not to be in bed or evacuated when the plague that had become the bane of the universe came to Earth. She was staggering unevenly around her room in Fengate Hospital, demonstrating to the good doctor Lazarus that she had the ability to stand on a ship's bridge... but Celia wasn't having any of it.

"It's my recommendation, but it's also an order from the top. Setter Caine thinks you'll be much more important at New Halifax," the doctor shot back at her patient, and Liz shook her head.

"Why would I be better there than here, exactly?"

The frustration of having lost a leg again was almost a surprise to Liz. She'd managed to keep her perspective all through the lead up to the battle for Krogg 'A', but now that she'd been knocked out of action yet again, she was losing her calm.

She always seemed to get wounded and thrown out of wars. She was supposed to lead, to help her people through and to die if necessary. Instead she always ended up in bed.

Celia couldn't answer her question, either — the doctor wasn't a strategist, as much as her cures were going to affect the final fight against Omega. She'd been spending most of her time now trying to figure out how to repair Christine's fluxed DNA, since she'd made use of it to create the cure...

"It's not for her to explain, is it?"

The question came from the doorway, and Liz wheeled to take a strip off whoever had asked it. Halfway through her stumbled rotation, the former ArcGeneral and President realized she knew the voice.

She hadn't heard it in years, but she knew the voice so very well.

Andra Ursla had crossed the distance between the door and Liz by the time the human had finished turning, and with a broad grin the great bear took Liz's hand, "Welcome back to Earth."

Liz actually laughed, "I've been here five days, you could have stopped by sooner!"

Chuckling, Ursla shook her head, "Sorry, it's been busy with getting the plan squared away."

"The plan, yeah I heard about it," Liz's elevated spirits dropped. "I heard you're going to Genesis with Setter."

Ursla's smile faded away, and the great bear nodded, "I am. And you're going to New Halifax."

Liz shook her head, "I'm staying here. I'm not missing this fight."

You have to. We really need you at New Halifax, Ursla's words went straight to Liz's mind this time, and the human froze, still unaccustomed to having Earthers do that to her.

Look, we're not trying to send you away so that you don't get hurt... we're sending all the last pieces of human society out there. They're going to need a leader, and Sarah is not that person.

Liz's face tightened instantly, and detecting a new tension in the room, Celia elected to leave the two old friends — the first Earther-human friends, come to think of it — to deal with serious issues. Hobbling back to her bed, Liz hopped up onto it with a wince and shook her head.

"No, I... President was not a good job for me. Probably ended up being the worst years of my life," Liz said that sharply — bitterly. "I'm not doing that again. I'm supposed to fight and die here with you."

Ursla studied her friend, "That's what you want to do, I know. You hate not being in the fight, and you hate having the weight of leadership on your shoulders."

"Don't make me sound like a shirker," Liz protested, and Ursla held up her hands.

"Not what I meant to do. But Liz, it's *you* who has to do this. We'd love for you to be here... Lab and Fox would love to have you. Ed Jeffries would love to have you in command of the human ships. But if we fail, and we might, then the escapees from New Halifax are going to need you."

Liz hated the words as much as their meaning. Ursla was asking her... *telling* her, actually... to miss a fight, yet again. During the Krogg War, Liz had been painted into the same corner. It had been said that only she could lead the Navy, and then the Naval class... only she could handle that much responsibility.

So back then, Sarah had been the one to command the Genesis Fleet to war, right until the end when Liz had forced her way in.

But now it was happening again. She was the responsible one, so she had to leave her friends to die while she went to the rear and looked after the civilians.

She wanted to fight and to *die*, dammit. She'd had a long run, she could go out now, fighting Omega... it was only by some minor miracle that she'd survived his attack at Krogg 'A' in the first place. She'd been ready to die. She still was. She couldn't run.

You're not running, you're going where we need you to go, and where your people need you to go.

"I'm sick of doing what my *people* need me to do," Liz started to vent, and Ursla realized she was going to need backup.

"I want to do something for myself for once... dammit, I'm staying here and I'm fighting this bastard alongside all of you. You're my friends, and I'm... going..."

Liz's words trailed off when she realized she was standing in whiteness, and Ursla was standing opposite her.

"Telepathic plane, sorry to abduct you but Andra said you were causing trouble," Setter Caine's voice came from behind Liz, and she turned sharply to see him walking towards her.

Then she realized that, in turning, her leg had been quite fine — not the achy and tender, recently-reattached encumbrance it really was.

"So this is the plane," she said, taking it in for a moment as Setter came to a stop in front of her. "You're at home?"

Setter nodded, "Phealan and I are just about to head out for a hike. I was going to come see you tomorrow before I left."

"Ah..." Liz looked from Setter back to Ursla. "Well you probably won't need to... this is... as good as being there, I think."

"Certainly can get used to it," Setter agreed. "But either way, Liz, you need to go. I know you don't want to, but we need you to. So please don't fight us on this."

Ah, they were trying to tag team her — she'd show them...

"Show us what?" Ursla rounded Liz to stand next to Setter, and the human mentally kicked herself. Of course they could hear her thoughts up here... and everywhere now. Earthers as telepaths were just scary — scary in a good way, but scary all the same. They'd been able to see so much with just instincts... now to have the capacity to read minds, that was just mad.

"Listen, Liz, *please*. You know what we're planning... you know how much of a long shot it is. We need you with the humans at New Halifax, so that we know there's still a chance, no matter what," Setter's earnest words drew Liz's gaze back to him, and she stared for a moment.

There was something in the old wolf's eyes... she wasn't sure how to explain it to herself, but she saw it. She felt like she'd seen it before...

Once, before Harvey Bingham had died on Genesis. He'd looked right at her, and said that the planet would fall... that he'd failed to do what he'd set out to do. He'd known then that Pious and Paine — the old Church bastards — were going to pull something, and they had. Their coup had cleaved Genesis wide open, and left the opening for Omega to exploit.

That look of dark tragedy was so similar to the look in Setter's eyes now...

the look of certainty that said he knew he'd be facing death and destruction, and that he desperately wanted someone to be spared from it.

And to pick up the pieces.

Once again, that someone had to be Liz.

With a long sigh, she closed her eyes and nodded.

They stayed on the plane to catch up for a while — to remember the good old days, and some of the bad ones — but the decision had been made: Liz was going to New Halifax, and from there she'd take up the leadership reins yet again.

It was her lot in life, it seemed.

CHAPTER 10

It wasn't the most classically beautiful day Setter had ever seen... it was about average, really. The clouds were in, the wind was up, it was raining and it was still unusually muggy for Newfoundland. If he'd been asked what sort of weather he'd have wanted for his last day on Earth, this wasn't it.

But it didn't really matter. Rain was only water, and muggy or not, the wind was crisp, the air fresh. This was his home, and no weather was going to take that away from him on his last full day here.

Phealan climbed ahead of him, the rain bouncing off his son's shield with a smattering of light flashes.

"We're near the top now," Phealan called, pointing forward towards the summit of the large hill they were climbing.

Setter had been up this way a few times before — there was a clearing at the top that looked out over the coast. The vista was incredible, and Setter hadn't seen it in so long, he'd decided he wanted to see it today.

On this, his last full day on Earth.

Last day on Earth...

So many times he'd heard that string of words together in various contexts, but rarely had they been so literal. It was rare that someone really knew that a day was going to be his or her last on Earth, but when the knowledge did exist, the person could make the most of it. And that was what he was determined to do.

He and Phealan were hiking around the estate, and while it wasn't the most adventurous hike they'd ever shared, or the most spirited, it was still a good one.

Father and son emerged into the clearing just as the rain broke, and Setter smiled to himself as the cool air from the higher altitude relieved some of the mugginess. As the rain halted, he and Phealan both turned off their shields, then together they looked out to sea.

This place was so beautiful. Here, on this very island, over seven centuries prior, Alpha Caine had been born. Newfoundland was, in the final analysis, the birthplace of Earther civilization... a truly incredible place.

And staring out to sea, over the rocky cliffs, the forests, the grassy clearings and the bogs, it seemed right to Setter. He took a deep breath and felt some peace. This was his last day on Earth, he was lucky enough to know it, and he was at home, in the place he loved most, with his son.

Couldn't really ask for anything more.

"The idea of a last day always scares me more than anything else," Phealan adjusted his stance slightly, his gaze directed out towards the horizon. "The thought of this being the last time I do something... the last time I pull on these walking boots, or the last time I see this view... the last goodbye... all of that, it scares me more than the thought of the end itself."

Setter nodded, "The 'lasts' are a stark reminder of what you're losing."

Phealan took a deep breath.

This was the last day, and the last hike, and the last afternoon. Soon it'd be the last sunset, and the last sleep at home... all the things that had made life so good were going to be at an end. Setter was going to walk away from them... that part he was fine with. Once he left, it would be easy.

But leaving was going to be so very hard. Leaving all these things he loved, and obviously, leaving his son...

This is the last day.

"Did you ever wonder what you'd do on your last day? Think of what you'd do, and how short it would seem?" Phealan couldn't help but ask, and Setter blinked a few times as the wind sharpened against his face.

"I did. Maybe we all do. When you're waiting for a battle, the hours are so long you just want them gone. Now they're the only hours that remain to you... thinking about how little time you have left is the most frightening thing. How not to waste that time... trying to do everything you need to..."

"Easy to get caught up figuring out what you want to do, and to forget what's most important," Phealan finished Setter's thought for him, and the elder wolf agreed telepathically.

We're lucky, people like you and I... we can see what's the most important essence of our life. We know that whatever else we are, we're from this place. We love being here... so we know how to spend our last days. I think all Earthers have that... but Sarah and Graham clearly don't. They're not so lucky, and that saddens me.

Phealan nodded slowly.

They were lucky. Despite the grim odds presented by the plan, and the probability of death ahead, they were fortunate. They'd known this day was coming, and they'd even *chosen* the day. Many people never got that chance. Elandra hadn't.

So this was good. If they had to be parted, and probably killed, then this was the way it should happen.

That thought was common to them both, and now they each took great lungfuls of the cool breeze and closed their eyes.

If you want more time, we could go to the telepathic plane, Phealan thought to his father, but he knew that prospect wasn't really appealing.

It wasn't how much time he had that mattered to Setter, but where and how it was spent. A telepathic plane couldn't compare to this place and this time, and his thoughts revealed as much.

Didn't think so, Phealan smiled to himself.

"I don't understand the human obsession with more time, when the quality is what matters," Setter admitted quietly, and Phealan opened his eyes and shook his head.

"You just said it, they often don't understand what's at the core of themselves. I don't think you or I would be at peace about this if we didn't know our deeper selves. I guess they want more time hoping they'll find the understanding... or fearing death..."

Opening his eyes too, Setter smiled at his son's words, "Deep talk for someone so young."

Phealan laughed, "You don't know the half of it."

They sat in the long grass in the clearing for what felt like hours, letting the wind run over them, ignoring the rain as it returned for a few minutes, and watching a fog bank appear far out on the horizon, drifting south before clearing again.

This was what was right. Sniffing the air like the wolves they were descended from, enjoying the moves and gasps of the planet to which they felt so connected. Being here at home, and being together. For the last day. For the last time.

"It's going to hit me like a missile once you're gone," Phealan said quietly after those hours of silence. "I'm not feeling it yet, but after you're gone, and after Omega's gone... I'm going to be completely lost. I'm going to have to try to hold to the beliefs I have right now, and do the things you've taught me... But it'll be very hard."

"I don't envy you that," Setter agreed quietly. "Even when you're as aware as we can be... you're never quite ready for how it feels to lose people, and to have to command."

"I expect not."

"But you know you'll survive it."

"I'll just have to weather it, and see what I'm like on the other side. That's something we can never predict, isn't it?"

Setter nodded, "Completely impossible to foresee... but I know you'll be fine. You know more than I've ever taught you. Sometimes I feel like all I've ever done is just set you up for something so great I couldn't even comprehend it. I hope that's the way it is."

With a smile, Phealan shook his head, "We'll see where things go once Omega's gone... once you're gone."

Again Setter nodded, and then he sighed. The sun was beginning to dip behind their backs as the day wore on. They simply sat and looked east.

"I wish the wolves had come back. I'd have liked to say my goodbyes," Setter murmured, and Phealan frowned and looked around the clearing.

"That would be... that... look at this."

Setter blinked and forced his eyes away from the horizon, turning his head just in time to see one of the wolves appear next to him.

He tried to think a question to Phealan — *where did they come from* — but his mind didn't seem able to actually process the query, or more precisely, to send it. His relief at seeing the wolves... a massive pack of maybe thirty... overwhelmed that ability, or so he assumed. He hoped it wasn't a case of him losing his telepathic ability when he was distracted... but he refused to worry.

Even if he and Phealan were telepathically deaf for a moment, the wolves needed no clever thinking to be understood. Earther instincts meshed with wolf instincts, and as the leader of the pack seated himself next to Setter, the Supreme Consul rubbed the grinning predator's neck, then extended an instinctive greeting, and offered his thanks.

This was the last time he'd see the wolves, and that hurt as much as anything else.

A couple of pups, lanky with big ears and paws, came to play again with Phealan, and he enjoyed the warmth of their presence. The wolves always brought with them a feeling of serenity and security. Even if Omega was coming, they were at peace.

But, Phealan realized abruptly, when the minions landed, the wolves would have to hide. Animals wouldn't be the plague's first target, but they'd have a hell of a time looking after themselves if he took over.

Yet another reason this plan had to work. Phealan couldn't stand the thought of losing his ancestors too...

Setter held his head close to the alpha wolf's, and breathed deep, "I'm leaving soon, and I won't be back, my friend. You need to look after your pack, and Phealan... I'll miss you."

The wolf looked Setter squarely in the eyes, closed his mouth, and then flicked his ear. Thanks to instincts, if nothing else, the wolf understood his humanoid cousin.

Things will be safe here, Setter thought to himself, evidently able to focus after all.

Then the wolves departed, the pups leaving an instinctive promise in their wake — Phealan would play with them again, they seemed to say. The younger Caine smiled and nodded to himself, "They may not realize all that's coming, but it doesn't matter to them."

"It's not how much time they have, it's the quality of the time," Setter remarked quietly. "That's where we get it from, I think. If they all died tomorrow, they wouldn't lament it. Just part of the experience of being here... they live simple, rich lives."

Phealan huffed a sigh and looked back out to sea, "Not quite an option for us, is it?"

"Our lives are different," Setter noticed the dying light. "And mine's almost over. We should get back home."

Without further words, the Caines got to their feet and set off for their house. For the last time, Setter had seen the horizon from his favorite place on Earth. For the last time he'd seen the wolves.

For the last time he'd enjoyed a day at home.

It was a fine last day on Earth.

Tomorrow he would leave for Genesis.

CHAPTER 11

The morning of Setter Caine's departure wasn't nearly as quiet as his last full day on Earth. He left his house for the final time, wishing the very best to Claire and then traveling to Halifax by pinnace, where he was to meet with Lab and Varnon at Admiralty House. There were final arrangements to be made before *Orion* left Earth space later in the day... and everyone on Earth knew that.

Millions of Earthers crowded the streets of Halifax as Setter and Phealan walked from the Citadel Landing Field down towards Admiralty House. Millions. They were silent — verbally and telepathically — as they filled the city with a feeling of great hope, and pride.

Every Earther knew the plan. Setter, Lab and Varnon had considered trying to keep it from them, but since they all were a part of it, the idea had made no sense. Certainly there was a security risk — Omega could pluck the details from an unguarded mind, perhaps — but the marines and officers guarding Omega-King in Fengate were focusing their new telepathic powers to jam that avatar's receptors.

The Earthers had a right to know, so they'd been told.

They knew that Setter Caine, their great leader, was preparing to leave Earth for the last time, and those millions who could make the trip came to Halifax to show their solidarity. Many were old spacers and marines who'd fought the Krogg War under his orders, turned out in their uniforms in a great sign of silent respect.

Setter couldn't help but smile gratefully as the crowds parted for him on street after street, all the way to Admiralty House. It was the greatest vote of confidence he'd ever received, and it made this all somehow easier.

Arriving at Admiralty House, he found a welcoming committee as grand as the reception outside. Cadmus Howler had drawn up his Second Battalion of the 54th Regiment of Foot on the lawn, and with the precision they were known for, those 500 marines came smartly to attention.

Beckett Lupus stood before them, with Varnia next to him, and both smiled warmly at Setter. Next to them were Varnon, Lab, Fox, Jax, Artie Tigar, Ami and Zed Dune, Dran Nightclaw, Minnie Maximane, and Ursla. Standing off to the side were Kragran, Narosh and Novash.

So many old friends. So many great warriors.

Phealan stepped up next to his father, smiling broadly, *I don't think they want a speech.*

Good, the only one I have I recorded for later, Setter thought back warmly.

He pulled a disc out of his pocket and handed it to his son, "That's my contribution for the speeches before action. It's pretty good, I think... though yours will be better."

Phealan laughed, still happy enough — still not saying goodbye. They had hours before he'd have to do that.

Setter stepped forward, and all his friends seemed to collapse around him, surrounding him and wishing him well.

For hours, the meetings went on, and each of Setter's old friends was able to say a personal goodbye. Ursla, who was the second Earther on the mission to Genesis, was able to say her goodbyes as well... it was a strange, strange morning.

"This is a strange sort of morning," Fox Magnus craned his neck to look way up at Ursla, and she smiled.

The pair was striding down one of Admiralty House's corridors, preferring to walk and talk instead of spending even more time in one of the briefing rooms they'd been situated in all morning.

"It's very strange," the great bear agreed. "A lot is going to be riding on you in a week... you know that, don't you?"

Fox laughed, "That fact occupies every waking and sleeping moment."

Ursla grinned, "I suppose it does."

The two old Admirals sobered after that, and they continued to pace in silence for a little while.

"Remember when we went to Genesis together... Chronos and Lang and I scouted the place in *Flame*, and then you sent us back here for help... and then we ran into the Freetowners on the way..." Fox's words trailed off.

All those adventures, written up by Pat in his *Alien Equation,* were dead and gone.

"Hard to believe it, but those were *good* days," Ursla stated with some irony.

Fox nodded, "And we'll make more good days. You do your part, and I'll make sure enough of us come through to make more good days."

Ursla's smile returned almost painfully, "Yes. Make sure of that, Fox. We're counting on you..."

"I know," the dapper First Space Lord replied. "Believe me, I do know."

When the meetings broke, and departure time neared, a line formed outside the briefing room that Setter Caine was occupying. One by one, all his old warriors came to pay him their final respects, and the mood was not bright.

Dran Nightclaw shook Setter's hand, then left him to look for Ursla. Ami and Zed Dune came up to the Supreme Consul and shook his hand in turn.

"Good hunting out there, sir," Ami looked into his eyes, her white face tight. "We'll miss you."

"Very much," Zed immediately followed her words, and then with parting nods they exited.

Chronos Claw smiled at Setter and shook his hand, "We'll look after things here."

Minnie Maximane had no words as she clasped his hand tightly in her own, before turning quickly to leave.

Artie Tigar came by next, "Glad you'll be able to put *Orion* to good use… all these years later."

"Glad your museum looked after it so well, Artie," Setter smiled at the cat, and Artie laughed.

"Somehow I knew we'd need it again one day."

Shaking Setter's hand, then, Artie moved after Dran Nightclaw to find Ursla.

"Like a damned funeral, and you're not even dead."

That tone was unmistakable, and Setter grinned as Jax Furgus sauntered over to him with folded arms, "By the Earth, you sure know how to make an exit."

"Don't get any ideas. After all this is over I want you to be alive and crotchety as ever. If your ship goes up, you better be in an escape pod… just like old times," Setter shot the words right back at the grizzled lion, who'd had countless ships shot out from under him during the Krogg War.

"Deal," Jax nodded, then unfolded his arms to extend his hand to Setter. "I don't plan on getting killed by some damned overblown flu."

Setter chuckled, "I'm going to miss you, Jax."

The lion's eyes softened, and he stepped closer to the wolf, "Not nearly as much as we'll miss you. We'll look after things, but by the Earth we'll miss you. It's been a real honor, and I mean that. You do what you always do… you beat that bastard. And we'll see you there in the end."

The earnest tone was not one Jax often used anymore — at his age, irreverence was his chosen tone of interaction.

But the old cat couldn't be irreverent about this — about Setter and Andra's departure.

Old friends riding off to their last battle… Jax knew what sort of sacrifice that was.

"And say hi to Savanna for me, if you end up meeting him. Tell the old tiger I'll see him again one of these days… but not too soon," Jax added with a grin.

Setter smiled again, and nodded, "I will."

Jax stepped back, and with a touch of class he threw a casual salute at his old war leader. Then he left the conference room.

• • •

"Wish I was going with you," Artie Tigar had convinced Ursla to stop pacing the corridors and join him in another of Admiralty House's briefing rooms, citing the tenderness of his reattached legs and arms.

Ursla smiled at her former Flag Captain's sentiment, but shook her head, "I don't need to tell you that you need to be here. And you... I never got to give you credit for it, but you're the only one who really predicted Omega's moves. Back when he hit New Halifax, you knew he was coming."

Artie smiled and shrugged, "Guess I still have the knack."

He did indeed. During the Krogg War Artie Tigar had predicted Krogg plans quite well... now he was doing it again. The cat had a gift, and a fearsome fighting ability to go with it.

"I'm flying my flag from *Agamemnon*, still. Battered and bruised, but it'll fight in the old style. Do you proud," Artie observed then, and Ursla nodded.

"That's good. That's very good."

The pair stared at the table before them for a moment, and then Artie's eyes darted up and caught Ursla's gaze, "You do good out there, alright? And if you get a chance, tell that bastard I say hello."

Getting to his feet, Artie noticed that Dran Nightclaw had come to the conference room door. Extending his new hand to Ursla, he said his farewells, then nodded to the waiting black cat, "Another old friend to say goodbye to, Andra. You... good luck."

Ursla smiled sadly, and nodded back to Artie, "Good luck to you too."

She and Artie shared a stare for another moment, and then with a parting nod the tiger left, passing Nightclaw as he went.

Rising from her chair, Andra turned as the Comptroller of the Navy — her former Flag Captain on *Cerberus*, and then successor in command of the 111th Flying Squadron — came into the room.

Dran Nightclaw was a cool, collected officer, always composed and with instincts tuned perfectly for a fight. Surprising Ursla, he stepped forward with the biggest hug he could manage around her massive frame.

"We'll remember you while we fight the frigates. I'll remember you until I die. Thank you for everything."

Ursla could say nothing but, "Thank *you*."

"I'm getting tired of goodbyes," Setter collapsed into one of the chairs opposite Lab Forepaw's desk, and the First Lord smiled at the remark.

"You've only done the Earther fleet officers so far — not even the marines. If you leave without saying something to Krag and Narosh, the alliance might fall apart."

"And you're not getting out of here without saying goodbye to us too," Varnon was standing in the corner of the First Lord's office.

Setter rubbed his forehead and nodded, "Yeah. Part of the plan I didn't really prepare for."

Lab shrugged, "There's always something you overlook."

"If saying goodbyes is the only thing we've overlooked with this plan, I'll be very, *very* happy," Setter said to his old Flag Captain.

"Very happy."

CHAPTER 12

Phealan Caine was waiting on the lawn of Admiralty House, enjoying the Halifax weather as his father and Ursla finished their goodbyes and their last minute planning. He, Lab and Varnon were destined to accompany Setter and Ursla up to *Orion*, and they'd say farewells there... but in the meantime, Phealan just had to wait.

"It's Phealan, right?"

The younger Caine's ear twitched as someone behind him asked his name, and he glanced back. A gray and white wolf in a tan marine uniform was pacing up to the picnic table he was perched on. Phealan recognized the officer — the *Colonel* — quickly: it was Cadmus Howler, the CO of 2/54th, and Beckett Lupus' trusted old friend. Cadmus had been in charge of the battalion when it had interceded on behalf of the government at Darymanis City, saving Claire and Christine, and then had led the unit into *Genesis One*, where it first met Omega's minions.

This wolf had, in many ways, influenced Phealan's recent life, but as was so often the case, they'd never actually met.

"Cadmus Howler," Phealan nodded back to the Colonel and verbalized his recognition.

Cadmus smiled, "That's me. Mind if I join you while we wait?"

"By all means," Phealan shuffled over on the table, and with the exceptional and precise grace of an elite marine, Cadmus hopped up and sat beside him.

"I've got a meeting with Beckett, but for now everyone's in there saying goodbye to your father. I paid my respects, but he and I never really knew each other well."

"Ah... it'll probably be going for a while yet in there..."

Reaching out with his mind, Phealan saw that Setter and Ursla were speaking with Beckett Lupus and the Generals. After that it was Krag and Narosh...

Yeah, it'll be a while.

Cadmus Howler frowned as the thought entered his head, then blinked and shook himself, "Sorry, still haven't gotten used to that."

Really? Phealan grinned.

"Yes..." Cadmus forced himself to switch to telepathy. *Yes... after all these years of fighting on instinct, having all the new telepathic data can be confusing. Still trying to figure out how much of it to let in when I have to fight the minions... too much data and I could slow right down.*

"Not a problem I have," Phealan admitted. "I don't envy you it."

Cadmus cracked a smile and shook his head, "Believe me, as challenges go that's the least of my worries."

"No kidding."

The two wolves chuckled, and inside Admiralty House Setter and Andra went on with their goodbyes.

"I have to say, Krag... you've really made this all possible. Thank you, and thank your people for me," Setter bowed his head towards the Warlord as he spoke, and Kragran bow-nodded back.

"You were our greatest inspiration... everything we do now is to honor you and your people. I thank *you*. It is our privilege to be here," the Krogg replied.

It was such a strange thing to hear from a former enemy... from a foe Setter had spent so much time and so much grave energy trying to finish.

We are a good deed that has born fruit, Krag added telepathically, and Setter smiled.

"Your words, not mine."

With a laugh, Krag carefully shook Setter's hand, "Kill well, Lord Caine."

"You too," Setter shook the Warlord's hand, and then they parted.

Narosh waited across the room, and as the wolf drew nearer the Larosian, the Admiral-of-a-Fleet gestured a request that they talk outside. Setter followed him out of the room, while behind him, Ursla and Novash laughed about old times.

The bear and the Admiral-of-a-Division had been the first of their respective races to meet. Novash now looked at the great bear and offered a smile that he'd practiced for many decades, "It was an honor to meet you, and to fight alongside you, Andra."

I wish your Empire a great recovery when all this is over, Ursla elected to respond telepathically. *And you keep yourself safe.*

Standing on one of the back porches of Admiralty House, Narosh looked out at Halifax harbor and shook his head, "You have a remarkable planet, my friend. I'll visit here more when Omega is finished."

Preparing himself for another somber exchange of farewells, Setter nodded, "Narosh, it'll be our honor and pleasure to have you here, once this is done."

The Larosian laughed, then turned back to Setter and folded his arms, "I once knew a human, the Son of Praaxus, and he had a mission not unlike yours. He was going to fight the Queen — we thought at the time that she was the senior Queen, but of course she was just an under-Queen. This was just months before your people and mine met. When he left, every Admiral and Captain-Elite in the fleet lined up to give him honorable farewells. He hated it."

Setter smiled, "It does get a little tiring, I won't lie. But these are all old friends. I could hardly say no to any of them... they've all earned the right to some of my time."

"That's what he told me, but he was a bit more frustrated about it than you are. He was human, of course."

"I remember the story you told of him, yes."

Well, Narosh switched to telepathy, *I'll tell you what I told him. Your mind is the strongest I've ever encountered. Go and use it, and your sacrifice will be remembered.*

Setter nodded to his Larosian friend, *I'll do that.*

The two stood in silence for a moment, but Setter then shook his head, "You and me... who would have seen this coming? I remember that day we nearly came to blows."

Narosh laughed again, "I'm glad you convinced me. We'd all be dead now otherwise. Did you realize then... how important saving the Kroggs would be?"

Setter opened his mouth, then closed it again.

I don't know. I knew saving them was right. I knew I had to save them or I could never face Phealan as the wolf I needed to be. But I don't think any part of me knew something like this was coming.

Narosh offered telepathic signs of agreement, *None of us could have. I'll miss you Setter.*

With a chuckle, Setter shook his head, "The only thing I *won't* miss is hearing how much I'll be missed."

Sharing a last laugh, the Larosian and the Earther parted ways for the final time.

That was the end of the farewells.

Two hours later, Setter looked out at the sea. The view from Citadel landing field was wonderful, if not as magnificent as the one at home. He stared at the gleaming ocean and the bustling city of Halifax, and its cross-harbor twin of Dartmouth, both rebuilt from destroyed old human settlements.

This was the last he'd see of Earth, the last he'd see of sky or smell of wind. This was the end of the goodbye. From here on, he'd be moving towards the inevitable and inexorable conclusion of this battle.

The time for fond memories and sentiment was ending. Now they all had to fight.

So taking a last lungful of air... and then one extra last lungful, Setter smiled and held up his hand, waving to the horizon, "Goodbye, home."

He turned away from the planet that had borne him and for which he was still fighting... and he stepped up the ramp of the pinnace.

He was leaving Earth for the very last time. And now there could be no more reflection or worry: Omega was at hand, and the plan would either end the plague, or the Earther race would die.

CHAPTER 13

"*Orion* is pulling out in about four hours, and I'm supposed to be up on *Guardian One* to watch," Christine was explaining her seeming haste as she followed Celia Lazarus through the corridors of Fengate Hospital, and the doctor took the hint.

"Don't worry, this is just a quick meeting — you'll be up there with time to spare," Celia smiled at the young human's seeming eagerness, then at last turned the corner and reached her office. "Here, have a seat."

Christine seated herself in a chair opposite Celia's and as she did, the doctor activated the holographic projector in her desk.

"We've been focused mostly on the Type 2 Omega cure, but because we were using some of your fluxed cells as a template for that, I've had a chance to look at your data. I *think* everything that's happened to you can be reversed, if we use one of these..."

Keying one of the controls on the desk console, Celia floated a hologram of some sort of molecular compound into view.

Christine stared at the compound... whatever it was... for a moment, then frowned slightly and started to nod, "I see..."

Celia detected the human wasn't actually saying what she meant, and as soon as the doctor's telepathy confirmed that, Christine looked up with a shrug, "...yeah, I have no idea what that is."

Chuckling, Celia sat down and laced her fingers, "It's a regen compound, but with a new template plugged into it. Basically, it could undo everything that was done to you... return you to the way you were just before we gave you the crash regen."

"Including the fried brain?" Christine's frown deepened. "Or would that stay fixed?"

"It'd be as it was before the accident. We can pull a genetic scan from your Genesis file, and use that as a template to work from. We've never tried it... we've never had anyone want to undo regen... but I think we can make it work, and still preserve your mind and memories."

Everything back to the way it had been. Human again, at long last...

Well that didn't sound half bad. And yet it sounded horrific.

Christine blinked at the contradiction. Part of her was desperate to have her carefree innocence back, another part was completely satisfied with her growing Earther character...

Oh Gods, I could go to war with myself over this...

"After we fix the mutation, we could give you regen again — properly — and you'd be where you are now, just without the nerve sensitivity," Celia continued her explanation, and Christine's eyes darted up to the wolf's.

"What about... well, my *other* changes. Since the regen I've been feeling more and more... *Earther*. I... I don't know if I should give that up or not."

Celia's eyebrow climbed. Every Earther who came across Christine was finding that her mind and her instincts were not those of the average human, and while medical scans weren't showing a genetic change that would account for this, it seemed obvious that the regen must have had something to do with it.

As had happened with Narosh, it appeared that the Earther DNA, when introduced during a trauma, had a way of deeply affecting the person who received it. There had been some cases on Freetown that had suggested such a thing might actually be happening, but no one had taken the time to study it closely... and now those people were probably dead.

Would this recursion treatment take those Earther qualities away?

"I don't know," Celia shook her head. "Sorry. It's a risk, certainly, but we just don't know. Even with all the scans we run, we still can't tell what aspect of our DNA accounts for those things... if it's DNA at all. Changing DNA might have no effect on them... or it might erase them. It's a risk."

Christine swallowed and shifted uncomfortably in her seat. Her future — even if it was only another week of living — was questionable here...

She stopped herself at that thought.

"How long would it take? You know the plan... Graham and I go to Freetown in a week. So maybe this is a moot point."

Celia's smile twitched almost sadly, and then she opened her desk drawer and pulled out a box, "It'd take me an hour to modify this shot accordingly. The repairs would take just a few minutes after injection."

Christine leaned back in her chair and shook her head, "Does physics not even apply to you people?"

With a laugh, Celia shrugged, "Sorry, Christine... it's what we do."

The young human nodded and looked away in frustration, "I know, I know. And most of the time it's fantastically good. Right now... though... dammit. I don't know what to say."

The decision was not an easy one, for so many reasons. Her desire to feel human was selfish — reinforced powerfully by the feeling she'd had again when she'd been reunited with Claire. She missed some of that, even if it could leave her ineffective before Omega...

But she was going to Freetown with Graham in a week, and the Earther aspects of who she was could prove useful when she was there, fighting Omega-Gillian...

Either she was going to be her most capable, three-quarters-Earther self when she fought Omega, or she was going to be her less capable human self.

No, that didn't sound like much of a choice to her.

"I should wait... if we come back, then I'll take it," Christine said that with a somewhat dejected tone. She wanted to be a sister again... but to have the chance to do that, she had to beat Omega first.

To beat Omega, she had to be part Earther. If he was done, she could take the risk of losing her Earther edge... but only then.

Celia nodded slowly at Christine's words — it was, as far as the doctor was concerned, the best decision that could be made under the circumstances. Graham was counting on Christine for this dangerous (perhaps insane) mission to Freetown, so unraveling who she'd become in a vain attempt to get back some of the innocence of a dead past wouldn't have made much sense.

But, of course, Celia had to offer the opportunity. Some humans probably would have concealed the existence of this possible treatment from Christine, fearing she'd take it and thus jeopardize the plan, but Earthers couldn't do such a thing. Freetown wouldn't have existed in the first place if Earthers had been as controlling as humans.

Whether that was a good thing or a bad thing was not for Celia to decide; she'd made this offer to Christine, and the young Schaeffer had made her choice.

"I'll prep the compound for you, in case I'm dead when you get back. I'm copying the research and forwarding it to New Halifax as well, so if we all die here but you survive, there'll still be a chance to get it done."

Christine blinked and caught Celia's gaze as those last promises were made. The doctor was such an exemplar of Earther life-giving, it sounded odd to hear her saying so much about death. But it was prudent thinking, as ever, from the doctor who'd done so much for Earther genetic science.

Narosh owed this wolf his life, as did Christine... and now the cure for Omega, ridiculously long shot as it might be, had come from her. Elandra Caine had probably been the Earthers' greatest geneticist, but Celia Lazarus was rapidly gaining ground on her fallen friend.

Now it was Celia Lazarus versus Omega, in the strangest sort of battle.

Christine took a deep breath, then nodded, "Alright. Thank you, Celia. Sorry I can't just take the cure and be more grateful..."

Holding up her hand, the wolf shook her head, "I agree with your decision. Just had to offer you the choice."

A smile twitched to Christine's lips, and she came to her feet, "You sure know how to make a girl feel not too badly about being part Earther. You enlightened people..."

Chuckling, Celia pressed on, "We get by. Now you're due on *Guardian One*, aren't you?"

Nodding, Christine let Celia lead her out of the office. She had a departure to witness.

CHAPTER 14

The mood was almost business-like on *Orion's* flight deck. Setter and Andra were aboard the ship that would take them on the ten-day journey to Genesis, and the only Earthers left to see them off were Lab Forepaw, Varnon Broadpaw, and Phealan.

Varnon was the first to say his in-person goodbye to Setter, as the two paced well away from the pinnaces that had carried them to the cavernous flight bay.

"The people will be ready... did you give a recording to Phealan for them? Hearing your voice right before Omega comes will probably help," Varnon had his hands linked behind his back as he paced next to Setter, and the Supreme Consul nodded.

"Phealan has it. But you'll have a speech of your own, old friend. And so will Phealan... and they'll be just as good," Setter replied confidently, but Varnon snorted a laugh at the compliment.

"Not likely. You don't admit it, but you have the gift of dramatic rhetoric. I just talk."

Smiling, Setter found his eyes drawn up to the scorched walls of the tired old bay, "Talking is all our people will need. But Phealan... I expect whatever he says is going to get noticed."

"I don't doubt it. Your son is the most precocious Earther I've ever known," Varnon concurred. He meant that, and Setter couldn't help but agree.

Phealan wasn't even fifty yet, but he was already leading from the very front... that was unique in Earther history, and Setter was certain the credit was due to some intrinsic qualities within his son. It wasn't how he'd been raised, though Setter hoped that he and Elandra had helped Phealan along... it was just something about the young Caine. His spark for leadership was greater than Setter's own.

Hopefully, in a week, that would help turn the tide.

"You feeling comfortable with the defensive plans?" Ursla was walking across another part of the massive bay with Lab Forepaw, and the First Lord nodded uneasily.

"At least this time we know for certain where he's going. I'm not looking forward to it, but I think we'll have a good chance. That said, you two really will have to do your stuff. We can slow him down... by some miracle we might destroy his fleet... but he could build another faster that we can."

Lab's somber words reflected his true, deep-seeded concerns — concerns he could only reveal to a handful of people. The plan was solid, if massively risky... but there was so much that could go wrong, even if it was a success.

Those possibilities weighed now on Lab the way they'd once laid on the shoulders of Setter Caine, and Ursla almost felt some déjà vu as she recognized them, "Well, just do what you do best, Lab. You're the greatest officer the Navy's ever had... and I mean that. Do what you do."

"I will," Lab nodded, still not convinced the compliment was accurate, but knowing that his self-assessment was irrelevant.

The officers collected at the bottom of the pinnace after long minutes of talking, and then Varnon and Lab changed chatting partners for a few more minutes. After that, they said their goodbyes — the physical ones, anyway.

"Good hunting, Lab," Setter shook the hand of his old Flag Captain and friend. "Believe what you want, but I know you'll do well."

Smiling, Lab answered, "I think so. See you up here..." the First Lord tapped his head, and Setter nodded. Then Lab went up the ramp of his pinnace.

Varnon extended his hand next, and smiled, "I'll see you on the telepathic plane. We'll get it done here."

Setter shook the First Consul's hand, and then Varnon strode up the ramp too.

That just left Phealan, and the young wolf was smiling at both Ursla and his father. He gave Ursla a hug, "Good luck."

The big bear squeezed Phealan carefully, then pulled away, "You're going to do amazing things, pup."

Phealan laughed, "I'll settle for 'good things'. But thank you."

Ursla nodded to him, then glanced at Setter, "I'm going to warm up the automation circuits. See you on the bridge."

Setter nodded and then he and his son watched as Ursla set off across the bay.

"Taking a ship on automated circuits to a planet called Genesis... I'm sure I've heard that somewhere before..." Phealan said absently as they watched the great bear Admiral leave the bay. "Maybe an old human movie..."

"I think I remember the one. Captain named Burke or something... April... Pike, maybe..." Setter nodded. "But as I recall, the circumstances were a bit different."

Phealan chuckled, "They always are."

They remained silent for a moment after that, and their smiles faded away.

"So, listen, you have a safe trip, right up until the duel. And I'll see you on the telepathic plane in the meantime," Phealan said after that pause, his matter-of-fact tone sounding entirely forced.

"Yes. And you have fun with the house to yourself, and find yourself a good wife at some point, and have a good life running the planet. You'll be great at it," Setter matched that tone perfectly, and the two looked at each other.

There was no way this could be easy, even for Earthers.

They hugged for a long time, for the last time, and then as they parted Setter took his son's hand, "You're going to be incredible, son."

"You are too, dad," Phealan replied. "I'll be there when you need me."

Setter nodded, their grip parted, and Phealan took one last deep breath, closed his eyes, and headed up the pinnace ramp.

Watching the hatch on that craft shut, Setter swallowed hard, then locked his mind onto the mission. As the pinnace left the flight bay, he watched and knew he'd said goodbye to everything. The days of lasts were over: the mission was starting.

He turned and headed for the bridge.

Lab, Varnon and Phealan watched from *ENS Venerable* as *Orion*, the greatest old titan of the Earther Fleet, turned away from Earth and slid into energy drive.

"The clock starts running now," Lab said softly. "Let's get moving."

CHAPTER 15

There was no hiding the fact that Caine and Ursla were on their way. Hell, even if there had been no avatar of Omega camping out in Fengate Hospital, the self-righteous, goody-goody, heartfelt goodbyes emanating from Earth would probably have been detectable to his avatars at Freetown and Ecclesia.

Couldn't the Earthers do anything without the violins playing?

Well, probably not.

Omega-Natosh smiled at that thought as he stood in the middle of the Krogg War Memorial on the surface of Genesis. His minions had finished clearing it of bodies, so the chief avatar was alone in the giant, sunken space. The dramatic cenotaph seemed a very suitable setting from which to send his own fleet to war.

But, of course, Omega wasn't going to make nearly as big a production of getting his ships off to Earth as the Earthers had in sending two of their leaders to him.

Seriously, they do love their self-righteous self-congratulations, Omega-Natosh continued to smile. *But maybe they also know they're going to die when they get here. Perhaps I should cut them some slack...*

Omega-Natosh laughed aloud at those thoughts. All the meaningful, emotional buildup the Earthers had gone through was going to do them no good at all. It would just make things that much more crushing when their plan fell on its ass and died.

And while Setter was trying to hit Omega-Natosh with the 'cure' that the not-so-brilliant Celia Lazarus had vomited up, the black ships of Omega's new fleet would be raining death and an army on Earth.

"Time to get them moving," Omega-Natosh said to himself, and then looked skyward.

Sitting in orbit over Genesis, and stretching out into the local space beyond, 5,012 warships were swimming around like a school of fish. In their midst were nine massive vessels hauling undulating sacs, each about the size of an old Krogg Mothership.

This was Omega's mighty fleet, and his army of nine billion minions.

In a move that felt to him like a flex of the muscles, Omega parted his ships in a great rush, and then brought them back together. They swam, wove and dove amongst each other, somehow never colliding while they moved with speed and coordination that even Earther ships couldn't match.

A little practice goes a long way, Omega decided, placing a smile on the face of every one of his avatars around the galaxy.

He'd been bested by the Kroggs when he'd attacked their world, but that had been his first genuinely big Naval fight with the black wave ships. Now he'd seen his new vessels' shortcomings, and knew better how to use them.

This fleet was going to wipe the Earthers out of space.

And then those Mothership-sized sacs, each one packed tight with a billion minions, would hit Earth's atmosphere, flatten out in the sky, and burst open. It would rain invaders, all of whom — hardened by Krogg exoskeletons and sustained by Omega's cells — would survive the descent, and land ready to fight.

It was a fight the Earthers could not possibly win.

Omega could visualize it all unfolding just as he expected. There was a chance the Earthers would manage some sturdy defenses — he'd expect no less — but their clever technology, their determination and their drive would not be able to stop his onslaught.

No matter how good Setter made them feel about themselves.

It was going to be awesome.

But excited daydreaming wasn't going to get Omega's ships into position to attack. As much as the plague enjoyed watching and feeling his massive school of deadly fish weaving and flying through Genesis local space, it was time to get them moving towards Earth.

With no more effort than it would take a human to walk across a room, the plague catapulted his entire, massive fleet into his improved version of flux drive. More than 5,000 ships were now bound for Earth.

Standing in an open field beneath the night sky on Ecclesia — a place which was now being prepared for the duel with Sarah Manchester and Pat Conroy — Omega-Paine paused as the fleet went into flux.

It was going to be very interesting to watch Sarah squaring off in a duel with the body of Paine. Omega had subsumed the mind of the man, but when she looked at him, the layers of her hate would be two-fold. His body, under its previous management, had been responsible in large part for the coup that ended her world, and for so much of the pain and strife before that. Under its current management, it was an avatar of Omega. She'd probably be breathing fire, which Omega expected would be highly amusing.

And if Pat showed up too, as Omega's telepathic scans of Earthers in Fengate suggested was the plan, then it would be highly entertaining to kill him in front of her, so she could feel one more crushing sense of failure before she died.

Omega-Paine would have to be creative in killing Pat. He'd have to do it in such a way that allowed Pat to live long enough to make eye contact with Sarah, and gurgle out a last apology, preferably with blood coming out of his mouth.

Hmm, a challenge... But Omega had no doubt he would figure it out.

Omega-Gillian was standing on the beach at Freetown, looking out at the beautiful waters of the tropical world. She'd taken the head of General Colin Brawn on this strip of sand, so it seemed the best place to receive Graham and his slut secretary.

Like his sister, the younger Manchester sibling was staying true to his family traditions, and running into a fight he had no chance of winning. Omega-Gillian was going to enjoy killing Graham.

But only, of course, after she tortured him as much as she could... and really, torturing the man wasn't going to be tough at all. Graham was coming to kill his wife: there was a whole keyboard of buttons to mash, all of which would make him reflect on what he was doing.

And Christine — the annoying little half-Earther girl he was keeping close to him — would be handy leverage too. The source of the *cure*.

Omega-Gillian cackled at the thought that anyone could hope that the stupid little Schaeffer, the bitch from the Panatorium, could be the key to defeating the most powerful god-plague in the history of the universe.

There was a reason David and Goliath was a *story* from the *Bible*. It was fiction, after all.

Laughing, Omega-Gillian ran towards the sea and dove in. Swimming was an interesting and rewarding sensation for Omega as a whole, so he made sure his avatars engaged in it whenever possible.

Bible, the plague thought to himself. *Imagine if I met God... how long would he last?*

Ah, hubris. It felt good. Especially since Omega knew it was deserved.

Nothing in this universe could stop him. He was bigger and more powerful than everything else around him. And seriously, if something tried to come from another universe to stop him, that'd just be pathetic.

No, the only one who could stop Omega was, well, himself. And shockingly, he wasn't going to be using much self-control over the coming weeks.

Omega-Gillian swam through the sea while, light years away, Omega's fleet swam through space.

CHAPTER 16

"I'm going to operate from here, I think," Varnon Broadpaw squinted against the bright sun that was shining over the Antarctic Plain, then slowly looked around the landing fields of Antarctic Base.

It seemed like as good a center of operations as any for the First Consul when Omega came down.

Beckett Lupus looked at his father-in-law, then surveyed the landing fields and shrugged, "Alright. If you like."

Frowning, Varnon looked back at the General, "Think there's a better place?"

Beckett smiled and shook his head, "I don't think there are going to be too many good places. But if you're in the headquarters building here, you'll be able to see what's going on everywhere... it'll give you the most control of the situation."

That had been Varnon's thought too.

"Until Omega overruns the base," Beckett added after a pause, and Varnon chuckled.

"Yes, until then."

Setter and Andra had been gone for a day, and the countless details of planetary defense were absorbing every Earther's time. Whether they were simply training to fight, or trying to figure out the minutiae of the defensive arrangements, the days were full.

"How long do you think we'll be able to hold here?" Varnon moved to stand next to Beckett, and the General frowned thoughtfully.

"Hard to say. We're going to have several layers of shields. I was going to try to get Naval guns pointed down to use as artillery, but Zed Dune says close-proximity energy fire might destroy the glacier... so they'll just be pointed skyward. We'll have plenty of firepower, though. So based on what happened to Freetown..." Beckett's voice trailed off briefly.

He looked to his left and then to his right, up and then down, as if adding up how much time each layer of defense would buy. He reached a total and then offered it in a frank tone, "I'd say an hour. Or maybe twenty minutes."

Varnon Broadpaw stared at the side of Beckett's head for a moment, and then looked back out at the Antarctic Plain, "That long, really?"

With a shrug, Beckett shook his head, "Well, I might be being optimistic."

Scratching behind his ear, Varnon winced, "Great."

"Not the word I was thinking," Beckett said wryly. "But it'll be a hell of a twenty minutes."

Vice Admiral Chronos Claw and Rear Admiral Zed Dune were trying to look nonchalant on the bridge of the Krogg Hyper Mothership *Death* with Kardrath, the Warlord of the fleet. That two Earthers were trying so overtly to appear casual was itself unusual, but these Admirals — two of the best engineers among the flag officers of the Earther Navy — were again participating in something they both had long ago decided was impossibly dangerous.

"We're entering energy-hyper now," Kardrath glanced back, favoring them with spoken warnings instead of telepathic ones.

Chronos swallowed and nodded, and Zed Dune tensed and glanced at his fellow engineer and Admiral, "Did I mention that when I tried this in anything bigger than a sloop, it cost me a frigate from the 142nd?"

"Yeah," Chronos replied uneasily. He'd been through two of these flights before, and it still unnerved him. "Yeah, you did."

There was an abrupt rumble, and then telepathic reports from the crew on *Death's* bridge began scrolling through the Earthers' minds. The Hyper Mothership was indeed in energy-hyper... they could both see it.

"Kardrath, I have to compliment your engineers again... we gave up on this decades ago," Zed Dune offered the compliment in a tone that revealed his continued anxiety.

This was the return run for *Death*; they'd left Earth that morning, bound to pick up several new squadrons of Dreadnoughts from Krogg 'A'. A few hours later and they were on their way back to Earth — they'd be home by dinner.

A trip that, in any conventional ship, would have taken at least a month was done in a day, including loading time. And, just to add to the incredulity of the whole thing, *Death* was about the size of a small moon, able to carry hundreds of warships within its hull.

All those years that we tried every trick we knew to make energy-hyper work... and we just couldn't get it going... Chronos mused quietly. He, of course, had originated the concept of sending a ship into energy drive while it was in hyperspace. It had been a reckless, creative solution to communication problems around the time of the Battle of Gibraltar... but since then, it had been discovered that large Earther ships weren't able to survive transit, and that even agile little sloops couldn't withstand the strain for long.

And yet here was *Death*, a ship the size of a planetoid, having no trouble at all...

"Do you want me to explain it once again, Chronos?" Kardrath appeared in front of the cat Admiral with a smile and a pleased twinkle in his eye.

The Kroggs, it had to be admitted, seemed to enjoy having accomplished something that had baffled the Earthers for so long.

Chronos blinked and then shook his head, "No... no I think... well. Yes."

Zed nodded as well, "I could sure use it again."

Kardrath immediately entered both Earthers' minds, and took them into a telepathic plane where they were surrounded by visuals of hyperspace.

"You see, the instability of an energy field in hyperspace is not absolute. With a living ship, we can adjust to the eddies of hyperspace travel, and telepaths can further stabilize the hull against the currents of hyper..." the Krogg began his explanation, and Zed and Chronos looked around at all the phenomena on display in this telepathic environment.

It was still very confusing — to both of them. Earther science could pull off a lot. With Wyndhymn physics, the Earthers had always been able to accomplish things that seemed almost magical to humans — it was as though they could program energy itself... and they could, after a fashion...

But this was something else entirely. The Kroggs had certain abilities and understandings that were a step beyond, and for the two engineer-Admirals, that was an eye-opener.

"You need not be so surprised," Kardrath recognized the continued shock of his guests. "We've spent centuries relying on hyperspace as our primary means of transport... our advantage here might be compared to a whale."

Chronos blinked and glanced at Kardrath, "A whale?"

The Krogg nodded, and then Zed helpfully projected a vision of a swimming whale into the telepathic plane around them.

"Precisely, one of those," Kardrath said with a smile. "You understand."

Chronos and Zed both opened their mouths at the same time, but neither of them could quite decide how to respond. They clearly didn't understand what the alien was alluding to... unless whales had an understanding of advanced physics that the Earthers had never given them credit for.

Kardrath laughed at that thought, and shook his head, "No, I'm sorry. I mean, if you were to create a submersible vehicle of metal, it could travel under water with success. But a whale, born in that environment, and living there, would naturally be more flexible and at home."

"Aha, so ships that live in space and hyperspace are probably going to be able to deal with hyperspace currents better than a ship of the line?" it sounded painfully obvious as Zed repeated the thought to himself. Ironic that the natural connection between an animal and its environment hadn't occurred to the Earthers.

A smile came to Chronos' face as he read that thought from Zed's mind, and he looked at Kardrath, "My friend, I'm really, *really* glad you're on our side now."

The Krogg laughed with a slight hiss and nodded, "Yes, me too."

Death surged on through hyperspace, carrying its load of warships to Earth's defense.

CHAPTER 17

Colonel Cadmus Howler flipped a bear over his back, and then quickly turned his sword over and laid it across the fallen Earther's chest.

"It's all about transferring momentum," Cadmus said as the bear let out a wheeze and nodded.

Standing in a ring around the Colonel and his sparring partner, a dozen Earther civilians watched with interest. These were wolves, cats and bears who had never participated in war before — they'd never felt they had an aptitude for fighting. Now, though, they were all certain that they would have to fight, aptitude or no. So they were getting a crash course on how to translate their natural instincts into hand-to-hand skills that could give them a chance against the minions.

Drawing his sword away, Cadmus extended his hand towards the downed bear, and helped the big fellow up, "Now, get practicing on each other for a little while. It takes some getting used to, but once you get the hang of it, they'll be in trouble."

The Earthers nodded simultaneously, and then began their own sparring. Cadmus left them to it, stepping out of the circle so that he could survey the other training groups nearby. He and Sergeant Major Ernile Cutter were in Cairo this afternoon, while the rest of 2/54th was scattered across the planet, teaching similar sessions.

Cuttar was emerging from his own ring of trainees when Cadmus caught his eye, and the Sergeant approached with a nod, "Hot out here."

Cadmus looked skyward and agreed aloud, "It is. Given the choice, I don't think I'd pick this place for our last stand. I'd much prefer somewhere cooler."

"Any word from Beck about where we'll be posted?" Cuttar replied with the question, and Cadmus shook his head.

"All I know is that he and Varnon Broadpaw will be at Antarctic Base. I guess we'll be there with them... so it'll be cooler."

Cuttar smiled, "Yes. That'd be a neat piece of symmetry, wouldn't it? Remember when we were all in the *Cerberus* squad... chasing Sarah Manchester and Pat Conroy down into the tunnels when the Crusaders had the base?"

It seemed like a lifetime ago, but Cadmus nodded. He and Cuttar had been part of Sergeant Lupus' squad back in those days. And they'd thought facing 100,000 Crusaders had been daunting...

"Long, long time ago," Cadmus said softly.

"Back in the beginning," Cuttar agreed.

Rear Admiral Ed Jeffries looked down at Egypt through the observation lounge windows on *Aboukir*, trying to decide if there was much point to defending this planet. That was a pessimistic question, but he couldn't help but wonder. The Allies had very handily lost Freetown... what chance did Earth have?

Well, there's more of us than there were of you on Freetown.

Ed blinked and looked up from the planet, wondering who had thought that into his head. He was alone in the lounge.

I'm coming up the hall, be inside in a minute.

Well. That was weird. Ed frowned and tried to identify the voice... he still wasn't used to having Earthers in his head.

The hatch opened, and Jax Furgus stepped in, "Ta-da."

Managing a half-hearted laugh, Ed waved to the crotchety Earther Admiral, "I thought we'd covered everything in the meeting, Jax."

The lion nodded, "We did, but I was coming up here to stare morosely at the planet, and then I realized you were here too."

"Ah," Ed nodded. "Well, I can leave. Was just taking a break before I headed back to *Felix*."

"Nah, stand around for a while. I'd ask how you're holding up, but now that I can invade your brain I don't actually need to," the lion paced towards the window.

"Yeah, I suppose that must be a conversation killer," Ed turned back to the view of the planet as well. "Eight days and we'll all be fighting for your home."

Jax nodded, "Yes we will. It's strange, looking down there at it... you know there's billions of people getting ready for the fight, a billion different little stories happening right now. The scope is incredible."

"Bigger than anything I've ever imagined," Ed agreed.

"A whole planet getting ready to fight," the old lion shook his head. "You know, I never thought I'd find anything else particularly impressive after the Battle of Krogg 'A'. But this, well."

Ed didn't need to be telepathic to recognize the genuine awe that was fixed in Jax's mind. Two *billion* beings all preparing for the same fight. An enemy who still outnumbered them. It defied comprehension.

"Whoever writes the history of the battle is going to have a hell of a time," Ed observed. "If Pat survives and tries it... well, I don't know how he could cover the preparations of two billion people."

Jax chuckled, "He'll probably have to have a bunch of vignettes with secondary characters all over the place, carefully laying down plot threads but not spending too much time with any of them. Otherwise the book would be unreadable."

"I don't know if he'd cop out like that," Ed smiled.

"Ha, I would," Jax shook his head, then glanced at the Freetown Admiral. "But that's why I'm not writing any damned books. I'll just complain when whatever gets written makes me out to be too pleasant a cat."

Ed chuckled, "I don't think there's much danger of that happening."

Jax Furgus laughed.

Artie Tigar, Minnie Maximane, Dran Nightclaw and Ami Dune were sitting in *Agamemnon's* briefing room, the holo tank at the center of its mighty table presenting a glowing map of Sol space.

"I'm pretty sure Lab is just going to put us in a ring around Earth..." Artie was frowning at the images. "Seems like the safest call to me."

Ami Dune had seen Omega appear out of nowhere before, when he'd destroyed the Genesis refugee convoy. She couldn't help but agree.

"We try to get cute, he can get around us," she concurred. "So it's just a matter of dividing the local space into quadrants... we can each take one with the recommissions, and Minnie and Dran can be our mobile reserve... go to meet him wherever he comes in."

Ami made eye contact with both of those other Admirals as she spoke, and the panther and the lioness nodded in turn.

Nightclaw then added a few words, "This defense is not complicated... there is no way or reason to make it complicated. We know how best to protect Earth. The difficulty is we may not succeed, even if our plans are correct."

He said what the other three Earthers in the room already knew, but what needed saying anyway. Omega wasn't going to outsmart them here — there was, in the end, only one way he could land his army on Earth, and that was by getting into orbit. There were different ways to do that — different vectors and approach tactics — but in the end, he absolutely had to get into orbit. That meant the Earthers knew where to meet him.

Cleverness on either side could not change the objective... but as the panther had said, it didn't matter whether the Earthers knew where he was going. There was every chance he could blow right through the defenses.

"We'll just have to make sure we give him hell when he tries," Artie read those thoughts from Nightclaw, and the panther nodded.

We will. Andra is relying on us.

Tigar and Nightclaw, Ursla's two Flag Captains from the last war, nodded together at that sentiment. The plan called upon the Earther Navy to do as much as it could to stop the plague fleet, before being swept aside.

It wasn't an optimistic sort of job, but it was one they'd do.

The meeting continued.

CHAPTER 18

Fox Magnus sat in his office in Admiralty House and stared out at Halifax harbor, lost in thought. Sarah, Pat, Graham and Christine would be taking their ships out in another thirty-six hours, and after that it would be just two days before the fight with Omega. It was as though some inexorable force was pushing the Earthers into the battle… the past week had evaporated in no time.

Someone's speeding up time?

Fox blinked and recognized that the thought in his head was not his own. Glancing away from the window, he saw Kragran standing on the other side of his desk.

"Oh, sorry Krag, didn't hear you come in."

The Warlord smiled and shook his head, "For beings of our size, we do like to move quietly, my friend."

"I'll say," Fox agreed, turning his chair. "We're supposed to be meeting, right?"

Krag nodded, then looked around him for a place to sit. Because of the blades that jutted out of the back of his carapace, a regular chair — even bear-sized — wouldn't work, but Fox had a big box in the room to serve as an alternative. The Krogg sidled over to that and perched himself only slightly awkwardly, smiling as he did.

"Once we have defeated the plague, I will send you some specifications for chairs suitable for Kroggs."

When? More like if…

Fox was surprised by the cynicism of his own thought, and Krag chuckled.

"I believe you're supposed to be the most optimistic Earther in the Admiralty, Fox. So yes, *when…*" the Warlord's confidence did seem quite firm.

Fox held up a hand and shook his head, "I try to be confident, my friend. Some days it just slips a little. I'm not pessimistic exactly… It's just been a bit different for me since Setter and Andra headed out. Feels like we're moving too quickly towards… well… the biggest fight in the history of the universe."

"It's marvelous, isn't it?" Krag bounced up and down a little on his box, and Fox's eyebrows went up. Chuckling, the alien shrugged, "Is my enthusiasm predictable?"

With a laugh, the First Space Lord shook his head, "It's refreshing. You really don't care if you all die, do you?"

Krag settled down again, but offered another shrug, "That might be a bleaker interpretation of our motives than I should ascribe to, my friend. We will enjoy the good killing when Omega comes, but we will hope... we will *fight* for victory."

Fox realized he'd pushed it a little far, and he scowled at his own overstep.

Please don't worry Fox, you've not offended me. The more I interact with the Earthers, the more I see how fundamentally different we remain. I think ours will be a fine partnership, once Omega is gone. We are alike in many ways, but we have differences that will round out our combined abilities nicely.

"I like your optimism, Krag," Fox smiled slimly. "I should be right there with you..."

"Seems to me, you won't get 'right here' if you don't stop kicking yourself for not already being here," Krag observed, his tone surprisingly dry.

Fox frowned at the words — that sounded like positively Earther advice. It made a great deal of sense, and it was coming from a Krogg.

If Krag read that thought in Fox's mind, he didn't comment on it, so Fox took a breath and looked back up at the alien. Then he clapped his hands together and leaned forward in his chair, "Alright, so talk to me about why we can't use telepathic explosions in the fight."

Gears changed quickly from a philosophical discussion of optimism to a practical discussion about why the Kroggs or the Earthers couldn't use the massive telepathic explosions that, forty years prior, had made the attacks on the Krogg home systems so dangerous.

Not that anyone was planning to blow up Earth in its defense, but the ability of Earthers on a crippled ship to blow up themselves and any nearby plague vessels would undoubtedly be useful.

Krag smiled and shook his head, "Telepathic weaponry isn't as flexible as it would need to be, my friend. Given all the efforts that have gone into the plan, there's a good chance trading telepathic explosions with Omega would be a waste of time and effort."

Fox's ear twitched, and he leaned back again, fingers steepling before him, "Run through it with me again, though, Krag. How does it work?"

"Easier to do on the telepathic plane, if you don't mind," the Krogg suggested, and Fox nodded.

Seconds later, both fleet commanders were standing next to each other in the white light of the telepathic plane, and the taller alien looked down at the Earther.

"When, for instance, the Son of Praaxus and the under-Queen fought their last great battle, shortly before all our races met, they did it here. When a telepath seeks to set off an explosion, he or she must come here, and then collect all of this light around us into a massive orb of energy."

Fox narrowed his eyes, then reached out with his mind, discovering that he could indeed take hold of the surrounding light and pull it closer to himself.

"It is like charging one of your energy canon... you gather enough energy in its capacitor to fire a shot. The difference here is that, instead of releasing the energy in a controlled fashion, you keep collecting. More and more and more... as much as you can stand. And once you have all that energy, you do not let it go gradually: you release it all at once. The result is an explosion equal to the amount of energy you have collected around you."

Krag's explanation drew a nod from Fox. It was like a rainy season filling up the reservoir behind a dam: if the dam didn't release excess water with a gradual and controlled flow downstream, it could burst.

But for a telepathic explosion, a *burst* was exactly what was needed — it was the point.

"Fox, you must not think of using one of these yourself."

The First Space Lord frowned and glanced up at his Krogg counterpart, "Well, it doesn't seem that difficult."

The Krogg tilted his head, "No, but you forget our enemy. Omega's mind is so powerful... if he were to realize what you were trying, he could contain the explosion with the power of his own telepathy. If he did that, all this light would simply burn your brain. And you would have died for nothing."

"But if there were several Earthers trying this... could he contain all of us?"

Krag nodded, remaining patient, "Remember, Fox, if the minds are cooperating to collect the light here, then all he needs to do is destroy one of your bodies, and then all the energy that mind was controlling would flood into the minds of the others, burning them out and killing them as well. It is not worth the risk — you're better off with your guns, my friend."

"Ah, right. I... obviously," Fox kicked himself for not immediately recognizing that possibility.

The plan couldn't stand these sorts of antics, appealing as they might seem. The job of the Earther Navy and of the Earthers on the ground was simple: Omega's forces had to be delayed, and no hint of Setter's mission given. Playing around on the telepathic plane would serve neither end.

Sighing heavily, Fox left the plane and returned to his office, Krag right behind him.

"Oh well," the First Space Lord shook his head, "at least we can ram them if the going gets tough."

Krag smiled, "We are very alike, my friend."

"That may be, but we certainly have different tailors," Fox countered

The Krogg hiss-laughed, and Fox glanced back out his window at Halifax harbor.

Not too much longer to wait...

CHAPTER 19

The days had passed far, far too quickly. Between all the preparations for the mission to Freetown and all the preparations for the defense of Earth, Christine had been working without halt, and the time had evaporated. Tomorrow, she and Graham would head to Freetown, alone on the Larosian Battleship *Carnarvon*, and Sarah and Pat would go to Ecclesia on *Joseph Barron*.

Tomorrow.

As Christine watched the ocean race by through the pinnace window, she tried not to dwell on the word. She was trying not to focus on the fact that this could be *her* last day on Earth. Leaving this world for the final time really shouldn't bother her; obviously, the planet wasn't her home. She loved it, but she wasn't as connected to it as Setter was.

She'd much rather be troubled by the fact that this could be her last time seeing Claire. She wanted to be terrified, or inconsolable... one of those things she'd have been when she was human. She wanted to be upset that today could — likely *would* — be the last day she'd ever see her sister.

But it just wasn't happening.

"ArcLieutenant Schaeffer, we'll be putting down in the field in two minutes," a report over the intercom cut into her thoughts, and she nodded back to no one in particular.

"Thank you."

She'd be at the Caine estate soon, and then she'd say goodbye to Claire.

Graham Manchester stared at Omega-King.

The avatar of the plague was still caged in the basement of Fengate Hospital, and he studied it dispassionately.

"Come on, Graham, you're going to be seeing the one you want to see in a few days, aren't you?" Omega-King hissed with a smile. "Seriously, I know this King body is tasty, but your wife is pure hotness. You have to agree."

The avatar was trying to get to him. He just stared at it in return. Omega was quite correct — in a few days, he'd be fighting a duel with Gillian... a duel for the fate of humanity, and for personal revenge. Or liberation. Or both.

"Staying quiet, Graham? Come on now, won't you play with me?" Omega-King tossed another jeer at him, but he didn't respond. "What, you a fucking mute now?"

The avatar was growing frustrated, but Graham remained unresponsive. He just stood there, as if he were carved out of stone, and the avatar banged on the energy shield that caged her.

"You think you can keep this stony hero act up when you see her? We'll see, won't we? It'll be a lot of fun..." Omega-King finally delivered a parting shot. "And maybe when I cut Christine open right down the middle, you'll react."

That last line was unexpected, but Graham was too firmly locked behind his emotionless wall to respond. He stared dispassionately at the avatar, and Omega at last gave up trying to goad the man. Why bother, when three days hence, the scenario would be perfect to break him?

The avatar went to the back corner of her cell and sat. Satisfied, Graham turned and left the holding area.

Climbing the stairs beyond the door, the junior Manchester exited onto the hospital's main floor where Celia Lazarus, General Karyn Kudlee, and Captain-Elite Tovarrin were waiting for him.

"Did it work?" Celia asked immediately, and the General and the Captain-Elite both looked on with interest.

"It did," Graham nodded in reply, then rapped his fist lightly against the Larosian-manufactured armor breastplate he was wearing over his uniform. "She couldn't get into my mind."

Tovarrin nodded eagerly, "Excellent news. You and Christine will be protected against mind control."

The armor was, as Tovarrin had promised during their visit to Laros, manufactured with the Genesis ore that had proven effective on Freetown in disrupting Omega's ability to telepathically control humans. Though it wasn't paired with a helmet, it seemed that the breastplate was able to provide the same telepathic protection that Genesis-pattern riot gear did. So Graham and Christine wouldn't have to wear cumbersome helmets when they landed on Freetown.

General Kudlee glanced at her Larosian counterpart, "Do you have any more of those? Sarah and Pat might need them."

The Larosian halted his nod, "We offered breastplates to both, but they elected to use their 'riot gear'."

"Oh. Well, whatever they prefer. Won't tell them how to do their job, eh Graham?" Kudlee asked in a friendly fashion, and the junior Manchester nodded impassively.

"Of course."

Christine emerged into the clearing around the Caine house, wondering why the base of her spine was tingling. Her skin suit, still working tirelessly under her jumpsuit, seemed to be functioning properly... and yet she was getting a sensation that she wasn't accustomed to.

There was no one evident at the house. It was a cool and drizzly day, so it seemed likely that Claire was inside, and perhaps didn't know her sister had come to say goodbye...

What *was* that?

The feeling was intensifying, and Christine stopped, concerned that it was some sort of malfunction.

Not today, not just before the mission... Graham can't be sent alone...

It's not a malfunction.

That last thought came with surprising clarity, and then she felt something nudge the back of her leg.

She nearly jumped, but she managed to mute her reaction as she turned to see what was happening. A black wolf with yellow eyes — one of the pure wolves, not an Earther — gazed up at her with a curious expression.

"Are you always around here?" her question bore a nervous edge, and she looked down at the wolf as if it could answer her. Instead it just sat down, seemingly amused that it had startled her, and continued to study her.

"You wolves are evil," she protested, shaking her head, then looked around to see if there were more. But this one seemed to be alone.

"Don't mind him, he's always getting up to mischief. He was bugging Pat a few weeks back," Phealan appeared on the house's deck, and Christine nodded, then narrowed her eyes for effect. With a grin, the wolf hopped back onto his feet and vanished into the woods.

Christine stood still for a moment, and realized the tingling in her spine hadn't left with him.

My guess is you're anxious, but in their current state your nerves can't put butterflies in your stomach, Phealan offered telepathically, and with a sigh, Christine turned back to him.

"Probably."

Phealan said nothing as he studied the young woman's face, but after a moment, he waved to the door behind him, "Come on in. She's waiting."

"You should take this with you."

Graham followed Celia Lazarus with his eyes as she rounded her desk and lowered herself into her chair. She extended a hand across her desk, and in it was an injector gun.

"What compound?" Graham leaned forward in his seat and took the gun from Celia's hand, studying it impassively.

She sat back and steepled her fingers, "That's Christine's cure. She refused to take it before the mission because she was worried she wouldn't be much help to you if she did. But if something goes wrong up there, she might need it."

Graham stared at the gun for a moment, then glanced back at Celia, "How quickly would it take effect?"

The wolf tilted her head, "All our simulations say it'll take about five minutes, and during that time it'll be pretty rough for her. But after that, all the damage is undone. It'll be as if she never had regen."

"I see," Graham lowered the gun to his lap and took a breath. "So it could diminish her current skill level."

"It could," Celia agreed. "But perhaps she'd be less vulnerable as well. I have no idea what's going to happen when you two face Omega, Graham, but I want you to have every option I can offer."

"Beyond the cure, you mean?" Graham's question sounded sharper than he'd meant it to, but thanks to her telepathy, Celia understood that he wasn't criticizing her contribution to the plan. Not that it would have mattered if he was.

She smiled sadly, "Yes. Beyond that."

Phealan watched silently as the sisters spent their last hours together. He'd never had siblings, so he didn't know what it must be like for them. He just stayed out of the way, and watched with both his eyes and his mind.

To his surprise, seeing their reunion didn't make him miss his father any more than he already did... though he had a hard time believing it would actually be possible to miss Setter any more than he already did.

I'm sure I'll discover it can hurt even more, once all is said and done...

He'd find out, one way or another.

He stayed out on the deck for most of the day, occasionally slipping in unnoticed to check for news from Varnon or Lab, but mostly relaxing and engaging in mental preparation.

From time to time, he'd look in on the sisters. It was remarkable how they comforted each other. They clung together. Sometimes they cried, sometimes they laughed, and sometimes they appeared outwardly calm. They went through cycles of happiness and pain, bolstered by each others' presence.

And they didn't think of what was to come. Or they tried not to. Phealan couldn't quite understand why they were ignoring that subject. He couldn't imagine finding comfort in pretending something wasn't going to happen. Denial of reality... how could there be peace and happiness in that?

But it was in their moments of denial, when they were just two sisters together, that Claire and Christine were at their very happiest. As soon as thought of the battles ahead returned to their minds, they struggled to drive the musings away.

It was different than what Setter had done. It was different than acknowledging what was to come, and enjoying the last day fully aware of its significance.

One day Phealan might be able to comprehend the human perspective on this, but for now he just watched in occasional wonderment, and let the sisters say their last goodbyes.

CHAPTER 20

Sarah stood up from the table and silently cleared her dishes. She didn't even look at Pat as he sat finishing the last of his meal.

They were alone in the ArcColonel's dining room on *Pope Joseph Barron*, the veteran Superdreadnought that would carry them to Ecclesia for the final part of this damned plan. The ship was empty — like *Orion*, it had been rigged up by the Earthers so that it could be flown by just two people, with virtually everything on automatic. Despite the changes, Pat still found the ship felt like home.

But Sarah didn't seem to be comforted by the familiarity. She remained distant, tolerating his presence only out of necessity.

Looking down at his plate, Pat pushed around some of his remaining food with waning interest. As much as he tried to retain his positive outlook, this was not a good day. They were leaving in the morning, on this damned mission that was angling to kill both of them, and she wasn't even talking.

"I'm going to check on the engineering automations. Zed said the AI has been improved," Sarah announced as she headed for the door, and Pat looked up.

"Wait, I'll come along."

"You're not finished eating. I'm fine alone," Sarah didn't even look at him as she spoke.

Then she was gone.

Pat froze for a moment, staring at the hatch as it shut behind her. His eyes then fell to his plate, and he tossed his fork into the middle of the dish in disgust. Patience was not an infinite commodity, even if he had it stockpiled in vast quantities. At some point, he was going to lose his cool... but he didn't know if that'd help things.

Leaning back in his chair, he rubbed his eyes with the palms of his hands and let out a deep sigh. He loved Sarah very much. He was flying to almost-certain doom here, and yet he was happy enough to do it because he was with her.

He even loved her stubborn detachment. He couldn't have loved her and married her if he hadn't seen something remarkable in the strength that let her always lead, always take responsibility... but he hated how much that strength drained from her emotions.

If someone had asked Pat Conroy how he'd want to spend his last three days before a dangerous mission, he would have replied instantly: alone with Sarah, in peace.

He was getting the 'alone with Sarah' part. Peace, however, didn't seem forthcoming. And damned if he knew what he could do about it.

Sarah was determined to continue to feel nothing.

This was her mantra, tried and true. As she strode through the corridors of *Joseph Barron*, she took no time to appreciate the comfort that came from being back on her old flagship. She didn't acknowledge the warmth and the familiarity. She refused to accept anything that might make her feel.

Like a broken record, bent against any sort of emotion, she silently told herself to be robotic.

Wordlessly, she obeyed.

This had been her way for so long. Since she'd been fourteen. Since the Church had killed her parents. Since she'd joined the Navy and fought the Larosians. Since she'd fought at Antarctica against the Crusaders. Since she'd rescued Pat during the Battle of Gibraltar.

And it had to be her way now. She couldn't afford to risk making bad decisions because of warmed emotions.

Not now. This was the most important fight in the history of the human and Earther races. Omega had to be stopped by this plan — there was nothing else in the universe that really had a chance to defeat him.

If it failed, the Earthers would be gone, and without the Earthers, there was no chance of stopping Omega. They were the key, so she had to suspend her emotions and help them.

She couldn't be weak. She just had to hold on for a few more days.

And then, if she got her way, she'd be relieved of her torments in the most final way possible.

Pat hung his broadsword in its sheath from a hook on the wall of the ready room. Next to it was the riot gear he'd be wearing during the landing, to shield his mind from Omega's telepathy, and on a nearby table were the energy rifle and personal shields he'd drawn from Earther Marine stores.

A very strange feeling began to settle over him as he stared at these things. This was the equipment that he could very well die in. For years, he'd assumed he'd die on the bridge of a ship somewhere, or better yet, at home in bed. But looking at this kit, he couldn't help but wonder what it would feel like if he had to go while wearing it. Riot gear. Sword. Marine weapons.

"Not how you envisioned going out, eh boyo?" Pat asked himself in a whisper.

He continued to stare at the equipment for a while, then noticed a scuff on the breastplate of the riot armor. Looking around he found a rag, then approached the black vest and started trying to buff it.

His armor and equipment had to be pristine. If he was going to fight for the fate of his race in this equipment, then damned if it wasn't going to be tip-top. He couldn't die looking shabby...

Pat stopped himself at that thought.

Gods wept, I need to stop being so morbid. And if I'm dying, who gives a damn how I look...

That thought halted his buffing for a moment.

And then he started again. He was going to be best dressed and ready for his battle with Omega, whether that was foolish or not. It wouldn't be long now until they left...

CHAPTER 21

Christine felt cold as she dropped her kit bag onto her bed aboard *Carnarvon*. Her cabin remained the same — the modified living space which, thanks to stasis fields and atmospheric painkillers would allow her some freedom from her skin suit. That, in theory, should have made her more comfortable here, but at the same time the alienness of this room, and this ship, were more striking than they had ever been before.

She'd just come back from seeing her sister on Earth, and juxtaposed against that experience the austere silver corridors and cabins of the Larosian battleship were suddenly too much. Her Earther-like calm wavered when she saw them.

But she couldn't allow herself to be hung up with such concerns. Instead, she opened her kit bag and began unloading it. It was a slow and methodical process. She'd packed in a bit of a daze down on Earth — after her last goodbye to Claire, she'd been too caught up to think carefully about what she'd carry with her on this final mission.

As if it matters how many outfits I have.

The sharp thought caused her to close her eyes and let out a breath. She was twenty years old and bound for a fight that could determine the fate of the galaxy — a statement that was remarkable because it was in no way hyperbole.

But as soon as the thought crossed her mind, her Earther calmness — as alien to her as this ship — returned. She was once again inhumanly confident about this whole situation...

Because I'm not really human anymore.

She'd first come to that realization when she was back in the Larosian galaxy, but the circumstances now were making it all the more striking. She found herself hoping and believing that all the changes the Earther regen had inadvertently created in her would make a difference in the final battle.

There had to be some *reason* for that accident — something that would make her torment worthwhile to the universe. There *had to be*.

"Aside from keeping me alive in the first place, I suppose," she muttered to herself at that thought, piling jumpsuits on the bed.

It was true enough — if not for the accident on *Genesis One*, Christine would never have had regen, and Beckett Lupus would never have come down to Darymanis City with her, and she and her sister would not have been saved from the Crusaders' coup...

Maybe the point of all this was to let her sister live. Christine was at great risk by being a part of this mission, but at least Claire was going to be relatively safe. Maybe that was the point... perhaps Claire had a destiny.

"Maybe I'm not being a bad sibling, just leaving her," Christine continued to narrate her thoughts to herself, using the words as a buttress against any unease that did try to creep through her.

"You've never been a bad sibling."

The young ArcLieutenant froze as those words came from behind her, and after a few seconds she slowly straightened up.

"I, on the other hand, have been very poor in that role. And in all my other roles."

Graham's dispassionate statement caused Christine to lay the jumpsuit she'd been folding down on the bed, and to turn slowly.

The junior Manchester's expression hadn't shifted, but as he stood just inside Christine's door, she could instinctively sense that there was a little more feeling behind his words than she'd heard in a long time.

"Don't be too hard on yourself," was the only flimsy response she could manage, and Graham shook his head.

"It's the simple truth, Christine. I abandoned my duty, and have isolated my sister, and we will not reconcile before we leave. I have failed in many respects... all I see now is this quest for revenge. And while I'm sure you don't want to die, I desperately do. The pain of all this... it's too much for me."

Graham hadn't opened up to her — or anyone she was aware of — at all.

And he wasn't yet finished, his gaze having locked onto a piece of bulkhead just past her shoulder, "I have to kill her, you understand. Gillian... I love her so much. For so long we've been together. But we didn't start our family until now... just when he needed us to. Now I have to kill her, and I *want* to. If I kill her, and cut her off from me, then my destruction will be complete. I can die, completely destroyed... do you understand?"

Christine blinked, "Um. No, I don't." She wasn't sure if anyone could.

Graham's eyes leapt to hers, "Probably best that you don't. If either of us is to survive this, Christine... it must be you. You do understand that, don't you?"

Feeling had definitely bled into those words, and Christine frowned slightly, "I'm not going to start talking about who should die, Graham. It's a sure way to get fatally disappointed."

The junior Manchester's face tightened, "You're so much like an Earther now."

It was neither an insult nor a compliment, just an observation, and Christine let out a sigh, "So I'm discovering."

Then she crossed the distance between them and firmly took one of Graham's hands in hers, "Whatever you think you've failed at, you're doing your duty right now. We're going to play our role in this plan and fight Omega. This isn't just you on a revenge quest, you're doing your job for all the Allies now. Just happens what they need you to do overlaps with what you want to do."

Graham stared at Christine, and though she found the gaze uncomfortable, she didn't look away.

"When we get down there, we'll do what needs to be done. And you'll get your chance to kill her. If you survive, or I survive, we can worry about what to do next. But only then. There's no point worrying about it right now."

Graham's stare didn't break, and he didn't say anything, so after a moment, Christine released his hand and stepped back.

"Are you alright with that, Graham?"

He stared at her still, and then he looked down at his hand and nodded shortly, "I am. You, Christine, are not just acting like an Earther, you're acting like a very wise Earther."

A small smile twitched to the corners of her lips, "Hopefully it helps on the day."

Graham closed his eyes and shook his head, "I'm sorry about having to take you with me. Because being less enlightened than you, I cannot stop thinking that, should you survive, you will change humanity forever." His eyes opened again, "I will do all I can to make sure you walk away from this. You're free to think that I shouldn't focus on that, but I will. Because after everything, I do remain... human... and..."

Graham's words trailed off, and he thought back to a feeling that had settled over him when his old friend Savanna Felix had died at Krogg 'C'. Savanna, who never should have died, because he was too great an Earther... but whose death had inspired the other Earthers to battle on. Christine reminded him now of Savanna. And he didn't want to cause her death.

"We'll see what happens when we get there," Christine said softly.

Looking at her again, Graham nodded, "Yes. I'll go unpack."

His words and departure were abrupt, and Christine found herself staring at the silver door as it closed behind him. She sat slowly on her bed, letting her head sag forward.

The junior Manchester was in a dire mental state, but he had been right about her. As her gaze locked on her feet, she could feel the calm that was flowing through her... the abnormal, almost unthinkable calm.

She wasn't human anymore.

Though he was wrong too: she'd never change humanity forever. Only the Earthers could do that. Maybe she was just their test case.

She went back to unpacking.

CHAPTER 22

Phealan decided to watch the departure of *Carnarvon* and *Joseph Barron* from the holo tank in his living room. He'd spent most of his time over the past three days moving around the planet, helping with the final preparations for the arrival of Omega, so he wanted to take this last moment to be at home and at peace.

And to offer some support to Claire, if she would accept it.

He sat in a chair in the living room while she slouched on the couch, intently playing with her hair in a bid to distract herself as they waited. It was another ten minutes before the ships were scheduled to depart, so they were just waiting, watching the icons float aimlessly in the plot.

"Why did Omega use wolves, cats and bears?"

Phealan blinked and looked at Claire surprised, not just at the question, but at the soft tone in which it was asked. Her edge was gone. He'd not heard her say anything since her sister had left, and while he'd detected more quiet in her mind, he hadn't expected it to translate immediately into words.

"We don't know," he answered. "Omega could have picked anything... fish or birds or cattle... but he picked us."

She looked across at him, "Are wolves and cats and bears more like humans than all those other things you just mentioned?"

With a shrug, Phealan shook his head, "I don't believe so. And the other species were more numerous... still are. But he chose us."

She stared at Phealan for a moment, then looked back at the hair she was toying with, "Bad luck for him."

Phealan wasn't sure if that was a compliment or not, but he decided to try to press the younger Schaeffer for more civil conversation.

"So, are you packed for the flight to New Halifax?"

Claire was, of course, to be evacuated to New Halifax, along with the other humans residing on Earth. When Omega landed here, humans would be in no position to survive.

"I'm not going."

Phealan blinked, and his eyes moved back to Claire. She wasn't even looking at him.

"I'd have to... strongly suggest that you do," he sounded genuinely surprised, and she shook her head, still refusing him eye contact.

"No. I don't want to run away. And I don't want to live if Omega wins. So I'm staying here."

Claire had never given a reason for her actions or decisions before, and now she seemed no more inclined to elaborate. Perhaps what she'd already said was reason enough… though Phealan wasn't sure if she could truly grasp the risk. He wasn't even sure if *he* could truly comprehend it…

Quite abruptly, her eyes turned on him, "You going to try to force me?"

With another blink, Phealan shook his head, "No, of course. That's not in our nature, Claire. You know that."

"Well your nature is strange that way. If you were human, you'd tell me I had to get on the ship and go."

Phealan cocked an eyebrow, "I'm not human. Thought the ears were a giveaway."

He'd been half-hoping to earn a smile from her with the joke, but his optimism was not rewarded. She simply shrugged, "I still don't know how you do it. I mean, you let me choose to die, basically. You won't try to stop me?"

"Do you want to be stopped?" Phealan didn't skirt the question, and she looked away.

"I don't know. Can't you tell me what I want?"

Phealan studied her for a second, and shook his head, "I could scan you and find out what you're thinking… but what you're thinking isn't always what you want. Even with telepathy, I don't think I could tell you that. You have to make your own decision — decide how to act on what you're thinking. It's not my place, or any Earther's to do that for you."

It was true, that hadn't changed. Earthers believed in the importance of personal choice above all else.

"What if you don't know what you want?" Claire's words were uneven.

Again, Phealan was silent for a second, "Then you ask yourself. You think about it, you reflect on it until you know."

She snorted an unsympathetic laugh, "Like it's that easy."

"It really is," Phealan countered. "You just may not want to admit it."

The firm words drew her gaze again, "I want to be with my sister. That's what I want. And I can't have that, so what do you say now?"

Phealan smiled sadly, "That you can't always have what you want. But you can always react to your circumstances the way you want to."

It wasn't what she wanted to hear, though Phealan couldn't have predicted her rapid loss of civility.

She scowled, "Stop with the philosophical bullshit. You Earthers are so fucking frustrating, do you realize that? What do you think we do — try to be miserable, just so you can come and save us? It's not easy, and you just don't understand what it's like."

She didn't fully understand what she was saying, that much Phealan could detect. Something wasn't easy, but she was too exhausted and distraught to understand what that something was. Or why it was difficult.

"You're right, I don't understand," he said simply. "My mother is dead, as your mother is. My father is out on the same mission as your sister. I wish I could be with them both, but I can't be. There just isn't a way. I could be dead in three days, too. We all could be. And yet here I sit. You know what the difference is between us, Claire? Despite all of this, I'm determined that these next three days... the days that could be my *last* days... will not be sad or miserable. Despite all that's going on, I'm going to do everything I can to find joy in the little things. Because this could be my last chance to do so. We always have choice. We always have responsibility. And even when we can't control circumstances, we can control how we react to them."

Claire's eyes fixed on his, and she didn't have an immediate reply.

He stared back at her, carefully studying her mind, and feeling her pain and confusion for himself. The torment that was running wild through her... the unchecked anger and anguish. Some humans, like Pat, had always seemed more Earther-like than others. Those humans who could find peace at times like this... who were determined not to be as miserable as Claire was now.

But Claire couldn't bring herself to take that approach. It wasn't in her nature.

She thus looked away from Phealan, "You're too good to be true. All of you. Humans cannot be like you. It's impossible."

Phealan opened his mouth to counter her pessimism, but she held up her hand.

"It's not pessimism. Impossible things can't happen, and while it's nice and well for you to be happy and enlightened when this shit is happening all around you, we can't be. We'll never be like you."

The words had an air of finality, so Phealan decided nothing would be served by trying to press an argument.

Impossible? Impossible was this plan... was the attempt to defeat Omega. Did humans really believe that it would be equally impossible to better themselves?

He didn't know, and he didn't feel he could ask Claire just now. So he changed the subject back to the origin of the discussion, "So you're staying?"

She nodded, "Might as well die sooner."

Phealan's ear twitched, but he kept his eyes on the plot. A few moments later, *Carnarvon* and *Joseph Barron* left Earth space.

That was it: the plan was completely in motion. Omega would arrive in three days.

CHAPTER 23

Omega was due in two days, so Earth was being prepared for its greatest fight.

"Every flag officer who will participate in the defense of this planet is here right now," First Lord of the Admiralty Lab Forepaw stood at the front of Admiralty House's briefing room, Fox Magnus next to him. Before them was every Earther flag officer in the solar system, along with representatives from the Krogg and Larosian Fleets, and Ed Jeffries from Freetown.

"The Genesis Fleet has been sent on to New Halifax under Liz Hastings," Fox picked up where Lab left off. "They'll be in charge of evacuating the galaxy, should we fail here. The Battlecruisers of the Freetown squadron have remained with us, and we're very glad to have you."

Ed Jeffries was feeling awkward as the only human in the room, but when Fox's comments drew a chorus of approving cheers that eased his anxiety.

"Great to have you, Ed!" Fox confirmed with a smile, and Jeffries waved back in thanks. The five advanced Battlecruisers from the Freetown squadron were still ready for action, and would be his squadron during this desperate last fight. He expected that neither he, nor any of his people, would survive.

"In orbit," Lab picked up the briefing, "we'll have every ship the Earther Navy can put to space... that's 150 *Venerables* and just about 1,000 other classes. We have 50,000 gunboats as well. Warlord Kardrath will command the Krogg Navy alongside us..."

Kardrath was perched on a box-chair with the other Kroggs at the front of the briefing room, and now he looked back to the assembled officers with a wave.

"His fleet, as you know, numbers some 1,200 ships, and includes these excellent new Hyper Motherships, which have already proven how formidable they are," Fox seamlessly followed Lab's words again.

Lab returned the favor, "And alongside our Krogg friends, the Larosian Navy has recommissioned 200 of its great Battleships and Warcruisers. Novash will hold command of those squadrons."

The Larosian sitting near the Krogg held up his hand as well.

"So that gives us about 2,600 ships total. And we're reasonably certain Omega is coming with twice that many hulls," it was Fox's turn again. "Now, as you all know, we've been kicking around deployment options on this for days.

We've tried to think of every angle... every possible outcome... and we've come to a decision about how we think it's best to run this defense."

"Of course, nothing is written in stone. Anyone has a brilliant idea, we're always happy to hear it. Even a not-brilliant idea," Lab added the last remark with a wry smile, that surprised him with its ease.

The Earthers in this room had not all been present for the lengthy planning discussions — many were less experienced or more junior than the officers who had been. If any among them saw an option that the elder, more senior officers hadn't, it would absolutely be considered.

"So the idea is this..." Fox took over again, "...we're all going to stay right here. At Earth."

The First Space Lord then paused to let a rumble of thoughtful noises subside — it was almost humorous that everyone going 'hmm' at the same time could be so loud.

"There are many disadvantages to this approach, of course," Fox continued. "It will be virtually impossible, for instance, for us to deny Omega the chance to land his troops. He'll be able to dart through our defensive lines with his transports, and down the minions will go. We know he's very good at pulling off those landing drops... he did it at Freetown and at Krogg 'A'. So we're just going to accept that he'll do it here too. Beckett Lupus will be in charge of dealing with that. I don't envy him."

Another chorus of agreeing sounds met that remark — there was no denying that dealing with nine *billion* minions was going to be a tall order, even if they only needed to be delayed long enough for the plan to work.

"Our job in orbit is not going to be to stop those landings," Lab reiterated the point as he took over again. "Our task is to tie up those 5,000 ships. Looking back at every battle we've been in with Omega so far, we see a pattern: he likes to move fast and hard... he likes to ram. When we let him fight that way, we pay for it. We have a hard time keeping up, and we lose the advantage of our guns."

Earthers in the room nodded, and Fox glanced at Kardrath.

"So our plan is simple... we're in a defensive position, we're going to make him come to us. We'll pick a spot in orbital space, and we won't move around too much. Our Earther ships, and Novash's Larosian vessels, will be a solid force, moving in pre-arranged formations, but basically keeping tight and pouring out a huge volume of fire. While we do that, Kardrath and his fleet will be doing the melee fighting, because Omega is not used to dealing with our Krogg friends."

Kardrath nodded to Fox before looking at the Earthers assembled in the room, "It is our privilege to take on this challenge."

Another round of approving sounds came from the Earthers, and Lab took over right after.

"The idea here is pretty straightforward: because we're not preoccupied with trying to keep his minions away from the planet, we can deploy and fight in a manner that best suits our survival. Everything we do will be designed with that in mind... because we absolutely *must* last as long as we can. The longer we hold his focus, and keep his ships tied up, the better. He has to be as preoccupied as we can make him, while Setter Caine and Andra Ursla are doing their stuff."

Fox took over again: "Now it's quite possible that, with the exception of Jax and his fine escape-pod-finding skills, we could all die in this action. Unfortunately, that's necessary. And you know I don't say that lightly. We've already lost many good friends against this plague... but you and I know that there's never been a more important fight to be a part of."

That drew even louder approval, and Fox took a step back so Lab could resume, "Whatever happens, though, we need to be mindful of the plan. When Setter, Andra, Sarah, Pat, Graham and Christine hit the Omega avatars with the cure, we need to be ready to do our part. And a lot of this hinges on us being in the right *frame of mind* at that moment. We'll pounce on any chances, and if his command and control starts to break down because he's losing concentration, we'll exploit whatever weaknesses he shows."

"And," Fox pitched back in, glancing at the Kroggs in attendance as he did, "there'll be no use of telepathic explosions. We don't want to give him a chance to wrestle with one of our minds like that. We don't want to tip our hands. So if it's looking bad, ram him, but don't try to blow him up with your brain."

That last remark actually drew laughter, and Lab Forepaw grinned, "Fox, I think we'd all be mightily impressed if your brain could blow up a balloon, let alone a ship."

The laughter increased and Fox joined in, kindly shaking a fist at Lab.

It was a lame joke, but it was appreciated by everyone in the room. As the humor quelled, Lab Forepaw looked back out at the assembled Commodores and Admirals.

"I'm glad that we're laughing again," he said. "For too long, this plague's kept us from doing that. Now that we have a plan, though, we're in good shape. He's not going to expect what we have waiting for him... and I think we can beat him yet."

More sounds of agreement came from the assembled officers, and the meeting moved on to the details of battle group and squadron command assignments. Preparations for the space battle were well in hand.

CHAPTER 24

Omega was due in a day and a half, so Earth was being prepared for its greatest fight.

"Nine billion minions is what they tell us, and I'm pretty sure you can't count that many on one hand," Beckett Lupus was standing out on the landing fields of the Antarctic Plain with all the senior officers of the Earther Marine Corps, along with Tovarrin of the Larosian Stealth Guard, and Kragthar and several of his legion commanders from the Krogg Army.

"When did you start thinking you were funny?" Colonel Cadmus Howler was at the front of the large collection of officers, and Beckett and the other Earthers present laughed at the question.

"I didn't realize I thought I was," the General protested, then moved on with a smile. "Now, I think it's clear to everyone that Omega's just going to rain down everywhere. I wish he'd be as helpful as Shappa Bactule once was, and land his whole force here... but then I'm not sure you could fit nine billion minions on Antarctica in the first place. And he certainly won't try to find out."

"So we'll spread out," Lieutenant General Garnet Wiskar of the fourth division offered his comment, and Beckett nodded.

"That's exactly right. Most of you have your assigned cities... if you haven't seen the overall map yet, the basic idea is that we're fortifying major population centers across the planet... multiple shield lines, ground-based energy cannon... everything we can do, we've done. Your task as marines will be to assist the populations of those cities in their defense."

A murmur ran through the crowd at Beckett's words. No one liked the idea that civilian Earthers would have to participate in the fight against the plague's minions, but of course there was no alternative. And Earthers, even if they'd never fought in their life, were still naturally-skilled combatants.

"So if you do the math, there's nine billion of him, and two billion of us," Beckett continued. "This is going to be the biggest ground battle... well... ever. And we can add eleven million Krogg warriors, and 121,000 Larosian Stealth Guards to that for good measure."

There were loud sounds of approval at the last point, and both Tovarrin and Kragthar waved in acknowledgment.

"Throw in half a million of our own marines... well, we're in for a big one, my friends," Beckett reiterated the point, then pressed ahead. "Now, let me explain how this will go. You'll be holding a city... say... Beijing. That's Karyn's post."

General Karyn Kudlee held up her hand at mention of her name.

"Karyn's going to mobilize all the local resources, and the resources of her own Eighth Division, to defend that city. If, once the minions land, she starts to feel that she's going to be overrun, she'll red flash headquarters. I'll be based here, I'll see the flash, and if there are reinforcements available, I'll send them."

The marines assembled nodded.

"Now," Beckett continued, "that's very easy to say, but here's the hitch: the Navy is not going to be fighting for overall control of orbital space. We're going to be using gunboats to protect transports carrying reinforcements, and in higher orbit I believe the Freetown Battlecruisers will be looking out for us, but moving our troops will not be easy. That's the first point. The second is that it's quite likely we're all going to red flash pretty quickly. Reinforcements might be tapped out very fast. So there's no guarantee of help."

A cool silence descended for a moment after those words. These marines understood very well that the situation was dire, and that at least some cities would inevitably fall... it was not a pleasant thought.

"Who will the reinforcements be?"

The question came out of the crowd, and Beckett pointed towards Kragthar, "The Kroggs will be our cavalry. We'll hold them back and then deploy them as needed."

Kragthar stepped in quickly to explain further, "We have strong drop-craft available to us, another benefit of the lessons we learned from the last war. We'll be using those to move quickly into position. I will spread our legions out to bodies of water around this planet. Our drop-craft can wait beneath the waves for a call, then deploy."

"Use water as cover, the way Omega did on Freetown?" Garnet Wiskar sounded impressed as he asked the question, and Kragthar bowed, Larosian style.

"I doubt we will be completely safe by hiding from him, but it will keep us out of sight in the beginning."

More sounds of approval met that explanation, and then Beckett continued to elaborate, "In the meantime, here at base, we'll have the Heavy Division, somewhat reinforced, along with the Eleventh and Twelfth Divisions working as the security force on the perimeter. And backing them up will be our friends the Larosians — all of them."

Tovarrin held up his hand at the mention of his Stealth Guardsmen, and after nodding to the alien, Beckett pressed on, "Our goal will be to keep command and control functioning for as long as possible. If we go down here,

General Lion will have secondary facilities in place at Arctic Base, and Karyn will be tertiary at Beijing. If we all go down, any undeployed Krogg legions will be left to their own devices... you'll have to try to contact them directly."

"We will be hungry to kill, so by no means be shy in your requests!" Kragthar said eagerly, and the marines all felt a bit of discomfort at the words. Kroggs being eager to kill was something the Earthers might never get completely used to...

"Bottom line is this: we have to keep these minions busy while Supreme Consul Caine and Admiral Ursla finish the plan. They're going to be fighting a duel with Omega-Natosh on Genesis... I've fought that avatar, and I will tell you their task is difficult. But you know the plan. We have to keep him preoccupied with the battle here. The Navy will be tying up as many of his ships as possible, we'll be tying up his minions... and hopefully the distractions will give Caine and Ursla the edge they need to hit him with the injector gun. After that, our job is to get to grips with all the minions we can find, so we can take advantage at the moment."

The marines all nodded again — the plan was no secret to anyone, but what it demanded of the fighting wolves, cats and bears here would be daunting indeed.

"How will we know the moment?" Cadmus Howler asked the logical question with a frown, then uncreased his brow before Beckett could reply. "And if you say 'you'll know it when you see it', I might smack you."

A laugh broke out again, and Beckett shrugged, "Well, I don't know if you'll *see* it, but telepathy being what it is, you'll figure it out."

The crowd sobered and nodded at that.

"And be assured, friends, that when you are locked in combat with the plague, we will be in support of you, wherever we are. We will do all we can to assist as you take advantage of that moment against him," Kragthar added immediately.

Tovarrin offered a stoic nod, "As will we Larosians."

Voiced words of thanks rumbled from the marines again, and Beckett took a deep breath as he looked over his troops.

"This is going to be... unlike anything we've ever done before. Ever. Not that I really need to tell you that... but. We're going to do our jobs well. We'll do our old friend Andros Grieve proud. And Omega isn't going to have the fun he's looking for."

More sounds of approval, and Beckett nodded.

"Alright, so let's confirm city assignments. If you haven't already, you're going to need to familiarize yourself with your defense zones..."

Preparations for the ground war were well in hand.

CHAPTER 25

Phealan Caine walked through the corridors of Admiralty House, looking for the conference room to which he'd been directed. Somewhere around here, the First Consul was working...

Stopping at an open door, Phealan caught sight of Varnon Broadpaw, sitting at a table with a pad of paper and a pen, looking somewhat frustrated. The young Caine approached the door and knocked on the frame to announce his presence. Varnon looked up.

"Phealan, I was just thinking about calling you!"

Phealan frowned and stepped into the room, "Well I was just coming to find you... what do you need?"

The First Consul stretched his neck and leaned back in his chair, rubbing his eyes as he did so, "I'm trying to come up with a speech."

Approaching the table, Phealan looked down at the pad, "Speech?"

Varnon nodded, "Yes, *the* speech."

"The speech?"

Varnon's eyes darted up to Phealan, "*The* speech."

Phealan's eyes darted back and forth in confusion, "*The...*"

"Speech!" Varnon threw his hands into the air in a rather animated fashion. "See, this is why I'm having problems. I'm just too nonsensical!"

"What's the speech for?" Phealan elected to broach the subject another way, and Varnon leaned forward in his chair.

"It's the rousing speech... like the one your father always does when people need to be fired up. I'm writing mine now... I mean, a day to go, I know I left it late. But still... how does your dad write these? For that matter, how do you? He told me you'd have one too."

Phealan's eyebrow climbed, "A rousing speech?"

Varnon nodded again, "You know... just before the big battle, we give a few speeches that remind everyone of everything they know. They're eloquent and powerful... we all roar afterwards. Feels good. Gets us ready to fight... you know?"

"Er... sure," Phealan was sort of following, so he frowned thoughtfully. "Well, I don't think my dad ever wrote one of those beforehand... I think he did them off the cuff."

Varnon groaned, "Oh great... now I'm really in trouble."

"Well, no... no I think you can give a very good speech..." Phealan stammered. He couldn't really believe he was having this conversation...

"I should have asked him before he left... how does your dad come up with those uplifting turns of phrase? I mean, what's the trick...?"

Phealan's ears twitched.

"I don't think it matters what words you use... the message is the important part. A speech is about communicating ideas... if you speak the truths that people believe in, it doesn't matter how you say it," he suggested.

Varnon's eyes narrowed, "Maybe... I suppose..."

The First Consul fell silent for a moment, then settled back in his chair again, "I read somewhere that a rousing speech was as good for morale as having an extra seven billion soldiers, and an extra 3,000 warships."

Phealan tried not to let his expression convey his confusion at the absurd remark, but unfortunately, being both instinctive and telepathic, Varnon picked up on it anyway and groaned again.

"Where'd you read that?" Phealan asked with a shrug.

Varnon pointed at a crumpled up piece of paper on the floor next to the waste bin at the door, "It was the first line of an earlier draft."

"Oh."

Phealan couldn't think of anything else to say, so he remained silent. Varnon dropped his pen on the pad before him and let out another groan, "Well, I could try winging it."

The young Caine nodded his agreement, "And maybe try not trying too hard. Like I say, I don't think the mechanics of the wording matter... it's the message."

Varnon nodded, then looked up, "I suppose so. That what you'll be doing for yours?"

"Since I haven't thought about mine at all, I suppose that's exactly what I'll have to do," he shrugged back.

"Ah, that makes sense."

The two fell silent again for a few moments, and then Varnon frowned and looked up, "So... wait. Why are you here? Were you looking for me?"

"Hmm?" Phealan wasn't paying attention in that second, his mind instead trying to wrap itself around the idea of his speech — what could he, as a youthful wolf, say to his people on the eve of this fight?

What could he say that his father and Varnon between them couldn't cover?

Rousing speeches certainly weren't going to make up for the differences in numbers... but perhaps they'd help anyway. Phealan would have to think about this...

Hey, you've tuned me out.

Phealan blinked at the telepathic intrusion, and shook himself back into reality with an apologetic grin, "Sorry."

Varnon chuckled, "I think it's fun we can do that now. I don't know if I'll ever give up talking... I do love the sound of my own voice, after all... but telepathy has certain advantages."

"It'll more than help against Omega, I suppose," Phealan agreed, his tone growing more somber as his mind started to drift back to the reason for his search for Varnon. "Anyway, I was looking for you. I wanted to let you know that I won't be in Antarctica during the attack. I'm going to stay on the estate."

Varnon's eyebrows rose sharply, "There's no security planned for the estate."

Phealan nodded, "But Claire is determined to stay, and I don't want to leave her on her own. There's a good chance, too, that Omega won't expect me to be there... he might ignore it. We can be pretty certain he's going to hit Antarctic Base with a strong force."

"Aye," Varnon drew out the word. The First Consul was going to be at Antarctic Base, along with Beckett Lupus, for the last fight... he'd assumed that Phealan would join them.

But if the young Caine believed he needed to be at his home when the battle came, it was hardly Varnon's right to deny him. Indeed, if Phealan thought it necessary, Varnon was inclined to believe that there was a very good reason... whether the young wolf realized it or not.

That said, if Omega did decide to go after the estate...

"Well, we know Omega really hates you and your dad, so he may well attack the estate, just out of spite. I'll get Beckett to assign some protection... not too much, but enough to hold the house, maybe."

Phealan wasn't sure he liked the sound of that idea, but Varnon shook his head, "I'll insist on that one, my friend. I don't want to take any chances that you get killed. We're going to need you at that moment, and we're going to need you a whole lot more afterwards."

When my father is dead? The question was asked by Phealan's mind instead of his mouth, and Varnon nodded.

We'll really need you then.

With a grim expression, Phealan nodded, "Alright then. Just have Beckett get in touch with me when he knows who he's sending."

Varnon nodded, "Will do."

The wolves paused again, and at last Phealan nodded and headed for the door, "I'll let you get back to your writing."

Laughing, Varnon picked up his pen, "Yeah... we'll see if that happens or not."

Phealan headed for home.

CHAPTER 26

Colonel Cadmus Howler stepped into Beckett Lupus' office, "You need something, Beck?"

The General looked up from a pile of pads he'd been working on and nodded, "Yes, just heard from Varnon Broadpaw that we'll need to secure the Caine estate. Phealan is going to be staying there for the battle."

"Really?" Cadmus' eyebrows went up. "Well... if that's where he needs to be..."

His voice trailed off as he realized the implication of Beckett Lupus telling *him* this.

"You want 2/54th for the job?"

Lupus sat back in his chair, a studied expression on his face, "He needs the best protection we can give him. That's you, Cadmus. I'd say put the squad in as his personal bodyguard, and the battalion will hold the perimeter... hopefully Omega won't realize there's anything important in Newfoundland, and won't trouble you..."

"But," Cadmus smiled sadly, "we both know he's more than smart enough to realize Newfoundland will be the center of the world for this battle. We'll be ready for him."

Beckett nodded to his friend, then stood up and rounded his desk, "We may not get to see each other again before it gets started, so... good luck, Cadmus."

Cadmus Howler's sad smile increased in size, and he extended his hand towards his General, and longtime friend, "Remember all those years ago when the Crusaders landed here?"

"I do. And when we stormed that empty Queen's Hive in Genesis, and when we were shot down with Pat, and when we stormed Krogg 'A'... it's been a long run," Lupus took his friend's hand.

Cadmus chuckled softly, "Always giving us the easy jobs. I'll see you after this is over, Beck... and hopefully we won't both be dead at the time."

Their handshake held for a moment more, then Cadmus Howler left Beckett's office, and prepared to round up and transport his battalion to the new center of the world: an island called Newfoundland.

Minnie Maximane, Artie Tigar, Dran Nightclaw, Ami Dune, Zed Dune, and Jax Furgus were sitting together in *Galahad's* briefing room. As host of the meeting, Minnie was at the head of the table, but there was very little to discuss. The fleet deployment arrangements had already been made, and now it just remained to wait one more day until they'd be put into action.

Into *hot* action.

"Empty chairs," Jax Furgus cut through a brooding silence with those words. "A number of empty chairs."

It was indeed surprising that between them, these six Earthers were nearly all that was left of the Earther senior officer corps. There were others, obviously, but they were tied up with organization... and many more were dead.

"Going to be a tough day tomorrow," Minnie Maximane observed, the comment only partially related to what Jax had said.

Everyone around the table nodded, and a cool silence returned. This was not so much the dire, grim feeling that had seized these officers before the recent battle at Krogg 'A', when they'd believed all was lost, but more a quiet certainty that the end was near.

"I, for one, am glad to have another shot at him," Artie leaned forward in his chair and took some pleasure in lacing his fingers together. "And look, we all know we can fight him. Minnie and I managed to take a strip off him at the corridor, and we've all done our piece of the fighting. So tomorrow, we just keep swinging. At the end of the day, we'll see who's left standing."

That was about all that could be said. Silence returned.

Ed Jeffries looked up from his desk at the knock on his door, "Yes?"

The hatch opened and an Earther stepped in, then saluted, "Garth Badger, sir, recently off *Venerable* and *Carnarvon*. They've assigned me to coordinate our gunboats with you."

Jeffries lowered the pad he'd been working on to his desk, "Indeed... the boats we'll be working with to help protect the reinforcement flights?"

Garth bobbed his head, "Aye sir. I did operations off a Larosian deck, so Admiral Lupus figured I'd be well suited to liaising with you."

Nodding slowly, Jeffries came to his feet, "I heard about your work out there. Excellent job, by the way. It'll be a pleasure to work with you."

"Thank you, sir, but the pleasure's mine. We're very happy to have you here."

Jeffries and the bear shook hands. They'd be working together closely the following day.

Fox Magnus appeared quietly on *Formidable's* bridge, intending to sneak up on his friend Chronos Claw. Unfortunately, the ship's Master saw the First Space Lord arrive, and barked out a crisp: "First Space Lord on deck!"

Then the ship's Captain, who had been speaking with Chronos, added a helpful, "Trying to sneak up on our Admiral."

Chronos turned with a smile and shook his friend's hand, "Come up to do the big fond farewell thing, the night before battle?"

Fox shrugged, "Seems appropriate. Big day tomorrow after all. Planet to save and all that."

Chuckling, Chronos nodded, "We'll get it done."

"As long as we don't let ourselves get blindsided somehow, like Lang did at Genesis," Fox's words were surprisingly less optimistic than they should have been. The pain of Lang Sandpelt's death still crept up on him now and then — the young canine had been with both him and Claw back in the old days aboard *Flame*.

Claw took the change of mood in stride, and dismissed it. "We won't get blindsided. Not after all this. It's gun on gun now... we'll make him pay. And keep him busy, as you and Lab said."

Fox took a deep breath, "Yes. That's exactly what we'll do. And no telepathic explosions."

Chronos Claw frowned, "If you keep saying 'no telepathic explosions', you're going to make me think you're planning a telepathic explosion."

Fox's eyes narrowed, "Well I'm not. I'm just saying, we don't want *any* telepathic explosions that day. Right?"

The way that was said confused his friend for a moment, but then Claw got it... or was pretty sure he did... so he nodded.

"Right."

"Good. Now let's get our last supper... or last before the plague shows up, anyway," Fox smiled, and nodding to his Flag Captain, Chronos Claw left *Formidable's* bridge.

Kragran was joined in one of the compartments aboard *Death* by his trusted lieutenants, Warlord Kardrath and Warlord Kragthar.

I wished for us to meet face-to-face one last time, my friends, Kragran thought somberly. *Tomorrow, I will join First Consul Broadpaw at the Antarctic Base. Kragthar, you and your warriors will be in the oceans of Earth, and Kardrath, you and our fleet will be here. We will see each others' minds, but as the Earthers seem to value the meetings face-to-face, I do as well.*

That is well, m'Lord, Kardrath thought in reply.

I agree, Kragthar concurred.

The trio of Kroggs stood in a triangle, then, mentally and verbally silent for a moment.

After no words or thoughts were exchanged for that period of time, Kardrath tilted his head in curiosity, *M'Lord, what are we supposed to do when we meet like this?*

Er. Perhaps. Talk? Kragran actually didn't know.

Talk about what? Kragthar asked with a narrowing eye.

Kragran stood still for a moment, *About. Things.*

They were silent and thoughtless again for a moment.

Perhaps personal meetings are more significant to the Earthers, Kardrath suggested. *Perhaps it is not a custom we need adopt.*

Kragran thought about that for a moment, and then nodded, *Perhaps you are right. Nice to see you both, I'll be off!*

So ended the Krogg experiment of visiting comrades on the night before battle.

Narosh and Novash met each other on the telepathic plane, neither feeling it necessary to leave their posts.

It will be quite a day tomorrow, sir, Novash observed, and Narosh nodded.

"Yes it will... er, sorry..." Narosh's reply started as words, then turned to thoughts: *Yes it will.*

"We can speak if you prefer, of course sir," Novash switched to his own vocal chords, and his superior smiled at him.

"Sorry, Novash... Being around all these Earthers lately has seemingly fired the Earther part of my blood. Speaking has become surprisingly natural."

"I don't see how that requires an apology, sir," Novash smiled back. "I do believe that the very point of us being here, and all we will do tomorrow, is to honor the good that the Earthers have brought us all."

Including speaking, now and then, Narosh agreed.

The Larosians continued their conversation telepathically.

Not long after Cadmus Howler departed, Varnia Lupus turned up in her husband's office, greeting him with a telepathic, *Hi.*

Beckett looked up at his wife, then came to his feet and was around his desk to hug her quickly, "Hi back."

"We're all set in orbit," she said as they squeezed each other and then parted. "I'll be in *Renown*, with the *Venerable* lines."

Beckett nodded slowly, failing to hide his relief. As far as he was concerned, those ships were the safest place to be for this fight. They'd proved their strength, so his wife would be as safe as she could be aboard hers.

Yes, but down here you'll be at risk, Varnia was reading her husband's mind, though even without her telepathy, his thoughts were quite clear from his expression.

"I'll look after myself, and your dad. You take care up there. That's all that matters."

"That's not all that matters," her tone was soft as she said that. "It's the least of what matters tomorrow."

Beckett Lupus couldn't honestly disagree with his wife on that point. He swallowed a little worriedly, then nodded, "Well... can you spend the night down here, or are you back to *Renown* immediately?"

She shook her head slowly, "Don't want to take any chances, I need to be up there tonight."

"Ah," Beckett nodded. "Okay. Well then…"

His mind reached out and pulled on hers, and they were catapulted to the telepathic plane.

"Let's talk for a while. You know, a minute or two real time… however long that is here."

Varnia smiled, "If Narosh explained this to me correctly, time means very little here. So it can be long enough."

Beckett's smile broadened, "Well, it's not as good as actual living, but that's not bad at all."

Jax Furgus was just settling down in his cabin on *Aboukir* when a call came in. He put it up on his desk holo plot immediately, and discovered it was from his daughter, "Hi dad."

"Joyce!" the old cat grinned at her. "You talk to your mother today? She's in the shelter in Cairo… she's even carrying a rifle."

Joyce Furgus, Captain of one of Cadmus Howler's companies of 2/54th, smiled back at her crotchety old dad, "I did talk to her, just now actually. I wanted to tell you, though, that things have changed and I'm posted to the Caine estate for tomorrow."

"Important job," Jax's grin faded, "you'll do it real good, cubbie."

"*Dad*," Joyce protested at being called 'cubbie', as she always did, and Jax chuckled.

"I'll see you the day after tomorrow, my little one. All my love is with you and your mom," Jax's tone became more serious, but its warmth didn't cool.

"You look after yourself, dad. Love you back… and yes, I will see you the day after tomorrow."

With a parting nod, Joyce closed the link.

Jax leaned back in his chair, wondering if he would see his daughter again.

Lab Forepaw and Varnon Broadpaw sat together in Lab's cabin on *Venerable*, an enduring silence covering them as they thought about all they'd been through to get here.

Finally, Lab broke the quiet, "Get that speech sorted out?"

Varnon snorted a laugh, "Sort of. Phealan told me to wing it. I'll say something as a preface to Setter's recorded message, maybe. And Phealan will speak after. You going to say anything?"

Lab shook his head, "I tried back when I thought Omega was hitting Freetown. It didn't work… I'll leave that job to the Caines now."

Varnon nodded slowly, "They know how to do it, alright."

Silence descended again, until Varnon looked at Lab, "Listen, Lab... if I go, you do all you can to look after Varnia, okay?"

Looking at his friend, Lab let out a breath, "I will."

"Good," Varnon replied. "Good. I need to make sure she'll be looked after if I go."

His repetition was a symptom of his unease, and Lab could sense that in his old friend.

"We'll get it done tomorrow. After all this, we have to. The plan... so help me... the plan will work," Varnon babbled a little there, and Lab closed his eyes.

"I hope so."

Everything would be realized tomorrow.
One way or another.

CHAPTER 27

Sarah almost looked as though she were at peace while she slept. It was the most like herself Pat had seen her in as long as he could remember... the troubles of the universe all gone from her mind, and a sweet fantasy giving her some respite. He enjoyed seeing the soft expression on her face, so it didn't bother him at all that he was losing sleep to watch it.

For two days of travel, she had stayed away from him, keeping her own counsel through most of the time, and only speaking in short, terse phrases at dinner. She was isolating herself from him, and from her emotions, willing to die without either.

Pat weathered it because he had to, and because he'd hoped — dreamed, perhaps — that maybe for a minute or three, she'd let the shields down. Just long enough to allow him to see a piece of her again, before they rode into battle.

She hadn't, though. They were pulling into orbit over Ecclesia tomorrow, where they'd face Omega-Paine... the bastard who represented their two most hated enemies. And then they'd kill him, or die trying.

It seemed terribly unlikely that Sarah would wake up in the morning and decide it was time to toss her beleaguered husband an emotional bone. No, this was as much as he could hope for — a peaceful look that reminded him of the best years they'd shared.

Sitting beside the bed and watching her, he found his own comfort.

He didn't even know what to think about tomorrow's mission... there was no point dwelling on it, he just had to do it. And if, by what might be termed a miracle, he survived it, perhaps they really could find a new life together.

But there was no point getting ahead of himself there. He didn't need to be distracted by hopes for a rosy future when he had a hard fight to focus on in the meantime.

The arrangements Setter had made with Omega had been clear: *Joseph Barron* would be allowed to go into orbit over Ecclesia, and Sarah and Pat could land. They'd sold this to Omega as Pat and Sarah's supposed need to fight their theatrical final duel with the avatar... which Omega had seemed to buy. Omega had promised no minions would attempt to intervene once they landed. Pat suspected no minions would be present at all, actually — the plague probably needed every soldier it could get for the landing on Earth.

But even with no minions to face, the task they confronted was next to impossible: they had to fight Omega-Paine to a standstill, and then hit the avatar with an injection containing the cure.

They absolutely had to kill him.

But Pat remembered all too well how powerful Omega-Gillian had been on Freetown... it didn't seem likely to him that anyone other than an Earther could pull that off. But he and Sarah would be motivated, and perhaps her coldness would pay off on the day — make her that much faster with her sword.

If not, and all else failed, he'd be carrying an energy charge with a dead man's switch.

They'd kill Omega-Paine, one way or another.

And if they managed to kill the avatar, and *if* the plague had inexplicably kept his word and left no minions on the planet to stop them leaving, they could retreat to orbit and take *Joseph Barron* back to Earth... or New Halifax, if the plan failed.

So would the plan work? It was an irresistible question. That Omega was letting it happen at all seemed so unlikely to Pat... the plague had the Allies in an impossible position, but his hubris and his twenty-first century mentality were his weakness. By letting these ships close to his avatars, and accepting bogus duels just because he'd enjoy them, maybe he was sealing his own fate...

Sarah stirred, and Pat instantly stopped his musing. He paused and marveled at his wife's genuine beauty. He hadn't stopped to admire her for so long... for years, it seemed, and this could be his last chance.

Then her eyes opened slowly, and locked with Pat's. He expected a volley of chastening words in that second, but her expression was still different.

"Mmm, Pat," she whispered through a smile. "Am I dreaming?"

"You were," he slid out of the chair he'd been occupying beside the bed, and leaned in closer. "Maybe you still are."

She smiled and closed her eyes again, "Well get in bed, it's cold in here without you."

The fact that Pat could barely believe he'd heard those words spoke to how distant Sarah had been over the past weeks. She was dreaming... perhaps she was in that blissful state that one finds after good dreams, when all the woes and agonies of the world seem to melt away, or are briefly forgotten. That might make her awakening the next morning a rude one, but for tonight, at least, maybe they could share a measure of peace and happiness.

Getting to his feet, Pat rounded the bed and slid carefully underneath the covers. Sarah shifted to give him more room, then snuggled back into him.

"We should get some sleep," she whispered, pulling one of his arms around her.

He found his face next to her cheek, so he kissed her gently, "Yes indeed. Good night, Sarah. I love you."

"Love you, Pat," she whispered back.

He hadn't heard her say that for a very long time — since before all this mess started. They'd come a long way, and now they had to find a way to get back what they'd left behind. It would never be the same — even if the plan succeeded, they'd never go back to Genesis...

But it could be just as good, or better, somewhere else. With all the darkness in the past.

As long as we get it done tomorrow, and safely...

He threw a roadblock in front of that thought. He'd worry about it in the morning; he'd enjoy this rare happiness right now. His hand on Sarah's stomach pulled her close, and he breathed deeply and tried to lose himself in the feeling of being at home.

He thought of all his Earther friends, who had been so good to him. He thought of all the luck that he'd enjoyed. Looking back, he couldn't complain. It had worked out well enough, and tomorrow would be no different.

No point worrying about it, or so his Irish ancestors might have said.

That thought jogged his memory, reminding him of a fine Irish saying he'd found in one of Garnan's histories of his ancestors. Smiling, Pat whispered: "In life, there are only two things to worry about — either you're sick or you're healthy."

Sarah didn't stir, so Pat went on, "If you're healthy, there's nothing to worry about. But if you're sick, there are only two things to worry about — either you'll get better, or you'll die.

Sarah's breathing remained smooth, and Pat continued, "If you get better, there's nothing to worry about. But if you die, there are only two things to worry about — either you go to heaven or to the gulags of Hell."

Pat reached up and touched his wife's cheek, "But if you go to the gulags, you'll be so busy shaking hands with your friends, you won't have time to worry."

Sarah remained fast asleep, so Pat closed his eyes and let his head sink deeper into his pillow.

Nothing to worry about tomorrow. Gods, the way they talked, my Irish forefathers might as well have been Earthers.

Maybe, Pat decided, that was why he liked the Earthers so much. Maybe that was why they'd win.

With that thought, Pat found sleep — a peaceful sleep that put his mind at ease.

CHAPTER 28

Christine was numb when she awoke in her cabin in the middle of the night. The numbness, of course, was necessary — if she hadn't been numb, she'd have been screaming in agony, every nerve ending sending far too much information back to her brain. So the absence of feeling was, theoretically, good.

But on this particular occasion, she hated it.

It wasn't the first time she'd felt that... it wasn't the first time she'd missed the ability to feel more than just the dull throbbing of the stasis fields on her skin, or the awkward cold of the atmospheric anesthetics that let her be exposed to the air in her quarters.

She wanted to feel cold water on her face again. Warm hands massaging her back, or a cool breeze in her hair. Not dull, muffled sensations that were just enough to allow her to operate. She missed feeling things like a human... or like an Earther.

But as she woke up this time, she realized that it could be her last night... the last time she would wish for these things. Her last night of sensory-deprived torture.

Chances were she would die today. And if she didn't, she could take the treatment Celia had sent along.

If she was honest, though, she expected to die. She knew that Omega-Gillian would be too much for her. And because of her disturbing sense of Earther calm, that expectation didn't cause her to feel a jolt of fear.

"Lights."

She called up her dim cabin illumination because she knew the darkness of her room felt even blacker due to of the grimness of her thoughts. It was the middle of the night and she was losing sleep she'd need tomorrow... but thinking that wasn't going to do her any good.

I guess I'm not Earther enough to sleep on the night before my death.

Like Pat and Sarah's mission to Ecclesia, her trip to Freetown had been part of Setter's deal with Omega. As was the case at Ecclesia, there were to be no minions here, just Omega-Gillian. They were to fight a duel with her, supposedly to gain their revenge. Then they'd try to hit the avatar with the injector containing the cure...

Christine still had a hard time believing Omega had let them through on such a flimsy excuse. He had to be suspicious, but perhaps his supreme arrogance factored in... Maybe he knew the cure was coming, but believed that it was impotent...

And he'd be wrong?

Christine shook her head and got to her feet. She headed for the bathroom, so that she could stare at herself again — it was something she was doing a great deal lately. Sometimes she couldn't help but feel as though she was looking at a stranger in the mirror... and other times, who she was seemed painfully evident.

Standing in front of her reflection, she peered deep into her own eyes. What would she do tomorrow? Would her Earther characteristics help her kill an avatar who had reportedly dismembered an Earther General? Would Graham's new skills, learned through endless and uncompromising training during their time in the Larosian galaxy, make a difference?

It seems like a stretch to think two humans could take her...

Christine was realistic in that admission. Even if Omega had kept his word, and there were no minions on Freetown... what were their chances?

She didn't know. Graham wouldn't care, and she didn't know.

"So maybe I die tomorrow."

It was a possibility, but she wasn't being absorbed by it. On one level she was calmed by that realization. On another, she was frustrated by it. She feared that when she was inevitably struck by the harsh reality that her end was coming, the revelation might lessen her effectiveness in the final moments.

Then again, maybe it wouldn't. Maybe her Earther side would fortify her, and—

There was a knock at her door.

She blinked and turned to the hatch — Graham must not have been sleeping either.

"Come in," she answered quietly, and the brooding ArcGeneral appeared, his face impassive.

"I'd feared you wouldn't be able to sleep," he commented as he stepped in.

"It's a tough night for sleep," she agreed.

"Indeed," his expression didn't change. "I don't know if I will be in trouble tomorrow, when the reality of what we're doing hits me. But... I wanted to tell you, whatever happens... whatever weakness I end up revealing... I want you to carry through. Even if I crack tomorrow. If I plead with you not to kill Gillian, you still must finish her."

Christine's eyebrows went up, revealing her surprise at the suggestion — not that she should kill Gillian, but that Graham might crack.

"You worried you're going to lose your nerve tomorrow?" she asked evenly, and Graham's head tilted very slightly.

"I don't believe I will, but it's not outside the realm of possibility. As I say,

Christine, we can't take the chance. If I lose my nerve, I must be able to rely on you to finish the job."

Christine's gaze locked on Graham's, and she nodded slowly, "Of course I will."

"Good. Good," he nodded to her, distractedly repeating that word, "Thank you, Christine. I'll see you in the morning, as we prepare for the landing?"

She nodded, "Definitely."

He started to turn to go, then turned back to her, "I'm sorry about all this, Christine. I'm sorry that you were drawn into all of this."

That halted Christine's thoughts — Graham was, for the first time in ages, voicing a concern about her?

She turned his words over in her mind for a few seconds, and shook her head, "I don't see how you were responsible for it. I accepted the job... the rest... well, that was all of my choosing."

"Yes, but I offered the choices," Graham countered, and his point was valid enough.

If not for Graham, she would be with her sister now... but by the same token, if not for her own decisions, she would be in the very same place. It seemed unnecessary to dwell too much on who was more responsible...

"Let's not worry about that," she said slowly. "Let's worry about winning tomorrow."

Graham's eyes settled on hers, and he nodded again, "I will be very lucky tomorrow, to have your help. Thank you for that."

She stared at him and then replied, "You're welcome."

With that, he turned away for good, and left her cabin. Christine watched the hatch shut behind him, and was overcome by a feeling of uneasiness. Graham was saying his goodbyes, she realized... so he believed that tomorrow was the last day.

She still didn't know.

Either way, she'd have to be at her best.

"I must not panic tomorrow," she asserted in a low tone. "I must be ready."

But if Graham — with his icy fury — was concerned about not being able to finish the job, how could she be confident of herself?

Returning to her bed, she felt her blood tingle, and she closed her eyes. Hopefully the Earther in her would make it work. Her humanity, in itself, would not be enough...

She went back to sleep.

CHAPTER 29

Setter Caine looked out at the passing stars through the large windows of *Orion's* observation deck. Though the ship was in energy drive, the cosmos was still visibly passing by — one of the interesting quirks of this mode of travel. Setter enjoyed the view... he'd been across this incredible universe many times during his life, and this would be the last.

"Never fails to impress, does it?" Ursla was standing a ways behind Setter, and he smiled and shook his head.

"It really doesn't... for all the certainty we have about ourselves and where we're from, we know so little about everything that's out here," he replied, his voice revealing some wonder.

Ursla nodded, "In time, we'll know more. Well, our people will, not us."

Setter turned from the glass with folded arms, "That's true indeed."

While others had hope about their fates, Setter and Andra knew they would not be returning from Genesis. They knew what Omega-Natosh was capable of, and they knew that even if he followed the agreement and kept his minions away, they wouldn't leave that planet ever again.

An injector gun full of the cure...

Probably don't need to keep reiterating the whole plan in your head, Ursla thought to Setter, her smile broadening.

The Supreme Consul blinked and chuckled, "What would we have been like last war, if we'd been able to do that?"

"Telepathy, you mean?" Ursla queried in reply, and Setter's eyes narrowed. *You could read my mind... why'd you ask if that's what I meant?*

Ursla laughed, "Good point. I think if we'd been telepathic during the last war, we'd have used that ability to make jokes about each other."

Setter nodded, then glanced back out at the stars, "I suppose that's all. It wouldn't have made that much of a difference against the Queen... might have been more vulnerable to her, even."

"True," Ursla agreed. "But now we can use it for all it's worth."

Those words carried some finality, and Setter met them with a slow nod. The plan... this plan he'd cooked up. Would telepathy help it succeed? Or would it fail?

At this stage, it almost didn't matter. If they lost, there'd be no time to worry about what might have been.

"You know, we're not going to be able to do an equation at the end of this mess."

Setter blinked at the unexpected words, and glanced back at his large friend, "What?"

"You know, the equations that we used to come up with... where we'd always boil down the lessons we'd learned to three words..."

"Right, yes... I suppose you're right. Someone else will have to do the equation this time."

Ursla frowned, "Is that even allowed?"

Chuckling, Setter shrugged, "I didn't think there were rules for that sort of thing."

"Hm. Well what would the equation be... what do you think? What would we say about all this? About fighting Omega?"

Setter's expression turned thoughtful, and he looked back out at the stars again. What would he say about all this, were he given a chance in the end? What had he talked about in the speech he'd recorded for tomorrow?

"Destiny, I suppose," he said quietly. "It'd probably end up being the destiny equation."

Ursla cocked an eyebrow, "Indeed?"

Setter glanced back at her with a shrug, "Well all of this... Omega is convinced victory is his destiny. Otherwise he wouldn't be fool enough to let us get close to him. And we... well I believe it's destiny too... I just define it differently."

Ursla could have peered into Setter's mind for clarification, but she still preferred to *hear* the wolf's words, "Define it how?"

A gentle frown crossed Setter's brow, and he sighed, "Destiny... I talked to Phealan about it. I don't think it's preordained... I think it's something we assign later. Events push us certain ways... circumstances, the actions of others... they all impact us. We make choices, and steer ourselves around. But I don't know that there's one finite objective at the end... I don't think where we end up is, as I said, preordained."

Ursla nodded slowly, her eyes still fixed on passing stars as Setter took a breath, then finished his thought.

"We know our *destiny* is to fight tomorrow. That's where the circumstances have led us, where we're headed. But I don't think destiny dictates who wins or loses... tomorrow will decide that. And then afterwards, perhaps we can look back and call what happened *destiny*. But before the event, I don't think it's written in stone. Destiny is more about the choices you're given, and what you do with them, than it is about the final answer."

So in the end, a great deal of responsibility falls on all of us, Ursla thought. *In the end, it's down to us to pick... or to fight for... the destiny.*

"Indeed," Setter agreed. "So maybe Omega's right, maybe he's wrong...

I think he's missing the point. Either way, tomorrow it's you and me against him."

Ursla nodded again, "And we'll die."

"Exactly," Setter agreed.

The two old friends shared a nod, and some comfort at the certainty of what was to come. The precise outcome was unknown, but they knew that no matter what, the battle would be fought.

"I'll go first," Ursla continued after that pause. "I'll be killed first, I mean. But I'll try to hit him with the gun before I go."

A small, sad smile formed on Setter's face, "I know you'll get him."

"I'm rusty with the sword, though. I haven't done a whole lot of hand-to-hand since... well... has it been all the way back to the Antarctic Plain? No, there was the boarding at Krogg 'A', but that wasn't much..."

"I'm just as rusty," Setter said smoothly. "It'll be more than our bodies doing the job, of course... the telepathy..."

Ursla shrugged, "He's still going to kill me pretty quick. Better that way all round."

Setter nodded, "You're probably right."

They settled into silence again, neither of them terribly bothered by their grim subject matter, or the relaxed tone of their discussion.

Humans really wouldn't be able to figure out how we could be this calm, would they? Ursla sent the question with her mind, and Setter laughed out loud.

"They'd probably think we were insane. But I think some of them would understand... others would call us too good to be true, because they always call us that," Setter replied.

Yes, this perspective on death was peculiar to the Earthers... and whether the humans understood it no longer mattered. Destiny to deal with, and all that...

"Well, two old warriors, off to the last battle," Ursla said, again with some finality. "They might let us get away with it."

Chuckling, Setter nodded, then looked back at his friend and extended his hand to her, "And I should say, just once out loud, that I'm glad it's you and me, old friend. It's been a long road for the two of us."

A grin lit up Ursla's face, and she took Setter's hand in her own larger one, "It has been, and it's an honor. A real, genuine honor. There's nobody better than you for this job, Setter. I'm just proud to tag along."

Old friends, partners in crime for long years. Ursla and Caine had lost limbs together on safari, fought fleets together in the Krogg War, and built a new galactic order together during the peace. Now they'd be together as they fought the last great battle against Omega.

And as they stood there on *Orion's* observation deck, contemplating destiny, they were somehow certain that they would win.

CHAPTER 30

Phealan checked to see that Claire was asleep before he headed out onto the deck. It was a cool night in Newfoundland — one of the places on Earth where the night before the final battle was indeed *night*, thanks to the time zones.

The marines of 2/54th would be arriving in Newfoundland in the morning, readying the Caine estate for its stand against the plague, but for the moment everything was cool and quiet. As Phealan sniffed the air and felt the cold wind coming in from the sea, he took comfort in that.

Quiet and alone, he thought to himself as he filled his lungs. Even the wolves were gone from the woods around the house… only he and Claire remained. A peaceful night on Earth… a final peaceful night.

Phealan didn't know if he was going to die in twenty-four hours. He didn't have any particular sense that he would… but then, many had died without expecting to. Only tomorrow would tell.

In the meantime, he looked up at the stars overhead for a moment before closing his eyes. His mind reached out, far across space, and he pulled himself into the realm of light — the telepathic plane.

When his eyes opened again, he was surrounded by the trademark whiteness of this place, and standing opposite him was his father.

"This telepathy really does make things easier," Setter said brightly, smiling as he approached his son.

"You're right about that," Phealan agreed. "I'm on the deck… it's a nice night."

"Good," Setter nodded. "I hope it won't be your last."

Phealan shrugged, "So do I. Things ready on *Orion*?"

The father nodded to the son, "They are. As long as Omega keeps his word and lets us land, the plan will be on. Any word from Sarah or Graham?"

"Nothing, but we've done telepathic spot-scans, and they seem to be on schedule. Everything should be ready to go for tomorrow."

Setter nodded approvingly at his son's words. The plan required a certain amount of precision: Sarah and Pat, Graham and Christine, and Setter and Andra all had to land and start their duels with the avatars at roughly the same time.

Then they had to count on Omega deciding to attack Earth simultaneously.

It would probably be illogical for the plague to divide his effort that way, but Setter was relying on a mix of Omega's hubris and his own goading ability to make it happen. And even if it didn't, in the end, the plan could still work.

"So... you hit the avatars with the cure..." Phealan reviewed in a soft tone, and Setter nodded.

"And we'll all need to be ready for the moment. Keep him occupied and engaged..." they'd been over the plan so many times now that Setter's sharp, short phrases were enough to carry the meaning.

"Exactly. We'll all do our part," Phealan smiled, then sighed deeply. "It'll be a big day. I... I wish it hadn't come to this. But it'll be a hell of a day, anyway."

Setter concurred with his son's sentiment, "You know, it will be. Andra and I were talking earlier about it being our destiny... not to win or lose, but to fight the final battle. That's our destiny."

"Destiny *equation*, maybe?" Phealan grinned, recognizing when his father waxed philosophical.

Chuckling, Setter shrugged, "Could call it that. And since I won't be around to do the equation at the end of this, feel free to use it."

"I may," Phealan's grin grew, then he paused and sobered slightly. "I... wow. You're going to die tomorrow. I might too. That's going to be a big day."

Stating the obvious seemed to be all Phealan could do in that moment — and understandably so. Few had ever faced such a strange array of circumstances, and none before these two Caines had done so with such a fundamentally Earther perspective.

"It's a great joy that we can talk together like this before it happens, isn't it?" Setter asked softly, and Phealan had to nod.

"We're very lucky to be where we are."

The irony — that they thought themselves lucky to be in such grim positions — was lost entirely on both of them.

"Do you think you'll see mom when you die?" Phealan asked. "Being closer to it give you any more sense of what comes after?"

Setter shook his head, "I really don't know. Sometimes I get a feeling that there's more to come... but sometimes I feel like I'll just cease to be. Only one way to find out."

"Indeed. Well, if you get any insights, you just let me know. I'd love some advanced warning," Phealan grinned again, and Setter laughed.

"Right, as if we won't be a little bit busy at the time."

They laughed again, and though humans would have called their humor dark, to the father and the son it was light and true. They really were fortunate: they knew what was coming, and they had the chance to prepare for it together.

"How is everyone back there?" Setter turned his next question away from them, and Phealan's eyebrows furrowed slightly.

"A lot of people saying their goodbyes. There's a quiet sense of certainty around here... all the Earthers I see are ready for tomorrow. They trust the plan, and they're calm."

Setter nodded slowly, his expression reflecting his approval, "We are privileged to enjoy great comrades."

"None better," Phealan agreed. "And... I'll do all I can for them when you're gone."

A smile settled again on Setter's face, "I wish I could stay around, just to see that. You're going to be an incredible leader."

With a shake of his head, Phealan breathed deep, "I'll do what I can, just as you did. But there are many great leaders... our people are going to live on."

"And write great histories of what was done..." Setter concurred.

The two fell into a comfortable silence.

After that, Setter closed with his son, and hugged him, "So you had better get some sleep. I'll see you tomorrow."

Phealan hugged his dad back, "You too... good luck with the duel. We'll be ready when the moment comes. And I'll be ready when you need me."

They hugged for a few seconds more, and then they both faded from the telepathic plane.

As his mind reoccupied his body, Phealan's eyes, which had been swirling with blue light, returned to their amber hue. He peered into the darkness, and for a second could have sworn he saw movement in the trees below. His instincts reached out, as did his mind, but they detected nothing. Just shadows.

Shadows of what was to come in a little less than a day.

Phealan breathed deep the air again, and his hands gripped the railing that ran around the deck. Omega would likely come to this estate tomorrow evening... and either way, Phealan would fight him. The plague would face more opposition than he ever believed was possible.

And, Phealan decided, the monster would be destroyed.

The price of victory will be high. But it will be victory.

He nodded to himself at that thought.

Good luck.

That thought made him frown, as it didn't feel like his own. But he didn't worry, and instead peered silently into the night.

Omega was coming. The end was at hand.

CHAPTER 31

Varnon Broadpaw hadn't stopped to watch the sun come up over the Antarctic Plain in many, many years. He'd been to Antarctic Base often throughout his career, but rarely had he stopped to enjoy the stunning sunrises at the pole.

This morning he had decided he'd make the time.

The continent's cold wind gusted at him as he walked amongst the shield generators and gun emplacements that surrounded the base. He paused occasionally to look out at the ice mountains that stood far in the distance, breaking up the horizon in the growing light. The penguins had been herded out beyond those mountains...

Penguins. I'd nearly forgotten them, Beckett Lupus appeared beside his father-in-law, offering that thought with a smile.

"I know. Seems like one of those little details you can forget about the last battle fought here," Varnon spoke his agreement. "Our old friends the penguins."

Nodding, Beckett inhaled deeply, and then closed his eyes to bask in the sharp wind. This was a remarkable place, and Beckett felt comfortable making his last stand here.

"So," Varnon turned away from the horizon. "We set?"

Beckett held up his hand towards the perimeter, then drew into his mind the image of what the Antarctic Base... the *fortress* really... now looked like. Five separate layers of shields, huge numbers of pulsar positions and small Naval guns for clearing the air... millions of millions could be crushed on these defenses.

"What about billions?" Varnon read the General's thought and asked the question with a wry smile.

Beckett chuckled, "Humans say in-laws are demanding... I never got it until now."

Varnon frowned at the remark, "Wait, was that supposed to be a joke?"

A shrug was Beckett's answer, "Might be the last chance I get to be funny."

"Why aren't you, then?"

Beckett groaned, and as the sun rose the wolves enjoyed the morning.

• • •

Lab Forepaw appeared on his bridge aboard *Venerable* at an early hour, expecting that he was perhaps the only flag officer in the fleet to have failed to sleep. It wasn't typical for Earthers — peace of mind and sleep were never far away for them... or almost never, at least.

But Lab hadn't slept, because today was the day.

Waving to his Flag Captain, Lab moved over to the plot and looked in. The fleets were in position, formed up and ready to receive at any time. The Kroggs and the Larosians were where they needed to be... everything was in place.

"Message from *Victory*, sir," the Signal Officer announced, noticing that Lab had arrived. "First Space Lord Magnus says he couldn't sleep either."

A smile slid onto Lab's face, and he reached out towards *Victory* with his mind, *Morning to you too, Fox.*

Right back at you. Unusual as it is, I don't think any of us slept, the answer came directly back into Lab's mind, and for a moment the First Lord of the Admiralty marveled at telepathy.

Today, perhaps, it would turn the tide.

"It's snowing."

Claire Schaeffer's statement drew Phealan's eyes to the glass walls of the Caine house, and he nodded his agreement.

"It is... the marines will have to layer up a bit," he said, moving towards the door.

As he came to the glass panel, he looked down over the deck to the ground below, where the wolves, cats and bears of 2/54th were forming up and preparing to defend the estate. Sure enough, Cadmus Howler was already reminding his marines to maintain a comfortable temperature. Some among them were from cold climates and were undoubtedly enjoying the weather, but some were from the warmer zones of Earth — it'd be an adjustment for them.

Looking down at those marines, Phealan paused in thought. They were here to protect him, and the plan... and soon enough, they'd have a very hard fight ahead of them.

Almost as though his thoughts were matching, Cadmus Howler turned away from his marines and looked up through the glass at the younger Caine. The Colonel smiled and waved at Phealan, and the Deputy Supreme Consul did the same in reply.

Soon enough...

"You're doing a speech, right?" Claire was abruptly beside Phealan, and he glanced at the girl.

"I am."

"What are you going to say?" her tone remained free of the insolence of past days... now she sounded resigned.

"Does it really matter what I say?" Phealan put the question to her, and she looked at him. It seemed a long time since she'd actually looked squarely at him, so he stared at her for a moment.

She shook her head, "Not to me."

We'll see, Phealan thought to himself.

Soon enough...

A few days' hard travel away, *Pope Joseph Barron* slid smoothly from flux drive. The Superdreadnought had arrived at Ecclesia, and as Pat Conroy stood on its bridge, he couldn't help but be hit by a feeling of some regret.

This was the first time a Genesis warship had visited the once-home of the Commonwealth of Faithful Humans. Maybe — just *maybe* — if the civilian government on Genesis had taken this place seriously decades before, there'd have been no coup... no easy way for Omega to walk onto their now-dead homeworld.

Maybe they should have brought warships here sooner, and destroyed this damned place...

But Pat knew better than most that dwelling on maybes was a fruitless endeavor. Instead, he turned to Sarah, who sat now at the helm position, controlling all of the ship's functions through the AI and a number of automation systems.

"We've arrived at Ecclesia," she said simply.

"Yes. We've left the mortal realm, I suppose," Pat's answer was oddly cryptic. His mind had drifted sideways into things he'd once read.

Sarah glanced back at him, "What?"

"Ecclesia et mundus," the Irishman pointed to the screen. "Ecclesia meant heaven, and mundus meant the mortal realm... to one of the old Churches, that is. The ones that came before ours."

"Ah," Sarah looked back to her controls and shook her head. "And I would have called this place Hell."

The almost-joke drew a snorted laugh from Pat, and then he nodded, "We'll find out in an hour."

Sarah didn't reply, but instead directed *Barron* into orbit over the orange world.

"Entering Freetown orbit."

Graham answered Christine's report with a very shallow nod, while his grip on the hilt of his sword tightened. The holo plot that had been installed on *Carnarvon's* bridge for this mission showed the paradise planet of the renegade Freetowners, and indicated the Larosian battleship's course as it circled above.

"We're due to disembark in one hour," Christine turned away from the Earther control surfaces that had been added to the bridge. "Presuming he doesn't shoot us down first."

Graham's eyes shifted to his aide, and he nodded, "Let's hope he isn't wise enough to do that."

Christine didn't have an answer; she simply tugged at her armor and waited.

Orion arrived silently at Genesis.

Setter and Ursla stood on the bridge of the great, battered First Rate ship of the line, and watched on the holo plot as the lush green globe that had once been home to the human race spun lonely before them.

Neither Earther said anything — or thought anything, for that matter. It was entirely possible that this plan would be stopped dead in its tracks, and that Omega would shoot them down well short of their landing...

But somehow, they believed that unlikely. The plague wanted his final showdown. He wanted his chance to out-drama all the movies he'd grown up on... all the history he knew. He wanted a chance to face Setter Caine in a Shakespearean duel... in an epic, climatic showdown.

And Setter was going to give him exactly what he wanted.

The plan was on...

"Oh no, they have a plan!"

Omega-Natosh looked to the sky of Genesis with a mocking grin as he spoke aloud to the empty arena. The Earthers needed to get better at shielding their thoughts... not that it would have improved their odds.

"Honestly, why don't we just upload a virus to their Mothership?" Omega-Gillian, looking skyward on Freetown, intoned for the plague.

"Kill the Queen and all will be okay," Omega-Paine added, as he too gazed up at the stars above Ecclesia.

This should be fun, the plague as a whole thought to himself. And then he reached out across space, and began pushing his invasion force out of flux drive just short of Earth.

"It all starts now," he said.

Yes it does.

The plague stopped at that thought. It wasn't his own.

"He's pretty observant," Andra Ursla smiled at Setter Caine, both of them peering into Omega's mind as he made his moves.

"Noticed us needling him right away," Setter agreed earnestly. Then he turned his thoughts back to his foe: *It's going to be a long day, Omega. You ready?*

• • •

On the surface of Genesis, Omega-Natosh laughed. On Freetown, Omega-Gillian did the same, and on Ecclesia, so did Omega-Paine.

In the space near Earth, the billions of minions appearing out of flux drive laughed too.

"Oh yes," Omega replied in one galactic, horrifying voice.

CHAPTER 32

"They're coming out of flux about twenty minutes short of orbital space," Fox Magnus observed from the holo plot, and Lab Forepaw nodded, his eyes shifting between the projections of his other fleet commanders.

"He's probably trying to draw us out to fight," Artie Tigar put in.

"Indeed," Ami Dune agreed.

"Then he's in for a surprise," Minnie Maximane finished the thought.

It would be a surprise. The Earther Navy was abandoning its old doctrine — there'd be no raiding, no fancy flying, no Earther timing. They'd just sit still and wait. And when Omega finally came into range, the raw firepower of 150 *Venerable*-class ships of the line, 1,000 Krogg War ships, and 50,000 gunboats would be unleashed.

"He's accelerating now," Dran Nightclaw pointed out the beginnings of movement. That was clear enough: Omega was moving, twenty minutes out and closing...

"Time for speeches, then, right?" Zed Dune suggested.

That drew a grunt from Jax Furgus, "Yeah. Here's mine: let's kill him."

Varnon Broadpaw stood in the Command and Control Centre of Antarctic Base, his eyes fixed on the holo plot. There were definitely 5,000 Omega ships out there, the plague hadn't been bluffing...

"Message from *Venerable*, sir," one of the Signal Officers near Varnon interrupted his thoughts, which was probably just as well.

"Put it in the tank," Broadpaw said, then waited as Lab Forepaw appeared. "All set, Lab?"

"Just waiting on the speeches. Jax is particularly excited."

Varnon grinned and shrugged, "Great, so I get to die twice today."

Lab frowned for a second, not getting the joke.

"You know... die... as in giving a bad speech?"

The explanation didn't help, and Lab simply smiled, "Well, you may not have many more chances to be funny, so don't waste them."

"I said the same to Beckett a couple of hours ago."

"I'm sure he was funnier than you," Lab's smile remained, and for that brief moment, both canines enjoyed themselves.

Very brief moment, though.

Varnon turned back to the Signal Officer who'd reported, "Alright, I need to say some rousing words. Put me on all the comms, please."

The Lieutenant nodded, and the great transmitters of the Antarctic Base began to fire up. Looking back to the plot, Varnon took a deep breath.

"Just tell me when I'm on," he added.

Those words boomed out to every comm in the solar system — to every Earther and Allied ship, and to every personal comm unit. Since every Earther was carrying a comm today, everyone heard the introduction.

"You *are* on," Lab said helpfully, and Varnon blinked.

"Oh."

"Probably would have made sense to do this telepathically," Lab added. "But this is tradition, isn't it?"

"Yep," Varnon agreed. "Telepathy just doesn't seem to have the gravitas. Well, it probably doesn't... but we probably shouldn't be talking about this now. Even if it is our last chance."

Everyone was hearing this exchange — and Varnon knew it.

"Listen, hi everyone. It's Varnon Broadpaw here. I'm the warm-up speech, because we have one recorded here from Setter Caine, and then one from Phealan too. I'm just the opening act... so I'm going to be brief."

Earthers everywhere smiled at the First Consul's bluntness, and chuckled at his low opinion of his own oratory.

"So. Today's possibly our last day alive. I want to recommend you all take every chance to find the beauty in things today. All day... every chance you get... remember how beautiful this planet is. Remember how wonderful your friends and family are. These are things that are always near and dear to us... they're things that I believe are ingrained in us. But since today could be the last day, let's just pay more attention to them. Because really, there's no point facing Omega morose or depressed. This could be our last chance to be happy. And as long as we can manage it, I say we keep it up. We do that, we may just win today. Or we might still lose. But I, for one, would rather die laughing."

The sentiment was unexpected, but it was compelling all the same. Earthers nodded their approval, and feeling a certain satisfaction that his meager contribution had been well received, Varnon glanced back at the Signal Officer, "Alright, that's my share. Let's put on the first real speech. Load up Setter's, please."

The Lieutenant nodded as he activated the recording Setter had left for the Earthers, and loaded it into the broadcast buffer. Varnon had no idea what the Supreme Consul had said, but it was Setter... it had to be good.

As the figure of Setter Caine appeared in the Antarctic Base C&C plot, Varnon thus found himself holding his breath. He needed to hear these words, the same as everyone else did.

"Hello my friends," Setter began. "It's plan day. It's the day that we've been anticipating for some time… and if all is on schedule, I'm in *Orion*, closing on Genesis right now. I'll be facing one avatar, while our human friends face the others. It's going to be quite something. Omega believes, and I don't think he'll mind me paraphrasing him, that today will be a day of destiny. He believes completely that this is the moment towards which his entire creation has been building. And I can see where he gets that impression. Think of it: he created us, and though we didn't turn out as expected, we carried him to the stars. We gave him access to a power greater than he ever dreamed possible when he appeared in a twenty-first century lab. And now, as far as he's concerned, he has the chance to put us back in our place. He intends to reign supreme."

The smiles generated by Varnon's words slowly faded.

"By the same token, it can be said that it's our destiny, here and today, to make a stand against the plague that created us. We're fighting our would-be God, today, making a stand for who we are, and for our home. So many strange coincidences have brought us to this point — so many accidents and random occurrences have played out to put us all where we are, with the skills we have. The Larosians have come back to us, the Kroggs have joined us… our good deeds of the past have brought us strength today. We are rallying to fight for our home… we could say, I think, that it is *our* destiny to win today."

Silence fell over Earth space.

"Well, a friend of mine once pointed out to me that hindsight always lends itself to destiny. When you look back, you can always see the circumstances that led you to a certain point, and you can always imagine that there was no other way things could have turned out. No matter what, *destiny* is destiny, isn't it?"

Setter looked down in the recording, then shook his head.

"You know, I don't think it is. I think if destiny exists, it's not an absolute, it's a possibility. Today is our destiny. Not tomorrow, not what happens here, but simply getting to this point. Getting to the place and time when the decision is to be made. So many things have brought us to this place, and so many things have brought Omega here too. Whoever wins can look back and think that there was no other way things should have turned out, but really, I think we could win, or we could lose. Our *destiny*, simply, is to fight. To find out. We can worry about the rest tomorrow, if we're privileged enough to be here."

Looking back up, Setter took a breath, "Destiny is something you add after the fact. The result… you work for that. That's the destiny equation. That's why we're all here. You choose to fight and then you throw all you have into the fight, not because you're destined to win or lose, but so you can find out whether history will say you were destined to win or lose."

He paused again, and smiled, "And honestly, I could never have hoped or dreamed for better friends to fight alongside. Because being an Earther… being one of you… that means more to me than anything else. We know who we are, at our very cores. That makes it easier. We do what we say we'll do, and we do it in a way that reflects us. Today we're going to stand together against Omega's presumed *destiny*. We're going to fight for each other. Today, maybe for the first time, is a day when we fight for ourselves, not others. We have allies fighting with us, but today we have to look after our own friends, our own family, and our own homes. This is a great and terrible day for us."

Setter breathed deeply again.

"And it's one we're ready for. To all of you, my friends, I say good luck. When the moment comes, we'll all be together."

He faded away.

Earthers everywhere stood in silence — no roar, no thunder, just absolute quiet and absolute certainty. Varnon stared at the plot, wondering what the day would bring. Setter was right — for all the coincidences, for all the beliefs that things *had* to go a certain way, there was no certainty.

It was down to the Earthers, and to their plan, to choose their own fate. Later, someone would write the story, and explain how it had all been destined to go a certain way...

"I hate to disagree with my dad, but I have to."

Varnon blinked, his eyes darting back to the plot. Phealan had appeared, and Earthers everywhere abruptly remembered that there was one more Caine left to speak.

"There's one thing he said that isn't true, and I need to tell you why," Phealan's words were slow. "Destiny is a tool of hindsight, that's true. And we'll all be here together, that's certainly true. But today, my friends, I have to remind you that we are not fighting only for ourselves. I thought we were. For a long time I thought we were. But I have a friend here, a human friend, and she reminded me of something. I know my dad just said today we have to look after ourselves... but I think it's worth saying: we're not just looking after ourselves."

Phealan was standing in his living room as he spoke, and now he turned his eyes to Claire, who was sitting silent and dispirited on the couch. She didn't return his gaze, but Phealan knew she was listening.

"I was asked a little while ago how Earthers can live the way we do — how we can handle all of this agony, all of this destruction. How we can cope with that and still keep moving forward, without bitterness... without forgetting to laugh sometimes. To my young human friend, it makes no sense. To her, it's beyond human nature. It's impossible."

Finally, Claire looked at him, and he smiled at her.

"Today, we have to do something impossible. We have to make our stand against a plague that created us, and that occupies billions and trillions of cells across two galaxies. We have to fight Omega. And many people, myself included, have rightly said that defeating him could be impossible. As impossible for us as living the Earther way seems to our human friends. As impossible as that."

Phealan looked back towards the camera that was recording him, "Well, that's what we're fighting for, isn't it? Not just for ourselves, not just to stop the plague... but to prove something. Today we need to prove to our friends, to all of our friends, that some days, the impossible really can happen. And that no matter what, it's worth trying. There is nothing wasted in reaching for great ambitions, or chasing dreams. We will struggle, and we may fail, but today we're fighting to do the impossible, so that we can prove to our human cousins that, in the end, the impossible can be done. If we win, we can prove to them that maybe — just maybe — they'll one day be able to live the way we do."

Straightening himself squarely, Phealan nodded to the camera, "So my dad isn't right. Today isn't a day when we fight just for ourselves. It's a day when we do what we've always done... we fight for ourselves, and for our friends, and for what we think is right. We fight for the impossible. We make this battle into something greater than a struggle about ships and minions and all the rest of it. This, now, is about how we see the universe. And sharing that view with those who still don't understand it. I certainly hope we win."

His words trailed off for a moment, and then his smile broadened, "So, all of us here today. Earthers. Humans. Larosians. Kroggs. I say we do the impossible. I say were dare to chase our hopes... our dreams. A wise Earther — the first Earther, my ancestor — once said that you should chase your dreams with a smile, because you'll never regret the adventure. I'm smiling. We all should smile. And if we lose today, that'll be a shame. But if we win, and I think we will... that'll be worth it. That'll be our *destiny*."

There was an upswell. Phealan could feel it in his mind — the communion of Earther minds and thoughts that seemed to glow around the planet and in the space above... it shone so blindingly.

Phealan smiled a wise, lonely smile.

Earthers all around the world began to roar, and began to look to the sky. They were fighting today for themselves. They were fighting today for their allies. And they were fighting against the impossible because there was no reason *not* to.

Phealan felt all that strength, all that defiance of Omega, and then he glanced back at Claire.

"That's what I said today," he said. "And just you watch out. If we win this, you'll have no excuse not to try being happy."

She didn't know what to say to that, so with a gentle smile, Phealan looked away again, and then reached out with his mind.

Speeches are done, dad. Time to go.

Days away, aboard *Orion*, Setter Caine nodded.

And Omega nodded too. His ships raced towards Earth.

CHAPTER 33

"They're moving against Earth," Setter Caine said to Andra Ursla, and the bear nodded in reply.

They were at the controls of the only pinnace left aboard *Orion,* preparing to depart the First Rate's flight bay for their last trip down to a planet. There was no time to become sentimental about the journey, though: thanks to the strength of his telepathic link with his son, Setter knew that the battle was fast approaching at home.

No time to waste.

"Firing up the drives. Automation circuits active for *Orion*... here..." Ursla pulled a wristband off the console nearby and handed it to Setter. "All set up. Put it on the opposite wrist to your main shield."

The wolf nodded, donning the wristband quickly, and then double checking that his wrist shield and his backup belt shield were both on and charged. Satisfied, he leaned forward and activated the console before him.

"You want to fly the pinnace or run the automation?" he asked as he started calling up command screens.

Ursla glanced at him, "Doesn't matter... but I think maybe *Orion* would prefer it if you gave the last orders."

Setter thought about that for a second, then smiled. It was impossible to quantify whether a ship like *Orion* had a soul, but Setter felt a strong connection to his old First Rate. He appreciated Ursla's sentiment, so he nodded, "Yes, alright."

With that, Ursla took over the flight controls, and the pinnace rose easily from the deck. At the same time, Setter took command of *Orion's* systems through an automation screen that he called up on his own console, then began winding down most of the First Rate's systems. Life support, lights, artificial gravity... none of them would be needed.

Orion would be left in Genesis orbit, silent and dark... a headstone to the grave of a planet... perhaps...

Ursla guided the pinnace forward as Setter keyed open the flight bay doors. She hadn't helmed a pinnace in many, many years, but it was still almost second nature to the great bear Admiral. With finesse that implied no rust on her skills, she guided the small craft out of and away from *Orion*, then down towards the planet below.

Locking down the last of the ship of the line's non-essential systems as they cruised, Setter didn't even think a final goodbye. The farewells were done with. Instead his eyes fixed on the planet rushing up before them, and he found himself suddenly struck by the beauty of the place.

"I never stopped to look at it... all the years we came through here, I don't think I ever paid attention to this place," he said quietly, and Ursla shrugged.

"If we'd had the time, and if the Church hadn't been against it, we could have safaried here... seen a whole new world. Would have been fun, I think."

Setter smiled, "All's fun until some crocodile rips off your leg."

"Or arm," Ursla added, grinning too.

The pinnace dove down into the atmosphere, and somehow neither Setter nor Ursla wondered whether Omega had been lying to them — wondered whether he'd shoot them down. It seemed impossible now... the plague was too melodramatic and too arrogant to pass up a chance to see them both face-to-face. Whether he really had sent all his minions away, though, was a question.

"Genesis City locked on," Ursla continued to smoothly work the controls as the pinnace slid down into gray skies. The land below, which had seemed beautiful from space, lacked luster when they neared it. It felt burnt somehow... like its life essence had been hollowed out.

"The planet's dying slowly," Ursla observed, her tone soft. "It's like it's been poisoned."

"It has been," Setter agreed distantly.

They skimmed lower, their craft racing over the planet's main continent, heading for what had once been the capital. Gradually — and yet somehow all-too-quickly — the buildings of the capital appeared on the horizon.

Setter and Andra had both been here many times over the years. They'd visited the world that Harvey Bingham had started to unite, and that Liz Hastings and later Sarah had tried to move forward.

Now it was a shell of itself.

Ursla slowed the pinnace as they arrived over the city, and banking the craft, she and Setter looked down through the windows. There was no movement in the streets — no sign of minions... not that Omega would have been fool enough to leave them in the open during the landing approach.

"The cenotaph's to the east, right?" Setter checked the sensor screen that sat between him and his friend, and she nodded in return.

"We can set down in the park right next to it... here," she pointed to the spot she had in mind, and Setter gave an approving nod. They'd be close — not far to walk.

The duel was to take place in the monument to the Krogg War... in the symbol of human unity. Setter remembered hearing about all the political fighting that had surrounded the building of that monument — one that creatively remembered Crusaders and Genesis Navy personnel as victims of the same Krogg War.

The Crusaders, of course, had been victims of Earther arms... a piece of rewritten history that Setter didn't approve of. He never hid from the fact that he, as First Space Lord, had been responsible for millions of deaths.

Today, in fact, he could be responsible for billions. In a way.

"Coming down..." Ursla didn't need to say that aloud, as the descent was quite evident, but Setter didn't mind the narration. This whole flight felt mildly surreal.

As the landing feet came down on the grassy park, Setter keyed into *Orion* one last time, and checked its orbit and status. He wanted his old ship to be at peace now, while it still could be.

The pinnace engines began to wind down, and Setter and Ursla stood without speaking. Their swords were in the locker behind them, and they collected each and belted them on slowly, methodically. They left the energy rifles where they were, but Ursla pulled a pack from the locker floor, then added it to her belt.

"I have the cure," she said formally, and then a smile creased her face. "That almost sounded absurd."

Setter chuckled softly, then collected an identical pack from the case and put it on his own belt.

"Whatever happens," he said, "one of us gets a shot of this into him."

He didn't need to say that — of course they both knew the plan — but he wanted to, nonetheless.

Ursla's smile broadened, and she reached out and put both her hands on her friend's shoulders, "I'll take care of it."

Reaching up, Setter rested his hands on the outsides of his friend's mighty arms, "Thank you."

They stood there for a moment, staring at each other.

"I'd say this telepathically, but I think I prefer actually hearing it..." Ursla's smile saddened. "You are my friend. My very best friend. And this is the right way for me to die, here with you."

Setter's grip on his friend's arms tightened, and his smile saddened too, "I couldn't say it better. Ready?"

"Ready."

They turned and left the cockpit. The pinnace ramp began to lower as soon as its exit hatch opened, and both Earthers then stepped out into the Genesis air. It stank of death, tasted bitter and dry. Ignoring that, they descended to the ground and looked around them.

Still no minions.

They turned for the monument and began to walk. Soon enough, the plan would succeed.

Or fail.

CHAPTER 34

"I've buttoned up *Barron*," Pat Conroy dropped into the co-pilot's seat of his and Sarah's pinnace, then glanced at his wife. "It'll be up here waiting for us when we're done."

Sarah was working the controls and didn't bother to look at her husband. Her reply reflected her state of mind, "It'll be disappointed and lonely."

Pat couldn't contain his sigh, but he said nothing, instead turning his eyes back to the orange world that was lying beyond the ship. They were about to depart their trusty old Superdreadnought's landing bay, and the space doors were open.

"Strap in," Sarah's words were sharp, and after just a few seconds she hit the accelerator.

Pushed back into his seat by the hurried launch, Pat simply watched as the planet grew before him, and then glanced at his wife. She hadn't taken her eyes off it.

"You're ready for this?" he asked.

"Of course," she didn't hesitate.

Pat frowned, "Well, I don't know if I am. But here we are, aren't we?"

"Do you need to keep talking?"

The chill on those words drew a wince from Pat, and he looked away. So much for trying to indulge in a last few moments of connection before the show started.

A dark feeling was creeping over Pat. He was in a Genesis-ore lined pinnace, so he knew it wasn't Omega — at least not yet. No, he wanted to say something to Sarah, just one thing that would retrieve the warmth and comfort of last night, and remind him one more time of the last fifty years of his life.

But what the hell could he say? Sarah was beyond listening now — she was charging the guns, just as the plan demanded.

True to form. True to bloody form.

Pat stayed silent for a few minutes, watching the orange, Church-poisoned planet get closer and closer.

Something to say... what to say?

"Just want to say this for the record, Sarah... I love you, and I know you love me. And I know you can't think about that right now because you're busy. We're busy, I mean. I understand that. And I don't expect anything different.

But just so you know... I want to live through this so we can try to find some sort of happiness again. That sound fair?"

He blurted it all out, and began turning red almost immediately.

Sarah looked at him, and for just a second, her eyes softened. That was it; she didn't smile, she didn't tear up... she just looked at him.

And that, in itself, would have satisfied Pat.

But she went one better. Through a force of will that came from the graveness of the moment, Sarah replied, "You should have found a better wife. But thanks."

Pat thoroughly disagreed with her first words, but that didn't matter. He felt a weight come off him — one so acute that it surprised him. She was still in there.

That was enough to fight for — and to try not to die for.

Sitting back in his chair, Pat took a deep breath. They were headed to the night side of Ecclesia, to the colony's capital city, and as the darkness spread over them he found his attention absorbed by all that was here.

The place was not beautiful. It was no resort... it looked like Hell. Perhaps that explained why the Churchers had loved it...

"City ahead," Sarah's emotional phase was over, and her cool professionalism had complete control.

Pat leaned forward in his seat and squinted, trying to see the buildings ahead of him, but it was too gloomy. The city seemed lost in the darkness, lacking lights or signs of civilization...

Then one shaft of light shot upward.

"I suppose we're expected," Sarah observed, slowing the pinnace. "That looks like about where we were supposed to land."

"Nice of him to switch on the lights," Pat grunted, then reached down to the floor, hefted his riot gear helmet and placed it on his head. They were close now — no point taking any chances.

Seeing that Sarah had her hands full with the controls, the Irishman then picked up her helmet and planted it on her. She said nothing; she landed the pinnace instead.

Sarah hadn't flown one of these in years, and there was a slight jar as the craft hit the hard ground. As the craft's engines began to wind down, Pat started collecting the key items that had been piled in the seats behind them.

Swords first — his medieval-style broadsword and Sarah's katana — and then the backpacks that they would carry, each with a critical payload.

"One of us hits him with one of these," Sarah reinforced the mission as she held up her backpack. "Nothing else matters."

Pat didn't need to be reminded, but he didn't protest, "He'll get it. That bastard Paine."

"His family killed my parents," Sarah added evenly.

Ancient history. A bygone saga.

"We'll kill this bastard," Pat reiterated, sounding hungry as he pulled his pack on over his shoulder. "And Omega will suffer."

Sarah nodded her agreement, then grabbed a case containing two energy rifles from the floor. She opened it and handed one to Pat, along with a pair of shields and a pack of extra energy cells.

"And," the Irishman added as he strapped up the Earther kit, "if I have anything to say about it, we'll be back on *Barron* at day's end."

Again Sarah didn't look at him, "That's not the mission... don't count on it."

"Just... trust me. I have a feeling we'll be together."

This time Sarah did look up, "Yes. In death."

Pat let another sigh go, then shrugged, "We'll see. Ready?"

"Ready."

Hefting rifles, backpacks, shields and swords, Sarah Manchester and Pat Conroy headed out into the night on Ecclesia, wondering what they'd find when they reached Omega-Paine.

Their part of the plan would soon be effected.

CHAPTER 35

"I've never tried flying off a Larosian deck before... hope I don't do any damage..." Christine Schaeffer slid into the pilot's chair of the Earther pinnace that had been seconded to *Carnarvon* for the mission.

"I don't expect it'll matter if you do," Graham Manchester had returned to his icy demeanor, and for once Christine was glad of that.

She needed him to be cold today. Today would be the most important day, and if he cracked...

But he wouldn't. For him, everything had been leading to this. Everything since Genesis. He was fueled by a deeper despair than she could comprehend, and even Omega couldn't hope to overwhelm that now...

"You're probably right," she replied to him as she called up the flight controls. "It must be the Earther in me, but I know there's a good chance this is a one-way flight... and it doesn't bother me."

Graham lowered himself into the co-pilot's seat as she said that, his eyes fixed ahead on the silver space doors before them. Soon he'd be able to see the planet... see where his wife had been taken... been made into an avatar.

Where he'd kill her body.

"Do you find it strange that it's not bothering me?" Christine asked gently.

Graham didn't answer, so Christine resigned herself to silence. Calling up the flight controls, she opened the space doors and lifted the Earther pinnace off the deck, marveling both at the ease of its handling — unsurprisingly, it was much better than the trainers at the Genesis Fleet Academy had been — and at her natural ability with it.

Again, she thanked her Earther side for that.

The pinnace slid unceremoniously from *Carnarvon*, and no effort was made to shut down the Larosian battlewagon. It would wait for them in space, whether they returned to it or not.

Before their eyes lay a tropical-paradise planet. Christine had never been to Freetown, but she'd seen movies... it had always looked wonderful to her. Water with a balanced acidity level you could swim in, sandy beaches, endless sun. As it grew before her, Christine felt some sadness that she wasn't here for a romantic holiday.

What a ridiculous reminder to have to give myself.

She chided her naïve thoughts, then almost laughed at herself for bothering to.

Under the circumstances, you get to think whatever the hell you please.

"It doesn't surprise me, at all."

At first she didn't register Graham's response, but after a moment her subconscious nudged her out of musing and into reacting. He'd answered her question from before.

"Really?" her response was simple and direct, and the junior Manchester nodded.

"You've always had steel in you, I think. The Earther biology has just brought it to the fore sooner. The Earthers do that for people, Christine. They show us the best of what we could be... what we can aspire to be. And that's incredibly important. Even if we can never be as great as they are, we'd be better off as a race if we just tried to be like them. If we just got a little closer to what they are."

The unexpected soliloquy caught Christine by surprise, but she managed a reply, "They are... the best of us."

"Too good to be true. Absolutely too good to be true. You have some of that in you now, to complement all the good that was there already."

His tone was still detached, but what he said actually touched Christine in a way she hadn't expected. It was good to hear someone say that... someone she was close to... someone who knew her. And someone who wouldn't be served by lying to her.

"I'm sorry you have to be here today," he said again. "I'm sorry it had to be you."

Christine looked at Graham, almost hoping to see some emotion on his face. There was none. But in reality the words were enough.

She looked back to the planet as the pinnace glided down into the atmosphere without incident. The computer had them on course for the Freetown capital, which had been so hastily evacuated just weeks before. They'd fight this duel on the beach there...

"I'm not sorry."

She spoke with all the cool certainty of an Earther.

"This needs to be done, and I'm the one on the spot, Graham. I'm at peace with that. The peace surprises me — I mean, look at me. I'm just a kid... but I'm not. Not anymore."

Graham nodded, "You're not."

Christine felt a little swell of pride at the compliment, and then she took better hold of the controls as the pinnace started skimming lower over the ocean. It was such a gorgeous day here — Freetown had indeed been a paradise. It never would be again, though. Even if the plan worked, no one would want to come here to relax. It was a planet infected by death.

"Coming up on the island," Graham leaned forward in his own chair. "Land right off the beach, in that industrial park strip."

His reminder about the landing zone was — unsurprisingly by now — not needed. The plan's final details had been nailed down long before they arrived here. But Christine didn't mind the words.

As they coasted over the beach, both of them looked down to see if Omega-Gillian was in sight. She wasn't. The capital seemed abandoned. Parts of it had been flattened by Jax Furgus' broadsides, and much of it was destroyed or burned during the riots that led up to its abandonment... it had an eerie quality that juxtaposed the beautiful landscape.

"Coming down," Christine dropped the pinnace's speed and turned it easily in an arc, finding a flat piece of what had once been a cargo loading zone on which to set down. She gently eased back the throttle and used the Earther counter-grav pads to lock the small craft into a hover, then lowered the feet right onto the ground.

Smoothest landing I've ever done... and for Gods' sake, don't think 'saved the best for last'.

Smiling at her thoughts, Christine came to her feet and tapped her knuckles against her armor breastplate. The Larosian-made kit would save her from Omega-Gillian's telepathy today...

Graham was on his feet too, turning to the locker at the back of the cockpit and drawing out their swords. He handed Christine her saber, then strapped his own mortuary sword to his hip. Next he collected the shield belts and wristbands, before pulling out the backpacks.

This was the same kit Sarah and Pat had — the kit for dealing with the avatars.

Holding one pack out to Christine, he locked eyes with her, "I won't repeat it again."

She smiled, "Of course you won't. We'll get it done."

He appreciated the simple confidence of those words, and as she took the pack from him and turned to pull it over her shoulders, Graham took a second to really look at his young aide. They'd been through so much together. He admired her. He trusted her. He cared about her. And he knew that with her assured, almost Earther-like movements, she'd come through for him now.

Gillian would die. Her body, at last, would stop being a walking abomination — a cruel insult to her memory.

And then, at last, Graham could die too.

"Ready?" Christine asked the question as she turned her eyes back to the junior Manchester.

"Ready."

"Let's go for a walk on the beach," she smiled again, seemingly irrepressible in her determination to be positive.

Graham stood aside and let her lead the way, and together the two damaged humans made their way from the Earther pinnace, and out into the warm paradise city of Freetown.

On a sandy beach under the sun, they would play their part in the plan.

The duelists were in place, soon Omega would be defeated...

Or he'd survive.

Soon...

CHAPTER 36

"They're two minutes out. I'm not going to lie, Lab, this feels weird."

Fox Magnus' words came to Lab Forepaw through the battle plot, and the First Lord of the Admiralty flicked his ear and shrugged, "Yes, it certainly does."

Waiting for the enemy… just sitting and waiting. That was quite opposite to the tactics the Earthers had painstakingly perfected during the Krogg War. But despite feeling wrong, they knew it was the right way to deal with this situation.

Venerable's bridge had gone to battle lighting — everything was noticeably darker, leaving the blue light of the holo tank shimmering uncontested before Lab's eyes. In that plot, the black wave of Omega was coming closer and closer.

"All *Venerable* squadrons report ready for mass fire," the Signal Officer announced as Lab folded his arms.

"Very good. All Krogg War ships to tuck in close, stay under the curtain," he reiterated that point because it was such a foreign one — none of these ships and crews were accustomed to just sitting. Just waiting.

"If we do this right, you know, we could kill all 5,000 of his ships," Fox spoke up again from the plot. "We just need to kill his ships at a rate of two to one… if we all stay tight…"

"Signal coming in from *Death*, sir," the Signal Officer cut in again, and Lab looked over at the Lieutenant with a second's surprise before he reminded himself that *Death* was the Krogg flagship, and not a morbid metaphysical force.

"In the plot," the First Space Lord looked back to the display, and Warlord Kardrath appeared next to Fox Magnus.

"We are prepared to advance to meet them, First Lord. We will draw them in and onto your guns, as planned," the Krogg's words were steady, and though Lab still wasn't entirely accustomed to hearing these aliens' voices in friendship, he nodded.

"Best of luck to you, Warlord. We'll… we'll be sitting here."

"As you must be," Kardrath bow-nodded, Larosian style, then vanished.

As soon as the space was vacant, the Signal Officer reported that a message was incoming from Novash, and that transmission was directed to the same place in the holo display.

The Larosian appeared, "First Lord, we're closing our formation off your port quarter. We await any deployment orders you deem necessary," the Larosian said quickly, with his customary smoothness.

"Thanks, Novash. I'll be in touch when the time comes."

"Of course," the Larosian bow-nodded, then vanished as well.

Lab took a breath, then his eyes drifted back to Fox Magnus, who'd remained in the plot the whole time, "One minute now, Fox. All set?"

The dapper First Space Lord cracked a grin, and for effect he scratched his ear, "Now what sort of question is that at a time like this? Hope at least one of us lives, Lab. Well, hope both of us do, but at least one..."

He fell silent, and Lab nodded.

That was it, Fox ordered the feed closed down.

"All ships, open gun ports, run out your guns. Stand by for roll and fire," those orders were a formality now, of course, but Lab gave them anyway. In the space around *Venerable*, nearly 1,200 Earther warships opened their gunports.

On the gundecks of those ships, millions of Earthers activated their targeting computers, and ran their mighty cannon out into space. Deeper in the vessels, Earthers stood ready at their stations, prepared to do everything and anything to improve the chances of victory.

It seemed impossible. But then, as Phealan had said, that was part of the point.

"Time to fight," Lab whispered to himself.

His eyes fixed on the plot, he watched as the Kroggs prepared to begin the battle.

All ships, begin advance by squadrons. Priority targets are Omega's troop-carrying vessels, Warlord Kardrath issued that order with his mind, and as it went forth, the ships of the mighty Krogg Navy began to swarm.

Aboard *Death*, the Telepath appointed as Captain began issuing orders of his own — his mighty Hyper Mothership had no corvettes to send forth, but its massive batteries had to be aligned, and made ready to spew their deadly streams of spines.

Closing now, m'Lord. Combat effect range in thirty seconds.

It would be a glorious battle. It would fulfill the Kroggs' need to kill for generations. No battle ever conceived could be so important and so right as this one. The Kroggs could kill with abandon, and harm only those who deserved to die...

The Krogg Fleet's squadrons were carefully balanced to that end. Superdreadnought and Dreadnought groups were teamed with clusters of Destroyers, the latter ships positioned to keep Omega's ramming vessels away from the more powerful combatants. This was a Krogg escort tactic left over from the old war, but refined and enhanced with the help of Earther thinking.

Omega would not enjoy his attempt today…

"I'm going to enjoy this," Omega spoke through every mouth he had.

He was referring both to the imminent planet-based duels, and to the massive battle in space. In a bit of a plot twist, the Earthers were sending their Krogg bitches forward first… using up the underlings, apparently. The Kroggs probably loved this job, though, because they loved dying.

It wouldn't matter. Nothing did. The Earthers were about to be crushed.

Range in ten seconds, the plague thought to himself.

They weren't even trying to stop him short of the planet. They'd resigned themselves to letting his minions land… a huge, huge mistake. It was an easy one to make, probably, but no defenses ever built could quell *billions* of warriors. If it was that easy to kill billions of people, Omega would never have been created in the first place.

Poor dears. They're dependent on their plan…

Soon enough, that plan would fail.

Five seconds.

Four.

Three.

Two.

One.

CHAPTER 37

It was a silent ballet of death.

In space, against a black mat pierced by stars, the Krogg Fleet met the Omega fleet in elegant, brutal carnage.

The lead echelon of Krogg Superdreadnoughts came into range at the very same moment Omega's leading pack of black wave ships unleashed its first salvo of spines. Like animals, then, the Kroggs and the Omega ships chased the wakes of their projectiles.

Free of Omega's blockage of their minds, the Earthers could hear every telepathic scream, hiss and roar from the Krogg ships.

Lab Forepaw reached out of his body for a moment and tried to see it all with his mind — it was his first and perhaps last chance to see a fight the way the Kroggs and Larosians always had. The sight was blinding and incredible. He was floating in amongst the Krogg ships, and they were diving and twisting.

Neuro energy pulses careened at Omega ships, and because the plague was not as in tune with the Kroggs as he was the Earthers, many of those shots hit home.

But of course, hitting home was not the only key to victory — damage had to be done. And Omega had learned from his encounter with the Kroggs at their homeworld: his ships were better protected.

That was no deterrent to the Kroggs, though.

Lab watched with a certain wonder as their mighty hordes surged forward, almost seeming endless for a moment. A great mass...

Spines literally filled space. Lab could have walked from one fleet to another on them, always having a place to lay his foot. They came from both sides, like the arrows of archers from battles in the old human times.

And like arrows, they began to batter into each other in the space between the fleets. Lab watched as these mighty acid-laden needles snapped against each other, spraying their vicious chemicals into the vacuum to vaporize.

The ships, meanwhile, tangled — almost literally.

The Krogg squadrons came on in line ahead, like Earthers might, and then laced themselves around the Omega vessels. Throngs of ships, like vines moving with purpose, and spewing death. They flung spines and spent their energy, and Lab could feel an anger amongst them — the Warlords and Telepaths were making no attempt to cloud their desire to destroy.

It felt strange to Lab — not just to be sitting in space, with a telepathic window to the fight — but to have that anger on his side. He remembered what it was like to fight against such fury... he remembered how hard it was.

Was Omega finding it hard?

The plague's mind was clearly present here, but Lab felt no opening from it — no attempt by the disease to reach out to him. He was, after all, just another Earther, one among two billion in this system...

And he didn't dare try to touch Omega's mind. He couldn't take that chance.

No, he just had to watch.

The first deaths were happening now. The engagement was nearly ten seconds old, so the destruction was beginning in earnest.

Black blood was spilled on both sides — ships torn, wrenched, squashed. There was a vicious quality to the fight when seen up close like this — much different than when Lab watched it in the battle plot.

Nearby, a Krogg Superdreadnought was thrown from its squadron line when it collided with a black wave ship, and as one pierced the other a mighty scream sounded in the First Lord's mind. Lab telepathically reached out to that ship, and saw that the minions from the Omega craft were pouring into the Superdreadnought, where they were met by eager warriors. Looking inside, Lab realized he could also watch the fighting within.

Minions surged, and hissed, and like the disease that owned them they entered the living Superdreadnought, flooding its corridors as if they were veins. The warriors were having none of it. Outnumbered though they were, they were still Kroggs. They excelled at the business of death and killing.

It was a strange delight to Lab, seeing Krogg warriors *break* the minions. He watched as Krogg blades pierced joints, and as Krogg strength — raw and fueled by hatred — tore the minions and their once-human bodies to pieces.

Omega tired of the sport quickly: he detonated his ship, destroying it and the Superdreadnought in the process. Lab imagined the Kroggs died happy as he pulled his mind back out to look at the colliding fleets.

The battle was almost fifty seconds old now, and at least a hundred ships had been destroyed on each side: the Kroggs were giving as good as they were getting.

That, according to the arithmetic of death, was not nearly enough to bring victory in space...

Lab caught sight of a Dreadnought line, running near the edge of the combating fleets. It was aiming to destroy the Omega carrier ships — the ones destined to deposit the minions on Earth. Somehow, the sight of those minion-laden vessels drew images of Genesis Colonizers back into Lab's mind. He could see the last of the Crusader-crewed ships arriving in Earth orbit all those years before. He remembered the fear he'd felt then as 100,000 humans had landed on his homeworld.

Today, he would have welcomed them with open arms.

It was obvious to Lab, and probably to the Kroggs too, that no attack on those carrier ships would be allowed to succeed. The Omega fleet seemed to surge as though carried on a current, and instead of just sending ships to intercept the Krogg attackers, a whole wing of the black wave enveloped them.

Watching that fight, Lab saw the Kroggs die.

It had taken the mightiest First Rates of the old fleet — *Orion*, *Agamemnon*, *Algenon*, *Endymion* and *Poseidon* — to stop the Colonizers. No ordinary Dreadnoughts could do the same job now.

And though Lab doubted Kardrath could hear his thoughts in the din of war that was surrounding them both, it seemed he realized this.

Death and its mighty sisters — the Hyper Motherships — began to move, and their speed and their firepower was incomparable.

Their spine guns roared in the silent vacuum, steams of projectiles leaping through space with such frequency they almost looked like whipcords lashing out at animals. These powerful combatants picked a place in the Omega formation and cruised directly into it: no finesse, no caution.

With all their firepower, they punched straight into the black wave, and then began cutting their way through — bound, of course, for the minion-carriers. They were making headway. Nothing could touch them, it seemed.

Lab hoped the same would be true of the *Venerables*. He let himself hope, just for a moment, that this battle might be won in space. Maybe — just maybe — the Omega fleet had been overestimated.

"They'll be in weapons range in ten seconds."

Those words came from *Venerable's* bridge, and they drew Lab's mind back into his body. Ten seconds to war.

He closed his eyes, then opened them again to restore his visual grip on the battle plot. Here it was, the Earthers' turn. Because for all the majestic death the Kroggs were handing out, Omega came on.

This would not be stopped in space. There was no hope of that.

Five seconds.

CHAPTER 38

Any other day, this beach would have made Christine smile. Her skin was still numb, her face not sensitive to the breeze... but she could still appreciate its beauty. She could still remember what warmth like this would really have felt like to a body not betrayed by its own nerve endings.

It really was paradise.

But it was also harder to walk on sand. She hadn't counted on that — she'd never come across beach sand before. Genesis had little, and she'd certainly never trained on it. She would have to change the way she fought, and perhaps that was the edge Omega was looking for, having this duel here...

That's silly. He has more than enough advantages already. He won't care what surface we battle on.

Christine held her breath at that line of thought. If the plague retorted by planting a snide observation in her mind, that would be the end of it — her armor would have failed her. And if she didn't have armor blocking those telepathic assaults, she'd definitely fail today.

But there was no retort. Omega wasn't in her head...

He didn't appear to be here at all.

Christine glanced at Graham, checking to make sure the junior Manchester was still moving. He was. With cold purpose. Today he was an assassin...

"You might as well come out," he called sharply, his voice raising up on the wind.

There was no reply at first, but Christine's instinct drew her eyes to the surf.

Omega-Gillian. Standing where she hadn't been just a second before, knee-deep in the water as the waves rolled in. Dressed like a surfer girl, her eyes black, she grinned at Christine and Graham, and then began wading in very slowly.

She looks so human.

Christine was surprised that the avatar looked essentially normal — so ordinary and so beautiful at the same time. Omega had clearly done that for effect. He wanted to make it tougher on Graham...

Glancing again at Graham, Christine noted that his expression hadn't changed. He was seeing his wife again for the first time since the boardwalk on *Genesis One*, oh so long ago... and he remained frozen. His emotions were clamped down.

"Come on then," he said, his words loud but devoid of feeling.

She came out of the water, and stood on the beach a few dozen meters away from the two humans, her grin widening, "Those clever fucking Larosians. I figured it might just have been the King avatar being too much of a pussy to break through, but that's some serious shit you're wearing."

Graham didn't bat an eye, and Omega-Gillian fixed her stare on him. Christine had to get between them. She had to.

"Setter Caine was right... you do swear an awful lot," she said sharply, hand connecting with the padded grip of her saber as she stepped forward.

A gentle chuckle was Omega's answer, and the avatar's eyes shifted to Christine. Right, just as Christine had wanted.

Keep her from getting to Graham. Just keep her attention on you while this gets started.

"You know, Christine, you're a fine little specimen. Honestly," Omega-Gillian's tone was obscene. "I'd do you. Honestly, I'd love to. I don't even mean kill you... though doing both at once, that'd be fun. I can't believe Graham's being so fucking loyal to a walking corpse... if he had a brain, he'd be riding you all day 'til the universe ended."

Christine knew that was meant to throw her off. She could feel the embarrassment and the anger boiling up under her skin, but a cool, calming rhythm was pounding through her veins at the same time. An Earther harmony, keeping her level, and disrupting the response.

She didn't take the bait. She smiled instead.

"You're not so bad yourself."

Omega-Gillian looked surprised for a moment, then cooed with laughter, "Oh fuck me, any other day I'd keep you around for entertainment value. Well done little girl. Well fucking done."

"I have to say, every other word being 'fuck' just doesn't seem mature to me," the young human persisted, taking another step toward the avatar.

The plague's laughter intensified, "What is your hangup with swearing? Honestly, who exactly said this should be a family show? The millions of families I murdered weren't choosy. Your parents included."

That one pierced her Earther harmony, and got a twinge. Her parents were gone, and her sister would probably be alone after today.

Fine.

Christine stood her ground now, and at last she dragged her eyes to the right, to see Graham standing still in the sand. He appeared relaxed. His sword was gently resting in its sheath, his posture easy.

Omega-Gillian turned her gaze back on him and smiled sweetly, "Now, I'd try offering you one last moment to say your goodbyes and all that shit, but you wouldn't believe me if I tried."

Graham's expression didn't change, but that didn't bother the plague at all. The smile on Omega-Gillian's face broadened further, "It's going to be great breaking you down, you realize. It's never fun when they don't resist... it's only fun when I get some shit like you, who thinks he's tougher than me."

Again, no response. No reaction.

"Oooh, poor Graham got hurt. Poor Graham lost his wife and his baby. You used to be all lost and alone, but she settled you down. You remember that? If you weren't in that fucking armor, I'd put it into your head so you could see it. But you remember..."

The avatar took a step forward as she began to taunt, and Christine realized this might be her opportunity. Maybe Graham could drag Omega-Gillian close enough... just enough. He wouldn't be able to strike himself — the plague's eyes were on him — but he could give Christine the chance she needed to land the first blow.

She remembered how well avatars fought, how fast they were. It didn't seem likely to her that she'd be fast enough... but she *would* try.

"Got all icy, you did," Omega-Gillian mocked with a grin. "Thought you could kill me, or just die. Poor Graham wants to just die. You're such a fuckup, too. You leave all your humans behind for me to eat, and you fuck things up with your sister. Honestly, you didn't even say a proper goodbye to her, did you? Oh, mister emo Graham, your pain was too much to let you say your goodbyes."

She took another step forward.

"Now you're going to lose little Christine, too. Loyal pussy dog that she is. With her big doe eyes that look at you and beg you to love her, because she's smitten. You don't give her what she needs, the same way you didn't give Gillian what she needed. You weren't there to save Gillian from me, were you? Aw, now Gillian and baby Grahamina are fucked. Just fucked. And that's because you are a failure piece of shit husband."

No response. Christine's own calm was starting to shake, but Graham remained composed. Nothing Omega-Gillian said was touching him.

"Well fuck me, he's going to make this *real* fun," Omega-Gillian's grin widened greatly.

Christine took her chance.

Her saber was up and out and flashing in the bright sunlight, and she was crossing the sand between her and the avatar with a graceful lunge that was too quick to evade.

Well, it was supposed to be.

All she felt was a hammer hitting the back of her shield, and she was suddenly somersaulting over Omega-Gillian, and lying in the sand.

"First strike to the lap dog," the plague said with relish. Her eyes then shifted back to Graham, "Fancy your chances?"

Christine scrambled to her feet, then checked to see her first shield was down by nearly ten percent. She noted that, started forward, then stopped.

Graham slowly drew his sword, and then nodded his head, "I do fancy them. Come ahead."

Omega-Gillian hadn't expected that. She stared at him, "Seriously? That's it?"

Graham's expression didn't change, "Well, if you won't..."

He attacked. He didn't try to sneak it in, he didn't feint or misdirect. He went straight in on his wife, and she staggered back in surprise. His blade flew fast, and she tried to recover...

She did.

Because though Omega-Gillian was surprised, she was still more than a match for Graham.

This duel had begun.

CHAPTER 39

Chronos Claw stood at *Formidable's* plot with his arms folded.

"In range... *now*..."

"All guns commence firing," the ship's Captain gave the order, and Chronos could only stand and watch as the tactics he had pioneered in the battle for Krogg 'A'... the *second* battle for Krogg 'A', that was... were used by the entire Earther Navy.

The broadsides began to lash out, tightly packed and carefully aimed. In his mind's eye, Chronos could see it: blue light filled space, as though a new star had appeared. So much energy racing at Omega.

As they fired, the ships began to roll, and the new guns of the *Venerable*-class ships recharged so quickly that the first to fire were ready to strike again before the turns were completed. The gunners began to angle their weapons down just a little, so they could fire more easily, and so the force of the shot leaving the guns could accelerate their ships' spins.

From *Formidable's* bridge, it all felt smooth. The artificial gravity plating did its work very well, and Chronos simply stood.

Not far from *Formidable*, *Victory* was doing the very same. Fox Magnus had begun to pace around the battle plot, watching as the great diamond formations of the Earthers' mightiest battleships unleashed their tides of energy.

"That's a *lot*," he whispered, and Thena Magnus looked through the plot at him with a nod.

"Almost makes you think it might be enough," she said softly.

Smiling in dapper fashion, Fox met his wife's eyes, "Almost, you're right."

The Krogg War ships were starting to join in now, their older guns having a slightly shorter range and a longer recharge cycle. These ships were all tucked into the diamonds — while the *Venerables* formed the lines that gave the diamonds their definition and shape, the older ships filled in the spaces in between.

Their shot might tell, too.

"No incoming fire yet, sir," *Victory's* Sensor Officer said as he moved behind his consoles.

Fox frowned at the words, "Interesting. But I suppose the battle's only a minute old."

Thena nodded, "He'll start shooting at us soon."

...

Rear Admiral Minnie Maximane held onto the sides of *Galahad's* plot, her eyes locked onto the markers of her squadron's energy shot as it careened at the Omega formation. The gunners had been careful to target a section of the Omega fleet that wasn't eclipsed by attacking Kroggs — no one wanted a friendly-fire incident today, though in time, it seemed inevitable that there would be one. The chaos would take over soon...

"Impact in ten... count it down, sensors," Mel Ramsay, Minnie's longtime Flag Captain, appeared at the lioness' side.

This moment would give them a sense of how well they could do here... or how badly they could be beaten up. If some of that shot did damage, then Omega wouldn't be invulnerable... but if he dodged it disdainfully — as Minnie had seen him do back at Krogg 'A' — then even this defensive strategy could fail...

The count to impact reached zero, and Minnie zoomed the plot in on the section of the Omega fleet that should have been clipped by the energy shot. One of the plague ships shuddered and jolted, but that was all. That was all her shot had done.

The shot of the *Venerables*, which had gone in sooner, had torn up some of the plague ships, but *Galahad* and its older consorts hadn't proven as effective.

"Well, so much for beating him in space," Mel Ramsay said softly. "Guess we do this the hard way."

Minnie nodded, "Getting used to that now."

"Good," Mel smiled, then turned to her Cruising Master. "Keep us rolling, and hold station."

"Feels weird not to be going forward," Minnie mused aloud. "But all ships hold here."

They wouldn't chase their shot — they couldn't today. But there were more broadsides on their way out...

Chronos' jaw tightened as his plot showed the harsh fight going on between the Kroggs and the Omega fleet. He felt a strong connection to his Krogg allies now — he'd spent more time with them than most Earthers, and their redemption felt to him almost like a personal victory, an accomplishment he'd had a hand in.

He hadn't really, but even so, he felt close to them.

And now they were most certainly dying.

The numbers were slowly beginning to turn against them, too. No longer were they giving as good as they got, because the plague was pushing forward more of his black wave. He had the edge in numbers, and he was growing more accustomed to fighting Krogg vessels.

Kardrath, Chronos reached out with his mind, seeking the Krogg Fleet commander. He heard no reply, and hoped that was just a combination of his telepathic inexperience, and the sheer volume of telepathic communication that had to be going on now in the Krogg Fleet.

Not to mention Omega's fleet — telepathy bonded every one of Omega's cells, so the amount of interference coming out of his ships was probably immense.

Death had gone deep into the Omega fleet, so it was probably lost in the din.

"Signal Officer, send to First Lord and First Space Lord that I recommend pulling the Kroggs back. We can maximize bombardment if we do."

Chronos wanted to race in after the Kroggs — to charge in under energy drive and start shooting — but he knew that was impossible, and unwise. The times of the glorious Earther melee were past...

Antimatter guns in range, sir.

Novash nodded telepathically at the report, then issued his firing orders, *All vessels, maximum destructive force. Open fire.*

The Larosian Navy today was a shadow of a splinter of its former glory, but its 200 ships would nonetheless burn away at the plague with all the antimatter they could throw.

The Kroggs are suffering heavier casualties now, sir. It appears that the plague's numbers are giving him a significant advantage in the close-quarter fighting, even against them.

Novash acknowledged the report telepathically, then his mind found the pertinent numbers: the Kroggs were down to 900 ships, Omega to 4,500.

This first minute of the battle was not going entirely to plan... the plague had a slight edge.

But soon Omega's fleet would not be eclipsed from the guns of the Earther Navy: if the Kroggs withdrew, indiscriminant firing — a complete wall of energy and antimatter shot — would cascade against him.

It was not a perfect beginning to this battle, but as Novash well knew, few battles had perfect beginnings.

Fox Magnus linked his hands behind his back and watched as the Kroggs began to disentangle themselves. They'd paid dearly for their close combat, but hopefully now the Omega ships were softened up. When they met the unfettered bombardment of the Earther Navy and the Larosian squadrons, that would give an indication...

"Signal coming in from Warlord Kardrath."

Thena responded before Fox could, "In the plot, Signal Officer."

The Krogg appeared, missing an arm from his left side, "I must report that we failed to destroy their troop carriers, Fox. I'm sorry."

Fox Magnus' eyebrows shot up, "Are *you* alright, Kardrath?"

"Nothing that won't mend. Our Hyper Motherships were heavily attacked, but we were able to force our way out. We did not get a shot at those carriers, though."

Fox nodded again, and just as he did he saw Lab Forepaw appear in the plot, being patched in on the signal.

"Their troop carriers are going to be tough to get at," the First Space Lord said to the First Lord of the Admiralty.

Lab Forepaw nodded slowly, "That's fine. We won't take his bait. Kardrath, reintegrate your fleet with us and prepare to cover our formations. When he charges in, you need to keep him off our backs."

Kardrath bow-nodded, "Gladly, sir."

The alien vanished.

Fox and Lab then exchanged stares.

"Seems so quiet so far," the former said after a moment.

Lab's ear twitched, "Really? Maybe. Either way, we're going to get into it in a minute…"

The Krogg Fleet fell back, and Omega's ships came on.

CHAPTER 40

Pat Conroy was fairly certain he was already in the outskirts of one of the gulags of Hell. It was a black night on Ecclesia, and with only the powerful shaft of light that Omega had sent up into the sky glowing on the surface, everything that remained of this former Churcher city was bathed under a haunting glow.

"Welcome to Hell," he muttered to himself as he walked forward slowly, energy rifle leveled and set.

"There could be minions anywhere," Sarah reminded him, and he nodded.

Of course Omega had promised no interference in the duels, but neither of these two experienced fighters expected to be given an easy crack at Omega-Paine.

Even though the night was cool, sweat was starting to collect on Pat's forehead. He'd have loved to wipe it away, but he wasn't going to lift his helmet and give the avatar any chance at getting into his head. Freetown was too fresh in his memory — that sick feeling as the plague invaded his mind, and the sheer destruction as it took over the people and made them into his mobs...

"Ahead," Sarah slowed, and Pat slowed next to her. His eyes snapped up, and then he grimaced: standing in the middle of the light shaft was a single, robed figure. Pat recognized the man's build instantly, and had to bite back a snarl.

The anger surprised him. He'd killed William Paine, once, during the old bastard's attempt to stage a coup after the war. He'd thought then that one death would be enough pay back to that man's family... but Gregory Paine, the old bastard's descendant, had come here and started Ecclesia, and tried to get his revenge...

Before all this had started, then, Pat wouldn't have minded killing Paine. Attach an 'Omega' to the man's name, and Pat realized that he *really* wanted this creature destroyed. The desire hit him suddenly, without warning... all the time he'd spent caught up in trying to be there for Sarah, and to be the positive voice for everyone else, had isolated him somewhat from his own anger.

Well, he'd enjoy killing Omega-Paine.

That in mind, he glanced at Sarah, and found her own face was as set as his. She wouldn't break — not now. She'd sacrificed all the humanity she had left so that she could be a cold and vicious killer at this moment. Omega would soon see that she was the fastest and deadliest human alive...

"Here they come, the poster kids of the Genesis Navy!"

Omega-Paine's voice was the same as Gregory Paine's had been, and Pat felt the anger building further within him.

"Let me guess, you're going to get into a taunting match with us," the Irishman roared back. "You're going to do everything you can to degrade us and belittle us. See if we're up to it."

The declaration drew a moment of silence from the avatar, and in that time Sarah and Pat came to a stop at the edge of the light shaft. Both humans took a brief second to wonder where the light was coming from — it was a circular shaft nearly ten meters across, but it appeared to have no source — it just shot out of the ground. Probably telepathic — Omega using some mental energy to light up his dueling ring.

They wouldn't step into it before they had to.

"Well, you pretty much summed up my plan, you fucking Irish," Omega-Paine started up again. "You think you can shut me up?"

A hungry grin formed on Pat's face, and he started to step forward...

Sarah's hand stopped him.

"I'll listen to your insolence," she said coldly. "You should probably get it all out of your system now, because you won't have another chance once we're through."

Pat blinked at the words, and looked at his wife. Her expression was cool and there was strength in her voice that he hadn't heard in... how long? She had an enemy to fight, right in front of her, and that was easier than dealing with herself and her guilt about her people.

Pain over the loss of Genesis was secondary now. Suspended.

Omega-Paine clapped once, eagerly, and turned to Sarah, "You know, you sound pretty tough. And even though I can't get into your head, I really, *really* believe that you mean it. That's impressive..."

He let his words trail off for a second, then sniggered, "No, actually, it's not."

Sarah's expression didn't change, but Paine took a step toward her, grinning, "Little Sarah, always making the wrong decisions. It was your fault mommy and daddy died, wasn't it? You led that spy right into their shop. You promised them she could be trusted. You said she'd never spy for the Church... whoops."

Pat's anger was escalating more rapidly now. Those were horrors from Sarah's childhood — things for which she'd long blamed herself, and for which she hadn't been responsible.

Still, they lurked in her... fueled her.

"And then you met the Earthers, and you had your little uprising, and yet you always made the same fucking mistakes. Always charging the guns, always having to prove that you're not the stupid little bitch who can't make a right decision. But then you left your crews to die at Gibraltar so you could rescue Irish asshole here. Let them all die. Was that a good decision, or another mistake?"

Omega-Paine came another step closer, and Sarah's breathing got harder. She was trying to stay calm. She was trying not to let the plague mash her buttons.

"You lost your planet to me. They were all counting on you, but first you let the Church outsmart you with their coup, didn't you? And then I showed up and ate your planet, stole your brother's soul, and then after that I seem to remember consuming most of the survivors. "

Her nostrils started to flare with each breath. Her hands started shaking. Omega-Paine *wanted* her to lunge. She had to resist.

"And all that incompetence of yours is costing the Earthers right now... my army, all those minions... they used to be your people. If you weren't such a fuckup, Earth would be safe right now. And you wouldn't be here with this bush league plan of yours."

Her knuckles were white and her hands were welded to her rifle by anger.

"But the biggest mistake — and you should have figured this one out — had nothing to do with planets or parents or any of that shit. You know what the worst thing you did was?" Omega-Paine lifted his hands before him, palms up as though he were preaching. He took another step forward, "You're such a coward that you spent all this time freezing out the only human in the cosmos who actually cares about you. I mean, Pat must have a severe fucking malfunction to see anything redeeming about you. But he does, so hats off to him. But he's been trying to help you and love you all this time, and all you're doing is saying you want to kill me? How does that even make sense? You should know you can't kill me... but you're treating your husband like shit so you can try?"

He laughed now, "That's very disappointing. Honestly. You are so damaged, you're probably not even good for breeding anymore. Pat, you're a fucking retar—"

Pat's broadsword very nearly took off Omega-Paine's hand, but the avatar leapt back just in time, keeping clear of the strike.

"Wha-ho! Didn't expect the Irish temper to go before the useless bitch," the avatar laughed.

Pat levered his rifle up and fired at Omega-Paine, but as he'd expected, the energy fire just bounced off some sort of shield.

"Power of the mind, Pat... if your brain wasn't shit, I'd try to teach you how it works."

After all his calm and cool dispositions of the past weeks, Pat was done now. No one — no plague, no Churcher, no avatar — went after Sarah like that. Not without him having a say.

He dropped his rifle, and with no finesse at all, he advanced on his adversary.

His turn, at last, to charge the guns as his wife so often did.

Standing behind him, Sarah was dumbstruck for just a few seconds, and then she realized what would happen next — Omega-Paine would tear her husband apart. Pat wasn't good enough to survive.

She had to act. She dropped her rifle, then she drew her katana. Without another thought, she raced into the pool of light.

Another duel had started.

CHAPTER 41

Artie Tigar held his breath as the Omega ships came right at his squadron. His pennant was still flying from *Agamemnon*, and now the old First Rate was joined by dozens of others in firing for all they were worth.

"Come on, plague… we'll hurt you again…" the cat whispered to himself.

Just as the words left his mouth, a signal came in from *Aboukir*, the old 74 that wasn't too far away. Jax Furgus appeared in *Agamemnon's* plot, "You feel like a rock right now, Artie?"

Tigar frowned, "Excuse me?"

"They're like a wave getting ready to break on the shore," the old lion pointed out gruffly.

Artie Tigar hadn't expected poetry from his curmudgeonly old friend, so somehow now he spared a smile, "That's really quite poetic for you, Jax."

The lion snorted a laugh, "Operative word there was *break*."

"Right," Tigar agreed.

He didn't get a chance to say anything else, as the warning from his Sensors Chief cut him off.

"Huge numbers of spines incoming!"

Dran Nightclaw was keeping the frigate *Cerberus* near *Agamemnon*, so Ursla's two great old ships could fight side by side this final time. As the spines appeared on his plot he nodded to his skipper, who'd been with him during the Krogg War, and then looked to his Signal Officer.

"All ships prepare to intercept rams."

The frigates that made up Nightclaw's new squadron were not the same old elite of the 111th Flying Squadron, but there were many fine vessels, and even more fine Earthers aboard them. He could rely on their dedication, even if they were all a bit out of practice.

It wouldn't take much practice to die…

As an 80-gun ship of the line, *Foudroyant* had been a powerful combatant in the Krogg War, but watching the cloud of spines coming at her ship and her squadron, Ami Dune knew her vessel was too small for this fight.

"We're not going to last long," she said frankly, and in her holo plot, her husband shook his head.

"Don't say things like that," Zed Dune protested. "We're staying right in close with you."

His frigate, *Hades*, was tucked in as an escort to the 80-gun ship — husband and wife would be as together as they could be when they died.

Frigates weren't going to survive this...

Or perhaps they would. The spines got caught in the last flight of energy shot that had flown from the broadsides of the Earther Fleet... only a few thousand came through. That made a difference: the shields and carronades could handle them.

"Well, we survived the first onslaught..." Ami began to say, but she stopped in mid-thought. Then she added the painful observation: "He's chasing them down."

The black wave ships were flying right down the wakes of their spines. The energy shot that crumpled the projectiles still wasn't damaging the warships. Maybe the plague's attack was being slowed by the broadsides, but if so, it wasn't slowed by much.

"Looks like he's going for close combat," Zed confirmed in the plot. "We didn't offer it, so he's coming for it himself."

Ami nodded, then looked back to her fellow white wolf, "Stay close to us, Zed."

"They're going to try to break up our formations. Once they're all around us, they can try to bring us down one at a time," Fox Magnus announced over the comm, and Jax Furgus gritted his teeth and nodded.

The wily old Admiral had been in enough fights now to have an instinct for what was coming next: chaos.

"Keep an eye on those troop carriers," he reminded his fellow Admirals over the comm. "They'll be using the melee as a chance to get through."

The Earthers who were patched into Jax's comm made sounds of agreement, and in *Aboukir's* reliable old plot, the lion watched as the storm came in.

It's like a swarm of bees... or a sandstorm, maybe.

Over 4,000 black wave ships began to collide with the Earther and Larosian formations.

"Hold tight!" *Agamemnon's* master adjusted the ship's roll to avoid a diving black wave ship — the big First Rate would have to move fast to avoid ramming.

But Artie Tigar's eyes remained trained on the plot, and he was already barking reminders to his Signal Officer, "All ships remember to stay in formation... we keep them tied up around us, so we can wear their numbers down!"

It felt so strange, to sit relatively still in space, just spinning and firing, but it was their only hope...

A third of Artie's squadron of Krogg War ships vanished — they simply hadn't moved fast enough, and had either been rammed or shot to pieces.

But every few seconds, despite the clouds of racing black wave ships all around them, *Agamemnon's* squadron-mates would unleash volleys of energy shot, and some of them struck home. Not all... not even many... but some.

Agamemnon was jarred sideways by a hit, but the mighty ship remained strong. Artie hung on...

"Remain close to the flagship," Nightclaw managed to maintain his usual, reserved-sounding tone despite the chaos, and *Cerberus* lunged and dove with all the elegance and speed of the old days.

But as Nightclaw clutched the sides of his old frigate's plot, he knew things were just too different — that a small ship of only 38 guns was not going to be able to make much of a difference now.

That wouldn't stop it trying, though...

"Omega Destroyer locked on, coming straight at us!"

Nightclaw's ear twitched at that warning, and his eyes darted to the plot: one of the black wave ships was coming on quickly, going bow-to-bow with *Cerberus*. Both broadsides had just fired; it would ram into the frigate before they recharged. The forward-firing chase guns hurled their shot at it, and carronades swept their beams over it, but it came right at them.

If they tried to evade now, they'd only be hit in the flanks...

Nightclaw took a breath, "Full forward shields, ram it."

He said that with an uncharacteristic amount of feeling in his tone — regret at the way his ship might die, right now.

Not one question; the Cruising Master gave orders, and Ursla's old frigate lunged straight at the Omega vessel. The two sailed at each other at barely-sublight speeds, and then the veteran frigate hit the black wave ship.

The explosion was unexpected — there seemed no good reason for the two to detonate on contact, but they did. Ursla's old frigate, carrying Dran Nightclaw, the greatest of the frigate officers, simply vanished.

Foudroyant was turning fast to avoid fire, and beneath the old second rate, *Hades* was doing the same. Zed's ship was a veteran 44-gun frigate from the Krogg War — it was faster and handier than Ami Dune's ship of the line, but standing at its plot, Zed hardly thought it was fast enough.

The white wolf kept his eyes on the holo projection — he and his ship were the spotter for *Foudroyant*. They'd identify any dangerous attacks coming in, warn the second rate, and intercede if needed. *Foudroyant's* more powerful broadside had to keep firing for as long as it could. Omega had to be as badly torn up as possible...

"Below-below-below!" the canine Sensor Officer repeated that warning three times quickly, and as he did *Hades'* Cruising Master saw the cruiser-sized black wave ship that had started to line up on *Foudroyant's* underside.

Without needing an order, the Master pushed her frigate into the path of the would-be ram, and gunners on the ship's port broadside unleashed their spite at the plague.

This plague ship, though, was determined not to crack: it drove right through the broadside, and right into *Hades*.

Zed Dune was catapulted from his place at the plot, landing with a sharp crack atop a console in the sensor section. The shrapnel that sliced through the bridge missed him completely, but he knew his spine was severed. He couldn't feel his legs.

He tried to drag himself off the console with his arms, but it was too late for that.

The Omega ship, carrying *Hades* on its bow, rammed right into *Foudroyant's* underside.

Ami Dune was launched sideways from her plot, but the second rate's Third Lieutenant managed to catch her short of going head-first into a console. She staggered, as did her ship, and then seeing a wounded pair of Earther hulls, a few more Omega ships dove in, spitting spines until what remained of the shields went away.

"What do we have left?" Ami called, just as the bridge went dark around her.

Her ship bucked again and she lost her footing, then went face down onto the deck. As she tried to struggle to her feet, she fell again, and she knew there wasn't anything left.

Kardrath watched the destruction that was beginning to unfold around the Earther Fleet with a twist of disgust. Omega was a vicious adversary... but the Kroggs weren't done yet.

Offer close support to all Earther ships in difficulty. Do not become overcommitted!

Those orders sent a Dreadnought and two Destroyers to *Foudroyant's* rescue, but by the time they arrived, the second rate was already breaking up into a few large pieces. The Krogg ships pushed on to help Earthers who were still in the fight.

Aboukir shuddered, but the wily 74 kept firing.

"Couple of Krogg Destroyers are attaching themselves to us!" the Sensor Officer reported, and that drew a grunt of approval from Jax Furgus.

"Good sort of close guards to have today," he muttered. He was still focused on those troop carriers, though... they were pushing forward with the rest of

Omega's fleet... surely they'd be making their way directly for Earth soon...

That's exactly what they started to do, just as Jax Furgus watched them.

"Put me on Fleetcomm again," Jax said quickly, and as his connection chimed, he barked his warning, "Everyone, the troops are starting to move in... get something in front of them if you can!"

Novash heard that warning, and noted in his mind's eye that his ships were on the nearest flank. If the Larosians could get into position, and unleash antimatter guns on the intruders...

All ships, prepare to reposition to port.

Omega must have heard the telepathic order: 500 fresh black wave ships turned instantly on the Larosian Fleet. The silver vessels couldn't redeploy while facing that much enemy fire.

Shaking his head in an Earther fashion, Novash turned his mind to a communications footing, and reached out to Kardrath, *Warlord, can you interdict?*

We will attempt to!

On *Death's* bridge, Kardrath decided that he had to try again: he ordered his Hyper Motherships out to the flank. They would deal with the troop carriers, or more likely, be destroyed in the attempt.

CHAPTER 42

Descending the steps into the Genesis War Memorial, Setter Caine couldn't help but feel a pang of memory. He remembered Liz Hastings explaining this place to him: it had been dug deep into a park in Genesis City, its walls lined with black stone. On that stone, the name of every fallen human from the Krogg War was engraved in the tiniest of print.

The monument was vast — it spanned hundreds of meters in each direction — and at its center was a statue of four humans, one facing each of the four cardinal compass directions: two Crusaders, a Naval officer, and a Genesis marine. They were the heroes of the war against the Kroggs, according to the unifying history that had been written during the peaceful years.

It had been meant to bring Church and technical classes together... now, as the monument sat empty but blood-stained, it was all too clear that the attempt to unify had failed.

Omega was here, and it had to be conceded that even had the Church and the Navy come together, this fate might not have been stopped.

"It certainly wouldn't have been stopped," a call came from the center of the monument, and Omega-Natosh emerged from behind the statues of the humans. "I wasn't going to be stopped by them, Setter. You know that."

Slowing his pace, Setter glanced up at Ursla, and she looked back down at him. This was it, then — this was where they needed to be. At last.

"So, I've already trash-talked Graham and Christine, and Pat and Sarah. They've started fighting their duels. And if you're not checking in regularly at home, my landing craft are moving in now. So it's all going according to my plan..." Omega-Natosh made his way towards the two great leaders, his demeanor so relaxed it surprised both Earthers.

"But I figure there's no point trash-talking you, now is there? You're not going to be any fun for me."

Setter smiled at the observation, and Ursla chuckled, "I didn't actually think you had that much sense. But you're right."

Omega-Natosh laughed too, and came to a stop about ten meters short of the pair, "Well, I am a megalomaniac. But I will admit, this righteousness you're all showing me... and all your confidence in your *plan*... it's hard not to take swipes at you for being such fucking boyscouts."

Setter's ear twitched, "Easy there, no need for the language."

Omega-Natosh threw his head back and laughed louder, "What *is* it with you? Why the fuck would a language be created with words that only some people can use sometimes? Honestly. A language is a bunch of fucking sounds that we make up, so why make up sounds we can't fucking say? Not that I'm complaining — it's fun pissing you off with it — but it's fucking strange."

Setter frowned gently, "It's a matter of preference, I'll grant you."

Omega-Natosh waved his hand towards the wolf, "There you go. See, we can have a civilized discussion."

The absurdity of those words left Setter with no immediate answer, but Ursla decided it was her turn now, "I see you've desecrated the cenotaph?"

"Of course," Omega-Natosh held up his hands and turned around to indicate the vast, bloodied memorial. "You know me. I started off with some sport down here... gang rapes and things like that. Entertainment that *never* gets old. Then I just started throwing bodies in after a while. I was going to cover it over eventually, but you called and I thought it'd be a perfect place for our overdramatic duel."

He was trying to slip the shocking statements into his smooth, almost casual conversation. Setter Caine didn't allow himself to be distressed by it.

"You cleared the bodies, just for us? Thanks very much," he countered.

"You're very welcome, my fine-furred friend," Omega-Natosh bowed in an absurd fashion. "So, while I'm killing the other two dueling teams and fucking over your planet, are we just going to stand here and chat?"

Setter glanced at Ursla, and she glanced back.

Then the Supreme Consul of the Earther people shrugged, "Well, we were going to destroy you, but if you want to talk first, we're open to that."

"Ooh," Omega-Natosh held up his hands. "I do like to talk first, usually. But I don't cuddle after."

Setter cocked his eyebrow, and the avatar laughed, "Joke from the old days."

"I see," Setter replied.

"So, no taunting? I was expecting taunting. I was waiting for you to start on me about losing Freetown," Ursla made sure she sounded genuinely disappointed.

"And me... well, you already started on me with that poor spacer King. I was expecting more of that. I'm a failure, millions dead, we're a lot alike... all the sorts of clichéd things you like to say. We getting a pass on those?" Setter joined in, and again the plague avatar laughed.

"You know, I was planning on it. The big old soliloquies. And believe me, your human friends got their buttons pushed... but you two... well. Why bother? You'll wax philosophical and call it an equation, and I'll groan."

Setter raised an eyebrow, "As I recall, when I mentioned the *nemesis* equation to you a few weeks ago, you just about had the King avatar rip off her own head in disgust."

Omega-Natosh sobered slightly, and the plague in general suddenly felt slightly defensive — absurd as that was, under the circumstances, "I was having a bad fucking day."

"Aha," Ursla folded her arms. "He strikes me as the surly type. Things go his way, he's like this... almost civil, in a sick way. We throw a wrench into his plans, he's suddenly shrieking about every injustice he's ever thought he's suffered."

"Sounds about right to me," Setter agreed. "Sounds very... human, actually. Not very even-keeled."

Omega-Natosh's humor was draining away, "Oh yes, here, push my fucking buttons. You're here because I think it'll be amusing."

Ursla's eyebrow went up, "And we're very grateful to be your playthings. And I promise you, we'll make sure you have fun while we destroy you."

Setter frowned and looked up at his tall friend, "Wait, we shouldn't promise that. It's a lie."

"Ah, good point," Ursla concurred, then looked back at Omega-Natosh earnestly. "I'm sorry for lying to you, Omega. We won't be making sure you have fun today."

The plague avatar was starting to lose his taste for the banter, and he knew that Caine and Ursla had meant for it to be that way. He'd had his fun pushing buttons, but being arrogant enlightened shit fucking Earthers, these two were trying to get some back.

He'd had enough.

"Say what you like. I can dish it but I can't take it? Fuck you. It doesn't matter if I can't take it when I can dish it this fucking way."

Setter perked up in surprise, "Do I sense some insecurity? Really?"

"Seems so," Ursla agreed.

"Talk shit while you can," the plague avatar hissed back. "Won't have another chance after you're dead."

Setter's smile remained, but he shook his head, "So quickly he makes that transformation. It's sad to realize that all this havoc has been wreaked by a petulant being with too much power at its fingertips and not enough maturity to understand his own state of mind."

"Cynical and jaded... a product of his times. And self-important too. I'm rather glad I didn't have to live with the humans of the twenty-first century... I wonder if any of them believed in anything at all, aside from how brilliant their cynicism was," Ursla nodded.

"We choose to believe there's no hope, so we won't even try. And that makes us smarter than those who..." Setter paused with a smile, thinking of his son, "...than those who try the impossible. That was the wisdom of those days, I suppose."

Ursla continued to nod, and then her smile broadened, "Good thing I'm the product of today. Willing to try the impossible and such."

As she said that, her massive sword came out of its sheath and she was moving forward. Setter wasted no time: he started to his left at a run, drawing his sword too.

Together, these two great Earthers meant to hurt the plague.

And the plague meant to hurt them right back.

The final duel had begun.

CHAPTER 43

"Looks like we're about to have company," Beckett Lupus turned away from the main tactical plot in Antarctic Base's C&C, and Varnon Broadpaw, Narosh and Kragran nodded.

"Warlord Kardrath is moving to intercept with his Hyper Motherships," Kragran pointed out. "But I do not expect he will be able to stop the landings."

The nine massive vessels hauling the undulating sacs that quite obviously held Omega's assault force were coming in, and the Krogg vessels sent to intervene somehow didn't seem equal to the task, despite their well-known power.

"Well, we knew we'd have to do our share on the ground... I don't know if the plan would work if we weren't keeping all those billions of minions busy," Varnon said with some finality. Then he looked to his son-in-law, "Alright, Beck, get the defenses ready."

"Roger that," the General nodded, then turned to the base Signal Officer. As he began issuing orders, Kragran stepped up next to Varnon.

"Narosh and I are contacting our respective warriors," the Warlord said, then switched to telepathy and reached out to Kragthar.

Lord Kragthar, landings are imminent. Prepare your forces for rapid deployment.

The Warlord acknowledged, *Very good, m'Lord.*

At the same time, Narosh alerted Tovarrin, whose Stealth Guardsmen were just outside the Antarctic Base command building, ready to give their lives to defend this place to the very last.

With them were the Earther marines of the Second (Heavy) Division, including its elite Guards Brigade — the same regiments that had led the invasion of Krogg 'A', forty years before. Along with those 10,000 troops were another 10,000 from the recently re-established Twelfth Division, which had long ago fought the Crusaders here in Antarctica.

Beyond those 20,000 were over 500,000 Earther volunteers: civilians mainly, whose cities across the southern hemisphere had been left unfortified. Beckett's deployment strategy in this regard had been quite simple: he could only protect so many urban centers, and the Earther civilians could choose to go to whichever one suited them.

Half a million had chosen to come here, and another half million were up at the Arctic Base, now shrouded in darkness. Cities like Beijing and Sydney held millions each — all across the globe, millions... *billions* of Earthers were standing ready to throw back the invasion.

They'd have to kill minions at a rate of nearly five-to-one to survive...

Perhaps that was possible. Perhaps between the heavy ground defenses, the shields, the pulsars, the gun emplacements, and then the swords and rifles of determined wolves, cats and bears, they could weather the assault.

Perhaps.

"This is Beckett Lupus to all protected cities: looks like the drop is about to begin. Stand by your defenses," the announcement went out. After a moment, Beckett glanced at the Signal Officer, "Give me Sydney specific, please."

There was a brief pause, then the transmitter realigned and reached out to Sydney, Australia, where Beckett had special orders for a certain officer.

Sitting in low Earth orbit, *Savanna Felix* and the remains of the Freetown Navy watched the battle going on overhead... and for once in his life, Ed Jeffries was truly glad he wasn't in the mix. The Omega ships were clawing at Earthers and Kroggs alike, and even with the enhancements that his human cruisers boasted, he couldn't imagine they'd survive the melee.

Theirs was a different job, and it looked like it was about to begin...

"They're coming in now, sir," Lieutenant Garth Badger was standing near the front of *Felix's* bridge, and he looked back from the main screen with a frown. "My guess is they'll scatter and drop planet-wide. We won't be able to stop all of them."

Jeffries nodded, "Agreed. We'll defend the bases then. Signal Officer, send to *Fox Magnus* to join us over Antarctic Base. *Andra Ursla* and *Setter Caine* to protect the Arctic. *Broadpaw* to guard Halifax. Garth, you're master gunboat officer."

The Earther nodded, then tapped his headset, "This is Lieutenant Badger aboard *Savanna Felix*, assuming control of Third Gunboat Division."

"Roger that, Lieutenant. Good hunting up there," the reply came back into his ear.

Of the 50,000 gunboats that were waiting in low orbit, 10,000 were now directly under the orders of the young Lieutenant. He'd seen Omega fight before in the Larosian galaxy: now it would be his responsibility to use those 10,000 craft to help Ed Jeffries guard the major bases on the planet's poles.

"They're engaging the Kroggs, sir!" a human on *Felix's* bridge reported sharply, and all eyes turned back to the screen.

Death shuddered under Kardrath's feet, and the Warlord quashed his own surprise as the mighty ship was hammered ruthlessly by the Omega carriers. They were already in orbital space — it seemed impossible to turn back the landers, just to slow them, perhaps kill some of their troops...

The Omega vessels are spreading out now, m'Lord. Preparing to release their minion sacs!

Kardrath acknowledged that report with an offhand thought, then watched as one of the Hyper Motherships was smashed by Omega's spines. That was no mean feat, and its scream was visceral in the Warlord's mind.

Attack the sacs! Attempt to destroy the minions in space!

Spines flew fast at the great, undulating bags of minions... but as the projectiles drove home, the elastic surface they were targeting repelled them.

The plague had been clever in his design.

The plague ships are entering low orbit now, m'Lord.

Kardrath would not give up: *Continue attacking the carrier ships, and once the bags open, close to neuro pulse range. We will attempt to kill them at low altitude!*

Varnon Broadpaw didn't like what he was seeing... and that wasn't a surprise to him. One sac each going to the Arctic and Antarctic regions, the other seven spacing themselves around the globe to shower regions with cities. If they burst at high altitude, minions would rain from the sky all over the world, all at once.

"All ground batteries are standing by," Beckett repeated that confirmation as he stood next to the First Consul.

Varnon nodded, then looked to the Signal Officer, "All remaining boat divisions to their assigned defense sectors. Shoot down as many minions as is possible."

The message went out, and Varnon folded his arms, "Nine billion targets."

Beckett nodded, "And we've only installed four million gun positions."

"The scope of this is *madness*," the First Consul said, then sighed. "But we'll cope."

Beckett smiled, glanced at his father-in-law, and then looked back to the plot, "That's one word for it."

Ed Jeffries settled into his chair as he watched the first sac fall from the sky on his viewscreen. The great bag of minions had defied the spines of the Krogg Motherships, so now *Felix* and *Magnus* were having a go with their long carronades...

But whatever the sac was made of, it wasn't allowing itself to be cut. Instead, it was slowly being dissolved, either by the atmosphere or some process of Omega's design...

"Four-twenty-seven Gun, commence your run," Garth Badger was ordering from his place on the bridge, and on the screen Ed watched an Earther boat squadron attempt its attack... with no luck. The energy shot was bounced away by the malleable surface.

"Whatever that's made of…" the human shook his head. "They're going to spill soon. Altitude?"

"We're sixty kilometers up, sir… that kind of drop…"

The Sensor Technician was about to point out that falling so far would kill any living creature… except for Omega. Somehow, the plague's minions had proved most adept at dropping from the sky. They'd done it on Krogg 'A', they'd done it back home on Freetown.

"Looks like they're going now, sir!" another tech barked, and all eyes returned to the screen.

"All weapons, start trying to slice them up," Jeffries said coolly.

"This is Badger to all divisional boats, begin rapid fire once the minions emerge."

Emerge they did.

Looking up at the sky outside Fengate Hospital, Lieutenant General Garnet Wiskar had to shake his head, watching the angry glow as energy shot punched out at high altitude, trying to kill minions.

"I'm afraid it's starting to rain, my friends," the dapper General announced, looking around him at the officers of Fourth Division, the formation tasked to protect this city. "Return to your commands and prepare for shield penetrations. I'll be at my HQ presently."

He nodded to each officer, then turned and headed into the hospital, waving his personal squad of marines to join him.

Moving quickly, the General headed for the stairs, then went down to the basement. The dimly-lit place was not terribly inviting to Wiskar, but he shook off any discomfort as his objective came into view. Omega-King was standing in her cell, and Celia Lazarus was standing nearby with an injector gun in hand, staring at the creature.

"My apologies, Doctor," Wiskar came to a halt and nodded to Lazarus. "Orders from General Lupus: we're to destroy the avatar."

Celia frowned noticeably, "We can't wait for the moment?"

She held up the injector gun to emphasize her point, but Wiskar shook his head, "Afraid not, Doctor. General Lupus is concerned that if we leave it too late, the city could fall. He doesn't want a fully-functioning avatar here to be rescued."

Looking very disappointed that she wouldn't get to inject the plague avatar with her vaunted cure, Celia stepped back with a nod. Omega-King, meanwhile, cackled, "It's all about to end for you…"

"Terribly predictable sentiment, I must say," Wiskar shook his head, then nodded to the marines of his squad.

One of the bears stepped towards the shielded cage and pulled an energy charge out of his backpack. As he began to arm it, the avatar hissed at him,

"And how the fuck are you going to get that in here with me, big boy? You going to drop the shield?"

Triggering the timer, the bear shook his head, "No ma'am. It's a one-way shield."

The avatar blinked, then hissed something else. It was too late: the energy charge was lobbed through the barrier of her cell, and then she, and the contents of her cage, were taken into energy drive, and reconstituted into atoms.

"Well done, Sergeant Cubdry. Take your marines up, I'll join you in a moment."

As the marines cleared out of the basement, Wiskar moved over to Lazarus' side.

"Finely acted," the doctor said, laying the injector gun on a nearby tray.

"You were very good too," the General smiled back.

They headed back upstairs.

Minions were falling from the sky.

CHAPTER 44

"They're not proving easy to shoot down... they're spread out. Way out. They're dropping from high altitude so they have time to spread. All our ground batteries are taking just one at a time!"

Artie Tigar wasn't sure who was making that report, but he was listening in since it was on Fleetcomm. Somehow he was managing to pay attention, even as *Agamemnon* leapt from side to side, firing its guns mightily, and occasionally hitting things.

By the sounds of it, the minions weren't falling in tight clusters... they were spread out in 'open order' as they plunged towards the ground. Even the massive guns the Earthers had installed all around the planet were only able to shoot down one at time — not handfuls or swathes of them, as they would have been able to had Omega dropped them in tight clusters.

Clever bastard. Unfortunately...

"We're down to sixty ships in the group, sir!" that report came from much closer to Artie, so he nodded fast.

The squadron around *Agamemnon* was being worn down... it was just a constant monotony of battle surrounding the ships. Every time they managed to gun down one black wave vessel, there was another, and another.

They certainly weren't defeating the plague ships at the necessary two-to-one rate...

Turning his eyes back to the ships in the plot, Artie gritted his teeth, "Send to Admiral Maximane: her squadron and mine to close up for mutual defense."

Galahad was hanging on, as were many of the *Champion*-class ships that remained with it. They were older than *Venerables*, but unlike their less successful showing at Krogg 'A', today they were fighting together in tight defensive diamonds, and it was making a difference. They still weren't killing many Omega ships, but they were staying alive...

"Signal from Tigar, ma'am... requesting we close up with his squadron for mutual support."

Minnie looked up at that report, first turning her eyes to the plot, then through the plot to Captain Mel Ramsay, "Looks like we're getting separated."

The fox skipper nodded, "Agreed."

Minnie's squadron had been next to Artie's not long before, but as both formations suffered losses and pulled tighter and tighter together to maintain the same defensive spacing with fewer ships, they were drawing further and further apart. Soon they'd loose the mutual protection of having friendly ships holding one flank.

"Orders to squadron, begin traverse to starboard, 50 pls. Hold formation," Minnie gave the command, and in seconds her remaining fifty ships were edging over to Artie's remaining sixty.

"We haven't lost a *Venerable* yet," Fox Magnus said to himself. Overhearing his words, Thena Magnus nodded.

"Not yet. But we've lost half the Krogg War ships."

That was true. The fight was so strange to Fox. Napoleon had once reportedly criticized Wellington for 'fighting sitting on his backside', and now Fox felt he was doing the same. It was almost *quiet* on *Victory's* gleaming new bridge. It wasn't visceral or anxious here: the ship turned, fired, and turned again. And no matter what the black wave threw at this section of the Earther line, it bounced off.

"Signal coming in from *Formidable*, sir," a report crossed the bridge, and Fox nodded, pointing to the plot in front of him.

Chronos Claw appeared, "This feeling too relaxed to you?"

Fox nodded immediately, "Glad it isn't just me... you think he's starting to route ships around us?"

Claw paused briefly before nodding, "He's not even below 4,000 yet... I think he's probably keeping us busy with some token offerings while he hammers the older ships and the Larosians."

That seemed likely to Fox — the biggest problem with sitting on one's backside was that the enemy could maneuver all around you...

"We can't do anything about that, though," Chronos added. "Eventually he has to come for us. He's taunting us now, trying to get us to break formation. If we do, he can pick us apart. We have to wait."

Fox sighed. His friend was absolutely right: even while their colleagues in older ships were dying and while the Kroggs and Larosians were suffering from more attention, the *Venerables* had to stay together. In the end, this battle was about killing Omega. And it seemed slightly possible that he wouldn't be able to break the mutually-supporting diamond formations of these mighty new ships, so long as they held fast.

They'd force him to find out...

"Signal from *Guardian One*," *Venerable's* Signal Officer gave that report, then stopped with a frown, planting his hand on his earpiece. "Cancel that, sir. Transmission just went dead."

Lab Forepaw ground his jaw: the *Guardian* defense stations that had surrounded Earth for centuries were now being picked off one by one, and the Allied Fleet was being ravaged. They'd survived ten minutes of hard battling so far — which was in itself an impressive accomplishment — but the First Lord of the Admiralty knew this was only the first phase.

The plague would be relentless, and even now, his minions were raining down...

"The Kroggs have lost four of their Hyper Motherships... looks like they're getting isolated, sir," that report came from his Flag Captain, and Lab nodded.

"Send to Kardrath, withdraw to defensive posture and preserve your ships. The minions are Beckett's to deal with now."

That gave him no joy, but it had to be said. The Navies of the Allies hadn't stopped the landings — now they just needed to save themselves... or, more precisely, takes as many of Omega's ships with them as they could.

"There, see that?" Captain Ronax Hobbes was standing next to *Aboukir's* plot, pointing out the movement of Omega ships.

Jax Furgus nodded as he followed his Flag Captain's finger, "Ground attack."

Aboukir was one of the last 74s left with the Earther Fleet now — of 1,000 old ships, barely 400 remained, most of them larger ships of the line or much smaller frigates. Neither the ship's skipper nor its Flag Officer seemed to pay any attention to that fact as their 74 writhed and sidestepped, avoiding destruction.

Instead, both cats were looking at Omega's deployment — he was sending nearly 500 of his ships away from the fight, to destroy the *Guardian* orbital stations, and by the look of things, to begin bombardment of the shielded cities on the planet's surface.

"Dammit," Jax shook his head. Each of those cities was protected by at least five layers of powerful dome shielding, but under heavy bombardment from the air and attack by millions of minions on the ground, those shields couldn't survive long.

Not even with the power grids for entire *cities* backing them. The onslaught would be too much... the defenses would be worn away slowly.

"Can we?" Ron Hobbes asked that question already knowing its answer. Seeing this move — seeing Omega virtually telegraph his intent to tear down city shields from space — was the greatest temptation of all: it was, traditionally, the Navy's job to protect orbital space so that nothing like this could be attempted.

But the plan didn't call for that. The plan required them to stand their ground, not get picked apart piecemeal.

As Jax thought that, Ron Hobbes read it directly from his Admiral's mind.

There really was nothing to do. Omega's ships would have impunity: they could strike Earth at will, and the Navy wouldn't try to stop him.

They wouldn't be baited into the trap.

"Send a signal to flagship," Jax turned away from the plot, "make sure Lab sees the Omega ships moving. Also remind him to tell Ed Jeffries not to get mixed up with those bastards, we need him and the boats to stay low for our own ground support fire."

A few seconds later, the signal was sent.

Turning back to the plot, Jax met Ron Hobbes' eyes, "I hate this sitting and spinning, but it maximizes the amount of killing we can do... and we need to—"

The rest of his sentence was drowned out by a giant metal moan, and then the front of *Aboukir's* bridge was torn off by what must had been a spine.

A few seconds later, the ship began to come apart.

"Acknowledge the message from Jax, and relay it to Antarctica," Lab was turning back to his plot after hearing the signal from his old friend.

Then he saw the holo marker for *Aboukir* go out.

He stopped breathing and let his instincts flare for just a second.

He *wanted* to move. Wanted to stop those bombardment ships.

But he couldn't. Because as soon as the Earthers broke their formations, they'd be overrun.

Discipline, he thought to himself.

And hope for Jax...

The tempo of the battle was picking up.

CHAPTER 45

Sarah landed hard on her back, and her first personal shield finally died. Pat's had given out minutes back, so he was down just to his backup forcefield. Now Sarah was too...

She struggled upward, keeping her grip tight on her sword as her husband kept Omega-Paine busy. Pat was no specialist in hand-to-hand combat, but he was furious, and he was protecting her. As she slid her feet under her, she watched the Irishman wield his broadsword with ease — the fitness he'd been maintaining over the years was paying off now as he swung that thing with both hands.

Omega-Paine weaved, and dodged, and tried to cross Pat with a fist, but it was expected, and Pat had moved away. They'd been at this for at least twenty minutes now — a very intense twenty minutes — so they were adapting to some of the avatar's ploys.

But neither one of them had so much as had a chance to think about their backpacks, or hitting the plague with their injector guns.

Sarah pushed herself up and forward again, realizing that Pat's energy on this attack was winding down. Their only hope as far as she could tell was to wear the avatar out... or to make him careless... *something*.

But as Sarah slid into range with a mighty upstroke that should have halved the diseased creature, she again found that he was not where he should be.

She controlled her frustration. She knew that Omega-Gillian had been a match for Colin Brawn on Freetown, and that Omega-Natosh had bested Beckett Lupus on *Genesis One*. She was nowhere near as skilled as either of those two... but she had to try.

Her muscles burned with an almost comfortable familiarity as she took over the attack, Pat staggering backward to recover his breath. Twenty minutes of this was testing his stamina, but there was more than enough driving him...

He watched Sarah now, and despite the circumstances, he still had to admire her.

She moved so *fast*.

The avatar backed away, grinning as he always seemed to, and Sarah surged forward, her katana a blur. She moved in short, controlled bursts of incredible power, her blade coming down, missing, recovering, returning to guard. It was like art.

But Omega would not be felled by art. The Paine avatar weaved and dodged, and at last when it suited him, his fist slipped right through Sarah's guard. If it wasn't for her shield — her second and final shield, now — he would have put his fist right through her face.

She was catapulted backward, landing a few meters from Pat. He watched her slide, and saw that she wore an expression of anger, not anguish. She was fine, her shield was still up... but how long would that last?

No time to wonder: Pat rushed ahead again, and Omega-Paine laughed at his fury. Pat knew anger was no replacement for practiced skill, but if his Irish temper could be good for anything, it had to be this, and it had to be now. He swung his broadsword, missed, and swung again.

Christine knew when she was being toyed with.

Omega-Gillian wasn't even trying to win this fight. Christine would already be dead if that was the plague's intent. The avatar was superior, if she'd wanted Christine and Graham dead, they would be.

Instead, the disease was relishing the fight... using it for dramatic purposes... using it as a way to break down the bodies of his victims, before starting on their minds.

That had to be it.

Christine had to find a way to win... she had to find a way to—

She was flying through the air again, so she turned her shoulder to the ground to help her roll when she hit the sand. This would be the end of her first shield...

As she landed, she carefully spun and rolled up onto one knee, her eyes following Graham as he went on the attack.

His anger was fueling him. His hatred... all the pain that had isolated him from her and the universe was now burning, and his speed was remarkable.

Every blow came with a sharp but contained roar of pain, every miss was recovered, and every hit he suffered was shrugged off in silence. Christine couldn't see his face, but she knew that every time he set eyes on his adversary, he could only be getting worse.

Because she'd been his wife, who he now had to kill.

He lunged and traversed, slashed, stabbed...

Then he was tossed through the air, just like that.

Omega-Gillian hopped and clapped gleefully, making herself look like an obscene version of an excited child. Christine didn't wait: she lunged again.

"Here comes the firecracker!" Chuckling, the avatar dodged Christine's first strike. "Jealousy's a hell of a motivator... you really wanted him to be your sugar daddy, right?"

Christine continued to ignore the taunts, continued to fight with all the strength and speed her Earther side could muster.

Continued to miss.

Two blows from Omega-Gillian felled her, one taking her legs out from under her and the second threatening to break her skull. Neither came through the shield, but the shield suffered.

Christine didn't expect it would last much longer... something had to work. Something had to keep them in this long enough to deliver their part of the plan...

Flying through the air after another throw by her adversary, Christine found her mind grasping at straws.

Graham went ahead to fight in her place.

Setter Caine and Andra Ursla hadn't fought together in years, but the old skills were not easily lost.

These two had never been the most formidable hand-to-hand combatants of their race, but they were driven by a great need to do their duties, and their telepathic abilities gave them an edge Earther combatants had never before enjoyed. They coordinated better than even instinct could have allowed, and they could predict and foresee things that would previously have been beyond them.

That, Setter decided, was why Omega-Natosh had not yet been able to fell either of them.

Ursla's great claymore sword was as long as Setter was tall, and it moved with the ease that a proper wolf moved its tail. Setter's own saber was quick and deft, and together their complimenting attacks left Omega-Natosh with no easy recourse.

"Fuck, you've gotten better," the avatar grunted as he dodged and weaved. "Of course, I'm just fucking with you for now. You won't win when we get serious."

Those words dragged a pause into the fight, with Setter and Andra both backing away slowly from their foe, swords still ready.

"And why would you be toying with us? What's the good of making us wait?" Ursla asked the question, knowing it was probably one that the plague had wanted to be asked.

The avatar before them smiled, "It's all about the journey, isn't it? Fuck the destination."

Setter's eyes narrowed, "It's more than that."

"Fuck off."

"He's concentrating in a lot of places at once. And I bet the minions aren't even on the ground out there yet," the Supreme Consul looked up at his big compatriot. "Must take a lot of focus to deal with us now... imagine how much worse it'll be in a minute, when all those minions are crashing into cities, and all those ships in low orbit are focusing on bombarding our shields. *And* our fleet and his fleet are still tangling."

Ursla grinned, "He'll be just a little distracted."

"Fuck you," Omega-Natosh snarled back. "I won't be fucking distracted!"

"Petulant again," Setter shook his head. "You should have thought this through, and killed us early and quick. It's only going to get easier for us now."

"No," the avatar hissed and started forward. "No, you're just going to fucking get to see how your people fucking die!"

Omega-Natosh tried to hit both Earthers, but his attacks missed as the two old Admirals got out of his way. That just piqued his frustration, so he slid to a stop and focused himself.

"You want a fucking good fight, fine. You'll see how stupid wrong you stupid wrong stupid wrong fuckers are!"

Setter cocked an eyebrow at the repetition, wondering if it was a sign he was losing his grip... but then the avatar came on.

Faster than before.

For the first time, both Earthers ended up on the ground. Their shields began to fall.

CHAPTER 46

"Bombardment incoming!"

The roar in the sky over Antarctica was unlike anything ever heard before on Earth — and soon it was heard over cities around the globe. Earthers looked up in open-mouthed shock at the sight and sound as thousands of spines rained down in long streams, and their powerful city shields hummed loudly in resistance.

Emerging onto the ice outside the Antarctic Base Headquarters building, Beckett Lupus looked skyward and shook his head. He'd seen a similar sort of bombardment from the Kroggs during the last war, but this was so much worse.

"Shield's starting to lose a percent every few seconds, sir," a report came into his ear. "This bombardment is *massive*."

The General took a deep breath and nodded, then spoke into his headset, "Save the backup generators for the last shield ring... it'll take him time to pound down the first four."

Varnon Broadpaw appeared next to his son-in-law, his eyes lifted skyward, "By the Earth... that's..."

Beckett nodded, "I know. You should stay inside, continue to command..."

The First Consul looked down and shook his head, "No. No orders left to give now, it's every Earther to the front. Novash and Krag have mobile forces to command... all I can do is fight."

Studying the wolf for a moment, Beckett Lupus acceded, "Stay close to me."

"Right," Varnon said flatly.

Beckett looked back to the base frontier, far across the landing fields, "Confirm with me that they're coming from all sides."

"Roger that, sir. Everywhere."

A circular perimeter had been established all around the base, with five layers of defenses protecting it. Even as the spines screamed down from the sky, energy cannon were roaring back, shooting high to try to silence the bombarding ships, or to burn away falling minions before they hit the ice.

Gunboats by the hundreds continued to swoop over the base, attacking whatever collections of minions they could. As the minions hit the ground, though, they all started charging towards the base.

Moving away from the Headquarters building with Varnon at his side, Beckett climbed the ridge to the artificially-designated 'north' — a ridge that Andra Ursla had once run down, scaring Crusaders and dispatching many in hand-to-hand combat. From this higher position he could see all that was coming.

"They're everywhere," Varnon whispered.

And they were. All around, in every direction, they were coming. There was no single great mass — they were generally quite well spaced — and they just kept coming. As far as the eye could see, there were first tiny black dots, that eventually grew into fast-running monstrosities that had once been human.

They just kept coming.

"When the shields start to go down, we'll keep withdrawing. Use the pulsars to kill as many of them as you can before we have to abandon your positions. Remember to deactivate the guns before you leave them, so he can't use them on us or the glacier," Beckett began making announcements to all his marines. "Volunteer defenders will hold at the inner ring. If he breaks through there, we'll go down to the underground complex, and try to hold there. Let's hope it doesn't come to that."

Even as Beckett said those words, he was hit by a sneaking suspicion that it would come to *exactly* that.

"First shield down to seventy-five percent now, sir. It's not going to last long."

Beckett ground his jaw, then replied, "Understood. The last shield will hold the longest... it'll be the smallest, it'll have all our backup power."

That wasn't actually reassuring, but a flight of gunboats was racing past as a pleasant distraction. Their carronades began slicing minions off the ice, but only a few dozen. The creatures weren't close enough together... Omega had learned lessons at Freetown and Krogg 'A'.

Damn him.

"You should go to the volunteers," Beckett looked back to Varnon. "They'll need you at their head. Stay in touch by comm."

Though he was First Consul and a veteran Admiral, Varnon was more than happy to take orders right now. This was Beckett's party.

And it was about to get bloodier...

The Caine estate seemed quiet.

In the distance overhead, Phealan could hear gunboats making defensive runs to protect the city shield at St. John's, but there was little activity up the coast at the home of the Supreme Consul.

"Think they've missed us, sir?" Lieutenant Ellen Arbear was walking a patrol circuit around the deck that Phealan stood on, and he glanced up at the marine.

"I certainly hope so, but I doubt that'll last. How many minions did he drop on St. John's?"

Arbear shook her head, "No one got a clear count, though I heard someone estimate about 50,000. Not too many."

"They're probably all focusing on Halifax, trying to get Admiralty House," Joyce Furgus appeared next to her Lieutenant, then nodded to Phealan. "But they'll soon figure out you're here. Any word on the timeline?"

Phealan's eyes narrowed as he reached out with his mind, connected silently with his father, and checked progress.

"I think... I think they'll be delivering the cure soon."

"Ahm," was Joyce's response. "So we have a while to wait yet."

Ellen Arbear cocked an eyebrow, "Let's hope everything works as it should."

Phealan's ear twitched, but before he could reply, Cadmus Howler joined them on the deck, his face grim.

"Joyce, just heard on comm: *Aboukir* is down. No word on pods."

The lioness Captain blinked at her Colonel's words, and Ellen put a hand on her shoulder. It was quite possible that her father was now dead.

"Esther's still alright, Ellen... for as long as that lasts," Cadmus completed his news, then fell silent.

There was no need for anyone to offer condolences: Joyce wouldn't have accepted them had anyone tried. Today, every Earther would lose someone, perhaps themselves. Jax Furgus, presumably, was now among the dead.

He may not be, but either way, I'm glad his daughter's here protecting us.

Joyce looked at Phealan as his thoughts entered her mind. After a moment, she nodded very slowly, "I should get back to my rounds."

"Me as well," Ellen Arbear agreed.

The pair moved off together, leaving Cadmus Howler next to Phealan, both wolves looking back out over the crisp Newfoundland night. A little snow had fallen before the clouds had moved off, and now it reflected the moonlight with a peaceful glow.

"They'll be coming soon, to answer your question," Cadmus said after a moment. "I got word from Brigadier Fish in St. John's... their sensors have at least 1,000 minions moving out this way."

Phealan nodded slowly, "Think he knows we're here?"

The elite Colonel of 2/54th paused before shaking his head, "It'd be more than 1,000 if he did. It's probably just a sweep... but he'll find us. And when he does, more will show up pretty quickly."

So they had a little time... perhaps enough...

"Listen, Phealan," Cadmus turned towards the young Caine, and the two wolves' eyes met. "If they break through our line, I'm attaching my old recon squad to you as personal guards. If they overrun our shields, you all need to make a run for it. You know this land… you can find a place, right? Survive until the moment?"

Until the moment…

"Yes," the young Caine agreed. "There's a clearing where my dad and I always went, up on the hill back there. And there's the beach. That's closer."

Cadmus Howler nodded, "Good. We'll buy you all the time we can…"

"And Claire… do everything you can to keep them out of the house."

The Colonel nodded, "We absolutely will. And if you could get her to hide in a lower level, behind a shield maybe… that might do it. They won't be looking for her, but if it's close to the moment…"

"They'll be after me," Phealan agreed. "I'll keep on the move."

That was all he could do.

Omega would be here soon…

CHAPTER 47

Artemis Tigar clutched the sides of *Agamemnon's* plot with all the strength his new limbs could offer. Things were not going well.

"Rear Admiral Maximane hailing!" the Signal Officer had to bellow over the moan of twisting metal as the great old First Rate writhed and absorbed a salvo of spines.

"In the plot!" Artie called back.

Agamemnon started to explode before he got a chance to see the signal.

"By the Earth... *Agamemnon's* breaking up!" Mel Ramsay had to pull herself around the edge of *Galahad's* plot because the ship was bucking too much for her to walk unassisted.

As she reached Minnie Maximane's side, the lioness Admiral started shaking her head, "Dammit. Signal all Admiral Tigar's ships to join my squadron!"

That order was the same one she had been planning to suggest to Artie — that they combine their two battered formations.

Omega was pressing in so close now... even if their formations merged, there'd be fewer than forty ships in this group, most of them of *Galahad's* vintage.

"Pull us in close to the *Venerable* squadrons... who else is left?" Minnie was struggling to keep track of all the icons in the plot as she clung to it, and Mel Ramsay used her slightly better angle to get a look.

"The Larosians... down to forty ships... Kroggs... down to about 400... all the *Venerables* are still there... aside from us... another fifty maybe."

It was too few.

"Omega... he's just dipping towards 2,000 now..."

The numbers were so massive. It felt impossible to track them all... but Minnie knew she had to try...

Galahad bucked hard, and Minnie Maximane and Mel Ramsay held fast.

Novash picked himself up off the floor of *Lycrotar's* bridge deck, suppressing the stab of pain that came from his chest. There was a piece of alloy sticking out of his armor — a piece of shrapnel released when the Warcruiser had taken that last hit...

Admiral-of-a-Division, are you alright?

That question came from one of the bridge officers, but Novash waved the questioner away.

I believe it is fatal, but it may not be. If it is, I will still have time. Report status!

We are suffering massive casualties now, sir. We have lost most of the Battleships.

What Omega had done here was as impressive as Novash had expected it to be — he'd fallen upon the Larosian Fleet, and despite the mighty armor and powerful antimatter guns of the old Battleships, they'd been picked apart.

Now only the Warcruisers — the fast and deadly survivors — remained.

Signal from the Earther flagship, sir.

Novash acknowledged that alert and opened his mind to the feed. Lab Forepaw appeared, still broadcasting his signal through energy comms and the translation buffer instead of telepathically. The Earthers likely weren't used to using their minds to pass on orders in combat…

"Novash, pull your ships in tight with Minnie Maximane's group, then collapse towards us. We'll all fold in together."

"Understood, moving now," Novash answered verbally, making certain not to reveal the discomfort of his wound.

Lycrotar trembled as more spines pounded its armor, but as Lab's signal faded, Novash was still able to order the ship, and its squadron, into flight.

Death was bleeding slowly into space, but the mighty Krogg ship continued to fight with all the anger of its race. The Kroggs were not easy to defeat, and Omega was rapidly discovering that even when they were defending someone else's home, they were most formidable…

Signal from First Lord Forepaw… he requests all ships close formation on his squadrons and combine maximum defensive fire.

That report almost surprised Warlord Kardrath as he stood upon *Death's* bridge, but he was able to stop himself short of questioning it. Lab Forepaw was, of course, correct: Omega had worn down the older Earther ships, the old Larosian ships, and was even succeeding in wearing down the Krogg Fleet.

It was 2,000 plague ships against barely 700 Allied vessels. They needed to stand together.

Order all ships to collapse back to final defensive positions. We will make our last stand amongst our friends!

"They're all on their way in… I expect it's going to get very hot here now," Fox Magnus said in *Venerable's* plot. Next to the projection of the diminutive First Space Lord, the image of Chronos Claw shared the sentiment.

"He's worn down everything but us now," Claw agreed.

Lab Forepaw stared at the two, his hands linked behind his back. *Venerable*, like all the ships of its class, remained strangely uncommitted — its guns were firing faster than any on the older ships, it was turning faster, and its weight of shot was spectacular... but it still felt insulated from the fight.

Now, though, Omega had no other targets to turn on. His full fury would be coming here.

"Artie, Dran, Jax, Ami and Zed are gone," Fox listed the missing, and he didn't need to say that he hoped some had escaped to their lifepods. Though Omega might not let lifepods survive... there was no telling.

"Omega overwhelmed the Larosian battlewagons," Chronos added. "And the Kroggs are hurting. They're not well suited to sitting still and shooting either."

Lab nodded at the observations, "Well. It'll be down to us then."

"Yes it will," Fox agreed.

"See how we weather the storm," Chronos added.

They would see — it would become very apparent soon enough...

"They're all collapsing back to the *Venerables* up there!"

That shout drew Ed Jeffries' attention for just a second, but immediately he looked back to the screen. The minions... over 100 million of them... were on Antarctica and raging towards the base, and because the continent was covered in ice Ed didn't want to chance too heavy a ground bombardment. No missiles, long carronades only — and even then, set on low power...

"Sir, looks like one of the black wave ships has noticed us!"

Ed frowned and his eyes darted to another screen beside the main one. Sure enough, one of the black wave vessels that had been sending streams of spines at the base shield was now closing with *Savanna Felix*.

Garth Badger was suddenly beside the human skipper, "We better move off. If we get shot down over the base..."

Nodding quickly, Ed came out of his chair, "Orders to squadron, redeploy immediately — get out over the oceans in case we get shot down!"

The signal went out, but it became clear that at their low altitude, pushing loudly through the atmosphere, the advanced Battlecruisers of the Freetown Navy weren't as fast as Omega's ships.

This particular plague vessel was looking to shoot down either *Savanna Felix* or *Fox Magnus* over Antarctica...

Ed made a decision.

"Helm, take us right at this bastard. We'll delay him while *Magnus* gets clear."

He was pretty certain *Savanna Felix* was going to die in battle today.

It wouldn't be the first time...

CHAPTER 48

Sarah realized her shield had collapsed because she felt the full impact of the ground when she hit it.

"My shield's gone!" she grunted so that Pat would know the situation, scuttling back from Omega-Paine as she did. The Irishman — whose shield was somehow still holding — did everything he could to keep the avatar busy.

Dammit, too soon... I should have been better!

Reaching for her backpack, Sarah tried to stop her inner scolding. Among other things, she was carrying an extra wrist shield — an extra ten minutes of fighting at this rate — but she'd never been certain she'd have time to put it on with an avatar bearing down on her.

Pat was doing everything he could to give her the chance.

The Irishman lunged and swung, then recovered with speed and determination, then lunged again and swung faster...

Too slow. Omega-Paine's blow to his back knocked him flat on the ground, and just as Sarah managed to get her shield band out of her backpack, she heard Pat scream: the avatar's foot was on his back — not on his shield, but on the riot gear vest covering his *back*.

Her eyes locked onto her husband, and horror shot through her.

Pat.

The Irishman was gritting his teeth against his scream, but the inhuman pressure of Omega-Paine's powerful leg was close to severing his spine...

"I'll make you a deal," the avatar sounded chipper, and it took Sarah a second to realize it was talking to her. "Take off your helmet. Take off your riot vest. Let me into your mind, and I'll let him live. For a little longer."

Sarah had a shield in her hand now. She could put it on, she could fight Omega again... alone. That would be tough, but it was the mission. It was what she had to do. She had to keep fighting him, wait for the moment... Pat was expendable.

It was all she had to do.

But no part of her could do it.

It's why I had to keep my distance from him. It's why I shouldn't have let him come here. I can't let him die like this. I never could let him go. Not him.

Pat tried to grunt something defiant, but the wind was pressed from his lungs. As the oxygen flow slowed, he struggled, but then fell unconscious.

"Patrick!" Sarah struggled upward, the shield falling from her hand. She left her sword on the ground too.

"He's got a few more seconds before I crush him," Omega-Paine offered helpfully.

Sarah said nothing, she simply removed her helmet, and then her vest.

The fate of the universe is at stake, and you give it up for hubby. I'll give you credit, you're fucking consistent. Gibraltar to here, you're an emotional fuckup.

Sarah cringed as Omega's thoughts penetrated her mind. The avatar stepped off Pat and then kicked the Irishman's limp body away with disdain. Turning back to Sarah, he wore a hungry grin, and he approached her with a slow gait.

"See, now we can have fun. *This* is why I let you come here. If I hadn't, you'd probably get blown up on some damned ship, and I wouldn't get a taste. This is *so* worth the hassle..." Omega-Paine came to a stop right in front of Sarah.

She tried to step back, but realized she couldn't. She didn't control her own body anymore. She'd taken off her Genesis ore protection, and as he'd done on *Genesis One* and Freetown, the plague avatar now held control.

There was no point struggling. He stepped in closer to her — this creature that looked like Thomas Paine with black eyes — and she felt his breath starting to graze her neck.

Revulsion bubbled through her. This creature, and his host, had destroyed her world... been responsible for the death of almost everything she truly cared about.

And she was impotent to stop him now.

Her eyes darted over Omega-Paine's shoulders, and she caught a glimpse of Pat lying face down at the edge of the circle of light. She couldn't tell if he was breathing, but as the desperation crawled up her skin, she wished he would. She wished he'd stand up and come help her.

She didn't want this... but she had to accept it. This bought Pat one more chance to live. Maybe if Omega-Paine was busy torturing her body... the way he'd tortured Audrey DeBrooke... maybe Pat could win. Somehow. Maybe Pat could still live...

I wouldn't count on that, Omega-Natosh sneered in her mind, then switched to spoken words, "And why would I carve you up like I did Audrey? Much more fun to take my time, since you're not as resigned as she was. And let's be honest, it's fitting — who better to have his hands on you than a Paine. And, of course, it was your decision to give me the chance. Poor Sarah, always making the wrong decisions. For the wrong reasons. Don't you ever get sick of being so completely useless?"

Sarah couldn't scream, she couldn't yell. Words wouldn't come out of her mouth — it was locked by Omega's mind. But even if she could have made her vocal chords work, she didn't know what she'd say.

Except, perhaps, that she thought he was right. She'd been wrong about everything for so very long.

Now she'd pay for it.

Omega-Paine's fingertips reached her neck.

Graham landed at Christine's feet, and she checked to make sure his shield was still running. It was — he still had time. Christine's second shield was near its minimum, but she should be able to last a little longer.

The important thing was that they were still fighting, and that Graham's cool desire to kill the thing in his wife's body hadn't faded...

He sat up slowly, but he was too stunned by his latest landing to get immediately back to his feet. Christine caught his attention, "I'll hold her for a minute."

With that, she leapt forward again, and found Omega-Gillian was grinning at her, "Listen to noble and mature little Christine. You think if you show you're a grown up, then he'll want you?"

Christine's answer to that came with the lunge of her saber, and again she missed. Omega-Gillian laughed sharply, and then did something new: she grabbed Christine and *held* her. For a second the young human didn't realize what was happening, but then she felt pressure like a vice squeezing her waist. She could almost *feel* the energy draining from her shield.

She struggled, contorting her body violently to get away, but Omega-Gillian had her locked in tight.

Oh Gods, if I lose this shield...

Seconds later, it winked out, and Omega-Gillian released Christine with a whoop.

"There we go, now it's fun time."

Christine staggered to the side and dropped to one knee, trying to keep her saber in the air as some sort of protection.

"Get back, get another shield!" Graham called to her as he charged in, but Omega-Gillian wasn't holding much back now.

As Graham landed hard on the sand even further away than before, Christine managed to get both legs under her. She got her stance back as best she could, and stared at the avatar over her sword. Her heart pounded, and only the Earther in her kept absolute panic from taking over.

She'd been here to look after Graham... now she was about to die.

Omega-Gillian moved, and Christine swung her saber as quickly as she could to get in the way. There was virtually no chance of her surviving this next engagement without an energy shield protecting her...

The saber was wrenched from her hand — she didn't see how.

Then Omega-Gillian was behind her, pulling her into a tight embrace from behind. Christine's head was abruptly next to the avatar's face, her temple pressing into Omega-Gillian's cheek. Wearing a wide grin, the plague creature locked Christine into that position with one arm tight across her neck, jamming back her chin.

Then the avatar's other hand started tracing up and down the sides of Christine's armor.

"This Larosian kit is really impressive, I'm not going to lie," Omega-Gillian repeated that sentiment. Then her fingers found the pressure points that released the molecular bond that held the front and back halves of the armor together.

Christine struggled again, but the pressure on her throat denied her much movement. She realized now that the plague had her, and worse than killing her, it meant to get into her mind. Would her new Earther side be enough to stave off the attack...

Not likely...

The arm came away from her neck, and she was flung forward into the sand. For a second she thought she had a reprieve — that Graham had come to her aid — but then she realized her armor had been torn from her in the process.

She was defenseless...

Against me, Omega-Gillian inserted the thought for her.

Christine looked down the beach. Graham was far away, and he still hadn't gotten up. She needed him right now — she needed all the skill and cold fury he'd built up...

"He doesn't really care about you, though, does he?" Omega-Gillian knelt in the sand next to Christine, then placed a hand on the girl's back in a mockery of comfort. "He's never even noticed you. Though looking at your thoughts, I see you've been denying that you have any feelings for him. That's either stupid or noble... but you realize, he doesn't feel anything for you. You're going to die here, and leave your sister all alone, for a man who doesn't give a fuck about you."

Christine gritted her teeth and tried to push herself up off the ground, but Omega-Gillian's physical strength was too much to overcome.

"There there," the plague mocked again, gently rubbing Christine's back.

The young human was about to struggle again when she realized abruptly what was going to happen next. Omega-Gillian's fingers began to play on the back of Christine's neck, caressing it gently, trying to tickle the stasis-numbed area... and then stopping on the stasis patch that controlled her suit.

"Oh Gods—"

Christine couldn't get out any more than that before the patch was ripped away.

The residual energy flowing through her suit meant the pain didn't come back all at once... but Omega-Gillian wasn't finished. She rolled Christine over in the sand and unzipped the front just past her collar bones.

Smiling, the avatar then took a handful of sand and sprinkled it on the exposed skin.

The screaming was so loud and ferocious it shook Graham out of his shock down the beach. He struggled to his feet and staggered towards Omega-Gillian... just in time to see his once-wife toss Christine into the waves.

Lying on her back as the waves rolled over her, Christine couldn't stop screaming. The sound cut through Graham like daggers. He ran, but it was too late... she couldn't stop screaming. The pain would have knocked a normal person unconscious, but as had happened when the change started back on *Carnarvon*, Christine's brain didn't react normally. She stayed conscious. All the water that ran over her suit and her body was like liquid fire. It was enough to shatter a mind.

Christine Schaeffer would be better off dead.

But, of course, Omega wouldn't make it that easy.

CHAPTER 49

Savanna Felix had the best shields ever mounted aboard a human-crewed vessel, and they bore up against a lot of punishment. As the Omega ship's spines continued to batter its forward quarter, the advanced Battlecruiser came on angrily, firing its long carronades.

"Looks like it lost some of its maneuverability in the atmosphere," one of the Sensor Officers called, and Ed nodded as his ship shuddered again.

"Missiles, full spread," he said.

The warheads raced out, roaring through the atmosphere seventy kilometers above Antarctica. They were shot down well short of their target, though, and Jeffries cursed openly.

"Neuro pulses..." the warning trailed off as *Felix* was buffeted by the impact of the cackling energy weapons.

This might almost be an even duel, thanks to the atmosphere. Maybe *Felix* could survive it...

"Look at that, sir!" one of the marines of the Guards Brigade pointed skyward, and Beckett Lupus followed the finger.

Way up high were the small, clear silhouettes of two large warships hammering each other. It wasn't the first time Beckett had seen such a thing...

"Second shield is about to go!"

That call was from the ground, and it drew Lupus' attention back to more immediate affairs. The base was still being bombarded by other ships in higher orbits, and there had to be a million minions right up against the perimeter now too.

Pulsars and carronades were firing to sweep as many of the creatures away as was possible, but more and more kept coming. The gunboats were still making runs, seemingly unscathed by orbital fire so far, but more minions filled the swathes cut by the air strikes.

"Withdraw to the third line, all marines!" Beckett called, and then joining the wolves, cats and bears of the Guards Brigade of the Heavy Division, he turned away from the front and sprinted for the next line of shields and gun emplacements.

It took the Earthers crewing the heavy weapons a few seconds to follow, as they needed to remove the command consoles that ran the guns, but they too made it away cleanly. The second shield fell, and the minions sprinted closer to the base... but a new wall of energy stood in front of them.

And each wall was a little stronger than the one before it, because it covered a smaller area with the same amount of power.

Beckett didn't need to give any orders: his marines simply started firing again. Everything they had — rifles, pulsars, guns... fire from all of them swept out over the ice and killed more minions. But never enough.

Joining in the assault, Beckett forgot the troubles above.

"Shields... *down!*"

Ed Jeffries struggled back to his chair, "Get us over the ocean, keep up all fire!"

Savanna Felix turned towards the coast and began to push its drives, but the black wave ship — still largely intact despite the gun duel — hit the advanced Battlecruiser hard, and then dispatched spines to hammer its engines.

Ed was thrown from his chair, and on the ship's bridge, only Garth Badger was able to keep his feet with typical Earther balance.

"Oh fuck Gods, we're going *down!*" someone cried out.

Badger helped Ed to his feet, and then they both watched the screen, open-mouthed, as the Freetown ship dropped its nose towards the ice and started a kamikaze dive... right towards Antarctic Base.

"Omega must have done this on purpose," Ed breathed.

A whole Battlecruiser... a battering ram that would crush even a city shield... maybe all three of the layers that remained.

Oh Gods.

"All gunboats, this is Badger, open fire on *Felix* — break the hull up before it hits the shield!" the Lieutenant was beyond worrying about the fate of the ship on which he stood. Thinking only of the base, he tapped his headset again, "Antarctic Base, we're dropping right on you. Prepare for massive impact!"

Ed Jeffries let out a long breath, his eyes fixed on the screen, "I thought some of us would survive."

Badger didn't look at him, but he answered, "Some of us will, sir. Maybe just not you and me."

All the human could do was nod at that.

Varnia Lupus remained silent on *Renown's* bridge as she watched *Felix* fall through the sky towards her husband's position. There was absolutely nothing she could do... she just had to hope the shield held.

Around the planet, the other Freetown Battlecruisers had already been shot down, all of them ending up in the ocean. But this wouldn't be an ocean impact; the entire ice shelf of Antarctica could melt if the blast was big enough.

Varnia closed her eyes. It seemed as though the ship was taking forever to fall...

• • •

Beckett Lupus looked up, and saw the dot in the sky grow bigger and bigger.

"Get as many people into the bunkers and buildings as you can. Activate all backups and prep the inner shield dome. All marines retreat to the last line!"

The General joined his marines — the elite Guards all around him — as they abandoned their carefully-prepared positions at the third line to fall back to the last one.

Their only chance was that the third- and fourth-line city shields would absorb most of the impact, leaving the fifth and final line intact. Then they'd be alright...

Not true. Then we'll be down to one defensive line against millions of minions.

Beckett ignored the reality check and focused on sprinting. They'd make it. They'd beat the falling ship to the inner perimeter. Beckett was almost there. He could see Varnon Broadpaw waving them in, and parts of the shield beginning to go up where marines had already gone through.

For a moment this whole situation struck Beckett as surreal. He could barely even remember fighting minions... it felt like everything that was going on here was so much bigger than anything he'd ever seen before...

He ignored that feeling too, and tapped his headset, "Lupus to Kragran and Kragthar. We're probably going to need every warrior you've got at Antarctica. We're going to lose our shield before anyone else."

"Understood."

Beckett slid across the inner perimeter and as the last marines from the Guards Brigade of the Heavy Division crossed behind him, the shield rocketed up.

The deafening roar of a falling Battlecruiser then drew all eyes skyward. Gunboats were making rapid passes, trying to blow the ship into more manageable chunks, but there was so little time...

Savanna Felix hit Antarctic Base mostly intact, but didn't explode. The great kinetic energy of the impact shattered the third shield instantly, the fourth shield milliseconds after, and then slammed into the fifth shield with a concussion not seen on the planet since the destruction of London and the British Isles.

But this time, the ship wasn't moving at anything approaching light speed, and it didn't detonate.

Every energy reactor beneath Antarctic Base groaned under the massive pressure, but the shield didn't fall. Instead the Battlecruiser — a modest ship by space standards, but quite massive on the ground — slewed sideways off the dome, its momentum causing it to skid over the ridge that Beckett had climbed minutes before, and sending it sliding over thousands of approaching minions before it came to a stop miles away.

Beckett Lupus actually managed to smile at that, and then he looked at his father-in-law, who'd appeared nearby, "How about Earther engineering."

Varnon Broadpaw grinned and nodded, "We sure do build them tough."

"The shield's at *four* percent, they'll be through any second!"

That call came over the comm, and it removed the smiles from Beckett's and Varnon's faces. There was no time to prepare — the marines turned to the shield perimeter, and the half a million Earther volunteers who'd been waiting there for their turn to fight suddenly found the battle was upon them.

A volley of spines felled the shield, and the minions came on.

As Beckett switched to his sword, he wondered how long they'd last.

CHAPTER 50

Setter Caine slid to a stop, his mind reaching back to Earth and finding much destruction. He then peered in on Freetown, and saw Christine Schaeffer writhing in agony. He looked last at Ecclesia, and saw Omega-Paine trying to destroy Sarah's soul.

His ability to go to those places through his telepathy was a gift, but it was an incredibly painful one.

"They're folding everywhere," he said aloud, drawing Ursla's attention.

She'd been engaging Omega-Natosh, keeping him busy, but now she fell back.

"My last shield's nearly done," she said as she came to a stop next to her friend. "It time?"

Setter blinked once, then again. He looked across the bloodied ground of the Genesis War Memorial at Omega-Natosh, and the avatar grinned back at him. The plague had been harder-pressed here than anywhere else, but even now, Setter knew the monster had reserves of strength that were yet to be seen.

If they tried to hit him with the injector gun, it would likely be the last thing they did.

Ursla was looking down at Setter, her breathing a little heavy. Never before had she fought like this... never had her great strength and speed been tested as it was being tested now, against the avatar. But she was ready for it... everything she had done, and everything she'd ever been, had prepared her.

"I can do it," she said simply. "I can do it on my own."

Setter looked up at her, and he wanted to shake his head, but he couldn't.

"Let her try, come on," Omega-Natosh called across the distance between them. "Come on, it'll make for an awesome fucking piece of melodrama."

Ursla smiled thinly, "See, even he knows it has to be done. You get on the line with Phealan and let him know... and I'll try it. I'll get a piece of him, and if need be, you can finish it off..."

Setter looked quickly back at the avatar. Omega-Natosh was letting them talk — he clearly wasn't afraid of either of them. He didn't care to stop their plotting. The arrogant plague thought he was invulnerable.

Maybe he was.

The gravity of this moment was starting to hit Setter, though, and it was harder than he'd expected. He was asking Andra Ursla, his dearest and best friend of all, to die. It was necessary, but it could never be *easy*.

Hey, you're not asking, I'm asking you, she thought to him, and her smile widened.

It didn't surprise him that she was ready to do this — and to do it in good spirits — but it still hurt.

"Oh get the fuck over yourself, Setter," Omega-Natosh taunted. "You're always acting so holier-than-thou. Let the big bitch try her luck."

Setter swallowed, then stuck out his hand to Ursla. Her smile widened a little bit more, and she took his hand, their shields recognizing each other and merging briefly to let the hands connect.

"Always a privilege," she said. "Make sure to finish him off."

"Count on it," Setter replied. "Good hunting."

Ursla turned back towards Omega-Natosh, and then, with more speed than she'd yet used on the day, she was beside him.

Her sword was swinging, getting set to cut him in half, but the avatar was ready, and was away from her before she could adjust.

"Using your telepathy to speed things up? That's pretty canny for a newb," the plague creature observed from a safe distance.

Ursla chased him again, and this time her sword nearly caught him. She wheeled quickly as he ducked aside, then she dodged two of his counterstrikes before the third one took her full on the chest. That one cracked the last of her shield, and she skidded back over the bloody ground.

Righting herself quickly, she leapt to her feet. She was a massive bear, three meters tall, and yet she was so fast and agile. Today, too, she was driven by the fate of her home, and of her friends. Everything that mattered in the universe was pushing her on, so when she lunged forward again, Omega-Natosh had to step back and right his balance, unable to counter.

It was that second's hesitation that gave her a chance.

The injector gun came our of her pack in a single fluid motion.

Omega-Natosh saw it coming, and moved to counter before it hit him, but he'd mistimed his maneuver.

Setter watched, almost feeling as though it were in slow motion. His breath caught, and he wondered whether she could do it... could she connect...

He reached out with his mind in the same second, and locked onto his son, *Ursla's about to hit him with the cure.*

Standing on his deck outside the Caine house, Phealan looked to the stars, his eyes instantly filling with a swirling blue light. His mind harnessed his father's message, and then passed it on to every open mind in the solar system around him.

Ursla is hitting Omega with the cure.

• • •

The split second between the beginning of the stroke that would hit Omega with the injection, and the actual injection itself, seemed eternal.

In his mind, Setter could see Earthers dying in space and on Earth. He could see Sarah and Christine in need of saving. All of that desperation... it all made the second endless.

And then Ursla's massive strength rammed the injector into Omega-Natosh's stomach, and there was a thunderously quiet hiss as the compound entered the avatar.

In the same second, the avatar's fist drove right through Ursla's beating heart.

They staggered apart, and Ursla turned away with a smile. She stumbled towards Setter — one step, then another. She fell to one knee, then forward. She propped herself up with her arms, and held her head up to her friend.

I'm dead now, she thought to him. She was using the last of her telepathic strength to animate her own corpse. *Good luck.*

She let go, and her body pitched forward to add its blood to the ground.

The cure has been delivered, Setter alerted his son, and the word was spread.

Setter stared at Ursla for a long second, then looked up at Omega-Natosh.

The avatar staggered one way, then the other, as though he was drunk.

Falling to one knee, he clutched his stomach, "What... what was that?"

Setter moved a little closer, "Elandra started developing it before you killed her. Celia Lazarus finished it. It's a flux-compound, using Christine Schaeffer's blood as a carrier."

The avatar's chin dropped, and he stared at the ground, "Little Christine... little Christine."

In his bloodstream, the cure compound began to spread.

CHAPTER 51

"Minions!"

Phealan blinked the swirling blue light from his eyes just as the warning reached his ears. The cure had been injected, and he'd pushed that notification out to every open mind he could find... but now minions were reaching the estate. There wasn't a whole lot more time...

Moving over to the rail of the deck, the young Caine saw flashes of light from energy rifles firing in the distant woods. From his higher position, he couldn't see down through the brush, but the bright bolts of energy were lighting up the night.

Cadmus Howler was beside him then, unslinging his rifle, "Cure delivered, right?"

"Yes. And Andra's dead," Phealan confirmed, unable to contain his regret at the last point.

The Colonel didn't allow himself to react to that, "So... how long?"

Phealan shook his head, "Can't say... will probably need a fair bit of time, though. Things will get worse here before they get better."

Nodding slowly, Cadmus looked past Phealan and waved a squad of marines up onto the deck, "Alright. Joyce Furgus' company is in charge of protecting the house. She'll defend this place as though you're in it... and because Claire is in there. Sergeant Ernile Cuttar and this squad will be with you at all times. If I give the word, take off."

Phealan's eyes moved between those of the wolves of Cadmus Howler's and Beckett Lupus' former squad — a team of Earthers whose reputation was unmatched.

"Thank you — all of you," the young Caine said.

Sergeant Cuttar nodded, "Our privilege to be here, sir."

Not knowing what to say to that, Phealan turned back to Cadmus, extending his hand, "And thank you, Colonel."

The wolf took the hand, then nodded, "My privilege too. I'll see you later, perhaps."

Then the Colonel descended the stairs from the deck, and began rallying more of his marines to join the defense of the estate shield.

Turning back to the house, Phealan saw Claire standing at the glass wall, looking out with wide eyes at the flashes in the night. He moved to the door and stepped inside quickly, then went over to her side.

"You need to go downstairs, to the bottom level, and lock yourself in the bunker room. Put up the shield. They're not going to be looking for you here... so if you stay there, and stay quiet, you'll be safe... at least for a while."

Claire stared at him, her defiance having long since disappeared, "All alone?"

"Nothing else for it," Phealan said. "All the Earthers must be out here. It's our only chance of actually winning today."

She blinked a couple of times, and Phealan expected a protest... but then, without another word, she turned and headed toward the stairs.

Looking at her back, Phealan felt a pang of sadness, so he called out to her one more time, "Claire... been an honor to know you. We've been lucky to have you around here."

Claire stopped, and Phealan wondered if he'd said something wrong, or she hadn't believed him. He started to reach towards her with his mind, but before he could she turned. She couldn't say anything, and she tried to wipe tears away with her sleeve, but her message was clear enough. She actually did like it here. She actually *had* benefited, despite all her anger and her refusal to settle in.

Phealan smiled, "Keep yourself safe."

She nodded jaggedly, then headed down the stairs.

Taking a deep breath, Phealan turned back for the door. How long...?

Beckett Lupus hadn't seen such chaos since the last battle on the Antarctic Plain. All through the Krogg War, the Earther Marine Corps had always been able to keep its formations neat. Even against the Queen on Krogg 'A', the battle had been closely controlled. He hadn't witnessed the chaos on Freetown or in the recent fight for the Krogg homeworld, but somehow he doubted they compared.

Earther marines and Earther volunteers were mixed together, over half a million combatants in a single great mass surrounding the bunkers and the buildings at the core of Antarctic Base. All around them, minions were coming on in droves.

The gunboats overhead had better targets now because the minions were packing closer together, but still... someone had said there were 100 million minions on the continent. Each Earther here would have to kill 200 to survive.

And that wasn't likely to happen.

But they'd fight for as long as they could...

"The cure's delivered!" Varnon Broadpaw was swinging his sword hurriedly, but his mind had managed to pick up that news from Phealan. He broadcast it loudly with his own thoughts, making sure every Earther on the Antarctic Plain heard it too.

Beckett managed to smile, cutting two minions in half while he did, "Good news."

He didn't get a chance to say any more: he was a popular target, and more minions threw themselves at him.

Perhaps it wasn't so different than that battle against the Queen's Guard. Beckett was fighting, buying time, waiting for something far away to change the tide of the battle...

"We can't handle too much more of this..." Varnon grunted. "But I think we're the only shield down. I think the others are still up for now."

Beckett didn't make any sounds of acknow-ledgement: a cluster came at him, so he went straight at them.

With his trademark pair of short swords, the elite General worked hard and fast. One came, and the left sword took its head, then the right sword cut another in half. He turned sharply, crouched, then raised himself, bringing both swords up on opposing vectors, slicing two more in half. He turned again, spun, and parted more minions from their waists...

The tide, though, was unending.

How many more?

On Ecclesia Sarah was allowed to scream. She tried not to, but it was impossible. She'd never thought pain like this was possible.

Only somewhere, back in the deeper recesses of her mind, did she hear a little voice: *The cure's been delivered.*

Christine's screams had died away, her vocal chords perhaps destroyed by the agonizing sound. Graham didn't know for sure... he hoped that somehow her mind had just let her go unconscious, or that she'd simply died.

He didn't have time to reflect on that hope, though: he attacked again, preparing to use up the last of his shield strength.

Then, in the back of his mind came a small voice from Phealan Caine: *The cure's been delivered.*

Venerable bucked more violently than it had so far in this engagement, but it remained largely stable. The mighty ship was virtually unassailable in its massive, powerful formation.

Standing on its bridge, Lab Forepaw couldn't help but look to the planet below. Minions everywhere, Antarctica now a complete brawl. Other cities' shields still holding... but not for much longer.

But the cure had been delivered.

Maybe... soon...

Venerable bucked again.

CHAPTER 52

Omega-Natosh was on one knee, clutching his stomach with one hand while the other propped him up.

"Little Christine..." he said for the third time.

Then, as Setter watched, he jerked back, clutching his throat and making a gagging sound. He writhed for a minute, then flung himself backward.

Setter watched with narrowed eyes.

Flailing on his back, the avatar fell still, his tongue lolling out the side of his open mouth.

Reaching out with his mind, Setter checked on his adversary. Then he took a deep breath, and collected himself, "I didn't think Larosians had tongues."

For a second, the avatar didn't answer, but then he decided to stop acting. His head came up, and his tongue pulled in, "I added one. Too much?"

Setter ground his jaw. He was trying to contain his anger, but he knew it was clear on his face. It was impossible to watch Andra die and not feel fury...

"So," Omega-Natosh sat up, dusting himself off rather absurdly, "let me get this straight. Your big plan was to get close and hit me with a shitty compound of fluxed cells from a clumsy girl with genetic defects that you caused? Even if, by some miracle, that 'cure' actually hurt me, how the fuck did you expect it to wander down through the trillions of other me's? Seriously, virus into the Mothership? Just asking."

Setter's breathing became sharper.

"You figured it wouldn't work, but you had to try. Typical Earther fuckup... though I'm not going to complain," Omega-Natosh hopped to his feet. "If you hadn't tried, I wouldn't have my hands in Sarah Manchester right now. You ever squeezed someone's kidney from inside her body? It's *awesome*. And young Christine is quite dead."

"I've seen," Setter replied, his dry words were quiet.

Omega-Natosh dusted off his hands, then stood staring at Setter, "So, you have a plan B, I'm sure. You'll probably try to fight me to the death, right? Or, because you're the big scary powerful Earther leader, maybe you'll try to use your telepathy to wipe me out."

Setter's anger was becoming less contained.

"You can try, wolf boy, but let's be clear: there's no mind as strong as mine. You fancy your chances?"

Setter blinked, and then his mind catapulted him to the telepathic plane. He found himself surrounded by whiteness, and watched as Omega-Natosh joined him.

"And don't think having any help would make a difference," the plague added. "I'm bigger than all the brains your side has left. Period."

Turning his thoughts away from the avatar for a second, Setter warned his son, *The cure failed completely.*

Then he looked back at the plague, "Let's start small then. Just you and me."

"Works," Omega-Natosh nodded, and what looked like a bolt of black lightning slammed into Setter Caine's chest.

He'd never fought a telepathic battle before, but that seemed to him like a bad start.

Phealan blinked as the news reached his mind, and then he looked to Sergeant Cuttar, "We're going to have to move soon."

The minions were piling up against the estate shield — it wasn't nearly as strong as a city shield, and soon it would fail. And apparently, the cure had too...

Phealan put aside thoughts of his current position just long enough to pass that thought along. The Earthers were going to have to win this the hard way — or not at all...

"We'll head for the beach. If we need to run further, there's a route from there to the clearing."

Cuttar nodded, and Phealan took a breath.

This really was going to get worse before it got any better.

Beckett staggered for a brief second as feet rammed into his back, but as he did, his father-in-law was right there, along with three other Earthers. Though Omega still had the edge in numbers here, it wasn't as it had been on Freetown — it wasn't *thousands* to one. The Earthers were staying close together, and they couldn't be picked off easily...

Turning, Beckett raised his swords to begin the fight anew. Varnon caught his eye, and the First Consul was smiling.

Then he was torn in half.

Beckett's eyes went wide. He hadn't seen his father-in-law's shield go down. He hadn't realized...

Varnon's torso landed at Beckett's feet, and the wolf was still breathing, a smile on his face.

He reached out to Beckett's foot with one hand, then managed to catch his eye.

"Survive," he rasped. "Give Varnia my love."

He died.

Beckett Lupus' mouth hung open for a second. He stared. Kneeling, he put a hand on Varnon's still chest. He looked up.

Rage.

The rage he'd once felt on Krogg 'A'. The anguish and the anger.

All around him, Earther volunteers were dying. The marines were faring a little better, but Earthers were dying. And Omega couldn't be cured.

And though he knew it shouldn't, a righteous fury burned down in Beckett Lupus' core... a desire to be living death.

It came at a propitious moment, because the sky filled with a great scream.

Overhead, black ships plunged through the air, perhaps 300 meters overhead. From those ships a rain began, and a mighty hiss filled the air.

"For the Earthers!"

The warriors of Krogg dropped on their adversaries, and as a million of them were delivered to battle, Beckett Lupus looked up.

There were plenty of minions to kill, and as the rage swelled in him, and began to spread to those around him, he lunged forward.

Novash heard that the cure had failed, and he closed his eyes and reached down to his commanding officer. Narosh was still in C&C at Antarctic Base, in a building protected by the Stealth Guards.

Narosh... I'm about to die. Our fleet is gone. I am sorry.

It took a second for the Admiral-of-a-Fleet to recognize Novash's voice over the telepathic din, but then he connected to his old colleague, *You have done very well, my old friend. I'm sorry this is the end, but thank you.*

And thank you, Novash responded. Satisfied with that, his mind released the last of its determination to live.

The silver blood flowed liberally from his body as he slouched on the floor on *Lycrotar's* bridge, and — as though it realized its leader was gone — the Warcruiser too seemed to finally let itself die.

That was the end of the Larosian Navy in space.

Kardrath could feel that he was down to perhaps 100 ships, and now they all sat still around the diamond of Earther survivors, trying to use their spines and neuro pulses to protect the *Venerables*.

The Kroggs had learned much from the Earthers, but in the end, Kardrath could see clearly that the wolves, cats and bears were still the masters. There was still more to learn.

In his mind's eye, he saw the great tides of energy that came from the mighty First Rates all around him. It was a wall of death that 1,500 Omega ships was still unable to pierce.

But even as he thought that, one *did*.

Venerable took the hit — another hit.

It would be attrition, but perhaps the plague really could wear them down…

More spines hit *Venerable*.

"Fire's increasing… we're starting to lose a little shield integrity," Lab reported in Fox Magnus' plot.

"Looks like they can wear us down… slowly," the First Space Lord replied, and in the plot, Lab nodded.

"Indeed. And the cure failed… let's hope we can kill them at a rate of ten to one."

Fox looked away from the projection of Lab, and met his wife's eyes. She didn't look convinced, and he knew he wasn't… but he was the dapper sloop skipper. He had to believe.

"Well, if anyone can do it," Fox looked back at his friend.

A smile spread on Lab's face, and he nodded, "Yes, if anyone can, it's—"

The signal winked out.

Fox frowned, then his eyes shifted to another part of the plot.

Venerable wasn't there anymore.

"What?" Thena asked the question not of Fox — she didn't ask what was happening, she asked what had gotten through to *Venerable*.

Fox's eyes widened, and then *Victory* began to buck.

"All ships, get tighter together right now!" the First Space Lord didn't sound dapper any longer. Lab was gone. Omega was closing in.

The *Venerables* began to suffer.

CHAPTER 53

The cure hadn't worked. He knew that much.

He wasn't surprised — not at all. There was nothing he could do about that. He staggered to his feet and he contained a snarl. He lifted his sword from the ground, then he unslung his pack. He'd need some of its toys.

Staggering ahead, he caught sight of his objective, and steeled himself against the screams. He didn't wait now, his temper was firing. He moved fast, counting on the bastard being just a little distracted with the agony it was inflicting.

Without hesitating, Pat grabbed Omega-Paine by the collar of his robe and physically hauled the bastard off Sarah. In the same instant, he swung his broadsword, and the avatar — off time by just a second — lost the top of his head. Right across the eyes, the blade struck, but the avatar stayed on his feet.

It started to move as if it could fight, but Pat let loose a war cry, "Damn you! You're dead!"

The Irish brogue tinging his words somehow magnified their fury, and then his sword parted the avatar at the waist.

That wasn't enough, though. Pat wasn't done.

He'd never been good in the kitchen — he'd never been one to carve meat well. He simply cleaved and cleaved and cleaved, the blood of the once-human body started to spread around him with a gore that failed to satisfy his anger.

It was only a single word that drew him away — Sarah said his name.

His eyes jolted to her, and he was too lost in his own actions to react initially to her condition. To the pieces of her insides that were lying on the ground next to her, as if she was being disassembled through a hole in her side...

She was holding up a hand waving to the edges of the shaft of light, and Pat looked back.

Minions were collecting there.

Perhaps Omega was a sore loser.

Pat dropped his sword and pulled two silver devices from his pack. The first he switched on and dropped amongst Omega-Paine's gore. The second he kept with him as he raced to Sarah's side. Planting it on the ground beside her, he keyed it active.

Just in time, a small shield dome extended up around the pair — a shield not unlike the one that had contained Omega-King in the basement of Fengate

Hospital, but which was working the other way. It would keep the minions out, not Sarah and Pat in.

As the small dome stabilized, the first silver box flashed — it was an energy charge, and it atomized the bits of Omega-Paine that Pat had left behind. The shaft of light winked out with the avatar's death, leaving Sarah and Pat alone in the darkness.

It took Pat a few seconds to find a hand torch and to set it up in an omni mode, to gently light the two of them. He scuttled over to his wife's side, then gently lifted her head up so it could rest on his thigh. Her backpack was still on her shoulders, so he tugged it off and fumbled through it until he found a stasis patch. He put that on her midriff and turned it on.

A sigh of relief escaped Sarah's lips, but as she looked up at him, her state of mind wasn't helped. There were minions surrounding their little shield dome now, testing it with their fists. Unlike at Fengate, this shield wasn't connected to a city power supply. It wouldn't last long.

Pat pulled Sarah up further, so that her back rested against his chest. He avoiding putting a hand on her side, fearing it'd find Omega-Paine's opening. He wrapped his arms around her, and pressed his cheek against hers.

"We got him," he said in a whisper. "We got him."

That hit Sarah hard: the job was done. The cure hadn't worked, but they'd destroyed the avatar here. That was good… that was…

"You should go," she croaked. She felt like the life was draining out of her — the avatar's mind was no longer present to keep her body functioning without the pieces he'd removed, and it seemed all too clear she wouldn't last long. Not even a stasis patch could change that.

Pat squeezed her tighter, "I'll stay."

"No," desperation crept into her weak voice, and her hand reached up to touch his other cheek. "No listen to me… listen… you… I've never deserved you. You… always are there for me. You've done enough. You have both our backup shields. You can make it to the pinnace."

"There's plenty of minions who'd disagree," Pat said soothingly. "And I'd rather be here."

"*No,*" that was more of a plea — the wounded words of someone who was losing her grip. "Pat please. *Please.* So many people have died because of me. My parents for a start. And everyone in the fleet… at Gibraltar… and *everyone* from Genesis… not you too. For me. You have to go so that I didn't kill everyone…"

Pat pulled her even tighter to him, and then turned her a little so their eyes could meet.

"Let me tell you something," he said softly, and smiled. "You'll never believe this, but I'll tell you. All of that… everything you blame yourself for… it was outside your control. The Church would have gotten your parents somehow.

Everyone would have died at Gibraltar. Omega wasn't going to be stopped, even if we were waiting for him. These things happened."

She started to shake her head, but her weakness left her no match for the hand Pat placed on her cheek.

"And I'm staying here because *I* want to. Because I love you, and you love me. I'm not going to leave now, understand. And I hope that proves to you that you're not all wrong and a mess... because you're not. Never have been. You're a mighty woman. You helped kill an avatar today."

Those words sunk in. They were perhaps the first words to really do so in a long time, and they hadn't even come from an Earther. A plain old human had said them, and Sarah absorbed them.

Maybe Pat was right.

Yes. Yes he was.

It was alright, at last, for Sarah Manchester to cry. She let tears out with some sort of relief that was beyond anything she'd known before.

Pat's words warmed her. She was at the end of the line, now. But she'd helped in killing an avatar. And Pat, despite it all, was with her. His choice. He made the decision, not her. He thought it was worth being here.

She felt such a fool for needing to have that pointed out for her. But at least she knew now.

As the life drained from her, she felt the great weight lifting from her shoulders.

She put her arms around Pat, and pulled herself in close to him, then kissed him. When the kiss ended, she smiled.

"You and me, Patrick Conroy," she whispered.

The pounding on the energy dome became more insistent, and the whine from its projector confirmed it was soon to fall.

"How about we take them with us?" she asked, and then she smiled.

Pat smiled too, and with one hand fished down into Sarah's backpack for the energy charge she'd carried. Finding it, he raised it up into her lap, and flipped open the control panel.

Sarah looked down at it, and found the right button for instant detonation. Her finger rested gently on it.

"Mind if I..."

"No of course, be my guest," Pat grinned.

They laughed together. For the last time they laughed together. There was nothing really to laugh at, but somehow they did. They were together, after all of this, in the last moment. It felt to Pat and Sarah both as though they'd been given a gift. In death, a smile, as Varnon Broadpaw had said.

And to be together, completely and totally. Them against the night.

"Love you," Pat whispered one last time.

"I love you," Sarah's answer was soft. "I really do."

It was the right way to die. Pat smiled, Sarah smiled, the shield fell, and she pushed the button.

Out in orbit, *Pope Joseph Barron* was left all alone in the Ecclesia system.

Sarah Manchester and Patrick Conroy were gone.

Together.

CHAPTER 54

Fox Magnus clutched his wife's hand as *Victory* turned hard to avoid incoming spines. The fire was coming through now, even against the *Venerables.* Mister Gunth, Fox's longtime Cruising Master, handled this new ship with great ease... kept it fighting... but Fox knew it might only be a matter of time.

Omega was down to 1,000 ships. That was a small victory...

But the Larosian Fleet was gone, only a few Hyper Motherships remained in the Krogg echelons, and three *Venerables* had been lost.

"Reports from Sydney and Beijing, sir... their shields are down. Fighting has begun."

That made eleven cities, along with Antarctic Base.

The Kroggs were dropping in support of those besieged strong points — warriors raining from the sky — but Fox knew the fighting was only going to get more desperate from here.

"Reports from Newfoundland, sir. The Caine estate shield is about to fall."

Fox blinked and nodded. It was coming apart. It was all coming apart...

Minnie Maximane struggled to stay upright as *Galahad* absorbed another massive hit. The *Champion*-class ship was the last of its kind, and was tucked in now next to Chronos Claw's *Formidable*, seeking whatever protection the newer ship might offer.

"Reactor two is about to redline!"

That call from across the bridge drew the gaze of Mel Ramsay, and the Flag Captain shook her head, "Shut it down. Prepare to abandon ship."

There'd be no surviving with one reactor down — *Galahad* was existing on the very limit now, and any slowdown in fire or maneuvering speed would spell the end of the ship.

Mel looked back to her Admiral, "Looks like we're done, Minnie."

Minnie Maximane heaved a deep sigh and nodded, "We did good today."

A smile stretched onto the face of her Flag Captain, "You bet we did."

As predicted, then, a volley of spines smashed through *Galahad's* weakened shields, and the ship began to break up.

Chronos Claw closed his eyes for just a second, then opened them. Minnie was gone.

The whole world was on fire, and here in space, what remained of the Earther Navy now had to huddle together, all alone.

The Larosians and the Kroggs had spent themselves against the massive Omega force, and had brought its numbers down... it was left to fewer than 150 *Venerable*-class ships of the line to destroy the plague's fleet.

Grinding his jaw, Chronos peered into the plot.

The plague was losing more ships, though. He'd spent his black wave against those 'softer' targets of the Allies and the Krogg War-vintage Earther vessels. Now he only had the best to challenge. Perhaps that was his mistake.

Chronos' grip on his plot tightened, and he looked to his Signal Officer, "Hail *Renown* and *Victory*, let's get all the Admirals we have left into the plot."

Varnia Lupus and Fox Magnus appeared in the holo projection, and Chronos looked hard at them, "It's absolutely down to us."

Fox nodded, "Yes it is. And he's going to regret that."

"Saving the best for last... not always a good idea," Varnia added. "My dad is dead."

Her tone there was so sharp it made Chronos wince, and then he closed his eyes again, "Alright. Close in real tight. Let's see if we can find a way to fire faster."

Captain-Elite Tovarrin of the Larosian Stealth Guard pushed his way forward through the crowds of Earther volunteers, seeking the front line of this battle for the Antarctic Base. His remaining guards were in position to hold the buildings, and were ready for when the Earthers retreated back into their underground complex, but he couldn't contact Beckett Lupus. He didn't know when the retreat would take place.

More Kroggs fell from the sky ahead of him, and he managed to marvel at their arrival as he advanced. They fell in squads — ten or twelve of the black soldiers would land together, and minions would be thrown away from them as they collected themselves. Tovarrin had yet to see a Krogg die, though he knew eventually they would.

But for now, they were buying time — much needed time. The Earthers had to draw back, and soon.

Finally Tovarrin found the front line, where Earther volunteers with varying skill levels — from those who were simply 'good' to the experts — fought against the minions who tried to overwhelm them.

There was no organization that Tovarrin could see, just Earthers fighting with all the instinctive prowess that made them lethal. Wolves, cats, bears... they attacked in turn, unceasing and sometimes untiring, until they died or until fresher fighters stepped forward to take their place.

Tovarrin felt privileged to be among these people.

Then he saw Beckett Lupus.

Then he *felt* Beckett Lupus.

The burning fury emanating from the Earther startled Tovarrin so much that he came to a stop. The wolf was alone, his two swords blazing brightly and flinging blood all around him. He moved with a speed that seemed beyond even an Earther, and no matter how many minions came for him, it was never enough. There simply wasn't enough physical space around him for enough of them to attack at one time.

No wonder he hadn't responded.

Tovarrin moved forward again, and realized now that several minions had noticed him. His two personal guards stepped in the way and presented their force shields — not the Earther-type energy shields, but the solid and impenetrable disc shields they wore on their arms.

I must relieve General Lupus. We must clear a path.

Those orders drove Tovarrin's guards forward, and a few Earther marines who'd been mixed into the crowd of volunteers pushed forward to join them.

Minions did not fall easily. Tovarrin attacked one with all speed, but his stroke missed completely, and he was forced to absorb a shocking blow with his shield. He learned from that oversight, and he did not miss a second time.

On he pressed towards Beckett, but it seemed as though the General was drawing further and further away, blazing his own trail through hordes of minions beyond counting.

"General Lupus!" the Captain-Elite called, but it was impossible to be heard over the din.

The Caine estate shield dropped, and Colonel Cadmus Howler drew his sword. The marines of 2/54th were all around him, and every one of these Earthers realized how important their task was. They'd been through the battle against the Queen's Guards, they'd fought the Crusaders in Darymanis City, and they'd faced Omega on *Genesis One.*

Now it was left to them to protect Phealan Caine.

Thankfully the minions weren't concentrated. They probably still didn't realize what exactly was happening here.

As the first Omega warriors came on, the marines cut them down with fluid strokes, swords glowing eerily in the moonlight. It was a silent exchange, and it provided Cadmus Howler a moment's peace. He knew the onslaught was coming, but for just a second he allowed himself to enjoy the presence of his trusty old battalion, and their nighttime defense.

Then the minions started arriving by the dozen, and then in groups of fifty.

The fight became bloody, very quickly.

Ellen Arbear glanced at Joyce Furgus as the pair stood on the deck of the Caine house.

"So we fight as if Phealan is in there behind us?" the bear asked the cat.

Joyce nodded, "As soon as they start showing up."

Looking back into the moonlit night, Ellen Arbear sighed, then nodded and stretched her arms, "Gotta love a rematch."

Joyce blinked, "Why should I love that, exactly?"

Realizing her friend had a point, Ellen shook her head, "In retrospect, perhaps you don't have to..."

The first minion bounded out of the trees. A pulsar cut it in half, but without delay, two more appeared. And then more.

"They're breaking through our line, Joyce," Cadmus' voice came into the lioness' ear. "We're still alive, but you'll have company!"

Joyce pressed her headset, "They just showed up."

There was no time to say anything else. The minions leapt forward, and Joyce's company charged into them.

CHAPTER 55

A bright, black light surrounded Omega-Natosh. In the real world, Setter Caine doubted such a sight could exist — a light that was somehow visible, bright, and yet black at the same time. The definition of light, to him at least, was the absence of dark...

"It's melodramatic, I know," Omega-Natosh caught a piece of Setter's musings, and grinned as he explained. "But admit it, it looks fucking awesome."

Setter admitted nothing. He had been knocked onto his back twice by the black lightning, but now he sat up and felt the anger pushing through him again. Forcing himself up onto one knee, he glared at Omega-Natosh.

"You... can make things look however you like," the wolf said.

Omega-Natosh laughed, "That's your comeback? Lame."

Setter gritted his teeth, then forced himself to stand.

As the blackness collected around Omega-Natosh, the creature shook his head, "Not going to work."

Reaching out his hand, he fired another bolt of black lightning.

This time, it was met by pure light.

Setter's eyes narrowed, and his heart rate — or whatever he actually had here on the telepathic plane — slowed. He forced all the power he felt in his mind to focus itself before him in a blinding, shining light, and it swallowed the bolt whole.

"Aha," the avatar opposite him grinned. "Now we have a little bit of a fight!"

Another bolt came... and another...

Graham's shield collapsed as he landed on the sand, but he didn't think anything of that. He knew he was going to die; that was inevitable. He needed to concentrate all his pain and all his fury... just once, he had to get through to what had been his wife.

Omega-Gillian laughed at him as he stood, then she folded her arms, "Look, if you want I can pretend to be her for a little while. Just pretend. Nothing of her is left in here. But I could try it. Kiss you, we could make out... I mean, you're going to die. You can go out defiantly, or we can pretend."

The buttons Omega was trying to press weren't connected to anything anymore. Graham realized, deep within himself, that since he'd lost Gillian, he'd done his work very well. The emotion was gone from him. Completely gone.

"Hmm," Omega-Gillian's smile faded, and she studied him with narrowed eyes. "You really might be tougher than your sister. She's dead, by the way. Killed my Paine avatar, I'll give her and Pat credit there. But they died too. So I don't give a shit. And I got to take pieces out of her."

Graham didn't respond.

"Wow. Now, honestly, you're doing pretty fucking good. But I guess you didn't love your sister. Not that I can blame you, she was a fuckup of the worst kind. And she got your parents killed. So I can see—"

Omega-Gillian stopped mid-sentence, realizing she was suddenly face-to-face with Graham Manchester.

And that his sword was sticking right through her breastbone.

"Fuck. You got fast, little Graham," she said, eyes wide with surprise.

Graham didn't know how he'd reached her, nor did he care. All his pain and rage was focused into that one moment. His sword was in the abomination that had once been his wife, and he stared into its eyes.

They had been Gillian's eyes. They still were, in a way. And her face... her lips, her cheeks, even her hair.

Graham's mind coolly analyzed what he saw. He should have wanted to break down now — to be so close to the beauty that he'd loved, and to let the pain of losing her consume him.

But he certainly didn't. He'd done his work very well... it had cost him every scrap of his humanity. All he had left was the goal which he had sought for so long: the death of this monster.

"Now," he hissed at her, "you lose your grip on her. You Godsdamned monster, you control her no more. She rests in peace."

He yanked his sword down, and it exited her torso with a sickening sound.

Omega-Gillian dropped to the sand, eyes still wide, and Graham staggered back from her, breathing hard.

"Graham," Omega-Gillian rasped, trying to emulate Gillian's voice. Graham wouldn't be fooled. "Graham... I'm so sorry..."

He turned away. He couldn't feel anything.

"...but are you fucking kidding me?"

He stopped.

"Colin Brawn nearly cut me in half and I ran away ten seconds later. One giant chop isn't going to do it. Pat Conroy had to mince the Paine avatar into little pieces and then hit him with an energy charge..."

Omega-Gillian's hands abruptly circled Graham, and she pulled him backward against her, then whispered, "See, I knit up one big slice like that quite easily. My bowels don't even drop out."

She yanked tight and Graham grunted, dropping his sword.

"So," the avatar smiled, "you just wasted your one chance. Now I wonder how best to torture you, since you're all cut off from your emotions. I've got time. I suppose I can act like Gillian and see if I can nurse the pain out of you..."

Graham's breathing sharpened, and his face twisted in a snarl.

With blinding speed again, he slammed his head back into Omega-Gillian's face. He didn't expect it to help, but somehow it did — she released him, and he scrambled forward across the sand, to the place where he'd dropped his backpack.

Wasting no time, he drew the energy charge he'd brought with him, and opened the panel.

Omega-Gillian staggered in surprise, then laughed, "Come on, really?"

Holding the charge up, Graham nodded.

Instantly, the avatar's expression changed. Her mouth rounded in shock, "No, not—"

Graham pressed down with his forefinger... but the charge was no longer in his hand.

He heard a thud, looked down the beach, and saw the silver box lying far out of reach. Then he looked to see who had taken it from him — some minion must have arrived to save the avatar...

"You are fucking *dead*," Omega-Gillian hissed.

Not a minion. Not a minion at all.

An impossibility.

Christine Schaeffer.

The young human stepped past Graham, dusting her gloveless hands. Graham stared at her as she went by, and saw for certain there was no stasis patch under her ponytail. Her gloves were off, her collar was still open, she was covered in seawater...

Omega-Gillian turned towards her, reaching out with her mind. Christine wasn't wearing armor — her thoughts had to be vulnerable.

Vulnerable to what, exactly? To you?

The thought slammed into the avatar's head like a battering ram.

"That's... not possible..."

Christine's words were harsh, "You realize how cliché you sound now, right? I thought you prided yourself on being cynical about those sorts of things."

"Fuck off, little girl."

"And honestly, the language," Christine closed fearlessly with Omega-Gillian.

Nothing the plague could throw was getting through to the young human's mind. It was as though she had the telepathic power of an Earther...

"Funny story," Christine offered helpfully. "When my change started...

back on *Carnarvon*, when I took that hit of UDRC in the face, and it started a new set of regeneration, Graham stopped it instantly. I was screaming in agony, so I understand why he did it. But he slapped on a stasis patch, assuming the change was only going to get worse. And after that, Celia Lazarus did everything she could to keep the process from continuing, because she figured the same."

Stopping almost nose-to-nose with the avatar, Christine's words came in a near whisper.

"But we should have realized, UDRC is made by Earthers. Earther medicine doesn't *have* negative side-effects. It's too good to be true. So it wouldn't start a change to my nerves unless it was working towards something positive... unless it was going to change my brain too. Make it able to cope with the heightened awareness. We stopped the process too soon... but you, my dear avatar, unfroze it."

Those words took a few seconds to sink in, both for Graham and for Omega-Gillian. Christine really was something different.

Something dangerous.

"You... fucking smooth-skinned Earther," Omega-Gillian's fist lanced out, meaning to puncture Christine, but the young human... or whatever she was... was not where she was supposed to be.

"I'm not an Earther. I'm something else completely," Christine was behind Omega-Gillian then, and as the avatar turned, she realized too late that the young human had found her saber.

"I do a number of things quite like an Earther, though," she added, and then she swung.

Two halves of Omega-Gillian fell into the sand, and then Christine started mincing both parts.

"Small pieces, as instructed," her words were cold and bitter. "*Many* little pieces. Graham, can you get the energy charge?"

The ArcGeneral was already arriving with the energy weapon, and Omega-Gillian — her face still intact — glared up at him, "You and your little whore..."

Graham said nothing. He keyed the charge and dropped it into the midst of the gore on the sand. He and Christine then backed away to a safe distance. Neither could make out what Omega-Gillian screamed before the blast.

Watching as she was atomized, Graham felt a twinge of something. He was overcome suddenly by exhaustion, and then he wondered why he wasn't dead. The shock hit him all at once, and he started to collapse, only to have Christine's arms encircle him, and keep him off the ground.

She pulled him close to her, pushing his head onto her shoulder, and then she reassured him, "It's done. Finished."

For a second, he hung limp in her arms, but then he found some strength and pulled himself tighter against her. The scream that he'd been unable to release earlier erupted now, but was muffled by her shoulder, and as minions began to turn up on the beach to menace them and find some revenge, she closed her eyes and held on to him.

Another avatar was gone.

CHAPTER 56

Setter Caine smiled at Omega-Natosh's obvious frustration.

The avatar lashed out repeatedly with black lightning, but it didn't penetrate the barrier of light that the Supreme Consul had raised before him.

"Don't get fucking smug you fuck," the plague spat. "I just need to focus more, so fuck off."

"You have a tell, Omega," Setter countered, folding his arms. "Whenever things stop going as you plan, you really do get petulant."

"Fuck!"

Setter laughed at the juvenile response, then shrugged, "So, you think you can finish me here? Come ahead."

The taunt was both transparent and effective — Omega figured Setter thought he had something up his sleeve, but nothing would matter. A mind of a billion-trillion cells could summon up more than enough energy to snuff out one Earther.

One Earther?

Setter grinned at the thought.

It was time to get some help.

Phealan stood on the rocky beach of the Caine estate, looking for just a moment out to sea. The thin blanket of snow here was glowing under the moonlight, and as the marines assigned to guard him waited silently, Phealan basked in the beauty of this place. Perhaps it would be the last time he would be able to do so.

Then he heard the thought he needed to hear. He turned to Sergeant Cuttar, and nodded once, "I'm going in."

Ernile Cuttar smiled back, "Glad to hear it. We'll make sure you aren't interrupted."

With a last, deep breath, Phealan closed his eyes. When he opened them again, they swirled with blue light.

"Cadmus, Phealan's gone in," Cuttar said into this headset.

"Understood. I'm coming to you," the Colonel of 2/54th responded.

"Ooh, black light. That's kinda ritzy."

Omega-Natosh's head whipped around, his eyes locking on the newcomer.

"Oh fuck off, kid," the plague snapped. "I don't want any father-son bonding shit. That's so pathetic."

Phealan smiled, his eyebrows climbing as he rounded the plague to stand next to his father. The two wolves shared a smile, and the son nodded approvingly, "This telepathic plane really does make things easier."

Omega-Natosh snarled, and as he did the blackness around him deepened. Wasting no time, the plague lashed out at Phealan — thicker, stronger bolts of black lightning careened at the young wolf.

"Nope," Phealan shook his head, and the wall of light before Setter suddenly widened. "Two of us now, Omega. You'll need to do better than that."

The avatar screamed his frustration, "You have *talent*. But let's be clear, you can't kill me. Neither of your puny fucking minds is big enough. Every fucking Earther could come in here and I could own you all!"

Setter raised his eyebrows and looked at his son, then pointed at the avatar with his thumb, "At least he admits to being melodramatic."

As soon as he said that, a new snarl came, and Omega-Natosh sunk into an even deeper blackness.

"Suit your fucking selves," he spat again. The darkness began to stream towards the Caines, and both of them gritted their teeth as it slammed into the wall of light before them.

Phealan let out a grunt, then glanced at his dad, "Well... he probably isn't bluffing."

Setter clenched his jaw and nodded, leaning into the light as if he was trying to hold a door shut, "That would have been too easy..."

As they spoke to each other, Omega decided to step up the attack on the Caine compound. He'd kill Phealan, at least. He'd save Setter to torture later, after all the other Earthers were dead.

Cadmus Howler slid to a halt on the beach, then turned to look behind him. One minion was coming, so he cut it in half. That wouldn't be the last of them.

"By now they're going to figure out he's here," Cuttar called, and turning, the Colonel agreed.

"Let's get a few shields around him!"

Each of the marines of the recon squad had a shield in his or her pack, and now they each started planting them around Phealan's feet... just as more minions arrived.

Cadmus had his own shield out, so he quickly moved over to the junior Caine's side, "I'll activate them, Ernile!"

The Sergeant nodded, then waved his marines forward.

The elite wolves of Beckett Lupus' old recon squad would make their last stand on this beach. All that mattered now was that Phealan was protected...

As Cadmus neared the young Caine, though, a minion drove into his back. The Colonel stumbled, and ran face-first into Phealan. One of the recon marines, Corporal Canit, noticed this and leapt to the defense, cutting the minion to pieces, but as he turned back to his Colonel, he saw something rather unexpected: Cadmus Howler was nose-to-nose with Phealan Caine, and both their eyes were swirling with blue light.

"Ernile, the Colonel got banged and I think he went in!" Canit called, then started activating the shield domes.

Ernile Cuttar had one second to look back in surprise, then he went back to killing minions.

Gritting his teeth, Phealan leaned into the light, and pushed hard against the darkness.

Omega-Natosh laughed, regaining his good spirits of earlier, "See, you can't resist me when I focus it all. And don't think you're distracting my minions. I can gather strength from all of their cells without slowing them down one bit."

"So you claim," Setter grunted. "But I tend to believe we're making a difference."

"Oh sure, and you're not biased," the avatar grinned, then summoned more energy into his mind. The blackness grew as the massive brain of Omega collected more and more energy, and placed it under the control of this single avatar.

There was no fucking way Setter Caine and the boy wonder were going to win this duel.

That thought brought a snarl back to Omega-Natosh's face, and he pushed harder, using more energy than he expected the two wolves could handle.

But the wall of light stood, father and son forcing it to remain bright and powerful.

Omega-Natosh grunted and pushed again, gathering more energy, "It's all... you can do... to hold me back..."

Another push, and both Setter and Phealan realized the light was starting to quiver.

"Push back," Setter said, as if the reminder was needed. He started to feel warmer, as though he was near a bonfire, but he pushed still.

Phealan grimaced and gritted his teeth, using every scrap of his mind to summon the light. It had to stand before Omega.

"Aw the light," the avatar cackled. "Really, and you call me fucking melodramatic."

"Well you picked dark," Phealan shot back, his tone unable to conceal the strain he was under. "We just took our cue from you."

"Pathetic. I'll break you down right now," Omega-Natosh returned to his threats, and the Caines braced themselves.

More darkness was hurled at them, and the wall of light thinned...

And then a little help arrived.

"I... er."

Cadmus Howler appeared next to Phealan and looked at the two wolves beside him with open-mouthed surprise. Both Caines returned the expression.

"Um. Cadmus?" Phealan kept leaning as he asked the question, and the Colonel blinked twice.

"I must have gotten knocked into you. Didn't mean to drop in here... but I must have gone eye to eye. Sorry about that..."

Phealan frowned, "No need to apologize..."

"Colonel, would you mind lending a hand?" Setter asked, pushing harder into the light. It felt now like his mind was starting to burn... he was putting every bit of himself into this.

"Oh, sorry, of course!" Cadmus nodded politely, and then he unleashed his own mind. The wall of light was buttressed, and Omega-Natosh rolled his eyes.

"Fuck, please. You wolves always do travel in fucking packs," the avatar was unimpressed. "Guess I'll just need *more* power."

Setter looked at Phealan, and then they both looked at Cadmus. The Colonel was pushing for all he was worth, but he smiled and then nodded, "Guess I arrived at the right moment."

"Yes," Setter agreed. "We'll need more soon, at this rate."

The last duel wasn't near over yet.

CHAPTER 57

"Phealan's gone in, just heard the report."

Fox Magnus nodded at Chronos Claw's words, then turned to Master Gunth, "You hear that, Master? Ready on the switches?"

The veteran Earther nodded, "Absolutely sir."

"Good. Might be a while yet, but stay ready."

The *Venerables*, minus their namesake ship, continued to roll and fire.

All Stealth Guards forward, we must give the Earther volunteers time to retreat!

Tovarrin continued to battle minions with all the speed and discipline he had available to him, which was a great deal indeed. Beckett Lupus, though, remained far away and out of sight.

Turning fast, the Larosian raised his sword, then halted himself. A Krogg warrior was beside him, and then three more.

We offer our assistance to your Guards, Captain-Elite, the warrior thought to Tovarrin.

Surprised despite himself, the Larosian bow-nodded, *Of course. It is our honor.*

The mighty Krogg grinned, and his single eye went wild. He hissed loudly, then spread his arms wide, "*Killllll!*"

His squad approved of the order, and went to work dealing death around Tovarrin.

"All Earther volunteers and marines, fall back to the complex! We will buy time!" the Captain-Elite yelled, and the Earthers who heard him began to spread the word.

But it would take time for the message to go forth...

Joyce Furgus dragged Ellen Arbear into the Caine house, leaving a trail of blood on the way. Shutting the glass door behind her, she raised the house's last shield — really just a barrier against bad weather, and collapsed to the floor next to her unconscious Lieutenant.

Both Ellen's legs were gone, and Joyce knew she herself had suffered internal injuries. She was losing blood... a lot of it.

She felt her head hanging heavily, and slouched back. Keeping an arm under her, she managed a few more seconds of consciousness. The minions would be up on the deck soon. Then they'd be inside... hopefully they wouldn't find Claire.

Hands were suddenly on the sides of Joyce's face, and the lioness' head swayed a little, changing direction to see the young human girl with a desperate look on her face.

"Hide," Joyce rasped, and then her mind was drained of its fuel.

In shock, Claire slid away from the unconscious lioness. She let go of the Earther Captain's head, sat down, and hugged her knees up in front of her. She was all alone. She was going to die all alone.

Sergeant Cuttar and Corporal Canit were all that remained of the recon squad. The elite Earthers had done all they could, and the snow on the beach was now almost uniformly red with blood, but they were at the end of their tether. A few more marines from 2/54th had fallen back to join them — probably the last survivors of the battalion, based on the number of minions that were pouring in.

Perhaps the greatest regiment in the history of the Earther Marine Corps had spent itself in just a few minutes of fighting in Newfoundland.

But it had been right to make that stand here. And they weren't finished quite yet.

"Have any shields left? They might buy some time," Canit suggested.

Cuttar's eyebrow shot up, "Good point."

Beckoning the other survivors to gather together, he pulled out a shield and activated it, setting it to spread a wall across the front of the beach. Another marine placed one just short of the shore, and a shield dome closed around them.

Another minute or two, perhaps.

Beckett Lupus found himself surrounded by Kroggs, and one of them nodded to him.

"Sir, we would be honored to fight with you. You are more powerful than even our stories suggested."

Beckett's mind was awash still with anger, but those words helped it subside. He was fighting the minions, and Kroggs were joining him.

He had been angered.

There was no time for him to feel guilty or reflect on that, because as ever, more minions were coming, so he simply nodded to the Krogg.

With both blades drawn, he flew onto the attack again. The Kroggs tried to keep up.

Emerging from the C&C buildings of the Antarctic Base, Narosh and Kragran found they were surrounded by Earthers.

"This is incredible," Narosh said quietly, his disbelief at the spectacle evident enough.

"Caine is fighting the plague now, I can feel it," Kragran observed. "The battle is not slowing the plague's minions down, though. The disease has incredible telepathic power."

"More than Praaxus, or the Son," Narosh agreed.

"And more than our Queen and her under-Queens," Kragran confirmed.

For a second they stood there, and then Kragran shook his head, "We will help them in our own way."

"It's all we can do," Narosh said.

Claire moved slowly to the glass walls of the house, and looked down the stairs to the clearing. More minions were ambling in, some stopping and taking their chance to mutilate fallen marines. They hadn't come up the stairs yet, but she knew it was just a matter of time.

She took deep breaths to try to calm herself. She didn't want to hide, she'd just get it over with and die. Hopefully they'd make it quick... hopefully she wouldn't have to suffer.

As she watched the minions, one looked up at her, and then hissed to the rest. She held herself tight as they moved slowly to the bottom of the stairs. She started to cry, but fought the sobs. She didn't want to die crying like a baby.

Then a black wolf walked across the deck in front of her, and sat down right outside the door.

Not an Earther, a wolf.

It looked back at her with golden eyes, and then looked down the stairs at the minions.

Claire panicked. The wolves were supposed to have gone away. She didn't want them to die trying to protect her.

She beat on the glass, yelled for it to go away, but it didn't.

Go and hide... why don't you go and hide?

Claire sobbed and slid down the glass, collapsing onto her knees. She didn't want all this to happen again — everyone dies, like had happened back home.

Please, just go and hide!

The wolf sat there, and finally Claire listened to the advice in her head. She crawled away from the window. She didn't want to see. She lay in a ball behind the couch, and waited to die.

CHAPTER 58

Darkness filled the telepathic plane, and only three wolves fought against it. Their wall of light was flickering, and Setter knew it had to be time.

"Now, I think," he wheezed, and Phealan looked at him, then nodded. "Now."

Now.

Fox Magnus heard the call, then looked to his plot. The Admirals shown in the holo tank had heard it too, as had Mister Gunth, "Switches on, all guns to automatic fire, all engines to automatic roll!"

Victory, and the other Earther ships that remained, switched to auto-pilot, and the Earthers aboard each one of them stopped what they were doing, and stood still.

Their eyes filled with blue, swirling light.

Now.

Beckett Lupus stopped with a jolt, and then hit his headset, "Now. Everyone it's now!"

He then stood still — right out in the midst of the minions — and his eyes filled with blue light.

Further to the rear, every Earther marine, and every volunteer, stopped and stood. Some were killed as soon as they stopped fighting, but the Kroggs and the Larosians had their part to play now.

The Krogg warrior who had joined Beckett Lupus looked to the sky and screamed out the command, "Now brothers! *For the Earthers!*"

A great hiss covered the Antarctic Base, and the Kroggs renewed their efforts to hold back the minions — millions of warriors against tens of millions of the plague's creatures. But the Kroggs would not be deterred: they fought to defend their friends.

Further down the ice, Tovarrin saw the Earthers around him stop, and he knew what was happening.

Larosians, now. All forward, all for the honor of our allies.

Narosh, standing well to the rear, joined the call, *For Praaxus, for the Son, and for our friends the Earthers! Stand now! Stand!*

Kragran's own thoughts were less poetic: *Deeaatttthhhhhhhhh!*

• • •

Now.

On the beach, the handful of survivors of 2/54th stood behind a failing shield. Ernile Cuttar had just been preparing himself to fight when the call came. He looked to the stars, and hoped that somehow he and the other survivors would not be physically killed while they went to the telepathic plane.

That seemed an unlikely hope, but they were needed, so they would be there.

The marines looked skyward, into the night, and the shield before them continued to be pounded by minions.

As the Earthers' eyes filled with blue light, and their minds left Newfoundland, a howl crossed the beach.

A few proper wolves trotted out of the trees.

Setter Caine stopped leaning into the light, and following his lead, Phealan and Cadmus did the same. They were themselves glowing, but they thought nothing of it. And the wall of light didn't weaken: it grew.

Omega-Natosh simply groaned, "Predictable. This becomes a story about community... bring all these here Earthers together and they's can defeat the big uh bad."

The strange brogue the plague mockingly used drew a frown from Setter, but he decided not to acknowledge it. Instead, he looked around him, and in a brilliant flash of light, a couple of billion Earthers appeared.

Earthers everywhere, from all across the planet, from the space around it, from New Halifax... they were all here, all at once.

The darkness Omega had generated was suddenly caged in light, and for a warm moment, Setter believed they could overpower the plague.

Fox Magnus and Chronos Claw edged their way forward through the masses of Earthers that now stood around in the artificial telepathic environment, then waved to Setter in greeting. Beckett Lupus found Varnia Lupus, and they stayed close to each other.

There were many faces not here... Lab and Varnon among them... but so many Earthers *were* here.

And their light was awesome.

"See, Omega? Here we all are," Phealan smiled brightly, taking a step towards the avatar.

Omega-Natosh laughed loudly.

"And here it comes, you're going to wipe the smile off my face."

Phealan blinked, and his smile reflected what he knew, "Worth a shot. How about it everyone, let's try to crush him like a bug."

There was a ripple of laughter, but it ended quickly as the Earthers focused their minds — all of their minds — and pressed in on the avatar. The blackness around him began to shrink, and he donned a look of fear... mock fear.

"Oh no!" he slapped his cheeks with his hands, then froze in place for a second.

On the battlefields all around Earth, minions froze in place too. Kroggs and Larosians took their chance to cut down more while the temporary paralysis set in... but then the beasts became active again. Omega-Natosh flexed his neck and shoulders.

"Alright," he said. His fists clenched, and there was a deafening thunder.

Two billion Earthers were thrown onto their telepathic backs. The blackness deepened and grew around the avatar, and a rumble filled the plane.

"I know all the 'pull together and we can win' clichés, and they're fucking useless," the avatar spat. "You cannot comprehend how large I really am... how powerful. I can collect more energy in one place than you, the Larosians and the Kroggs combined."

Setter was the first to pick himself off the bright white 'ground', and he stared at the avatar, "You think you can crush us like bugs? All of us?"

Omega-Natosh let out a frustrated sigh, "Uh. *Yes.*"

He collected more power, and more, and Setter realized the plague was committing everything now. All the power of his billions of trillions of cells... so much energy...

The avatar looked him square in the eyes, "I knew the cure thing wasn't your plan. But I thought you'd be a little less lame than this. Band together and we can kill our God? Did you miss the definition of a God?"

Setter let his chin dip for a second, then shook his head, "We try the impossible, Omega. We do what we say we'll do, in a way that reflects us. And we're not going to give up now."

Shaking his head in disgust, the avatar had had enough, "Well fuck you."

His hands reached out, and he pushed the immense darkness at Setter Caine.

The Earthers came to their feet again, all of them, and their light burned bright, trying to strangle the darkness, and to cage it. A thin shell of light started to form around Omega's power — just enough to hold it where it was.

Shuddering, the avatar gritted his teeth, "Really? Come on, even with all of you, you can't hold me back for long..."

Setter Caine smiled.

"Who said we needed *long?*"

Outside the telepathic plane, standing in the bloody Genesis War Memorial next to the body of his fallen friend, Setter Caine reached his right hand across to his left wrist, and tabbed the remote control band he had put on before leaving the pinnace.

In the space above Genesis, *ENS Orion* entered energy drive.

•••

Omega-Natosh blinked, confused at first. The Earthers all around him fixed him with their stares, and then Fox Magnus, the dapper First Space Lord, came up alongside Setter.

"What was it Kragran warned you about — why we couldn't use telepathic explosions against Omega?" Setter asked his friend.

Fox frowned thoughtfully, "As I recall, he said that if multiple minds were telepathically connected and gathered energy together... and if Omega here happened to destroy one mind in the collective... all the energy would be forced into the others. And that'd be more than enough to overwhelm those minds. Overload and burn out, basically."

Setter nodded, "And by that principle, a giant brain of countless cells, held together by telepathy, would be vulnerable to being burned out by an energy surge if, say, it collected all the power it could into the person of one avatar... and then that avatar's physical body was destroyed."

"Seems likely to me," Chronos Claw stepped up next to Fox. "All that energy we just trapped in him will be released into the rest of the cells of his brain, wherever they are across the galaxy. It'll be like blowing a dam. Or massively surging a reactor through a power grid."

"And since our friends killed all the other avatars that might have had enough telepathic power to control the flow of energy, it'll race out through every Omega cell, everywhere, and burn him to death from the inside out," Varnia Lupus added sharply.

Omega-Natosh was wide-eyed.

What they were saying... was impossible. Except that it was possible.

Because the one thing that made him so much better than everyone else — the giant brain, spanning galaxies, connected by telepathy — was like a giant power grid. He'd used it all to harness more telepathic energy in one place than the universe had before seen... and now Omega-Natosh was single-handedly managing the power.

If that avatar's body was gone, and all that energy washed out again, without Omega-Gillian or Omega-Paine to moderate the flow... his mind was vast, but it wasn't configured to handle it. A pile of concrete blocks wasn't the same as a dam; a spool of copper wire wasn't a power line... he'd have nothing configured to handle the flood...

"What, no comeback?" Setter interrupted Omega's panic with a smile, and stepped closer to the creature again. "You know we listened to you... you were right all this time. There was nothing powerful enough in the universe to destroy you... except for you yourself."

If Omega had had a heart, it would have stopped in that instant. Because the wolf bastard wasn't wrong... but he *had* to be wrong. Because even Omega wasn't powerful enough to destroy himself. Because he was too powerful to be destroyed by anything...

But he was also so powerful that he could destroy anything...

"Getting confused with your own semantics and arrogance?" Phealan read those thoughts with a wry smile, and asked the question.

"*No!*" his avatar snarled back, and then spat out his defense. "I collected the energy, I can handle it, even without the avatars!"

Phealan's eyes narrowed, "Maybe you can. In the end, you did collect all that energy, so perhaps you can diffuse it all. But here's a question: what happens when we — all of us here — add a little more to it? We might not have had enough light to beat you on our own, but we might be able to tip you over the edge into a burnout."

Omega-Natosh thrashed, resisting the notion. But the young Caine was right.

And Setter was suddenly in front of him. The veteran wolf glowed in the darkness now — light seemed to be pouring out of his body. His gray, furry hands reached up to Omega-Natosh's face, and with a smile, the great wolf looked at them.

"Look at that," he said, "the light's coming right out of me. How about I give some to you?"

Omega-Natosh couldn't throw him off. And all the Earthers standing around the plane — all two billion of them, reached out to Setter Caine with their minds. Their light joined his.

And Setter pushed it into Omega.

"Tell me, Omega," the Supreme Consul of the Earther people spoke softly. "What does it mean... to be full of light?"

Minions raced towards the Genesis War Memorial. They had to kill Setter Caine — had to destroy his body. It was the only chance now...

ENS Orion was faster than they were.

The great, mighty old First Rate had only one mission left to complete — the greatest mission it had ever embarked on. It had carried its two favorite commanders safely to their deaths, and now it would play its final part.

There could be no more fitting end, and had *Orion* been able, it would have smiled.

A ball of blue energy, the 175-gun ship of the line slammed into the Genesis War Memorial at 2,000 pls. The explosion fractured the main continent on Genesis, and obliterated all the minions there.

Omega-Natosh ceased to be, and Setter Caine's body was gone too.

And then all that energy the plague had so arrogantly collected into his one avatar washed out through all the other corners of his mind. It was an epic overload. With no avatars to control the flow, it ploughed through every minion, every *cell*, everywhere in the universe. The telepathic power that had connected

Omega across the vast gulfs of space became the carrier of his doom.

The light that the Earthers had sent rode with the darkness — all their power, all the hope they held, all the good they had done produced a massive surge of its own. The darkness overwhelmed Omega's mind, and then the light burned him down.

Every minion saw it. Their eyes flew wide open, their vision blinded by the searing brightness. For a fraction of a second, light seemed to spill from every Omega cell in their bodies — a brief flash, and then all-encompassing darkness.

Each and every piece of Omega's mind lost the ability to talk to each and every other piece. The basic blocks of the plague's existence fell apart.

On Earth, the Kroggs and the Larosians stood back and watched. The minions fell before them without ceremony, and the rush of telepathic brightness they released was unmistakable to the warriors of both those races.

The black carapaced aliens saw the victory immediately, and in an instant they hissed mightily, that noise covering the Earth in a chilling and yet warm celebration. The Larosians were more reserved, first lowering their blades, then lifting them in salute to their Earther friends.

Bodies fell before them. Minions that had once been human, and that now were nothing. Without Omega, and the power of his mind, they could not exist.

In the space above, Earther ships continued to roll and fire, their helms and their weapons cued to automatic destruction. Their adversaries fell limp, the mind of Omega having been all the command and control they enjoyed. Now, without him, they hurtled on inertia, colliding with each other, breaking up, spinning into oblivion.

From a nightmarish black wave, they began to dissipate like a black cloud before a wind. And the blue light of Earther energy shot had the same effect on them that the light of the Earthers' minds had on Omega.

Rendered to nothing by the energy of the Earthers — by their blinding light.

Across two galaxies, Omega burned away. Never had history seen so much energy harnessed from the telepathic plane; never had something so vast as Omega been defeated so absolutely.

All who could witness such things took notice: the universe was free of that particular darkness. And the Earthers, a young race with ancient wisdom, had more power than anyone could have imagined.

CHAPTER 59

Omega-Natosh burned last. Perhaps he was nothing more than an echo of the mind he represented, because as everything else died in his mind, this avatar remained on the telepathic plane, and dug his hands into Setter's arms.

"You don't know what you've done..." he hissed, and stared into Setter's eyes. "And you don't know where you're from."

The Supreme Consul of the Earther people stared back, and watched the avatar clench his jaw. Light spilled out of his skin now, and this last piece of the plague began to disintegrate.

"The Krogg Queen warned you about me being in your blood. It was no coincidence that she and I appeared at nearly the same time..." he rasped out, wincing as his body burned away. "Listen to me now. I chose your species for a reason... your ancestors aren't what they seem..."

"Stop," was Setter's answer.

He pressed his hands tighter against Omega-Natosh's disintegrating form, as though he could crush the being.

"Stop trying to get the last word in. Maybe you're telling the truth. Maybe there's more going on than we know. Maybe one day my son will learn what it is. But that's the future, and you won't be there."

The avatar's body was almost all gone, yet he snarled, "Neither will you!"

Setter Caine smiled, "No I won't. But my son will be. My people will be. And you know me well enough to know that's all I ever wanted."

Absurdly, Setter didn't actually want to say 'I've won', but Omega-Natosh read it in his enemy's mind, and let out a wail. His last words were a scream of rage and disappointment, and then the last resistance to Setter's hands vanished: the last corner of Omega's mind... of the galactic plague... was gone.

Overwhelmed by his own darkness; burned out by the Earthers' light.

Setter staggered back, and then looked down at his own body. It still existed here — though he knew for a fact that, along with just about every other living thing on Genesis, his physical form was gone.

Odd.

"Let's not complain about that right now, alright dad?" Phealan smiled as he came up alongside his father.

Setter nodded, but said nothing.

Instead, he turned around, and saw billions of Earthers looking on.

"I do believe we just won," Setter said, sounding almost surprised.

There was silence for a moment, and then the roar began. Earthers began slipping from the telepathic plane, and they took that roar with them.

For all their differences, the Kroggs and Larosians both were equally overwhelmed by the power of the victory cries that crossed the planet. Like thunder everywhere, a massive rumbling through the air.

Cheers, handshakes, and hugs. They had done the impossible today, and many of them were alive to see it.

While most Earthers withdrew from the plane, a select few remained. Phealan stood with Cadmus Howler, and then Fox Magnus, Chronos Claw, Varnia and Beckett Lupus joined them.

They all looked at Setter Caine, who somehow was still there, and he smiled.

"So... I suppose the plan worked after all."

The Supreme Consul looked down as he spoke, and saw that the glow beneath his skin was beginning to turn into some sort of evaporation — similar to what had happened to the avatar, but somehow entirely different.

He blinked, "Oh my. Not sure how long I have."

"No time to waste, then," Fox came forward and hugged him. "Thank you."

Each of the Admirals said the same, as did Beckett Lupus, and then one by one they departed.

Cadmus Howler went last, shaking the hand of the Supreme Consul, "It was my honor to turn up early."

Setter patted the Colonel's shoulder with his free hand, then looked him up and down, "You're glowing like Phealan and I are, Cadmus. No idea what it means... but you are."

Grinning, Cadmus Howler shrugged, "If it's permanent, I'll retire from night operations."

With a parting chuckle, the Colonel vanished.

Phealan and Setter were left standing alone.

"Phew," the younger one said.

"You got that right," the elder agreed.

As Fox Magnus reanimated himself on *Victory's* bridge, he found Thena already standing in front of him. They hugged immediately, and then as they parted, Master Gunth appeared next to him, hand extended.

"Great work, sir. Damned great work."

"You too, Master," Fox grinned. Much had been lost, but it was impossible not to find joy in this moment.

"We've secured from automated firing, sir," Gunth continued. "Fleet is beginning search and rescue operations."

Fox nodded, then frowned. Lab Forepaw hadn't been on the plane... he'd have come to the front if he had been, and no one had felt his presence. Either he'd been lost with *Venerable,* or was unconscious in an escape pod somewhere. That put the First Space Lord in charge... Fox was officially in command.

"Recall all remaining gunboats from the atmosphere, and have all ships join the search. Hopefully there are plenty of pods out there to recover."

"Aye aye," Gunth turned away.

Letting out a long breath, Fox looked back at Thena, "Am I mistaken, or did we just win?"

Thena Magnus smiled, "No, you're quite right. We won. Accomplished the impossible."

Fox paused for a second, then laughed, "About damned time too."

Tovarrin found his way through crowds of cheering Earthers back to Novash's side. The Larosian leader smiled at the approach of the Captain-Elite, "I'm glad you're well, Tovarrin."

"And you, sir," the Stealth Guard agreed aloud. Then he looked up at Kragran, "And Warlord, I must congratulate you and your warriors. They are... most accomplished."

Kragran bow-nodded to the Larosian, "I'm obliged for the compliment, Captain-Elite. It was very good for all of us to fight on your side today. A habit we intend to keep... should fighting ever be necessary again."

"With the plague gone, let's hope there isn't much more of that to deal with," Narosh remarked, and then squinted and looked up into the bright sky.

I believe all our ships have been destroyed, sir, Tovarrin switched to open telepathy as he sheathed his sword. *Is that correct?*

Narosh nodded, his expression losing some of its humor, *Admiral-of-a-Division Novash died.*

Died well, Kragran pitched in.

"Indeed," Narosh agreed softly. There was definitely consolation in that, though the Admiral-of-a-Fleet would rather have had Novash back than the consolation.

Alas, many could share such sentiments today.

"We should assist the Earthers, and find General Lupus. We'll need to determine how best to help in the cleanup here," Narosh looked back down from the sky.

The aliens started looking for the Earther commanders.

Ed Jeffries woke up with a start. A bear was looking down at him, and he realized quickly that it was Garth Badger, the boat officer.

"Sir, we've done it," the Earther said with a smile.

Blinking a couple of times, Ed looked around him. The bridge of *Savanna Felix* was canted over on a thirty-degree angle, and their were shafts of sunlight stabbing in through the ruptured ceiling.

It was also getting chilly.

"We... wait. We survived the crash?" Ed started to shake his head to try to get his thoughts to clear, but the action caused a stab of pain in his neck.

"Easy there, sir," Badger said smoothly. "You lost a leg, and you might have some hefty internal damage. SAR teams are on their way over from the base."

Ed looked squarely at the Earther Lieutenant, "Garth. Wait. We *survived the crash?*"

The Earther laughed, "Yes sir. And then the plan worked."

That didn't register — it didn't even come close.

Lying back against the wall he'd landed beside, he sighed, "Holy shit. We survived the crash."

Cadmus Howler blinked the blue energy from his eyes and found himself standing face to face with Phealan. The young Caine was still on the plane with his father, so the Colonel deactivated the shields guarding them both and stepped out onto the beach. Ahead he saw Sergeant Cuttar and Corporal Canit, two of his great old friends from all the way back to the Quest.

"We made it, sir," Cuttar called with a wave, and then he crouched.

Moving up the beach to the Sergeant's side, Cadmus frowned.

"They were here when we got back from the plane," Cuttar explained. "Shield was down, and they were just sitting here looking at us."

Half a dozen wolves were on the beach, grinning happily and projecting an air of calm and joy. It struck Cadmus as very odd — he'd heard that the wolves had fled to the deeper parts of the island.

But here they were, inexplicably. The Colonel crouched to greet them, and one of the wolves approached him with a grin... then stopped just short of him, mouth closing. They stared at each other for a minute, and then Cadmus frowned. Did the wolf see something wrong with him?

Very strange... not what I was expecting... oh well...

The wolf grinned again, then came up and started sniffing in a more traditional wolf-Earther greeting. Cadmus laughed and petted his distant relative with a firm hand.

Chronos Claw was on the line with Varnia Lupus when the Signal Officer interrupted him, "Sorry skipper, but one of the boats just picked up a pod with Rear Admiral Maximane and most of her bridge crew."

A smile appeared on Chronos' face, and he looked at Varnia.

"You hear that?"

She nodded back, a small smile joining her answer. It was some consolation, but the death of her father was still weighing on her. Beckett was alright, but Varnon was gone...

"Another one, sir... by the Earth... hang on, signal coming in. I'll patch it into the tank."

Chronos' eyebrow went up, and he waited until a new figure appeared in the tank.

"No one ever gets to tell me I'm too cranky ever again. How many damned ships is that now?"

Varnia's smile grew warmer, the same signal appearing before her in *Renown's* plot, "Does it really matter, Jax?"

The old lion thought about her words for a second, and then he smiled, "You know, I don't expect it does."

Jax Furgus had survived once again.

Beckett Lupus sheathed his swords as soon as his eyes cleared, and he found he was surrounded by Krogg soldiers.

One of them — the same one who'd spoken to him before — noticed that he was moving again, and he did what Beckett supposed was their equivalent of coming to attention, "Sir, your victory was most awe-striking. May I shake your hand?"

Blinking in surprise, Beckett shrugged, "Er. Sure."

He shook hands with the Krogg.

"Have a name, soldier?" Beckett asked, turning to look back at the base. He didn't want to think of how many were lost.

"No, sir."

Beckett started to nod, then he stopped and looked up at the Krogg with a frown, "What?"

"No, sir."

"No... name?"

"No, sir."

Looking away for a second, Beckett allowed himself to be confused by that pleasantly trivial matter. Then he followed up with a question, "Is that normal, soldier?"

The Krogg nodded, "Yes, sir. We didn't have much time after spawning, so we don't have names."

"Oh."

"We can get some, sir, if you need us to!"

Beckett opened his mouth, then closed it again. Looking back towards the base, he took a deep breath of the icy air and shook his head, "Suit yourself, soldier. Will you help me find the other senior officers?"

"Of course, sir!"

They set off.

• • •

Kardrath had only four ships left — *Death*, *Agony*, *Pestilence*, and with the utmost of irony, *Plague* — but with these ships he was determined to find survivors.

A piece of an 80-gun ship of the line is ahead, sir. Still pressurized.

Acknowledging the report, the Warlord reached out to the piece of debris with his mind, *This is Warlord Kardrath to the section of an 80-gun ship ahead, we are taking you into my Mothership's dock. Please stand by.*

An Earther appeared next to him as he sent that message, so he turned his attention away from telepathic matters for a moment. The white wolf smiled sadly at him, then extended a hand.

"Thanks for picking up my pod," Zed Dune said softly.

"Our pleasure," Kardrath took the offered hand. "Are you well, Admiral Dune?"

The white wolf swallowed, "I'm hoping—"

Telepathic signal from the debris, sir… it seems to be an Earther.

Kardrath held up a hand to Zed, "Sorry, just a moment."

The Warlord looked back to the front of his bridge as he reviewed the communiqué in his mind, then nodded slowly, his eye turning back to his guest.

"She's in that chunk we're bringing in now, Zed. And mostly intact."

Zed blinked.

"*She* being Ami Dune," Kardrath added for clarification.

Zed blinked again, and opened his mouth. Nothing came out.

Smiling, the Warlord waved to one of his junior officers, "Take Admiral Dune to the recovery bay."

As the white wolf was led away, Kardrath felt joy. A glorious day of killing, and now a reunion. It was a good outcome.

Joyce Furgus groaned and sat up slowly. She was still on the floor of the Caines' living room, but since she was alive, she had to presume that the plan had worked.

Pressing the palm of one hand against her ringing head, she let out a low groan and waited for her vision to clear. When it did, Claire appeared, standing at the door in front of her.

"Claire, you alright?" Joyce asked in a croak, and the girl nodded gently.

"The minions didn't get in?" the marine Captain asked, trying to get to her feet. She stopped when a shot of pain lanced through her.

"They… didn't. He showed up, and I hid, but they never came in."

Joyce frowned, starting to ask who had showed up, but instead her eyes dropped to the deck and she saw a black wolf with yellow eyes sitting out there, staring at her. She frowned, surprised to see him.

Then he winked... no, he blinked... and got to his feet.

Claire watched from the window as the wolf trotted down the stairs and headed off into the brush. She didn't know what had happened — she'd hidden, and the wolf hadn't. And the minions hadn't entered.

She didn't understand.

Before she could think any more on it, though, Cadmus Howler and the survivors from the beach appeared around the Caine house, and medical supplies were recovered for Joyce and for Ellen Arbear.

All around Earth, people were shaking off the battle, and trying to figure out what to do next.

They were alive, though. That was the key. They were alive — and they'd won.

CHAPTER 60

"Any idea how long you have?" Phealan looked at the light pouring out of his father's feet, and Setter Caine chuckled and shook his head.

"I'm taking it as a bonus that I have any time at all. I guess the telepathic 'me' lingered around for a while after the blast," he replied.

Phealan smiled and nodded back, "It certainly is a bonus."

The two Caines stood bathed in the light of an Omega-free telepathic plane, and breathed deep.

"Wait, are we actually breathing now? I mean, you especially?" Phealan frowned.

Setter laughed again, "You should get Narosh to write a manual on what's actually happening when we do things in here. I think we did pretty well for newcomers, but I get the sense there's a lot more happening than we've figured out so far."

"That's a safe bet," Phealan agreed.

They stood silent again, breathing deep — or whatever they were actually doing — and the light pouring out of the elder started to rise little by little. It was like he was evaporating from bottom to top.

"Good thing it didn't start on the top and work its way down," Setter laughed again, and then he kept laughing. Phealan couldn't help but join in.

They laughed and laughed.

You realize what we've managed to do? Phealan thought, even as he doubled over.

We won, Setter confirmed.

It was impossible. The plan had worked.

After a little while they sobered, and Phealan caught his breath — or whatever — and shook his head, "We tricked a cynical, know-it-all, would-be God into destroying himself."

"That's what we did," Setter confirmed with a grin.

It was an unapologetically great feeling.

And soon, they both realized, it'd have to be over. The persistent light was making Setter's knees disappear.

"You did incredible today, son. Your speech, your help here… all of it was incredible."

"You too," Phealan countered. "You made this all possible."

Setter opened his mouth to counter-compliment, but Phealan held up his hand, "I don't think we should spend the rest of your time trying to one-up each other with praise."

"Good point," Setter nodded, looking down. "Funny, I can still feel my toes."

Phealan frowned, "Maybe it's in the manual."

"Should have thought to ask for it sooner... anyway. Listen..." Setter sobered, though the joy didn't leave him. "Listen. You're their leader now. You have to be. They're going to rely on you, and I know you're going to make things so much greater."

Those words eased the frown from Phealan's face, replacing it with a steady gaze, "It's going to be a lot of work. After all this destruction... we can work with Liz and Graham to rebuild human society. And we'll bounce back, obviously. I see we still have over a hundred ships left. And we'll help the Larosians and the Kroggs... perhaps an alliance of all of us..."

Setter's smile returned, "By the Earth, listen to you. You've already checked in on everyone... you already have a vision."

Chuckling, Phealan shook his head, "I have an idea. It'll be a long road. But after this victory, how could we *not* take it? So many people died, we *have* to rebuild. Otherwise, it was all for nothing."

"Rebuild, and rebuild better," Setter concurred. "See if you can bring them all together... see if you can help the humans do the impossible, just like you said."

Phealan thought of his speech, "Yes. We'll do all we can for them."

Taking another deep breath, Setter looked down. The light was up past his belt, and his hands — which had been at his sides — were starting to disappear too. He frowned at that, and tried raising one hand over his head. It reappeared.

"Odd," Setter frowned, and Phealan then helpfully passed his foot through the space where his father's feet would have been. They definitely weren't there — they weren't just being masked by something.

"Oh well," dropping his hands back to his sides, Setter let them continue to vanish. "Looks like we're low on time now."

"Yes it does," Phealan's smile faded away.

"So," Setter glanced away for a few seconds. "If I see your mother, I'll tell her everything."

"Send my love," Phealan added. "If you see her."

Setter laughed once, very softly, "Indeed. If."

"You did good today, dad. You saved us all. And wherever you end up, don't forget that. We would have lost if not for you," Phealan's words had some finality.

Setter simply stared at his son, taking a lingering pause as the light worked its way up his chest.

Then he spoke: "And you remember, son, that without you, we'd all have fallen apart, and lost our way. You're going to be a brilliant leader. And wherever I go, I'll be proud."

Phealan looked down, nodded, and swallowed.

The light seemed to be moving a little faster now, and Phealan watched it for a second.

"What does it mean?"

Setter frowned, "Hmm?"

Phealan nodded at the advancing light, "What you said to Omega. What does it mean... to be full of light?"

Eyebrows climbing, Setter smiled, "You know, I don't know. Maybe... maybe that all our good deeds, all the good we've ever created... maybe that's powerful stuff. Maybe it comes back to us when we need it. Maybe believing in something actually fills you with a light that can't be darkened. Maybe that's why we won... because we're all full of light."

A smile returned to Phealan's face, and he shook his head a little, "Wise words to end on?"

Chuckling, Setter shrugged — just before his shoulders disappeared, "I'm evaporating here, you're going to grudge me some sage words?"

Phealan shook his head, then sighed deeply, "I think you may be right, though. Full of light... indeed..."

His voice trailed off as the light started to work its way up to Setter's neck. There was no more time. Again, the last goodbye.

"Love you, dad," the young Caine said at last, and the elder smiled brightly.

To Setter Caine, who'd fought one war for his son, and another with his son, that really was all that mattered now.

"Love you too, son. Have fun."

The light took Setter Caine, the greatest leader the Earthers had yet known. Phealan Caine watched until the tips of his father's ears had evaporated, and then he breathed deep again. He held up his hands before his eyes, saw light seeping out from under his skin. It was similar to what had happened to his father, but different. Less intense.

The light had consumed Setter. It was as though it was living inside Phealan.

"I really need to get the telepathy manual from Narosh," the young Caine muttered to himself.

No longer just the young Caine, he realized. *Just Caine now. I'm alone.*

He'd been ready for that, but he'd known no amount of preparation could soften the blow when the moment arrived, and it became the truth.

Letting his chin sink for a moment, Phealan longed for his father and mother. He longed for the days when he was tiny, when the humans were just a story, and Omega a ghost in the past.

But he didn't linger on those wishes, because he knew, deep down, that now was an even better time. Because Omega was truly gone. Because there was a chance to rebuild — to confront a future without hidden darkness.

With that in mind, he closed his eyes... and opened them on the beach in Newfoundland.

The marines had left ahead of him; there were bodies of their fallen comrades and of many minions yet to be recovered.

Phealan looked out to sea, watching it glimmer in the moonlight.

Then a wolf appeared next to him — the black one, with yellow eyes. It sat on the rocks and looked out to sea as well, and then when Phealan looked down, it looked back up. As their eyes met, the wolf's grin faded. They stared at each other for a long moment.

Very strange.

Very odd.

After that, they looked back out to sea.

Phealan was alone... and there was much to be done.

CHAPTER 61

Liz Hastings had been pretending to sleep when the messages began to pour in from New Halifax Earthers who had joined Setter on the plane. These reports could yield only one of two possible outcomes: either the Allies were victorious, or the human refugee fleet was going to have to run.

When *Unity Genesis'* ArcColonel had called her to the bridge, she'd rolled out of bed fully dressed and had run the whole way, testing her new leg to the limit. By the time she arrived, the bridge was full of cheers.

She didn't need to ask.

A warm feeling coursed through her, but it was tempered — victory was great, of course, but what about the duel teams? What about Sarah, Pat, Graham and Christine...

It took her nearly ten minutes to get in front of a screen and to find more details. By that time, word had spread to the whole fleet. There would be no need to flee: Omega had been destroyed.

But as Liz read the details sent telepathically from Earth, her hand gripped her jaw. Eventually, she read too much, and her hand slid up to cover her eyes. She stopped being able to hear the cheers, or feel much of anything.

Sarah had died. And Pat too. Liz sat back in the chair she'd commandeered and felt hollow inside. She'd never had children, but she could only imagine this was how it must have felt to lose one's child.

Of course the plan had been a risk — of course this had always been a possibility. But somehow, despite all her experience in war and death, Liz hadn't been ready for it. And she had somehow held onto the hope that her family, such as it was, would survive.

All Liz could hope was that, in their last moments, Sarah and Pat had found a little piece of happiness. Only that could be real consolation, so Liz chose to believe they did.

She was right.

Graham Manchester sat alone in his darkened cabin aboard *Carnarvon*. Christine had returned them to the ship without incident, her completed evolution helping her dispatch many minions, before the rest were killed by the plan. Graham was safe. He was alive.

He certainly hadn't expected that.

He didn't even want it.

There were so many layers to his torment.

He had helped kill Gillian. That was easier to bear, because it had been his intent the whole time. It had been what he'd been meant to do. It had been the only thing left to him after all Omega had done. And it had been necessary.

But he'd done so without torment or strife. He'd suspended so much of his humanity... and secretly he'd hoped that at one tragic moment, it would come back to him.

It hadn't.

Did I banish it permanently? Perhaps it would be better if that was the case... if I am to live now, doing so without guilt... would be easier.

Or perhaps he simply shouldn't live now. He'd thought about that — he could easily end his own life. Christine had asked him not to do so without letting her know first, so that she didn't walk in on his corpse without warning, but she seemed open to letting him do it.

But should he? He'd shirked his responsibility to his fleet for all this time, perhaps now he should pay them back... they'd need leaders.

Leading out of a misguided sense of obligation... perhaps that was a Manchester tradition. One that had to be preserved.

It seemed absurd, though.

Graham didn't have the answers yet. Perhaps he'd consult with Setter...

He stopped himself there. He knew Setter was gone. He shouldn't have thought that.

Perhaps Phealan, then. The young, wise Caine.

Until they could meet, though, Graham would continue to sit in the darkness. There was nothing else he could do.

Christine Schaeffer suspended any chance of angst. She refused to think dark thoughts. There'd been too much of that over the past days, and she had far too much to be happy about. Her sister was alive, she was heading home — *home* — to Earth, Omega was gone, and in a personal victory... she could feel.

Really *feel*.

Her transformation was complete — the change they'd all been afraid of, but in retrospect, they just should have let run its course. Because the Earther cells injected into her would never have sought to do her harm... if they had sentience, that was.

No, the Earther cells were to be trusted, and they'd restored her ability to feel... and added much to it.

In celebration of that fact, Christine filled her bathtub with plain water — no analgesics, no stasis fields, no *nothing*. Just hot water. She shed her skin suit and let the air touch her skin, and it felt the same as it once had... perhaps better. The very basic pleasure of *feeling* the air, she'd taken it for granted but now it was restored to her.

When she slid into the water, she let out a very satisfied groan, and she realized that most of her muscles had been tense. The hot water eased them, and at the same time it surrounded her, touched her skin and reminded her what it really was like to be able to feel. Again, she'd taken that for granted for so long.

Dipping her head under the surface, she let the water poke into her ears, and swim through her hair. The simple contact with water was heaven. She stayed down beneath the surface for as long as she could hold her breath, then she popped up laughing. She couldn't help but laugh.

These were the things she hadn't appreciated enough before, and now she had them back. And the Earther part of her mind was making certain she enjoyed them.

Is it an Earther part, though? Or am I all Earther now?

Despite what she'd said to Omega-Gillian, Christine wasn't really certain anymore. She no longer felt like a work in progress, though — she no longer felt that every time she looked in the mirror, something else would be slightly different. She was complete now, whatever that ultimately meant.

A new person... who still enjoyed the same, simple things, but a little bit more than she had before. She dunked herself back under the hot water, and tried laughing down there. It ended badly, but that was alright — she'd missed coughing too.

Carnarvon plied the space towards Earth.

Claire Schaeffer sat on the couch when Phealan Caine stepped back into his house. She looked up with a start, and then she leapt to her feet and was rapidly hugging him.

He held up his hands in surprise for a moment, then embraced her in return, "Your sister is on her way home."

Pulling back, Claire looked up at him. She didn't manage to actually ask for confirmation of those words, though she found them hard to believe.

"Really," Phealan added with a smile, then let her slide free and return to the couch. Looking down at the bloody floor, he frowned, "Wounded come in?"

Claire nodded, but said nothing.

Phealan plucked the memory from her mind very subtly, and noticed with some surprise that the same wolf he'd seen on the beach had been here too. Those wolves were very protective, it seemed. And lucky too...

But there was a whole lot of blood on the floor, so he stopped thinking about that and headed to the kitchen, where he found a hand cleaner. Returning to the bloody spot, he held it up and shot the floor. A very gentle, strobing energy pulse carefully broke up and atomized the dried blood. After a second, the floor was spotless.

Turning back to the kitchen to return the cleaner, Phealan realized Claire was staring at him, "So much dried blood and that's all it took? That's too good to..."

She stopped herself from blurting out the rest, because she realized how absurd it would sound. She hadn't meant it to be mean, either — this was just another example of Earther magic. A simple problem and an effortless solution.

"We just beat Omega... did the impossible, remember," Phealan reminded her with a smile, returning to the kitchen and putting the cleaner away. "I don't think our floor cleaning abilities are top of the pile for the things about us that are too good to be true."

Claire shrugged a little sheepishly, looking away again, "I didn't mean anything."

"I know. You've been snapping at us for a while now, it'll take some time to break the habit. I don't mind waiting," Phealan said, leaning against the counter. "As long as you do it, I mean. Obviously I can't force you to change... that's not what we do."

"No," Claire said. Phealan wasn't sure if she was agreeing or disagreeing, but it didn't seem terribly important.

"So," he went on, "when Christine gets back, you and she can find your own way... I just hope what I said registered a little. About the impossible."

Claire glanced up at him, and she shrugged, "You want us to try to be wonderful people?"

Phealan winced at the wording, "Not when you say it like that. Just... just."

"Try to live better lives?" Claire helped, her tone a little playful. "You're a real wordsmith, you know."

Chuckling, Phealan shrugged, "Maybe I should write books."

"Maybe you should," Claire agreed. "Maybe I should too."

A broad smile came onto Phealan's face, and he nodded, "Yes. Maybe you should."

CHAPTER 62

It took a week for things to return to some state of quasi-normality.

By no means was this regular normality, of course — nine billion bodies could not be recovered in just a week's time. But many places were cleared, and survivors from the space battle were rescued. Pieces of life were starting to fall back into place, and to further that process, Phealan decided to welcome many people to his home.

The gathering began on a sunny afternoon, the snow having melted in one of Newfoundland's typical weather shifts. As Phealan walked around his house, and outside across the grounds of his estate, he found many fine people around him.

The humans were all here — Christine was with Claire, Graham had come, along with Ed Jeffries in his hoverchair, and even Liz Hastings. Liz was suffering the loss of Sarah and Pat, and Phealan could well understand that. He'd talk to her later.

The aliens had come too: Narosh, Kragran, Kragthar, and Kardrath, along with Tovarrin were all sitting out behind the house, the Larosians in large chairs, the Kroggs propping themselves up on rocks to avoid shredding the furniture with their blades.

And everywhere else were the Earthers. Many faces were missing: Varnon Broadpaw was gone, and Lab Forepaw had never been found. Artemis Tigar had died in a lifepod from his wounds, and Dran Nightclaw had died with his ship.

Obviously, Setter and Ursla weren't present either.

But those who remained were all very happy to be there: from the Navy came Minnie Maximane and her Flag Captain, Mel Ramsay. Jax Furgus had come too, along with Chronos Claw, Varnia Lupus, Fox and Thena Magnus, Ami Dune, and Zed Dune.

Karyn Kudlee, short an arm after Beijing, joined the dapper Lieutenant General Garnet Wiskar and, of course, Beckett Lupus from the marine corps. Along with them were Cadmus Howler and Ernile Cutter, as well as Joyce Furgus — the defenders of the estate.

Celia Lazarus was in attendance as well, the only doctor to join the occasion.

It was a fine collection of guests, and it did Phealan good to have them all at his home. The place had felt lonelier to him of late, for very obvious reasons.

Making the rounds, then, he stopped first to see his alien friends. A couple of the wolves from the pack had ventured in to examine these guests, as neither Larosians nor Kroggs were common sights in Newfoundland.

Kragran stared at one as Phealan walked by, and waved to the young Caine as he passed, "Phealan, these creatures are your progenitors?"

Eyebrow raised, Phealan shrugged, "They are. We like to think of them as extended family."

Kragran smiled at the categorization, then nodded, "Yes, I can understand that. Very fascinating fellows. Closed minds."

Phealan shrugged, "We don't communicate with them telepathically... it's all instinct."

"Aha," Kragran nodded, then looked to his fellow Warlords. "Small wonder we understand our Earther friends so well. They remain close to their origins."

The logic of that assertion didn't make a great deal of sense to Phealan, but he decided not to press the question. Instead, he looked to Narosh, who lounged in a chair and seemed fascinated by the fact that he could see his breath when he exhaled.

"This is marvelous," the Admiral-of-a-Fleet smiled. "It's very cold!"

Phealan cocked an eyebrow again, "Don't see that much?"

Narosh looked up, "Not in many years. Laros is not a cold world, though there were some in the Empire. There shall be some again, too, once we reclaim them from the old plague."

"Aha," Phealan nodded with a smile. "Well, a little taste of home, then."

"Indeed," Narosh's smile broadened, and he went back to watching his breath.

Leaving the aliens to their amusements, and curiously eyeing the wolves again, Phealan went on his way.

Joyce and Jax Furgus were sitting together on some rocks, watching a couple of wolves watch them.

"Are they staring at us?" Jax asked after a while. "Honestly, we beat Omega and everyone starts gawking at us."

"Maybe they just think you're ugly," Joyce offered helpfully.

Jax croaked a laugh, then nodded, "Good point, they don't look blind."

Chuckling, Joyce agreed, and then they fell silent again for a little while. They were back together, father and daughter, and it felt great.

"Oh," Joyce slapped her knee as that thought reminded her of something, "Ellen got her first new leg on this morning. Her mom's at Fengate with her."

"Esther?" Jax asked, then grinned when he got the confirmation. "That's great. That really is great."

The Furguses continued their staring contest with the wolves.

• • •

Ami and Zed Dune were wandering in the woods well away from the house. They enjoyed the cold — it was natural to them as arctic wolves — and getting a chance to walk the terrain of Newfoundland was too good an opportunity to pass up.

After a couple of hours, they arrived in a clearing that overlooked the cove below, and Ami took a great lungful of brisk sea air, "I'm glad to be back down here."

"On the planet, you mean?" Zed asked, and she nodded.

"Yes. I love the Navy... but there's no air like this in space."

Zed cocked an eyebrow and smiled wryly, "Strictly speaking, there's no air in space at all."

Ami grinned and glanced at her husband, "Well, doesn't that just make me even more right?"

He laughed and nodded, "Sure, you go ahead and think that."

Standing in that clearing, the two arctic wolves enjoyed the beauty of Newfoundland.

Minnie Maximane rubbed her hands together and blew on them, drawing a frown from Captain Mel Ramsay, "You alright there, Min?"

The lioness frowned and kept warming her hands, "Nerve damage, the doc says I'll have cold hands for a while until it's fixed."

Mel Ramsay frowned, "There isn't a shot you can get to just... well... fix it?"

Minnie looked up with a frown, "Why would there be?"

The fox captain scratched her chin thoughtfully for a moment, then shrugged, "Well, we're Earthers. You ever heard of the common cold?"

Frowning thoughtfully, Minnie shook her head, "Can't say that I have."

"Exactly. We cured it. So..." Mel looked back over her shoulder, then saw Celia Lazarus. "Hey doc!"

Celia heard the call and came over quickly, "What's up?"

"Minnie says she has nerve damage... she'll have cold hands for a while. Isn't there a shot for that or something? A rapid regen cure?"

Celia paused for a moment, then shook her head, "Don't believe so, no."

Minnie Maximane smiled winningly at her Flag Captain, and Mel Ramsay scowled, "What? Really?"

Celia nodded, "Sorry. I did bring a pocket lab with me though. I can probably have a prototype for you in about half an hour."

"Aha!" Mel grinned, and it was Minnie's turn to scowl.

"Later, doc. Enjoy the party for now," the lioness insisted.

Chuckling, Celia seated herself with these two. They talked about the magical quality of Earther medicine.

• • •

Ernile Cuttar was passing Karyn Kudlee and Garnett Wiskar when he heard something odd, and decided to stop.

"So it's 'l-e-e' instead of 'l-y'?" Garnett asked with a very serious frown. "Do you know why that was the chosen spelling?"

Karyn Kudlee shrugged, "I suppose... it looks neat on the page."

Nodding in a proper fashion, Wiskar clutched his chin, "I must say, it really is fascinating."

Cuttar frowned as he closed with these two, "Talking about...?"

"Our names," Karyn smiled at the Sergeant as he joined them. "We were just remarking on how Earther names have evolved."

"Indeed," Garnett added. "For instance, my name *Wiskar* is rather an obvious choice. But... well, your name for instance, Sergeant Cuttar. Do you know where it came from?"

Ernile frowned, then shook his head, "My first name was the name of a human Admiral from the old days. But mine's spelled differently than his."

"Ernle Chatfield," Garnett nodded.

Cuttar blinked, "Er. Yes."

"Names like Caine and Lupus are sourced from the species, and Wiskar comes from a characteristic," Karyn continued. "Maximane, obviously."

"Howler," Cuttar added helpfully.

"Indeed," Wiskar maintained his thoughtful frown. "Do you think someone sat down at the beginning of our race, and started coming up with clever options? Or did we all just make it up as we went along?"

Cuttar glanced at Kudlee, and then they both looked at Wiskar.

"Made it up, I think," Cuttar said.

"Definitely made it up," Kudlee agreed.

"How very interesting," Garnett Wiskar said earnestly.

The marines chuckled at his seriousness.

Thena Magnus had left her husband to catch up with Chronos Claw, and was on her way to the house for a drink when she passed Ed Jeffries, sitting quietly in his hoverchair and looking out into the woods.

"Ed, you alright?" she asked. She didn't know Jeffries that well, but everyone at this gathering shared a common bond.

He blinked and looked up at her, managing a smile, "Oh I'm alright. Just sinking in. I... well, I'm the only flag officer from the human race to fight here last week. And I lived."

Thena smiled, approaching his chair, "No mean feat. You should be proud."

The dark-skinned human smiled sadly and shook his head, "You can see it from two sides. It's great that I'm still here... it's just numbingly horrible that I'm the only one."

Taking a deep breath, Thena put a hand on Ed's shoulder, "What we lose...

what we leave behind… often is horrible. But here we are. Might as well keep going forward."

"Yes," Ed said softly. "Here we are."

CHAPTER 63

Phealan found Liz Hastings down on the beach, wrapped up in a heavy coat.

She heard him coming, and for once turned the tables on an Earther — she identified him by sound.

"Hi Phealan," she called, and the young Caine chuckled as he moved down the beach towards her.

"Liz, warm enough?" he offered in greeting.

She smiled thinly and nodded, shifting her coat a little to keep it and its heaters tight to her, "I'm doing alright."

Phealan paused for a moment at her answer, folding his arms across his chest, "Does that mean you're warm, or that in the grander scheme, you're fine?"

Liz didn't register his words at first, then she blinked and glanced at him, "Hmm? Oh, in the grander scheme I'm not even close to fine."

"Oh," Phealan smiled. "Glad that's out in the open."

"Hmm?" Liz looked at him again, and seeing his smile she realized what she'd said and laughed. "You'd think an ex-fleet commander, ex-politician wouldn't speak her mind so casually."

Laughing, Phealan shook his head, "I don't think that was too bad."

They stood silently for a moment, watching the cold waves come in. Seagulls passed overhead, squawking their usual, unique song.

Liz let it all wash over her. Breathing deep the salty air, she tried to remember everything she and Sarah had talked about. She simply couldn't get Sarah off her mind — Sarah and Pat...

"You didn't have a husband or children of your own, did you?" Phealan asked openly, and Liz shook herself from her thoughts.

"No, never did. Never found any men I was interested in. Never thought I could bring a child into the world anyway... first it was the Church, then it was the Kroggs, then it was trying to rebuild Genesis..."

Her voice trailed off and Phealan nodded, "I understand."

"I'm glad, too," she added. "If I'd had a kid... well, he or she could be dead now. Better not to take that chance."

It was a comment born in pain, and Phealan understood the sentiment. But he couldn't agree with it.

Shaking his head, he turned to Liz. He remembered meeting her on this estate decades prior, when he'd only been as tall as her boot. She was a woman of age, grace, and knowledge... but the life she'd led had shaped the wisdom she now enjoyed. Or didn't enjoy.

"Well for us, Liz, it's never too big a chance to take."

Liz's eyebrows went up, and she looked at him, biting back a retort about Earther idealism. Most days such a counter would never have occurred to her, but the pain of late had brought her cynicism back.

"Better off never being born?" Phealan asked, shaking his head. "There's joy in every life, no matter how miserable. Even suffering, even death... you find moments, and they're worth so much. They're certainly worth the risk."

Liz shook her head, "Can't agree with you, Phealan. I just can't."

"Your choice, of course," the young Caine replied, looking back out to sea. "But I think you know there's truth in what I'm saying. It's just a matter of actually being able to see it, which isn't easy."

Quieting, Liz followed Phealan's gaze back out to the waves, then heard the wolf sigh.

"I've been around so much death, Liz. My dad brought the weight of millions of dead into our house when he came home from the war... and since Omega's return, of course, it's been so much worse. I can understand how you feel, particularly after what you've seen... the whole civilization that you worked to build with Harvey Bingham on Genesis. And Sarah and Pat. All gone. Why did you bother to try, right? If it was all going to be taken away in the end?"

Those words started to strike at the core of Liz's thoughts, and she nodded a little reluctantly.

Shrugging, Phealan looked back at her, "Well, in real terms, if you hadn't then Christine and Claire might never have been born. And they would certainly never have been saved from the plague."

Liz frowned. She didn't really know either Schaeffer kid, and on first blush, they weren't much consolation.

But Christine had kept Graham alive, and Claire had helped Phealan find his voice. That was something.

"They seem like only small things — small victories, insignificant when you compare them to all we've lost," Phealan said softly. "But because you tried, two people are alive, and possibly many more because of them."

Liz turned her mind on that vector. What would have become of Genesis if she hadn't tried? Would more have suffered, and died, or never had a chance to begin with... Would Omega have come anyway?

"Exactly," Phealan scooped those thoughts from Liz's mind. "When things go badly, it's always hard to accept that they could have been *even* worse if you'd done things differently. But there are ways they could have been, and while that's very small consolation, it's true. So we just have to hope we did the best we could, and enjoy the good things that came out of it all."

Liz blinked a few times.

"One thing my dad said to me before he vanished," Phealan added, his voice suddenly sounding more like his father's. "We're full of light... maybe that's all the good we've done, coming back to help us when we need it to. Even during some of the darkest moments. I'm convinced, Liz, that if you hadn't tried to build a new Genesis, Omega would have won. I don't know how, but he would have. We'd have had less light to stop him with."

Liz didn't know if she bought that, but then she also had a hard time doubting the words of a Caine — even one younger than her.

So she nodded, "Next you ask me to do it again."

Phealan smiled, "Next I ask you to do it again."

She had to start from scratch, and rebuild human society one more time.

"Aha," she sighed. "Well, regen gives me another century to play with. I suppose... I could..."

She halted, her attempt to puff up with inspiration not succeeding. Rebuilding human society for a second time, out of shards left by the plague, was a job so big and so difficult...

Phealan interrupted those worries, "You don't have to start right now. You need time to grieve, and to forgive yourself. But we'll need you and Graham both to do this... what's left of your race is going to need you."

Sighing deeply, Liz nodded.

This was her lot in life. She always missed the fight — always missed the fatal end — and was left to pick up the pieces, and try to build again. Matriarch of the Navy, the first President of Genesis... now the steward of a new human civilization...

"Steward, I like that," Phealan grinned, and then put a hand on her shoulder. "It'll never be easy. That's why it's your job."

Liz closed her eyes at those words, and then Phealan drew his hand away and left her on the beach.

She'd have to find her own peace, and then the reconstruction of human civilization would begin.

CHAPTER 64

Fox Magnus and Chronos Claw sat in the woods, and tried to keep each other laughing.

They told old stories, they made bad jokes, and all the while, they could almost feel the ghosts of old friends crowding around them.

Together on *Flame*, these two had helped start Freetown, along with Savanna Felix. He was dead, a long time now. With them in their sloop had been Lang Sandpelt, and he was dead too.

Then they'd parted ways, Chronos taking over *Flame* and Fox serving in *Atlas*. With *Atlas*, Fox had worked with Audrey DeBrooke and James Stanton, who were dead, to help Sarah find Pat, both of whom were also dead. On the same mission, he'd met up with Draco Maximane, who'd died years ago, and Garvin Jardaw, who'd died more recently.

Fox could keep going like that, and so could Chronos. Lab Forepaw, somehow, had just winked out of life. No one knew how he'd died, or what had finished off *Venerable*, but they'd been taken out. Varnon Broadpaw had died fighting on the ground.

"Artie... I never thought he'd go," Chronos said after a while, adding to the train of thought. "Did you hear what he said to Omega before the New Halifax corridor fight? He said 'you're about to lose everything I can take from you'. Great way to say it..."

Shaking his head, Claw let out a sigh and leaned back against a tree.

Fox looked away for a few moments, absently playing with a stick he'd picked up.

"Dran Nightclaw, too," the First Space Lord said after that pause. "I didn't think it was possible... remember when he bailed us out, with the 111th?"

"Right when we met James and Audrey," Chronos nodded. "Running from those Kroggs... I was so worried about our engines. Ha! I remember that. Then I turned around and did energy-hyper... what was it... a year later? Worried about the engines... I had no idea what worried meant..."

Fox managed a laugh, "True. Though on the list of things we didn't know back then, I'll mark that one as low."

Chronos chuckled and nodded, "That's fair enough."

They fell silent again for a moment, then Fox shook his head and pitched the stick into the dirt, "We were so young, weren't we? The excitement of chasing back to Earth with that call for reinforcements... that whole war, honestly."

"We were a young race," Claw nodded. "I think meeting the humans, and working with them, taught us a lot about ourselves. Before them, we always took it for granted. I think seeing them, and their problems... that makes us more conscious of ourselves. Makes us better at being who we are."

Fox's eyebrow went up, "Keeps us honest?"

A laugh escaped from Chronos, "Funny way to put it, but I suppose."

He stopped again, trying to order his thoughts.

"I don't know," he said at last. "We've grown and evolved, but not the way the humans assumed we inevitably would. We haven't gotten bitter, or changed how we do things. I think our idealism still drives them nuts..."

"Our tech frustrates them too," Fox injected. "They think it's too easy."

Chronos nodded, "Exactly, that too. So we haven't changed that. Science that they figure is based on magic, morals they figure are out of kids' stories... and we keep winning, so that hasn't changed either."

Fox frowned, "You're building this one up, my friend, so you had better deliver."

Claw chuckled, "Easy there, I'm no Caine."

"Subtle," Fox countered, and Claw shook his head.

"Seems to me, all we've changed is how we explain ourselves. We're still the same idealists with magical science, we've just figured out how to explain that to the humans a little better. Phealan Caine has in particular. Maybe we can bring them round."

Fox leaned back in thought, "Some always understood. James and Audrey did."

Chronos bobbed his head a little, "True. But still. In the grander scheme."

"Yeah," Fox agreed. "We tell our story a little differently than we used to."

"Exactly," Chronos said, satisfied.

The conversation tapered off after that. They sat in silence again for a while, fishing for more things to talk about — inane or brighter subjects.

"Ah, I have one," Chronos said. "Why do you think Omega picked wolves, cats and bears?"

"And foxes," dapper Fox Magnus added with a smile.

Chronos shook his head, "I don't think you lot were invited. I think you snuck in."

Fox paused thoughtfully, then nodded, "Does sound like something I'd do..."

They laughed together again, and as their conversation meandered along for the hours that followed, they laughed more and more. Old friends, together after the war.

•••

Not far away, Varnia Lupus sat with her husband on a rock, looking up at the trees all around them.

"Dad and I came here plenty of times over the years... we never got to sit and enjoy it, though," she said.

Beckett Lupus nodded, "Aye. But together you got to sit in plenty of places, and enjoy plenty of things."

Varnia's chin dipped, but she murmured her agreement, "True enough."

Holding onto his wife, Beckett traced his memories of that last battle, and to the rage Varnon's death had released. He didn't know where it had come from — he'd never figured that out. But it only ever seemed to come when death was inflicted on those undeserving.

"You shouldn't worry about the anger," Varnia said, picking up on those thoughts. "It never comes at the wrong time."

Beckett sighed, "I would like to know the source, though."

Leaning into her husband, Varnia shrugged, "Pain, I guess. And anger... righteous anger, if that doesn't sound too strange."

"It does sound a bit strange," Beckett shrugged. "But as long as you don't mind that I have that sort of anger within me..."

She shook her head, "One part of you is not the whole. And... well, when it was dad dying, I'd probably have done the same."

It came back to that for both of them. Varnon had been such a great wolf. Like Lab Forepaw, those two had been together with Setter, Ursla, Artie Tigar and Savanna Felix back in the old days. Now they were all gone.

Earth space felt a little emptier.

The quiet sadness that accompanied that revelation stilled both wolves, and they sat together in silence again. Everyone today seemed to be sitting in silence.

But then something occurred to Beckett, and he smiled.

Varnia sensed a slight change in mood, and she looked at him, "What?"

Beckett Lupus squeezed his wife, "He did what he said he'd do, though. He went out smiling."

Varnia Broadpaw Lupus smiled sadly, "That's the way it should be."

"Yes it is," Beckett agreed.

Together, those two wolves remembered their fallen father — the wolf who'd told all Earthers to enjoy what time they had, and who had followed his own advice.

CHAPTER 65

The sun was shining bright, but Claire was sleeping rather deeply. Standing in the doorway of the room her younger sister had occupied in the Caine house since her arrival on Earth, Christine Schaeffer enjoyed the sight.

Sure, there'd be nightmares, but maybe right now she wasn't having any. Maybe there was peace in her dreams.

You can actually look in on them, if you want to. I discovered that by accident... but you're right, she has had nightmares. And she's not having any right now.

Phealan's telepathic voice in Christine's mind drew an answering nod from the young, hybrid human. The wolf came to a stop beside her and looked in at Claire too, then glanced again at the elder sister.

So, thinking of yourself as a hybrid now? he asked, and she shrugged.

It's an economical word... probably as accurate as any.

Good point, Phealan smiled, then waved in suggestion that they close the door and head for the nearby exit to the deck. Christine agreed with a nod, then pulled Claire's door shut and followed the young Caine in silence, taking every chance she could to touch something along the way — to appreciate its texture and temperature. These were things she could enjoy again...

"You're glad to be back in the world," Phealan observed, and she nodded without looking at him.

"I really am."

"Well, Celia mentioned to me earlier that whatever happened to you... sorry, no, whatever you became... no, I mean... well."

The young Caine's inability to convey his meaning with words surprised Christine, but before she could reach out with her thoughts to clarify, he asked, "Can I show you something on the telepathic plane?"

That would sort out any confusion, so Christine nodded, "Sure."

Phealan's eyes immediately went blue, and Christine's did the same.

As they both appeared on the telepathic plane, Phealan began, "First of all, you can come up here on your own. That's beyond every other human we know about... except, according to Narosh, the Son of Praaxus."

"Who's dead," Christine agreed. "Yep, so this is one of the inconsistencies... one of my new abilities, I suppose."

"Exactly," Phealan said. "But there's something else. Look at me."

Christine did as she was asked, and her eyes went up and down the young

Caine. At first she wasn't sure what she was supposed to see — perhaps she was able to see things differently than a normal human. Or perhaps it was something about him...

Ah, he was *glowing*.

"There's light coming out of you... just a little. But it's there," she said, and Phealan nodded again.

"Yes there is. And I don't know why. So that's interesting... but what's more interesting is that there's light coming out of *you* too."

Christine blinked, then looked down. At first she didn't see it, but her eyes somehow adjusted, and then the short, soft rays became clear. She frowned, raising her hand up before her eyes. It was very subtle, but she *was* glowing.

"They say when a woman's glowing, she's pregnant," she observed dryly. "I guess now there's another reason."

Phealan chuckled, "I'm going to stay away from direct commentary on that particular point. But you *are* glowing."

Christine nodded again, "I am."

She absorbed that fact for a moment, and then voiced the natural concerns, "So. Obvious questions are: why, how, and what does it mean?"

"Was kind of hoping you had some insight," the young Caine countered. "Of course, it could be coincidence. I got this way after we wrestled with Omega... we were holding the light against his attacks, and I'm guessing long-term exposure did something to me. But you came by it differently."

"Through pain... and rapid evolution," she said.

Had what she'd been through done this? Or was it just a function of the modified brain chemistry that she now enjoyed... or perhaps an accidental side-effect? She was used to those by now...

"It's probably a question for a doctor," she concluded.

"And the doctors are stumped. So I guess we just wait and find out," Phealan shrugged. "Ready to go back down?"

Christine nodded, and they returned to the deck. Once they were back in the real world, she not-so-subtly held her hand up before her, and made sure it wasn't glowing.

"That's really weird."

The frank comment amused the young Caine, but he didn't answer it directly. There were other things he wanted to ask.

"So. You sticking with Graham now, or you have other plans?"

With that abrupt change of subject, Christine's eyes moved back up and caught Phealan's. She wasn't sure what to say.

"He has a long way to go before he heals. But he has a long time to do it, and in the meantime, he'll be able to do a lot of good for humanity. Working with Liz... you know."

"I do know. I'll help, of course. But is that what you were asking?"

Phealan's smile spread, *Part of what I was asking.*

Oh right. I need to get used to looking for double meanings via telepathy, Christine thought back. But she still didn't have an answer.

This is how I feel... she offered, and pushed all her emotions about Graham to the surface.

They were a bit of a jumble, and Phealan frowned as he picked through them.

You care a lot about him. Well, let's not mince words... thoughts... you do love him.

Christine nodded, *I think you're right. But I don't know how much. And I'm not just going to close in on him now. Not after all he's been through. Maybe we'll end up together one day... maybe we won't. We'll still make a great working team.*

"Ah," Phealan said, and then he shook his head. "Hybrid really is a good word."

"Hmm?" Christine was confused by the change of topic again, but then she did the smart thing and checked Phealan's surface thoughts. "Oh... yes, well I suppose I am handling it a bit like an Earther, aren't I?"

"You are. You really are. I hope... well, it's not my place to..."

"No, it is," Christine smiled. "We owe you enough, you're allowed to have hopes for us."

Phealan couldn't disagree, "Well, I hope more humans can gain your perspective. I feel awkward saying so... I don't mean to judge a species... but..."

"But we'd be better off if we wised up. You don't need to feel guilty about saying it. And I think, in time, we may. I'll do everything I can to make it happen... well, short of doing to other humans what was done to me. That was a bit extreme."

"No kidding," Phealan concurred.

Their conversation ended then, because they both immediately sensed Claire waking up, and stumbling out of her adopted room. She looked both ways down the corridor, then spotted Christine out on the deck. Rubbing her eyes with the palms of her hands, she came outside to join them, stifling a yawn.

"Sorry, I was tired," she said as she slipped an arm around her sister, and her sister did the same.

"No problem," Phealan smiled. "I'm just making the rounds. Well, I mostly have already. One more person to see."

"We won't keep you, then," Christine said. "Thanks for the info about the glowing thing. Hope we get more news soon."

"Me too," the young Caine agreed, then set off.

Claire frowned at her sister, "Glowing? You're not—"

"Don't even go there," Christine shot back.

It was too late, the sisterly teasing had begun.

And these two welcomed it.

They were two of the survivors of Genesis, and some of the greatest benefactors of Earther kindness. And they were together again, at last.

CHAPTER 66

Graham sat on the couch in the Caine living room, staring at nothing in particular. He had made no decisions about his life over the past days — he'd simply gone through the motions, shook hands... done all the things expected or required of him, while intentionally isolating himself from the world.

He hoped that this afternoon, and a visit with Phealan Caine, would make some sort of difference.

"Don't know what I can promise, Graham," Phealan appeared behind the junior Manchester... the only Manchester... and then rounded the couch and lowered himself into the chair beside it. He looked over at Graham and let out a long breath. "You and I are newly alone, aren't we?"

Nodding slowly, Graham glanced at Phealan, "I never expected to survive. Shortsighted on my part... but I think that's forgivable, under the circumstances."

"I'd agree, you really didn't have much chance of surviving," Phealan concurred. "But now you've come back from the suicide mission. Have you decided if you're going to finish it off — kill yourself, I mean?"

Graham blinked at the openness of the question, "You don't mince words, do you?"

"Ha," the young Caine shook his head. "Doesn't seem to be much point. You're either going to do it or not, so why be coy?"

"You make a very good point," Graham agreed. "I think that's something I'll appreciate about this new situation... I'll be dealing with more Earthers. I never really got to work with many after the war... it was all about the Carrier program, for all the good that did us. I never got to roll up my sleeves and work with Earthers."

Phealan raised an eyebrow, "You'll have your chance now. If you stay with us."

Pausing, Graham closed his eyes, "My thinking at this stage, Phealan, is that I'll stay, and help. Out of a sense of obligation, if nothing else."

Phealan laced his fingers in his lap and flicked his ear, "That's not the best motivation, but I won't complain about you staying around. There's been too much death for my tastes."

Graham stared at the floor before nodding slowly, "I suppose in time I might find another motive. But yes, too much death. Much too much."

He was thinking of Sarah, and regretting his coldness — as he and Phealan had both known he would. For all the opportunities he and Sarah both had been granted to make their peace with each other, they simply hadn't. They'd been too wrapped up in the importance of what they were doing, and their anger, and all those other aspects of humanity that led to bitter endings.

The Earthers clearly weren't suffering the same. They'd made their peace, they hadn't hidden from the direness of their situation, and that let them find each other before the end. Something more humans should have done. Something Graham now silently wished he'd done.

"No point regretting it," Phealan offered quietly, reading the human's thoughts. "No last day would be perfect, no matter how hard you tried to make it so. Just... well. You and Sarah lived sixty years as the closest of siblings. How it ended is secondary to that."

A small, sad smile came to Graham's face, surprising the young wolf.

"In time, I might evolve enough to have that perspective on things."

Phealan guessed Graham was right: there was no point trying to rush that realization.

"You'll come to that change in your own time. I understand why you'd feel an obligation to live. But it's ultimately for you to choose your path — not just if you stay or go, but what you want to do if you do stay. I think Savanna Felix once had a discussion with you about that... it's the way we do things. You make your own choices, and we'll support you, wherever you end up."

Graham didn't immediately react to those words, and Phealan saw that no thoughts passed across his mind, so he added one more thing: "If I had to guess, though, I think soon you'll be leading your people. Because when this pain passes, you're going to discover that's what you're best at. And your people will need you to be good at it."

Closing his eyes, Graham let his head fall back against the head rest, "What I'm best suited for."

"Yes," Phealan confirmed, and then they both fell silent.

Graham's mind drifted to those who were gone, and he wondered what they would have said. That was a question Phealan had something of an answer for, so he gave it, "My dad was really happy you came away alive."

Graham's eyes turned on Phealan's.

"And Sarah and Pat... I didn't get a good look, but my dad and I were keeping a connection to them. They were together when they died. And they were happy. They had *found* each other again, I suppose."

Graham sighed.

"That's enough for now," he said.

Phealan nodded gently, "Fair enough. Just understand that they were happy, and happy for you too."

That was good. And now Graham was alone again, which was fine. There would be a great deal of work to do, he supposed, which would occupy him soon. He could visualize that — working, and not worrying too much about what had been lost.

As Phealan was saying, there was no point in dwelling on the past, and regrets. He'd just move forward, and do his best. Working solo. He could do that...

"I'm sure you could. But you're thinking with a flawed premise," Phealan interrupted Graham's thoughts. "I know it might help now to just close yourself off, and to draw strength from being alone. But you won't be that way forever. I can already tell your old façade is melting, my friend. And some day, you're going to be back with us. We'll be better off for it."

Graham looked down again, feeling a dreadful certainty that Phealan was right. It was easy to hide in sadness, to cut oneself off and let misery guide one's actions... but eventually he knew he'd have to let people in again. Heal and move on.

"Yes, so since you know that's going to happen one way or the other, you might as well stop resisting it," Phealan smiled, coming to his feet. "You don't have to do it all right now. That'd be foolish. But you can do it one choice at a time. Over the next couple of years, you'll start to find your way back. And then one day you'll just be yourself again. Different, but still yourself. The pain won't leave you... but it'll join a bunch of other things, all of them equally valid."

Frowning at the certainty in Phealan's words, Graham looked up. He didn't even bother to ask the question that came to mind — it coming to mind was enough for the wolf to pick it up.

You sound like you've been through it already.

Smile twitching, Phealan nodded, "I'm an Earther, Graham. We're too good to be true, remember? I went through all that after my mom died. And again after my dad died. And I miss them both. But I'm still here, and they'd both be so happy about that. And I'm happy about it to."

He said that so simply, and then with an Earther sense of timing, he went on his way.

Frowning as those words replayed in his mind, Graham settled back into the couch, and wondered. He couldn't say those things himself. Not yet. Phealan seemed certain the peace would come... and the Earthers tended to be right about such things.

Happy to be alive. Happy to still be here. Why wasn't that enough already? Graham shook his head slowly at that.

The human equation seems to be patently inferior to the Earther equation...

Graham stopped at that thought. Such a ridiculously obvious thought. It made him chuckle — in spite of everything, he chuckled.

"Don't remember seeing you do that for a very long time."

Blinking, Graham looked up, and saw Christine Schaeffer considering him with a raised eyebrow.

He stared at her for a moment, and then frowned, shaking his head, "I don't suppose you have."

His good humor seemed to slip away, and seeing that, Christine dropped onto the couch beside him. Her arrival pushed him back into a more serious mode, so he took a heavy breath, "How's Claire?"

"Napping again," Christine answered promptly, folding her arms.

Graham nodded, folding his arms too. They both settled back deeper into the couch, looking straight ahead, wearing stern expressions.

"I think there are a lot of people who expect us to be consumed by passion right now."

Not exactly what Graham had expected his adjutant to say, but he still managed to stop himself from turning to stare at her.

"I expect they will be disappointed," was his answer.

A smile crept onto her face, and she nodded, "Yes they will."

They fell silent after that, eyes front and a tiny space between them on the couch.

Graham thought about Gillian, and felt a stab of pain as she appeared in his mind's eye. Christine could tell what was going through his mind — she could have figured it out even without her new Earther side.

Phealan — and many people, it seemed — believed she'd fallen in love with Graham. She probably had. And she knew that, in time, he'd probably reciprocate. One day, perhaps, they'd find each other, and that would be wonderful and such.

For now, though, they were both alive, and that was enough to make Christine very, very happy.

She was part Earther, so that made sense.

"Perhaps, two years from now, I'll kiss you," Graham observed distantly, Christine blinked, and this time she looked at him.

"Two years?"

The ArcGeneral looked at the ArcLieutenant, then shrugged, "Time enough to grow beyond the pain. After that, I expect the attraction should be automatic."

Christine's eyebrow climbed at Graham's matter-of-fact statement. She wasn't sure if she could detect humor in the words.

Then he smiled and shrugged, "In a couple of years, then?"

She laughed, "Well, I'll look forward to it."

In the meantime, Graham Manchester and Christine Schaeffer sat shoulder to shoulder on the couch in the Caine house, and let the day wind down around them.

EPILOGUE

Some hours later, the sun was beginning to dip, and most of Phealan's guests had moved inside to talk, joke, reflect… to continue doing all the things that had filled this quiet day.

Phealan, though, had spoken to just about everyone, so he headed for the beach — the familiar place where he'd spent so many important hours of his life.

He didn't have any other pep talks to give. There was no one else to help. It was just him, alone, looking out at the sea. As he arrived there, he saw clouds blowing in — the rain would start soon, and he loved that.

Sniffing the air, he smiled. This was his *home*, and that hadn't changed. One comfort he still had.

Other than that, though, he did feel alone. He had a feeling that might never fully change. His responsibility now was to lead… and that was a solitary task.

"What does it mean to be full of light?"

The young Caine blinked at the unexpected question, then looked over his shoulder in surprise. Colonel Cadmus Howler was pacing down the beach, moving with the typical silence of an elite marine. His hand was held out before him, his eyes fixed on it.

As he came to a stop next to Phealan, the Colonel glanced at his fellow wolf, "I'm still glowing too. I think… well, whatever fluke put me there with you and your dad, now I'm in the same boat as you."

Phealan nodded, "I didn't mention you to Christine, but I know."

Cadmus took a deep breath of the cold, damp air, then shook his head, "Well, it's my honor to be on the team. Though I'm sorry I'm not someone you knew better before this all started. Might have made it easier for both of us, if we'd been longtime friends."

Phealan frowned for a second, and contemplated denying Cadmus' words… but he couldn't. The Colonel had a point. Though Earthers inevitably got along well together, there was a deeper bond that existed between close friends — as it had between Setter and Andra — which made them natural partners.

Cadmus Howler and Phealan Caine had never been friends, but now they both knew they'd have to work together. Perhaps for a very long time, and on very important matters. It would have helped if they had a longer history, but they didn't, so they'd have to build a new friendship now. That would be essential.

They were both full light. And neither of them had any idea what that meant.

But over time, they'd find out, and both of them suspected they'd be veritable brothers at the end of the journey.

As that thought crossed his mind, Cadmus cracked a smile, "Well if we want to be more than 'veritable' brothers, I do have a sister about your age."

Phealan blinked, "Excuse me?"

"Just saying," the Colonel chuckled. "If you two happened to hit it off, then we'd actually be brothers…"

"Are you trying to set me up with your sister?"

Cadmus shrugged, "There are worse icebreakers."

Phealan laughed out loud, and then shook his head with a grin, looking into the wind, "Well. I won't rule anything out."

Cadmus took his turn to laugh, and the two wolves stared out to sea. The drizzle started to fall a moment later, and they both looked up into the dim sky, basking in the coolness. It was as though their home was reaching out to touch them, to remind them of where they were from, and where they were going.

After a few moments, Phealan opened his eyes.

"Long road ahead, Cadmus."

Cadmus Howler opened his eyes too, "Much to do."

Phealan nodded again, and then Cadmus frowned, "Is this when we're supposed to summarize all that's happened to us… look ahead and formulate an equation? That's how it went in Pat Conroy's books."

Glancing at his compatriot, Phealan frowned thoughtfully, "Well… I suppose it could be. But equations were my dad's thing. I don't think they're for me."

Cadmus shrugged slightly, "That's fair enough."

"Indeed."

Pausing again, the Colonel frowned, "So if equations aren't for you, what is?"

The Supreme Consul of Earth didn't have an answer, so he said as much: "You know, I don't know yet."

"Ah," Cadmus nodded. "But then, thanks to your dad… and to so many of our friends… you have the time to figure it out, don't you?"

A smile spread on Phealan's face.

He couldn't have said that better himself.

For all they had lost, and all they had suffered, the victory had been won. And there would be many days ahead to decide what would come next. They would build a brighter world, and enjoy all they had won. Sometimes they would suffer, too, but they'd have their chance to go on. They were alive.

And because they were Earthers, that was enough — more than enough. They could move on.

Setter Caine would be happy.

Looking up to the gray sky, and feeling the drizzle dampen his face, Phealan Caine breathed in deep lungfuls of air.

This was his home, and now it was his planet to look after, as he'd promised his father. And whatever came, he'd find a way to deal with it. He had the time to learn, after all.

"I do have the time, Cadmus," Phealan said.

"I do indeed."

POSTSCRIPT

There was an unexpected, sharp, blinding flash.

Setter Caine blinked, and realized his son was no longer in front of him. He was still on the telepathic plane... or at least it appeared to be the telepathic plane. He was surrounded by white, and it felt the same, but as he looked down he found that his body was no longer evaporating.

The afterlife?

He started to look around, but then a voice stopped him cold.

"What's this I see..."

He knew that voice.

"Setter, what's going on? They didn't get you too..."

Turning fast, Setter came face to face with Savanna Felix.

Yes, Savanna Felix. Who'd been dead for forty years.

Setter didn't have words at first — his eyes went wide, then a great smile came to his face, and he grabbed his old friend by the shoulders and shook him.

"Whoa... easy..." Felix protested. "What's going on? Did I just die?"

Setter eased off for a moment, then tried to figure out what exactly was happening. If he'd just died and come here, perhaps Savanna had too... even though he'd died four decades earlier. Maybe, somehow, they'd arrived in this post-death location at the same time.

"Savanna... no, I didn't die then... I mean, it's been over forty years. I just died defeating Omega..." he started to explain, but realized if Savanna had literally just been plucked from the bridge of an exploding *Tonnant* at Krogg 'C', it wasn't going to make any sense.

Convenient that he realized as much, because Felix's eyebrow was severely raised. *Severely.*

"Omega?"

Setter winced and scratched behind his ear, "Any chance you're telepathic? You weren't back then... but you're on a telepathic plane here, so maybe..."

"Telepathic?" the cat Admiral wasn't ashamed to make it clear that he wasn't following.

Can you hear me now? Setter asked with his mind.

"Of course I can," Felix replied. Then he paused, asked, "Wait. What?"

Try thinking to me. It's like using your instincts just... well, a little more language-based.

Felix nodded, *Okay... whoa. Okay. That's unexpected.*

"I know!" Setter realized he was excited, which seemed unusual, but he didn't care. He was getting a chance to see Savanna again, for however long it lasted.

And if Felix was here, others must be too...

But first, he had to bring his old friend up to speed, "Alright, let me catch you up."

Felix blinked, "Well. Sure. Always wondered what it was like for the Larosians..."

Setter projected the memories of the past forty years into Felix's mind, and over the course of a couple of minutes the cat digested them all.

"Good grief," he said.

"That's one way to put it," Setter agreed. "So... er. Don't see anyone else, do you?"

Felix and the wolf looked around for a moment, seeing nothing but whiteness in every direction.

"Nope," the cat confirmed after that.

"Nothing," Setter added.

"Just us. Not that I'm complaining," Felix smiled and patted Setter's shoulder.

The wolf nodded in reply, "Absolutely. So I wonder what we're doing here."

Felix frowned, "I would like to know that. But there's nobody to ask, so we may have to..."

He stopped, his eyes fixed on a point past Setter's shoulder. Realizing there must be something to see, Setter wheeled, and stopped in surprise.

There hadn't been anyone there a few seconds prior... but now.

"Maybe they know," Felix suggested.

Setter nodded, and stared at two humans who were, in turn, staring at the pair of Earthers. One of the men wore a green tunic, the other a black one, both of which looked rather like uniforms, but which certainly weren't Genesis issue.

Felix moved up alongside Setter, and they both eyed the humans curiously.

Then the human in black shook his head and glanced at the human in green, "So. Wasn't expecting this."

The one in green winced the way you wince when you were hoping for more insight from a friend but don't get it. He then glanced at his compatriot and let out a sigh, "Well, look on the bright side."

The one in black frowned, "Which is?"

"They're not raccoons."

The one in black paused, narrowing his eyes, "Really? That's what you come up with?"

"Well they're clearly not raccoons. They look like a humanoid wolf and a humanoid tiger, which is... well."

"A great big bucket of interesting," the one in black offered. "Bet you're regretting all the stupid jokes, now, aren't you?"

"Maybe I am. But I really hope they don't speak English, because first of all that would make *no* logical sense, and second of all, we're probably not making a good first impression if they do."

Setter and Felix looked at each other, and took that as their opening.

Holding his hand up in a wave, Setter Caine offered a greeting, "Good morning."

"Well crap," the one in black said.

"Good morning," the one in green returned the greeting, trying not to act sheepish.

Completely confused, and more than a little curious, Felix and Setter began walking towards the humans. Then, with a glance to each other, the humans came to meet them.

None of them had any idea where they were, or why, but somehow that didn't worry Setter at all.

Perhaps this was the afterlife, or perhaps there was new work to be done.

Either way, he looked forward to finding out.

APPENDIX A: CHARACTERS

We come to the end, and find that many of the friends we traveled with to get here are no longer among us. These are the ones who remain to fight in defense of the Earth.

Arbear, Ellen – Lieutenant
A marine with Cadmus Howler's elite 2/54th, Ellen is the daughter of venerable Krogg War Captain Esther Arbear.

Arbear, Esther – Captain
During the Krogg War, Esther Arbear was one of the Earther Navy's finest Captains. Having retired after the end of that conflict, she has rejoined the service in order to help battle Omega.

Broadpaw, Varnon – First Consul
Varnon Broadpaw is the First Consul of the Earther people. One of the most respected veterans of the Krogg War, he has a keen military mind and a bad sense of humor. He will need both in order to play his role within 'the plan'.

Caine, Phealan – Deputy Supreme Consul of Earth
Phealan has assumed the role of deputy to his father, and now must help with the execution of 'the plan'. He is the greatest Earther ever to have lived.

Caine, Setter – Supreme Consul of Earth
Setter Caine is the patriarch of the Earther people, and the originator of 'the plan' — the Earthers' only real hope of cheating Omega of his victory. Setter knows he will not survive the final battle, but as ever, his focus is on the fate of his people, not on his own well-being.

Claw, Chronos – Vice Admiral
A veteran (and subsequent Commander) of Fox Magnus' *Flame*, Chronos Claw finished the Krogg War as one of the Earther Navy's most distinguished sloop officers. Staying at Krogg 'A' after the war, he became one of the fleet's leading Admirals. His experience will make him a great asset during the final battle.

Conroy, Pat – Historian
Pat Conroy distinguished himself with hard battles during the Krogg War, and in providing assistance during the early battles against Omega. Now he must play his part in 'the plan', and hope that victory will bring a new lease on life for him and his wife, Sarah Manchester.

Cuttar, Ernile – Sergeant Major
Ernile Cuttar is the Sergeant Major commanding the special Recon Squad attached to 2/54th and General Beckett Lupus. Having fought alongside both Beckett and Colonel Cadmus Howler in the Krogg War, he is acknowledged as one of the most elite marines in the Earther service.

Dune, Ami – Rear Admiral
Ami (Cairn) Dune was one of the Krogg War's best-known officers, her exploits having been covered extensively by Will Rust and the Genesis Free Press. After the war she married Zed Dune, her fellow wartime Commodore, and joined the Earther Consulate.

Dune, Zed – Rear Admiral
One of the most innovative thinkers in the history of the Earther Navy Engineering Corps, Zed's fingerprints can be found on the first versions of Earther hyper charges and energy-hyper cutters. He is also an experienced frigate officer.

Forepaw, Labrador – First Lord of the Admiralty
Lab Forepaw is probably the best officer ever to serve in the Earther Navy, and now he leads the fleet as it prepares for its final battle with Omega.

Furgus, Jax – Admiral
During the Krogg War, Jax Furgus had many ships shot out from under him. Now he commands the recommissioned 74-gun *Aboukir*, and figures he may not actually survive if Omega destroys that ship.

Furgus, Joyce – Captain
Daughter of Jax Furgus, Joyce commands a company of Cadmus Howler's elite 2/54th. She will join all other Earther marines in defense of their home.

Gunth, Howard Percival III – Cruising Master
Mister Gunth was Fox Magnus' Cruising Master in *Atlas* during the Krogg War, and aboard *Chimera* when Omega returned. Now he joins the dapper First Space Lord aboard *ENS Victory*.

Hastings, Elizabeth – Group Captain
Liz Hastings survived the second battle of Krogg 'A', and now must take charge of her people as they struggle to survive against Omega.

Hobbes, Ronax – Captain
A carrier skipper during the Krogg War, Ron Hobbes returned to the service when Lab Forepaw asked him to serve as Flag Captain of *Aboukir* on a run to Freetown. He now serves with Jax Furgus aboard that ship.

Hodge, Gillian – Avatar
Gillian Hodge isn't herself anymore: her body belongs to Omega. The plague was able to infect her (despite the protection of Earther regen treatments) by infesting her unborn fetus, and now she is one of his favorite avatars. Omega-Gillian will soon face Graham Manchester in battle, as he plays his part in 'the plan'.

Howler, Cadmus – Colonel
Cadmus Howler had commanded Beckett Lupus' old recon squad on Krogg 'A', and since then he's remained at Beckett's side, turning the recon squad into a special escort unit for its former Sergeant, and eventually taking over command of 2/54th. He has returned to Earth space with *Renown*, and will be integral to the defense of his homeworld when Omega invades.

Jeffries, Ed – Commodore
A veteran of Pat's Pirates, Ed went to Freetown after the Krogg War, and rose to command of *Savanna Felix*, one of the colony's new Earther-hybrid warships. The only leader to survive the destruction of the privateer colony, Ed and his ships are destined to be the only humans participating in the defense of the Earth during the final battle with Omega.

Kardrath – Warlord
Kardrath is commander of the mighty new Krogg Navy, and very proud to be called an ally of the Earthers. He and his ships will fight viciously in defense of the Earth.

Kragran – Warlord
The leader of the new Krogg people, Kragran has led his race to new heights of mental and military power. He looks forward to helping the Earthers defeat the plague that threatened to ravage Krogg 'A'.

Kragthar – Warlord
The new legions of the Krogg army are commanded by Kragthar. A generally

agreeable Krogg, he looks forward to killing many Omega minions during the final battle on Earth.

Kudlee, Karyn – General
A distinguished veteran of the Krogg War campaigns at Avalon and Amaratsu, Karyn has worked her way up from her old command of 2/49th to her current post, General commanding the defenses at Earth. Karyn is decidedly aware of how her last name is pronounced, and she uses her considerable body size to make sure no humans give her grief for being a 'cuddly' bear.

Lazarus, Celia – Doctor
During the siege of Krogg 'A', Celia Lazarus was a medic aboard *Orion*, and it was she who stabilized Narosh after his crash landing on that ship's deck. Her actions saved his life then, and the injections of Earther drugs she gave him spared him from infection by Omega forty years later. Now she has created the cure — the foundation of 'the plan' which Setter Caine hopes to use to disappoint the plague.

Lupus, Beckett – General
Beckett Lupus has risen to the top of the Earther Marine Corps in the forty years since the end of the Krogg War, and is thus the overall commander of the service. When Omega comes to Earth, he will face Beckett's prepared defenses.

Lupus, Varnia – Rear Admiral
Varnia (Broadpaw) Lupus is the wife of Beckett Lupus and the daughter of Varnon Broadpaw, and up until the Church coup was the Earthers' senior ambassador to Genesis. She now commands *Renown*, and will be aboard that mighty ship for the defense of her homeworld.

Magnus, Fox – First Space Lord
First Space Lord Fox Magnus is the second-highest-ranking Earther in the Navy, and the most dapper by far. He and his wife lost their previous ship at Krogg 'A', but have taken over the newly-built *Venerable*-class First Rate, *ENS Victory*.

Magnus, Thena – Vice Admiral
Having fought alongside Fox during the Krogg War, Thena has joined her husband in command of *ENS Victory* and its Battle Squadron for the final battle against Omega.

Manchester, Graham – ArcGeneral
Graham wants to die, and he'll do anything he can to take Omega with him

when he goes. Particularly, he hopes to kill the abomination that the plague made out of his wife, Gillian Hodge. He is without feeling; this quest is all he has left.

Manchester, Sarah – President, ArcGeneral

Isolating herself from her emotions, Sarah is preparing to play her role in 'the plan'. She once commanded ships in battle; she once was President of Genesis. Now all she can do is fight Omega-Paine, and hope to win.

Maximane, Minnie – Rear Admiral

Daughter of Draco Maximane, Minnie followed in her father's footsteps and joined the Earther Navy. She now commands a formation of inter-war ships, flying her flag from *ENS Galahad*.

Narosh – Admiral-of-a-Fleet

Narosh was rescued from the clutches of Omega by *Renown*, and was returned to Laros. He now commands the Larosian forces dispatched to assist in the defense of Earth.

Natosh – Avatar

Natosh is no longer himself, but is instead the chief avatar of Omega. He was the vehicle through which Omega captured Genesis, and his physical and telepathic prowess is considerable. He is one of the plague's preferred vehicles for torture and mutilation, and he will be the figurehead with whom Setter Caine crosses swords during the final stages of 'the plan'.

Novash – Admiral-of-a-Division

The first Larosian to ever meet an Earther, Novash has spent the past decades commanding the defensive blockade of Laros. He now leads the Larosian ships assisting in the defense of Earth against Omega's invasion.

Nightclaw, Dran – Comptroller of the Navy Board

Acknowledged by one and all as the greatest frigate officer who ever lived, Dran is the Comptroller of the Navy Board, and will return to command of his old frigate *Cerberus* for the final battle.

Omega

The creator of the Earthers, Omega is coming for his revenge. The Earther immune system that he created in the twenty-first century was so powerful it defeated him, but now that he has been spliced with Krogg DNA, he's ready to show the Earthers just how nasty he is. He will crush the Earth, and the stupid Earthers, and force Setter Caine to watch. Being the most powerful telepath in the history of the universe, he plucked 'the plan' from Earther brains almost immediately. He thinks the cryptically-named strategy is pretty damned stupid, and he looks forward to laughing in Setter Caine's face when it falls flat on its backside.

Paine, Gregory – Avatar
Once the leader of the Commonwealth of the Faithful, Paine has become an avatar of Omega. Sarah Manchester and Pat Conroy will face him as their part of 'the plan'.

Ramsay, Mel – Captain
Mel Ramsay's parents served with Draco Maximane during their careers in the Earther Navy, though both survived the destruction of *Engadine* at Krogg 'A'. Forty years later, Mel commands Minnie Maximane's flagship, the *Champion*-class *Galahad* during the final battle in defense of the Earth.

Schaeffer, Christine – ArcLieutenant
Christine Schaeffer was just another cadet in her fourth year at the Genesis Naval Academy, working at a Panatorium to pay her tuition. Then she met Pat Conroy, who introduced her to Graham Manchester, who hired her as his new aide on a whim. In a freak accident on *Genesis One*, she was critically injured, forcing Doctor Celia Lazarus to give her a rapid regen treatment. Unexpected side-effects from that treatment have left all the nerves in her skin hyper-sensitive, and her biology in a unique state of flux. This particular mutation inspired Doctor Lazarus, and with cells harvested from Christine's mutated bloodstream, a potential cure for Omega was formulated. Christine remains attached to Graham, and when he faces Omega-Gillian as part of 'the plan', she will accompany him.

Schaeffer, Claire – Citizen
With her parents dead and her sister away, Claire Schaeffer is virtually catatonic, and under the care of the Caines. She intends to witness the end of the Earth from their living room.

Tigar, Artemis – Vice Admiral
Artie Tigar was Andra Ursla's Flag Captain through the entirety of the Krogg War, serving with her aboard *Agamemnon*. He flew his flag from that ship when Omega attacked the New Halifax corridor, and in the battle that followed he lost both arms and legs. Both limbs and ship have been restored for the final defense of Earth.

Ursla, Andra – Admiral
Andra will join Setter Caine as part of 'the plan'. Together, the old friends and leaders of the Earther people will battle Omega-Natosh, to their deaths.

Wiskar, Garnet – Lieutenant General
Garnet Wiskar is a veteran of the assault on Krogg 'A' during the Krogg War, and has since moved on to command the Fourth Division of the Earther Marine Corps. A dapper cat, Wiskar will be responsible for protecting Sydney, Australia — and Fengate Hospital — during the final battle against Omega.

CHAPTER ONE

A COMMODORE'S JOB DESCRIPTION

"Commodores aren't supposed to get themselves into trouble, you know. That's why they made you one," Karen McMaster's words came with their usual smooth elegance, and I smiled and glanced at her as she spoke.

Of course she was right — Commodores were supposed to stay out of the messy bits of Naval duty, and instead take care of squadron command and paperwork. My particular job description probably had 'stay out of trouble' written right into it.

But since when had a job description actually described what any Defense Command officer *really* did?

Seriously, I don't mean that in an arrogant way... for me it's just a question of my style when it comes to dealing with the Belt frontier. Generally, my approach with that rough side of space didn't fit the template of the academy playbooks. That's why I got my job done.

But thinking about such things at that moment was irrelevant, and besides, Karen was smiling at me. One of her trademark smiles. If you don't know what I mean by that... well, you will soon enough.

Containing a contented sigh, I managed to grin in response to her words, "You know, they really should know better than to think an extra rank bar's going to keep me from being stupid."

"Those were my very words to Admiral Noyce. He wasn't holding out much hope," her eyebrows rose playfully as she said it, and I chuckled.

"Yeah, so I'll take that as de facto authorization for this then."

Karen's smile stretched wider still, and I stared at it for a second as she looked down at her mag and slapped a fresh power cell into the pistol.

The way she could make anything look elegant never fails to amaze me. Even loading a pistol — how can that be elegant and still serious? Karen. That's how.

Sorry, I got distracted then; I get distracted now just thinking about it.

Oh and in case you're wondering, this was still early days of us being together all the time on the same ship. She'd only transferred over from *Lion* a week or two before this, I do believe. So cut me some slack for allowing my mind to wander.

Prying my eyes slowly away from Karen's smile, I slid my electromagnetic disrupter (mag) pistol from its holster on my hip, then tabbed the power cell release and quickly examined the conduit heads to make sure they were clean and free to send energy into the blast emitter. Satisfied, I pushed the cell back into the pistol and tabbed it online, then set its output to moderate.

The goal here was to take Jones alive, after all. Hopefully he'd go along with that plan...

"Matt's going to kill us both when we get back to the ship," Karen looked back up, satisfied with her own gun's state of readiness.

My eyebrows went up and I met her eyes, my grin remaining, "A Commodore and his Flag Captain are about to storm a notorious pirate's hideout with only sidearms and no immediate backup… and you think *he's* going to kill us? Our dear friend Matt is the least of my worries."

Somehow, Karen's smile brightened a little more. Let me tell you, she needed an overload switch on that thing. I was always sure that one day I'd just be staring and get hit by a bus or something.

Anyway, moving on.

She was referring of course to Commander Matt Baxter, First Officer (but until his promotion the previous week, head of security) of DCNS *Wolf*, my… well, now *our* frigate. He never liked it when we did stupid stuff. He actually called it 'stupid *stuff*' to our faces.

It was remarkable he hadn't given up on us already…

"Alright, ready?" Karen purposefully took the smile off her face. Her heart rate was still up, and so was mine. This was the exciting part — the moment that promised action and maybe even a shoot out, but which came before the mind-numbing terror of being caught in a crossfire. It only goes downhill from here.

"Yep," I raised my mag and settled my upper body into a good firing posture.

Karen did the same, turning her torso to get a good sightline down the barrel of her pistol, holding that weapon in both hands and shifting her balance to make sure she could move steadily.

She did that *really* well — with that elegance I keep blubbering about. She sells that gracefulness magnificently. Like a praying mantis; beautiful and so very lethal. Not that I'm saying Karen's like a bug… guess I should have thought that one through a bit better…

Sorry. Keep getting sidetracked.

"Here we go…" Karen's smile was gone entirely and her leg suddenly flashed forward in a blurred kick. Jones' old front door flew off its hinges and thudded into the room inside.

A stale, hot stench hit us both as Karen led the way in with quick, even steps, "Defense Command officers, everybody on the ground!" Her words go from smooth to steel in a flash.

I covered left and she covered right. The room was dark — there'd clearly been no lights on inside, and now we had to wait just a moment for our vision to adjust from the simulated daylight outside to the blackness of–

"Down!" I threw myself to the ground before I actually realized what I was doing; I'd seen the shape of a man taking aim with a shoulder-laser and just reacted.

Karen threw herself to the ground on the other side of the room, and just in time, too, as the frame of the front door and the wall surrounding it were disintegrated by a geyser of red energy.

That's right, Jones was defending his *house* with an *anti-tank weapon*. Hey, I guess it never hurts to think big.

Read the full chapter at:

WWW.DEFENSECOMMAND.NET

CHAPTER X *(Abridged)*

"There they are... looks like Freddie's leading them himself," Devlin pointed towards the closest street to the palisade, and Waller adjusted the vector of his glasses and nodded. Captain Kearsey's men were in position to watch the backs of the Canadian Rifles in the houses along the wall.

"Good man. Alright Jimmy, get down to your platoon, be ready to move if I yell, but leave me a section."

"Yes sir," Jimmy nodded quickly, turned, smiled at the ladies, and then left, putting on his hat as he did so.

Waller's glasses swept the palisade now — the man-like beasts were at 300 yards and that left little more time to watch. Soon they'd be under the protection of those palisades — the defensive arrangements here left no loopholes for firing through, and had no turrets to allow defenders to fire at savages as they piled up against the base of the long, straight wall.

Tucker would have seen that too, and positioned his men accordingly... the only place along the entire line where the defenders had the angle to shoot at savages piling up under the wall was on the roof of that train...

Waller stopped thinking for a moment, because before his eyes the savages seemed to all shift left — to the right from their own perspective — and head for the station. Over 1,000 at least, all heading there. Had they seen the weak point?

Devlin had just emerged onto the street, so Waller called down to him, "They may need you at the station, Jimmy. I'll send a runner if I need you elsewhere!"

Saluting quickly, Devlin barked orders and with three of his four sections, began a run to the station.

Smith saw them coming at the same time the Lieutenant, Quilty, did.

"Rapid fire! Fire at will!" the Lieutenant barked immediately as the savages began breaking from the woods. "Sergeant Kinley, the rest of the platoon immediately!"

While the last two reserve sections of the platoon raced up to extend the soldiers' line, Smith raised his Winchester to his shoulder and started choosing savages. Perhaps a dozen came out first, but the fast and very good shooting of the Newfoundlanders stopped them dead. More came, though — hundreds more. It was like a wave of beasts, more than Smith had ever seen, coming straight at him.

He pulled the trigger of his rifle, then levered the next round into the chamber and fired again, and again. The savages rushed forward, coming for the platform, seeing the stairs that would lead them up onto it.

Smith kept shooting, and in a minute his fourteen bullets were gone. The savages were 200 yards away and climbing over their dead to get at him. He started pulling .45 caliber bullets out of his belt and sliding them into the receiver of his Winchester, then turned to look for Tucker. They'd need more men in a minute. Because more savages were coming out of the trees.

As Smith turned, a man landed at his feet. He stopped and looked down in genuine surprise until he realized the man hadn't fallen, he'd dropped prone, and he had a monster of a gun in front of him on a bipod, with a round drum of bullets sitting on top. Another man carrying extra drums dropped next to him.

The soldier squeezed his trigger, and Smith backed up as the small machine gun started roaring away, spraying the horde as it came for the platform.

His rifle reloaded, he turned and started shooting again.

He decided as he shot another savage that he'd never in his life been surrounded by so much firepower.

•••

The station was definitely receiving the worst of it. It was as though they could smell the train, smell the way in. Waller watched through his field glasses as Devlin bounded up the stairs onto the platform, revolver in hand, and waved his men towards the far end of the station, which Waller couldn't see.

They must have been coming down the rail bed too. Dammit, all his men were committed to the south side of this town, now. If the savages flanked too wide, he'd be finished.

Turning his glasses back to the south wall, he saw the first beasts climbing up onto the palisades, and being thrown off by the fire of the Canadian Rifles from the houses. Two platoons of Kearsey's company were divided into sections, and had lined up in the intersections between the houses to fill the gaps. Presumably Kearsey could quickly redeploy to the north or east if it was needed.

At least the numbers of savages seemed to be dwindling. Looking back up to the fields beyond the town, the grasslands seemed to be carpeted with bodies. They looked so very human, like white men who'd gone native and naked, and yet their speed and power made it clear they could not be of the same species as Waller and the Newfoundlanders.

The sounds of fighting from the station grew louder, and Waller turned his glasses back there. He couldn't see the far end of the platform as it was eclipsed from this angle by the station building. Devlin would see to it...

"Fix bayonets!" Devlin barked to his men as he reached the end of the platform, discovering savages just yards away from him. He shot two with his Webley revolver, and waved his men forward. "Form a secondary line ten yards back! Quilty, get ready to displace!"

Smith watched the arrival of reinforcements and backed towards them, though he didn't stop shooting until his rifle was dry again. They weren't being overrun by the savages yet, but he figured that wouldn't take long if the men he'd been standing with ran out of ammunition.

They'd only been carrying 150 rounds each, and they'd been firing hard for minutes.

"Platoon withdraw behind secondary lines! Sergeant Butler, send two men for a case of ammunition!" Quilty roared the order, and as he did, his Lewis machine gun crew got to their feet and fled back to drop next to Devlin, while the men withdrew in good order.

As Smith came to stand next to the pleasant young Jimmy, the Newfoundlander was ordering his men to form a line two deep, and for the front rank to kneel again. This worked for them, and Smith had to say the hundreds of dead savages beyond the platform proved its worth.

"Rapid fire at will!" Devlin barked, and as the first savages bounded up onto the platform, the line erupted with fire.

This time, Smith realized, they were too close. The first savages hurled themselves at the line of men, and as they were only twenty yards away, they couldn't all be shot down.

"Hold them with bayonets!" Devlin roared, and behind him Smith heard the other Lieutenant rally his men.

"Fix bayonets! Charge bayonets!"

The Newfoundlanders began to yell and roar to get their spirit up, and then as Devlin's line collided with the savages, eighty men lunged forward with knives longer than Smith's own bowie locked onto the front of their rifles.

Smith drew his six-shooter and started blasting.

For more excerpts, visit: **www.newworldempire.net**

ABOUT THE AUTHOR

Born in 1984 in St. John's, Newfoundland, Kenneth Tam holds both a Bachelor's and Master's degree in history from Wilfrid Laurier University in Waterloo, Canada. His MA thesis examined the creation and operation of the Caribou Hut, a hostel for Allied servicemen in St. John's during the Second World War.

In 2006, Kenneth received a prestigious Canada Graduate Scholarship from the Social Sciences and Humanities Council of Canada. He was also awarded a Balsillie Fellowship at the Centre for International Governance Innovation during 2006-07. In that capacity, he worked for Mr. Paul Heinbecker, Canada's former ambassador and permanent representative to the United Nations. He presently serves as a Communications Consultant for Kitchener–Waterloo's federal Member of Parliament, Peter Braid.

Since releasing the first *Equations* novel in 2003, Tam has promoted his books across Canada, speaking with junior and high school students, delivering writing workshops, and doing book signings at bookstores and Iceberg-organized events. He frequently appears as a guest author at science fiction events across the country.

Kenneth is a partner in Iceberg Publishing, the company he and his family started in 2002. He has authored many of the company's existing titles, and is also responsible for graphic design, including the company logo, website, banners, advertisements, and other marketing materials. He acts as a primary contact with printers and suppliers, and is also key in new author development and recruitment.

He remains very lazy about writing his author bios. When they told him to make this one longer, he mostly copied and pasted it together from the Iceberg website, www.icebergpublishing.com.

www.ingramcontent.com/pod-product-compliance
Lightning Source LLC
Chambersburg PA
CBHW031604240626
47153CB00002B/627